THE LAST
OF THE JUST

A Novel by
André Schwarz-Bart

Translated from the French by Stephen Becker

MJF BOOKS
NEW YORK

Published by MJF Books
Fine Communications
Two Lincoln Square
60 West 66th Street
New York, NY 10023

Library of Congress Catalog Card Number 96-76472
ISBN 1-56731-140-7

Copyright © 1960 by Atheneum House, Inc.
Original published in French under the title *Le dernier des Justes*
© 1959 by Editions du Seuil, Paris

This edition published by arrangement with Simon & Schuster, Inc.

Manufactured in the United States of America on acid-free paper ∞

MJF Books and the MJF colophon are trademarks of Fine Creative Media, Inc.

10 9 8 7 6 5 4 3 2 1

CONTENTS

I

The Legend of the Just Men   3

II

Zemyock   25

III

Stillenstadt   83

IV

The Just Man of the Flies   143

V

Herr Kremer and Fräulein Ilse   205

VI

The Dog   255

VII

The Marriage of Ernie Levy   305

VIII

Never Again   351

This book is a work of fiction. In making use of historical fact the author referred principally to the following sources: DU CHRIST AUX JUIFS DE COUR: LE BRÉVIAIRE DE LA HAINE, by Leon Poliakov; ÉCRITS DES CONDAMNÉS À MORT, by Michel Borwicz; L'UNIVERS CONCENTRATIONNAIRE, by David Rousset; DE DRANCY À AUSCHWITZ, by Georges Wellers; TRAGÉDIE DE LA DÉPORTATION, by Olga Wormser.

How am I to toll your death,
How may I mark your obsequies,
Vagabond handful of ashes
Between heaven and earth?

M. Jaztrun, *The Obsequies.*

I

THE LEGEND OF
THE JUST MEN

OUR EYES register the light of dead stars. A biography of my friend Ernie could easily be set in the second quarter of the twentieth century, but the true history of Ernie Levy begins much earlier, toward the year 1000 of our era, in the old Anglican city of York. More precisely, on March 11, 1185.

On that day Bishop William of Nordhouse pronounced a great sermon, and to cries of "God's will be done!" the mob moiled through the church square; within minutes, Jewish souls were accounting for their crimes to that God who had called them to him through the voice of his bishop.

Meanwhile, under cover of the pillage, several families had taken refuge in an old disused tower at the edge of town. The siege lasted six days. Every morning at first light a monk approached the moat crucifix in hand, and promised life to those Jews who would acknowledge the Passion of our very gentle Lord Jesus Christ. But the tower remained "mute and closed," in the words of an eyewitness, the Benedictine Dom Bracton.

On the morning of the seventh day Rabbi Yom Tov Levy gathered the besieged on the watchtower. "Brothers," he said to them, "God gave us life. Let us return it to him ourselves by our own hands, as did our brothers in Germany."

Men, women, children, dotards, each yielded a forehead to his blessing and then a throat to the blade he offered with the other hand. The old rabbi was left to face his own death alone.

Dom Bracton reports, "And then rose a great sound of

3

lamentation, which was heard from here to the St. James
quarter. . . ."

There follows a pious commentary, and the monk finishes
his chronicle so: "Twenty-six Jews were counted on the watchtower, not to mention the females or the herd of children.
Two years later thirteen of the latter who had been buried
during the siege were discovered in the cellar, but almost
all of these were still of suckling age. The rabbi's hand was
still on the hilt of the dagger in his throat. No weapon but his
was found in the tower. His body was thrown upon a great
pyre, and unfortunately his ashes were cast to the wind, so
that we breathe it and so that, by the agency of mean spirits,
some poisonous humors will fall upon us, which will confound
us entirely!"

This anecdote in itself offers nothing remarkable. In the
eyes of Jews, the holocaust of the watchtower is only a minor
episode in a history overstocked with martyrs. In those ages
of faith, as we know, whole communities flung themselves
into the flames to escape the seductions of the Vulgate. It was
so at Speyer, at Mainz, at Worms, at Cologne, at Prague
during the fateful summer of 1096. And later, during the
Black Plague, in all Christendom.

But the deed of Rabbi Yom Tov Levy had a singular
destiny; rising above common tragedy, it became legend. To
understand this metamorphosis, one must be aware of the
ancient Jewish tradition of the Lamed-Vov, a tradition that
certain Talmudists trace back to the source of the centuries, to
the mysterious time of the prophet Isaiah. Rivers of blood
have flowed, columns of smoke have obscured the sky, but
surviving all these dooms, the tradition has remained inviolate down to our own time. According to it, the world re-
poses upon thirty-six Just Men, the Lamed-Vov, indistinguish-
able from simple mortals; often they are unaware of their

station. But if just one of them were lacking, the sufferings of mankind would poison even the souls of the newborn, and humanity would suffocate with a single cry.
For the Lamed-Vov are the hearts of the world multiplied, and into
them, as into one receptacle, pour all our griefs. Thousands of
popular stories take note of them. Their presence is attested
to everywhere. A very old text of the Haggadah tells us that
the most pitiable are the Lamed-Vov who remain unknown
to themselves. For those the spectacle of the world is an unspeakable hell. In the seventh century, Andalusian Jews
venerated a rock shaped like a teardrop, which they believed
to be the soul, petrified by suffering, of an "unknown" Lamed-
Vovnik. Other Lamed-Vov, like Hecuba shrieking at the
death of her sons, are said to have been transformed into dogs.
"When an unknown Just rises to Heaven," a Hasidic story goes,
"he is so frozen that God must warm him for a thousand years
between His fingers before his soul can open itself to Paradise.
And it is known that some remain forever inconsolable at
human woe, so that God Himself cannot warm them. So
from time to time the Creator, blessed be His Name, sets forward the clock of the Last Judgment by one minute."

The legend of Rabbi Yom Tov Levy proceeds directly from
this tradition of the Lamed-Vov. It owes its birth also to a
singular occurrence, which is the extraordinary survival of the
infant Solomon Levy, youngest son of Rabbi Yom Tov. Here
we reach the point at which history penetrates legend and is
absorbed by it, for exact details are lacking and the opinions
of the chroniclers are divergent. According to some, Solomon
Levy was one of thirty children who received Christian
baptism during the massacre. According to others he (ineptly
butchered by his father) was saved by a peasant woman who
sent him along to the Jews of a neighboring county.

Among the many versions current in thirteenth-century
Jewish stories we note the Italian fantasy of Simeon Reubeni
of Mantua; he describes the "miracle" in these terms:

"At the origin of the people of Israel there is the sacrifice accepted by one man, our father Abraham, who offered his son

to God. At the origin of the dynasty of the Levys we find again the sacrifice accepted by one man, the very gentle and luminous Rabbi Yom Tov, who by his own hand slit the throats of two hundred and fifty of the faithful—some say a thousand.

"And therefore this: the solitary agony of Rabbi Yom Tov was unbearable to God.

"And this too: in the charnel house swarming with flies was reborn his youngest son, Solomon Levy, and the angels Uriel and Gabriel watched over him.

"And finally this: when Solomon had reached the age of manhood, the Eternal came to him in a dream and said, 'Hear me, Solomon; listen to my words. On the seventeenth day of the month of Sivan, in the year 4945, your father, Rabbi Yom Tov Levy, was pitied in my heart. And therefore to all his line, and for all the centuries, is given the grace of one Lamed-Vovnik to each generation. You are the first, you are of them, you are holy.' "

And the excellent author concludes in this manner: "O companions of our ancient exile, as the rivers go to the sea all our tears flow in the heart of God."

Authentic or mistaken, the vision of Solomon Levy excites general interest. His life is carefully reported by Jewish chroniclers of the time. Several describe his face—narrow, pensive, somewhat childlike, with long black curls like a floral decoration.

But the truth had to be faced: His hands did not heal wounds, no balm flowed from his eyes, and if he remained in the synagogue at Troyes for five years, praying there, eating there, sleeping there always on the same hard bench, his example was commonplace in the minuscule hell of the ghettos. So they waited for the day of Solomon Levy's death, which might put an end to debate.

It occurred in the year of grace 1240 during a disputation

ordered by the sainted King Louis of precious memory. As was customary, the Talmudists of the Kingdom of France stood in one rank facing the ecclesiastic tribunal, where was noticed the presence of Eudes de Chateauroux, Chancellor of the Sorbonne, and the celebrated apostate Jew Nicholas Donin. In these singular disputations, death hovered over. every response of the Talmudists. Each spoke in turn in order to distribute equitably the threat of torture.

At a question of Bishop Grotius relative to the divinity of Jesus, there was a rather understandable hesitation.

But suddenly they saw Rabbi Solomon Levy, who had until then effaced himself like an adolescent intimidated by a gathering of grownups. Slender and slight in his black gown, he steps irresolutely before the tribunal. "If it is true," he whispers in a forced tone, "if it is true that the Messiah of which our ancient prophets spoke has already come, how then do you explain the present state of the world?" Then, hemming and hawing in anguish, his voice a thread, "Noble lords, the prophets stated that when the Messiah came sobs and groans would disappear from the world—ah—did they not? That the lion and the lamb would lie down together, that the blind would be healed and that the lame would leap like—stags! And also that all the peoples would break their swords, oh, yes, and beat them into plowshares—ah—would they not?"

And finally, smiling sadly at King Louis, "Ah, what would they say, sire, if you were to forget how to wage war?"

And these were the consequences of that little oration as they are revealed in the excruciating Book of the Vale of Tears: "Then did King Louis decide that our brothers of Paris would be condemned to a Mass, to a sermon, to the wearing of a yellow cloth disc and a sugar-loaf hat and, as well, to a considerable fine. That our divine books of the Talmud would be burned at the stake against an isolated tree in Paris as pettifogging and lying and dictated by the Devil. And that finally, for public edification, into the heart of the Talmudic flames would be cast the living body of that Just Man, that Lamed-Vovnik, that man of sorrows—oh, how expert in sorrows—

Rabbi Solomon Levy, since then known as the Sad Rabbi. A
tear for him."

After the auto-da-fé of the Just Man, his only son, the
handsome Manasseh, returned to that England whence his
ancestors had once fled.
Peace had reigned over the English shores for ten years; to
the Jews it seemed permanently enthroned. Manasseh settled
in London, where the renown of the Just Men set him at the
head of the resurgent community. As he was very graceful of
form and speech, he was constantly asked to plead the cause
of the Jews, who were daily accused of sorcery, ritual murder,
the poisoning of wells, and other affabilities. In twenty years
he obtained seven acquittals, which was indeed remarkable.
The circumstances of the seventh trial are little known.
It concerned a certain Eliezer Jefryo, whom rumor accused of
having stabbed a communion wafer, thereby putting the Christ
to another death and spilling the blood of the Sacred Heart,
which is the dry bread of the Host. This last acquittal disturbed
two powerful bishops. Shortly, arraigned before the tribunal
of the Holy Inquisition, Manasseh heard himself accused of
the crime from which he had so recently exculpated Eliezer
Jefryo.
He was obliged to undergo the Question Extraordinary,
which was not repeated—that being forbidden by the legisla-
tion in force—but simply "continued." The court records show
him infected by the evil spirit of taciturnity. And therefore on
May 7, 1279, before a gallery of some of the most beautiful
women in London, he had to suffer the passion of the wafer
by means of a Venetian dagger, thrice blessed and thrice
plunged into his throat.
"It is thus," a chronicler writes naïvely, "that after having
defended us in vain before the tribunals of men, the Just
Manasseh Levy rose to plead our cause in Heaven."

*   *   *

His son Israel did not seem bound to follow that dangerous path. A suave, peaceful man, he had a small cobbler's shop and wrote elegiac poems with the tip of his hammer. So great was his discretion that his rare visitors never arrived without a shoe in hand. Some assure us that he was well versed in the Zohar, others that he had barely the intelligence of a dove, whose gentle eyes and moist voice he also had. A few of his poems have become part of the Ashkenazic ritual. He is the author of the celebrated selihah "O God, cover not our blood with thy silence."

So Israel was quietly fashioning his own little world when the edict of expulsion burst upon the Jews of England. Always levelheaded, he was among the last to quit the island; they made first for Hamburg but settled later for slow progress toward the Portuguese coast. At Christmas, after four months of wandering, the caravel entered the harbor of Bordeaux.

The little shoemaker made his way furtively to Toulouse, where he passed several years in a blessed incognito. He loved the southern province; the Christian manner there was gentle, almost human. He had the right to cultivate a plot of ground, he could practice trades other than usury, and he could even swear an oath before a court as if, a Jew, he spoke with the tongue of man. It was a foretaste of Paradise.

There was only one shadow on the picture. A custom called the Cophyz required that every year on the eve of Easter the president of the Jewish community present himself in a plain gown at the cathedral, where the Count of Toulouse, to the strains of the Mass, administered a blow in the face with great ceremony. But over the centuries the custom had been singularly refined; in consideration of fifty thousand écus, the Count satisfied himself with a symbolic slap at six paces. So it went until Israel was recognized by an English emigrant and duly "denounced" to the faithful of Toulouse. They plucked him from his shop, blessed him, his father, his mother, all his ancestors and all his descendants, and willy-nilly he accepted the presidency, which had become a position of no danger.

The years flowed by with their train of griefs and small joys, which he persisted in translating into poetry, and on the sly he turned out a few pairs of shoes now and then. In the year of grace 1348 the old Count of Toulouse died; his son had been raised by excellent tutors, and decided to administer the Easter slap.

Israel presented himself in a long shirt, barefoot, on his head the obligatory pointed hat, two vast yellow discs sewn to the whiteness of his chest and back; on that day he had seventy-two years behind him. A huge crowd had gathered to see the slap. The hat rolled violently to the ground. According to the ancient custom Israel stooped to pick it up and thanked the young count three times; then, supported by his coreligionists, he made his way through the screaming press of the mob. When he arrived at home his right eye smiled with a reassuring sweetness. "It is only a matter of habit," he told his wife, "and I am already entirely accustomed to it." But over the cheek marked by four fingers his left eye wept, and during the night that followed, his aged blood turned slowly to water. Three weeks later he displayed signal weakness by dying of shame.

Rabbi Mattathias Levy, his son, was a man so well versed in the mathematical sciences, astronomy and medicine that even certain Jews suspected him of trafficking with the Devil. His agility in all things was notorious. Johanan ben Hasdai, in one of his anecdotes, compared him to a ferret; other authors sharpen the description, indicating that he seemed always in the process of fleeing.

He practiced medicine in Toulouse, Auch, Gimont, Castelsarrasin, Albi, Gaillac, Rabastens, Verdun-sur-Garonne. His condition was that of the Jewish doctors of the time. In Auch and Gaillac they accused him of poisoning sick Christians; in Castelsarrasin they accused him of leprosy; in Gimont he was a poisoner of wells. In Rabastens they said he used an elixir whose base was human blood, and in Toulouse he cured with the invisible hand of Satan. In Verdun-sur-Garonne, finally, he was hounded as a propagator of the fearsome Black Death.

He owed his life to the patients who kept him posted, hid him and spirited him away. He was often reprimanded but he always found, ben Hasdai says, "strange reasons for opening his door to a sick Christian." In several places his death was reported. But whether he was thrown into the Jew pit at Moissac, burned alive at the cemetery in Auch, or assassinated in Verdun-sur-Garonne, one fine day the ferret would make his sad appearance in a synagogue. When King Charles VI, on the good advice of his confessor, published the edict of expulsion of the Jews of France, Rabbi Mattathias Levy was hidden away in the neighborhood of Bayonne; a step or two and he was in Spain.

There he died very old, in the middle of the following century, on the immense white slab of the *quemadero* in Seville. Around him, scattered among the fagots, were the three hundred Jews of the daily quota. It is not even known whether he sang in his agonies. After an ordinary life, this lackluster death casts doubt on his quality as a Just Man. . . . "Nevertheless," writes ben Hasdai, "he must be counted as of the illustrious line, for if evil is always manifest, striking, good often dons the clothing of the humble, and they say that many Just Men died unknown."

On the other hand his son Joachim bore eloquent witness to his vocation. Before he was forty he had composed a collection of spiritual decisions as well as a dizzying description of the three cabalistic *sephiroth*—Love, Intelligence, Compassion. He possessed, legend says, one of those faces of sculptured lava and basalt of which the people believe that God models them veritably in his own image.

On that level the persecutions did not trouble him. Always noble and grave, he reigned over his disciples, who had come from all corners of Spain, and spoke to each of them the language of his death. In a polemic that has remained famous, he established definitively that the reward of the persecuted is the Supreme Delight—in which case it is obvious that the good Jew does not feel the horrors of torture. "Whether they stone him or burn him, whether they bury him alive or hang him, he remains oblivious; no complaint escapes his lips."

But while the illustrious Lamed-Vovnik discoursed, God, through the intervention of the monk Torquemada, concocted divinely the edict of permanent expulsion from Spain. Through the black night of the Inquisition the decree fell like a bolt of lightning, marking for many Jews immediate expulsion from earthly existence.

To his great shame Rabbi Joachim managed to reach Portugal without bearing personal witness to his own teachings. There John III charitably offered the exiles a sojourn of eight months in return for a mutually agreeable entrance fee. But seven months later, by a singular aberration, that same sovereign decreed that he would now spare the lives of those Jews leaving his realms without delay, and this in return for a mutually agreeable exit fee. For lack of savings Rabbi Joachim saw himself sold as a slave with thousands of other unfortunates; his wife was promised to the leisures of the Turk and his son Chaim promised to Christ and baptized abundantly in several convents.

A doubt hovers over the rabbi's death. A sentimental ballad locates it in China, by impalement, but the most cautious writers admit their lack of sure knowledge. They suppose that his death was worthy of his teachings.

The infant Chaim knew a prodigious fate. Raised in a convent and ordained a priest, he remained a faithful Jew under the soutane, but his superiors, satisfied of his apparent good conduct, delegated him to the Holy See in 1522 with a sizable group of "Jewish priests" assigned to the edification of the papal entourage. Leaving for Rome in soutane and biretta, he ended at Mainz in black caftan and sugar-loaf hat; there the survivors of the recent holocaust welcomed him with pomp.

Treated and regarded as animals, the Jews were naturally avid for the supernatural. Already the posterity of Rabbi Yom Tov had broken all the bounds of the ghetto. From the Atlantic coast to the interior of Arabia, every year on the twentieth day of the month of Sivan a solemn fast took place, and the cantors chanted the selihoth of Rabbi Solomon ben Simon of Mainz:

With tears of blood I bewail the holy community of York.
A cry of pain springs from my heart for the victims of Mainz,
The heroes of the spirit who died for the holy name.

The arrival of Chaim Levy, come surging from the depths of monasteries, seemed as miraculous as the deliverance of Jonah; the abyss of Christianity had rendered up the Just Man. Blessed, cherished, circumcised, he leads a life of ease. They present him generally as a tall, thin, cold man. A witness alludes to the unctuously monotonous flow of his voice, and to other ecclesiastical traits as well. After eight years as a recluse in the synagogue, he marries a certain Rachel Gershon, who shortly offers him an heir. A few months later, betrayed by a coreligionist, he is escorted back to Portugal. There his limbs are broken on the rack; lead is poured into his eyes, his ears, his mouth and his anus at the rate of one molten drop each day; finally they burn him.

His son Ephraim Levy was brought up piously in Mannheim, Karlsruhe, Tübingen, Reutlingen, Augsburg, Regensburg— all cities from which the Jews were no less piously chased. In Leipzig his mother died, out of breath. But there he knew the love of a woman and married her.

The margrave was not at all devout, no more was he greedy or wicked; he was simply short of money. So he fell back on the favorite game of German princes, which consisted of chasing the "infamous" and retaining their worldly goods. Young Ephraim fled with his new family to Magdeburg, whence he started for Brunswick, where he set out on the road to the death of Just Men, and was laid low by a stone that hit him in Kassel.

He is hardly mentioned in the chronicles; the scribes seem to avoid him. Judah ben Aredeth devotes barely eight lines to him. But Simeon Reubeni of Mantua, the gentle Italian chronicler, evokes "the undulating curls of Ephraim Levy, his laughing eyes, his graceful limbs moving as if in dance. They say that from the day he knew his wife, whatever befell him he never ceased to laugh, so the people named him the Nightingale of the Talmud, which perhaps indicates excessive familiarity toward a Just Man."

These are the only lines that describe the charming person of the young Ephraim Levy, whose happiness in love seems unworthy of a Lamed-Vovnik. Even his last agony failed to soften the rigor of the Jewish historians, who do not mention its date.

His son Jonathan had a more commendable life. For many years he crisscrossed Bohemia and Moravia—a peddler of the secondhand, and a prophet. When he entered the gates of a ghetto he began by unwrapping his glass trinketry; then, the day's small business over and the bundle done up and knotted at his feet, he lectured passers-by on the Torah, on the angels, on the imminent arrival of the Messiah.

A reddish beard covered his face even to the periphery of his eyes and, a more cruel disgrace still, his voice had a falsetto resonance, but he possessed, the chronicle says, "a story for each of our sufferings."

In those days all the Jews of Europe wore the uniform of infamy ordered by Pope Innocent III. After five centuries of this catechism, its victims were curiously transmuted. Under the pointed hat, the *pileum cornutum,* solid citizens thenceforth imagined two small horns; at the base of the spine, where the cloth disc began, the legendary tail could be guessed at; no one was any longer unaware that Jewish feet were cloven. Those who stripped their corpses were amazed, and saw an ultimate witchcraft in these bodies now so human. But as a general rule no one touched a Jew, dead or alive, except with the end of a stick.

During the long voyage that was his life, Rabbi Jonathan struggled often against cold, hunger, and the ordinance of Pope Innocent III. All the parts of his body testified forcefully to that. Judah ben Aredeth writes, "In the end, the Just Man no longer had a face. In Polotsk, where he turned up in the winter of 1552, he had to give up his bundle. A happy indiscretion having betrayed his quality as a Lamed-Vovnik, his sicknesses were healed, he was married, he was admitted to the seminary of the great Yehel Mehiel, where eleven years passed for him like one day."

Then Ivan IV, the Terrible, annexed Polotsk in a thunderclap!

As we know, all the Jews were drowned in the Dvina except those who would kiss the Holy Cross, prelude to the saving aspersion of holy water. The Czar indicating a desire to exhibit in Moscow, duly sprinkled, "a couple of wriggling little rabbis," his minions proceeded to the methodical conversion of Rabbi Yehel and Rabbi Jonathan. When all else had failed, they were tied to the tail of a small Mongol pony, and then their remains were hoisted to the thick branch of an oak, where two canine cadavers awaited them. Finally, to this oscillating mass of flesh was affixed the famous Cossack inscription, "Two Jews, Two Dogs, All Four of the Same Religion."

The chroniclers prefer to end this story on a lyric note. Thus Judah ben Aredeth, ordinarily so dry: "Ah, how the mighty have fallen!"

On Tuesday the fifth of November, 1611, an aged servant asked entrance to the Grand Synagogue of Vilna. Her name was Maria Kozemenieczka, daughter of Jesus, but she had raised a Jewish child and perhaps, she finished timidly, the Jews would act jointly to save him from conscription?

Assailed with questions, she first swore by all the saints that the child had been "engendered" in her by a peddler at the side of the road "in passing." Then she admitted having picked him up the day after the Russian annexation at the gates of the former ghetto of Polotsk, and finally she offered what was accepted as the truth: once cook in the household of the late Rabbi Jonathan, she had received the boy from the hands of the young wife as the Russians broke down the door. In the night she had fled to her native village. She would be old some day; she felt tender; she kept the innocent for her own; that was all. "And may you all forgive me," she concluded in a sudden shower of tears.

"Return to your village," the rabbi said to her, "and have the young man come here. If he is properly circumcised, we will pay for his release."

Two years went by.

The prudent rabbi of Vilna had breathed not a word to any man, and congratulated himself on it. But one night, leaving the temple, he bumped into a young peasant planted under the porch, haggard, his features drawn with fatigue, his eyes gleaming with an emotion in which arrogance battled fear. "Hey, you, old rabbi, I seem to be one of your people, so tell me what you have to do to be a dog of a Jew."

The next day, bitterly: "Pig in a sty, Jew in a ghetto, we are what we are, huh?"

A month later: "I'd like to respect you but I can't do it; it's as if I was disgusted, a feeling in the belly."

Started on the way of frankness, he told them of his anger and his shame, of burying himself in the Army. He had deserted in the middle of the night on an irrevocable impulse. "I woke up, just like that, and I heard them all snoring, good Christian snores. 'Jezry, Jezry,' I said to myself, 'you didn't come out of the belly you thought, but a man is what he is and if he denies it he's a pig!' " On that violent thought he had knocked out the sentry and then a passer-by, whom he stripped of his clothing, and like an animal off into the night he had headed for Vilna, a hundred and twenty-five miles from his garrison.

Men who had known his father, the Just Jonathan Levy, came rushing from all the provinces. First struck by his coarseness, they made overtures, analyzed his expression. They say it took him five years to resemble Rabbi Jonathan; he burst into laughter finding that he had Jewish hair, Jewish eyes, a long nose with a Jewish curve. But they were always worried about the crazy peasant who slumbered in him; now and then rages shook him, he spoke of "getting out of this hole," uttered blasphemies at which they stopped their ears. After which he enclosed himself in an attentive, studious, suffering silence for weeks on end. In his famous *Story of a Miracle* the prudent rabbi of Vilna reports, "When he did not understand the meaning of a Hebrew word, the son of the Just Men squeezed his head between his heavy peasant hands, as if to tear out the dense Polish gangue."

His wife revealed that he cried out in his sleep every night, calling now upon Biblical figures and now upon a certain St. John, the patron saint of his Christian childhood. One day when the service was at its height he fell full length, beating at his temples with his huge fists. His madness was immediately recognized as holy.

According to the rabbi of Vilna, "When the Eternal at last took pity upon him, Nehemiah Levy had replaced, one by one, all the pieces of his former brain."

The life of his son, the curious Jacob Levy, is nothing more than a desperate flight from the implacable "benediction" of God. He was a creature of thin, elongated limbs, a languid head, the long, fearful ears of a rabbit. In his passion for anonymity he hunched his back to the extreme, as if to mask his height from men's eyes, and as a hunted man buries himself in a crowd, he became a simple leatherworker, a man of nothing.

When the talk turned to his ancestors, he claimed that there had been an error in his case, arguing from the fact that he felt nothing within himself except perhaps terror. "I am nothing more than an insect," he said to his indiscreet courtiers, "a miserable insect. What do you want of me?" The next day he had disappeared.

Happily, heaven had joined him to a talkative woman. A hundred times she had sworn to keep silence, but always one fine morning, leaning toward a neighborly ear: "He doesn't seem like much, does he, my husband?" she would begin slyly. And under the absolute seal of confidence the secret made its way like a fired train of powder. The rabbi sent for the modest tooler of leather, and if he did not offer him his own ministry, he assured him that he was blessed of all men, dangerously radiating glory. So it happened in all the towns the couple passed through. "So that he could never savor the quietude of obscure men," writes Meir of Nossack, "God placed a female tongue at his side as a sentinel."

In the end Jacob, his patience exhausted, put away his wife to burrow into an alley in the ghetto at Kiev, where he quietly carried on his trade. They found him soon enough, but out of fear that he would disappear again, they only verified his presence now and then with a discretion equal to his own. Observers record that he straightened up to his full height, that his eyes cleared, and that three times in less than seven years he gave in to unfeigned gaiety. Those were happy years, they say.

His death fulfilled everyone's expectations: "The Cossacks locked a group in the synagogue and demanded that all Jews present strip naked, men and women. Some had begun to take off their clothes when a simple man of the people came forward whom a subtle rumor had identified with the celebrated dynasty of the Levys of York. Turning toward the tearful group, he hunched his shoulders suddenly and in a quavering voice broke into the selihoth of Rabbi Solomon ben Simon of Mainz: 'With tears of blood, I bewail . . .'

"They cut short the chant with one blow of a cleaver, but

other voices had already taken up the plaint, and then still others; then there was no one to sing, for all was blood. . . . So did things come to pass among us in Kiev on 16 November, 1723, during that terrible *hadaimakschina*." (Moses Dobiecki, *History of the Jews of Kiev*.)

His son Chaim, called the Messenger, was bequeathed his father's modesty. He gleaned instruction from everything, from rest as from study, from things as much as from men. "The Messenger heard all voices and would have accepted the reproach of a blade of grass."

And yet in those days he was himself quite a blade of a man, built like a Pole and so hale that the ghetto dwellers feared for their daughters.

The evil-minded insinuate that his unmarried state was not unconnected with his sudden departure from Kiev. Actually it was on the express injunction of the elders that he was obliged to take his place near the Baal Shem Tov—Rabbi Israel ben Eliezer, the divine Master of the Name—in order, they said, to add to his knowledge and to refine his heart.

After ten years of retreat on the most savage slopes of the Carpathians, the Baal Shem Tov had established himself in his natal village of Miedzyborz, in Silesia, whence his light streamed forth on all Jewish Poland. They came to Miedzyborz to heal ulcers, resolve doubts, or cure themselves of demons. Wise men and fools, the simple and the depraved, noble reputations and the run-of-the-mine faithful milled together around the hermit. Not daring to reveal his identity, Chaim Levy did his chores as a handyman, slept in the barn reserved for the sick, and awaited, trembling, the luminous glance of the Baal Shem Tov. Five years passed thus. He had merged so thoroughly with his identity as a servant that pilgrims from Kiev did not recognize him.

His only apparent talent was for the dance; when the reels formed to lighten the heart of God, he leaped so high in the air and cried out so enthusiastically that many Hasidim were offended. He was relegated permanently to the ranks of the sick; he danced among them for their pleasure.

Later, when everything was known, he was also nicknamed the Dancer of God.

One day the Baal Shem received a message from the old Gaon of Kiev. Immediately he ordered it proclaimed that a Just Man was concealed at Miedzyborz. All the pilgrims were interrogated—the sick, the wise, the possessed, rabbis, preachers. The next day it was noticed that the handyman had fled. Testimony streamed in immediately, each contributed his own anecdotes: the vagabond of the barn danced at night, took care of the sick, and so on. But the Baal Shem Tov, wiping away a tear, said simply, "That one was healthy among the sick, and I did not see him."

News filtered in as if drop by drop.

They learned that poor Chaim was wandering through the countryside preaching in public squares or practicing odd and humble crafts—for example that of the bonesetter, who used only his two hands (and who treated both humans and animals). Many chronicles point out that he preached only reluctantly, as if under the domination of an officiating angel. After fifteen years of that mad solitude, he became so popular a figure that a number of stories identify him with the Baal Shem Tov himself, of whom he was said to have become the wandering incarnation. In the abundance of ancient parchments we cannot separate entirely the commonplace from the miraculous. It is certain nevertheless that the Messenger often stayed in a village without delivering himself of any message but his medicine, so that he passed doubly unnoticed.

But his legend traveled faster than he did, and soon they recognized him by certain signs: first his tall lumberjack's build and his face ridged with scars, and then the famous missing right ear, ripped off by Polish peasants. From then on it was noticed that he avoided the larger cities, where his description was common knowledge.

One night during the winter of 1792 he arrived in the neighborhood of the small town of Zemyock, in the canton of

Moydin, in the province of Bialystok. He fainted away at the door of a Jewish home. His face and his boots were so worn, so hardened by the cold, that at first he was mistaken for one of the innumerable peddlers who crisscrossed Poland and the "zone of Jewish residence" in Russia. It was necessary to amputate his legs at the knee. When he was better they came to appreciate his manual talents and his skill as a copyist of the Torah. Every day his host trundled him to the synagogue in a wheelbarrow. He was a human husk, a poor unfortunate, but he performed small services and was consequently not a great burden. "He spoke," writes Rabbi Moshe Leib of Sasov, "only of material things like bread and wine."

The Just Man was in his wheelbarrow, like a living candle planted in a dim corner of the synagogue, when it happened that the village rabbi erred in the interpretation of a holy text. Chaim raised an eyebrow, rubbed his one ear, cleared his throat carefully, rubbed his ear again—to hold back the truth of God is grave, grave. . . . Finally, rubbing his ear one last time, he brought himself upright with one hand on the edge of the wheelbarrow and requested the right to speak on the text. He was then assailed with questions. Suffering a thousand deaths, he answered brilliantly to all of them. To make the disaster perfect, the old rabbi of Zemyock was transported into a sobbing ecstasy:

"Lord of the worlds," he cried between two sobs, "Lord of souls, Lord of Peace, admire with us the pearls that drop suddenly from that mouth! Ah, no, my children, I cannot now remain your rabbi, for this poor wanderer is a far wiser man than I. What have I said? Far wiser? Only far wiser?"

And advancing, he embraced his horrified successor.

II

ZEMYOCK

Hᴏᴡ Cʜᴀɪᴍ ᴛʀɪᴇᴅ to throw them off the track and was finally unmasked, what happened when he was married, and the diplomacy he exercised in order not to be carried to Kiev in triumph—no, lest the reader see a romance in it, none of that can be the object of a historical narrative.

It is nevertheless true that in spite of his most subtle hair-splitting, he immediately had to give up being pushed to the synagogue in a wheelbarrow.

A pious artisan had conceived a sort of rolling armchair, a veritable throne upholstered in velvet even to the inner faces of the wheels. They installed the Just Man in it with great pomp; a brocade quilt, placed across his thighs, covered his infirmity. The cantor walked at his right, the outgoing rabbi kept pace familiarly at his left so that he could command the attention of the Just Man's good ear. And the high priest pushed the rolling throne, leading a cortege of the faithful who offered their homage to the Dancer of God.

In the beginning the children displayed respect, but one day, doubtless emboldened by a young ringleader, they posted themselves along the line of march and burlesqued the old wheelbarrow.

Men rushed at them but Chaim was exultant. "Leave them alone," he said. "They're making fun of the throne, but they never laughed at the wheelbarrow."

That reflection was small consolation to the Jews of Zemyock, who felt that their dignity had been impugned. They took counsel, they spoke of wooden legs, and instructions were given the carpenter to construct a thoroughly dignified pair padded with leather and trimmed in fine silk. Solemnly offered to the Blessed of God—who had to train himself immediately to their use—the pair of legs proved to be a frightful instrument of torture; the stumps, instead of hardening with use, became more tender, more sensitive, until finally they infected. The villagers had to resign themselves: an ark was erected in the Just Man's room, which became a place of worship. So ended the humiliating journey to the synagogue.

Still infatuated with their great man, though a bit put out, they admitted privately, the villagers thought to glorify him still more with the reputation of a miracle worker (a campaign supported by the local businessmen). Chaim claimed immediately that he possessed no such power, except perhaps, *perhaps,* he emphasized, the power of tears. Nevertheless he received the sick, prescribed simples or other rural nostrums, and also received animals in a nearby barn.

And still, even when he could do nothing for a sufferer, he always conversed with him, not on higher matters, as one might have hoped, but on entirely anodyne affairs lacking in interest, such as the married life of the sick man, his work, his children, his cow, his chicken. A strange thing—people went away happy, saying that he knew how to listen, that by following your little tale he uncovered the grieving thread of your soul. When he could not hear you well he turned his left ear toward you, cupping his hand behind it, blinking in good fellowship. "How do you expect me," he asked, "to be interested in your soul if you don't trouble yourself about my ear?"

One day, to a poor old lady who was thanking him: "My old friend, don't thank me. My soul goes out to you, for I have nothing else to give you."

He might have established a school; solemn doctors of the Law, rich *tsadikim* in marten-lined capes or penniless wanderers sparkling with holy fire, hurried from great distances to dispute with a Lamed-Vovnik, but they encountered only his silence, or else a bad grace that unreeled itself in banalities on the mystery of knowing.

When the day was sunny, he forbade entry to anyone wearing the beard of a Talmudist, and dragging himself to the window he sniffed at the air, taking deep breaths with a nostalgic expression. On those days a discreet watch was kept on the house, for the urchins of the neighborhood liked to tiptoe even into the Just Man's room. They came because of his pillow, under which a heap of dried raisins, assorted nuts, almonds and sugar candies awaited them; the Just Man dispensed these to his young admirers. But in return the old man engaged the children in interminable conversations on the rain, the good weather, the quality of the snow, the tenderness of cherries eaten directly from the tree. "Ah! You give me back my legs!" he cried occasionally in the middle of a rowdy discussion. And sighing with pleasure, "My legs, yes, and *maybe even more* . . ."

Once they found two little boys under his bed; surprised by the arrival of a group of cabalists, they had spent the whole afternoon giving off mysterious sounds of nibbling that made the scalps of the wise men prickle. When the little jaws became too noisy, Rabbi Chaim said simply, "All right, little ones, don't forget that I am in important conversation." Bewildered, the visitors believed that he was admonishing familiar demons.

It caused a small scandal. They might have wished that the Just Man devote himself to occupations more worthy of him, and above all more worthy of the respect in which they held him. Shortly after this painful episode, they noted a certain amelioration: he requested ink, rolls of paper, and goose quills in great number. They rejoiced, and believed that the peasant had mended his ways. Informed persons announced that he was preparing an enormous commentary on the treatise Ta'anith; according to others, it was a fundamental exegesis of the Tsedokeh.

In the end it turned out to be simple tales for children; he went on writing them for the rest of his life.

At the birth of a first male child, Rabbi Chaim rejoiced, thinking that all was now consummated and the cycle of his life at an end. And how would he present himself before the Eternal? In a wheelbarrow, ho, ho! And then his heart contracted slightly in fear: O Lord, what a miserable gift it is that I offer you, and how will you put me to the sword? What death awaits me?

Outside, for the villagers, all things passed in good cheer under the cloudless sky of Zemyock, but musing on the multiple dooms of his ancestors, Chaim told himself that the resources of God are inexhaustible.

He was approaching forty; few Just Men had lived so long.

At first it was a matter of days, then of weeks. After six months the horrifying reality was borne in on him—Zemyock was so peaceful a town, so sheltered from the world, that there even a Just Man could die only in his bed!

The holocausts of life, they say, often follow the roads laid out for commerce and industry, but Zemyock was huddled in a valley, hidden from the world's eye; regional traffic went by beyond the hills, and as there was neither a nobleman nor a priest for at least a league in any direction, the peasants lived on human terms with these Jews, artisans and trimmers of crystal. From time immemorial, perhaps more than a hundred years, the faithful here had died gently, between two sheets, fearing only cholera, the plague and the holy name of God.

Chaim became a dreamer. Each night he took to the highroad on wooden legs or fled in a little amputee's wagon that traveled like lightning. But always the villagers found him in the end, tucked him willy-nilly into his great featherbed, and to the triumphal sound of the shofar, the bed hoisted on four shoulders like a coffin, they carried him back into their city of perdition.

When his wife's belly swelled again, all Zemyock was perturbed. There were anguished confabulations, followed by a solemn council. Finally a delegation comprising the principal personages of Zemyock betook itself to the Just

Man's bedside to make the general apprehension known to him. They said, in substance, "O Venerable Just Man, what have you done, what have you done? . . . *Your ancestors gave the world one son and then died.* . . . And tell us now, if this next child is also a boy, which of the two will be your spiritual heir? Which of the two will be the Lamed-Vovnik?"

"My good friends," Chaim answered, "I refrained from my wife for over two years, for I feared to go counter to the design of the Most High. And then I thought it is not good that a man conduct himself so toward a woman. If God wills it, this will be a daughter."

A young student of the Law insisted, "And if it is a boy?"

"If God wills it," Chaim repeated calmly, "it will be a girl."

A few months later it was a boy, and the delegation demanded immediate audience of the Just Man, whom it found prostrate in his bed of misery, his eyes grim, seeming himself to have undergone an intolerable accouchement. "Why do you harass me?" he complained. "It is not I who decide these things. I did nothing to retard my death."

"Or to retard this second child," the student remarked in obvious irony. "Your wife is pretty. . . ."

"She is also a good woman," the recumbent victim protested. "Possibly," he sighed, "I am not a Lamed-Vovnik. You built a throne for me, but I sat in it reluctantly. I have never received any confirmation from within, not the least sign, no voice telling me that I am a Lamed-Vovnik. As far back as I can remember, I have believed that the dynasty ended with my father, the poor Jacob, may God warm his soul! Have I accomplished miracles for you? All I wanted was a wheelbarrow."

"But you sat upon the throne," the student went on adroitly. "You could have told us that you felt nothing!"

"What can I say, my friends? I am only a man, alas!"

"Alas, yes," the student said with a certain smile, "and you made that quite clear to your wife."

A heavy silence fell over the room.

Two tears slipped from the hollow eyes of the Lamed-Vov-nik; slowly, one by one, they were lost in the wrinkled scars of his face.

"It is written," he answered calmly, "that God will satisfy those who revere him. And here he has satisfied your desire to find a way to ridicule me."

Those words transfixed the hearts of his audience. In the general stupor the student of the Law began to emit strident cries, standing erect, frozen in the attitude in which the Just Man's words had touched him. With calm restored, each of them approached the bedside, kissed the Just Man's hand, and tiptoed out. Of all those who were present at that scene, none ever spoke of it again. But the rumor spread over all Poland that God had not been able to resolve himself to take Chaim Levy, whose heart seemed that of a child.

In addition to a few daughters, his wife added three more sons to his perplexity.

The future Just Man, he judged at the beginning, would be easily distinguishable from his brothers, like a cygnet among ducklings. But as they all grew up, Chaim was forced to admit that the divine presence was not apparent in any of them. The mutual loathing usual among heirs divided the first four, who intrigued for the title—sufficient proof, Chaim thought naïvely, that they had no right to it.

The fifth was beneath any consideration: a pagan, an imbecile, an authentic schlemazl. They called him Brother Beast; he was unlettered, and only rarely did the wings of thought touch him. A man devoted to the soil, rather than pray or trim crystal he planted stupid vegetables that grow by themselves, requiring no skill except in the eating of them. He lived in a fetid hut amid a population of dogs, turtles, field mice and other abominations, which he treated as brothers—nourishing them, teasing them with protective gestures, blowing suddenly at their muzzles. From birth he seemed misshapen, with a glazed eye and a pendent lower lip. The arrival of an idiot is a manifest omen; poor Chaim saw in it a confirmation—God had rescinded his promise.

The brief final agony of the Just Man was made more sad by the absence of Brother Beast, who was wandering peacefully in the fields, walking his animals.

The patriarch had admitted only his sons to his bedside; they were wrangling over the succession, and Chaim wondered only if there would be one. And as they were also wrangling over the meager estate, it is said that Chaim wept to hear them, beating his guilty breast with both fists, indicting himself for having lived so long only to die in bed like a woman, like a Christian.

Suddenly, dropping back on his pillow, he gave way to little gasps of happiness.

"That's all we needed," the eldest son said coldly, stroking his beard in irritation. "Now what are we going to do?"

But already, with a sort of calculated slowness, the dying man had caught his breath and was murmuring gentle sighs of ease while beads of froth formed at the corners of his dark mouth. Finally, his eyes sparkling, his face lightly flushed: "My children, don't be misled," he said in an uncharacteristic tone of malice. "Only the smallest drop of life is left in me, but my mind is sound." Then, lowering over his blind eyes the worn veil of his eyelids, he seemed to withdraw into a region of being where the cohesion of his bones, his dead flesh, and the enveloping night ceased to matter. "My sons," he said dreamily, "sons of this clay, does a man not have the right to smile at his death if God makes it gentle for him? No, I have not yet felt the fluttering against my forehead," he went on into his gray beard, already matted in a terrible sweat, "of the wings of imbecility.

"Listen, open your ears, for this is my reason for laughing. Amid my tears I heard, 'Well-beloved Chaim, your breath is thinning; hasten therefore to announce that the Lamed-Vovnik is he whom your sons call Brother Beast, and so it will be for him at his last breath.'"

And laughing again in delight, old Chaim choked, gasped, exhaled a thin sigh—"Do you know? God is enjoying himself" —and died.

. 2 .

B ACK FROM THE FIELDS that night, Brother Beast wept
stupidly at his father's bedside when he should have
been rejoicing at the marvelous crown that was his legacy.

From the next day on, he threatened to leave Zemyock if
they insisted on naming him rabbi.

Nothing helped; neither veiled menaces nor the promise
of all earthly wealth could bring him to modify a single one of
his cherished habits. Every morning after swigging his bowl
of rude soup, the new Just Man swung a spade to his shoulder,
whistled for his dogs, and marched to a parcel of land granted
him by a Polish peasant. The gifts rotted in his hut: fluffy
tarts, honey cakes, pastries made with real cow's-milk butter—
whatever the dogs declined went to the children of the neighborhood. For himself he brewed enormous pots of vegetable soup
in which he soaked black bread—or, lacking that, cake.

Though he was thoroughly ugly, thoroughly dirty, thoroughly stupid; though he urinated as the spirit moved him
(except in the synagogue, where he sat rigid, as if paralyzed
by terror), the most beautiful girls of Zemyock now dreamed
only of him; each of his faults glowed now in the idealizing
light of his title. Anguished, ravaged, secretly enraptured, even
the men yielded to his charm. It is impossible to say what,
they agreed, twisting their curls spitefully, but he indubitably
has *something*.

The most desirable matches were offered him; motionless,
in a seventh heaven of delight, clasping his hands or foraging
in a nostril with his index finger, Brother Beast stood in contemplation before the beauty in all her finery, but he did not
approach her. The word alone, "marriage," sent him into
strange excesses. Thinking to give voice to unformulated desires, an audacious father leaned one day to the ear of the Just
Man and gestured toward his daughter: "Ah, Brother Beast,"
he whispered in an appropriate tone, "have you no desire to
nest that dove in your bed?"

The Just Man cast his humid glance at the girl, reassured her with a blissful grimace, and, raising his fist in the manner of a mallet, brought it hammering down on the skull of the foolhardy father. The question was not raised again.

He had only one friend, Joshua Levy, called the Absent-Minded. Still a child, and though normal in all respects (leaving aside a pronounced tendency toward daydreaming), little Joshua sometimes accompanied his uncle into the fields and watched him work. Later on it was stated authoritatively that the idiot and the child indulged in long conversations; still, no one ever saw them other than silent, the one digging, the other dreaming. One day the idiot made a gift of a little yellow dog to his nephew, and that was all. But later, much later, it was also remembered that the child never called his uncle Brother Beast, like everyone else, but by a singular aberration addressed him simply as Brother. And what was first attributed to childish inattention was later illuminated in a strange light. . . .

When Brother Beast lay down to die on a fragrant evening in May, he called for his dogs, his goat and his pair of young doves. But the Levys insisted that he first name his successor, and as he claimed to know nothing about it, they kept at a distance from him that menagerie, yapping, bleating and cooing at death.

They say—but is it true?—that as Brother Beast continued to refuse to give them a name, the Levys persecuted him to his last breath. "Pity, pity," he wailed. "I swear to you that I hear no voice!"

In short, some time after the tragedy uncharitable tongues claimed that the idiot, roused from his comatose state and fearing that they might retard his death indefinitely, only then resigned himself to naming his little nephew Joshua Levy — "You know, the one who has my yellow dog?"—before falling into the last sleep of the Just.

Thenceforward they knew that the crown of glory could "fall" upon any head. Cliques sprang up, a pitiless pressure was brought to bear upon the reigning Just Man—the life of

Joshua Levy was but one long calvary. He promised his second wife, "so young, alas," to designate a son of her flesh, and in the end, in his agony, the name of an undistinguished nephew escaped his lips. Nothing more is known. Nothing. The unfortunate Levys sought vainly to identify the signs by which God made his choice. Was it necessary to engulf oneself in prayer? To work in the fields? To love animals, men? To accomplish high deeds? Or simply to live out the miserable but so sweet existence of Zemyock? Who will be the Chosen One?

And from then on the childhood of each Levy was lived under the new sign vouchsafed by God to his people: a question mark, hovering over his skull like an uncertain halo.

While the sands of the days ran on, gently, grain by grain, the Jews of Zemyock persisted in thinking that the measurable time of man had ceased to exist in Sinai. They lived, not without grace, in the eternal time of God, which passes through no hourglass. What was a day? Even a century? Since the creation of the world the heart of God has pulsed only half a beat.

From those sublime heights, no one had eyes to see what destiny was weaving in the time of the Christians—a newborn industrial Poland, nibbling away squarely at the primarily artisan's life of the Jews. Like an iron heel, each new factory crushed hundreds of independent workers. At times the elders evoked the good old days, a time more propitious to the founding of families and synagogues. But unable to resign themselves to those sinks of iniquity, the factories—where the Sabbath was not respected, and where one could not observe in their plenitude and magnificence, as at home, the six hundred and thirteen commandments of the Law—they died of hunger, piously.

And then a few souls, audacious, not strangled by religious scruples, took flight toward Germany, France, England, often reaching even the two Americas. It was thus that about a third of the Polish Jews came to live essentially through the post office—which is to say, by the money orders from their "envoys" abroad. It was the same for the inhabitants of Zemyock, where the trimming of crystal no longer supported a Jew.

But the Levys received no support from the mails, and expected none.

It was known that to leave one's homeland was to place oneself at the mercy of American idols, to exile oneself from God. And if for Polish Jews God was more apparent in Poland than elsewhere, the Levys judged that he was particularly at home in Zemyock, in the territory assigned to the Just Men. So they would not leave him, and all of them remaining, all were with God, and all were miserable.

As they were the poorest and shabbiest in Zemyock, those who ranked a bare second to them in poverty spared them any sort of alms, for the rich pity only each other, no? In season the Levys hired out to the small farms, but the Polish peasants scorned Jewish arms, which are frail, and paid them a pittance in kind.

Toward the end of the nineteenth century, the Levy children were recognized by the pallor of their faces. . . .

Mordecai Levy (grandfather of our friend Ernie) was born into a needy family of crystal trimmers. As a boy he had an erect head, a lively, clear eye, and a big hooked nose that seemed to draw his whole face forward. But his adventurer's vocation was not yet entirely evident.

On a day when even the traditional herring of the poor was lacking at table, Mordecai announced that he would seek work the next day among the neighboring farms. His brothers stared at him astounded and his mother voiced shrill cries, swearing that the Polish peasants would insult him, would beat him to death, and God knows what.

To begin with, he was refused any work; they hired Jews only with reluctance and under pressure of the season. After long days of vain searching, he was taken on for the harvesting of potatoes, but at a very distant little farm. The foreman had said to him, "Jew, you're as big as a tree, and I'll give you ten kilos of potatoes a day. But will you be brave enough to fight?" Moredecai met the foreman's cold glare and did not answer.

The next day he was awake two hours before dawn. His mother tried to hold him back; something bad would happen to him, as it had to this one and that one and the other one, who had all come home bloody. Mordecai listened to her and smiled, remembering that he was a tree.

But when he found himself alone on the road in the gray dawn, in the vanishing warmth of his breakfast of tea and potatoes, the foreman's words came back to him. My God, he told himself, he was going there to work and would behave so well toward everybody that the Devil himself would not have the heart to insult him.

The morning was uneventful. Legs apart, he raised the instrument they had put into his hands and brought it down with redoubtable force all around the faded potato plant; then he searched the thousand-fibered clod and heaped its fruits at the edge of the open trench. To his left, to his right, the rows of Polish workmen advanced at much the same rate. Determined not to be left behind, he did not see the surprised and unhappy glares his neighbors cast at that immense Jewish adolescent, stiff and formal in his long black cloak, brandishing his hoe with the industrious eloquence of a priest, the blind intoxication of a blacksmith.

When he reached the middle of the field he took off his velours hat and balanced it carefully on two potatoes. But sweat still obscured his view, and ten yards farther along he stripped off his cloak and left it lying across the trench.

Finally, when the moving line of harvesters had reached almost the end of the field, a spider with an infinity of slashing claws came down on his back, suddenly arched in agony. Twisted and cramped, Mordecai raised his hoe in slow rigidity, saying in his mind, "My God," and brought it down desperately as other words saw light in him for the first time:

"Come be of aid to thy servant." It was to that invocation, renewed before each potato plant, that he attributed his heroic perseverance to the end of the row. He finished up dead level with the Poles.

At noon he went back into the field to recover his cloak and his hat, and shivering with the cold and with a formless fear, he approached the fire around which sat the workmen.

The farmhands fell silent at his approach. He squatted and slipped three potatoes into the embers. All those silent glances released a mortal anguish within him. The foreman had gone back to his own chores. Mordecai saw himself as between the jaws of the wolf, posed delicately on its quivering tongue; at his slightest gesture the fangs would close, ripping at him. Breathing heavily in fear, he plucked out a potato, jiggling it in his palms.

"Some people use the fire without even asking," a voice behind him growled.

In the clutch of terror, Mordecai dropped the potato and half rose, bringing his elbow fearfully up before his face as if to ward off an imminent blow.

"I didn't know, sir!" he babbled from below in his hesitant Polish. "Forgive me, I thought——"

"You hear that?" the Pole asked jovially. "Did you hear it? He *thought!*"

The peasant was about his age, but his arms were bare in spite of the cutting cold, and his half-open tunic unveiled the majestic beginnings of a taurine neck. His knotty hands, resting square and jaunty on his hips, accented his look of a stocky animal. Mordecai trembled; from a good-natured, ruddy face two delicately blue eyes stared at him with a placid, hating, Polish gravity.

"No help for it," a voice said from somewhere, "you've got to fight."

Mordecai rallied, "Why? What for? Fight for what?"

And turning toward the motionless group of peasants, he undertook his defense according to the methods recommended in such cases by the most ancient authors: "Gentlemen," he began, spreading his arms significantly, "ah!—I take you to witness. For I had no wish to insult this gentleman in using the hearth for my potatoes. Can you believe otherwise? And since there was no offense," he went on in quavering tones, on one knee, his chest thrust out by the force of his oratorical breathing, "and since there has been no offense, do you not think, farmers and gentlemen, that reasonable explanations might allow us to resolve the differences between myself and . . . this gentleman?" he finished on a sadly falsetto note.

"They do know how to talk, these Yiddls," said the young Pole in a voice of sincere conviction. And sweeping the air with an eloquent gesture, he flung Mordecai to the ground.

On his elbows Mordecai hastily wriggled a few yards. The smell of sod rose to his nostrils. Far off in space and time, the peasants were hugely amused by his dazed, terrified air. He plucked a scab of mud from his jaw; he had hit the ground chin first.

The young Pole took a step. Mordecai put his fingers to his cheek, where the blow had landed. He would have to show these people that they were in error; a man as religious as he could not be forced to fight, not a Jew all of whose principles set him against any manifestation so little in conformity with the teachings of the sages, not a young Levy who had never witnessed physical violence and who knew what a blow was only by hearsay. But because his oppressor was approaching, rolling his shoulders absurdly, Mordecai's imagination told him immediately that any such protestation was doomed to failure.

"And would he understand, *this monkey?*" he gibbered suddenly in Yiddish.

He was barely on his feet to flee when the kick caught him on his rump, depositing him face down in the dirt. The young Pole was repeating placidly, "Dirty Jew, dirty Jew, dirty Jew," and drove a foot against his rump each time he tried to rise. In his voice was so strong a note of triumph that soon Mordecai felt his contempt for the man transform itself into an aching flame that consumed him entirely, reducing him suddenly to a human body flexed and sinewy as a bow.

He never knew how it happened; he found himself standing, and flung himself toward the young Pole, crying, "What do you think you're doing?"

He was indignant.

· 3 ·

WHEN THE PEASANTS dragged him off his defeated foe, whom he was still hammering with his fists, his feet, his elbows—if possible he would have thrashed him with the whole stiffened mass of his body—Mordecai, haggard and almost drunk on blood, discovered that he had conquered the whole Christian universe of violence in one campaign.

"That one," a peasant said, "that one's not like the rest of them."

Slowly a dry shame invaded Mordecai. "Now," he said with a naïve arrogance they liked, "now I can use your fire?"

And that evening, home again, he knew that henceforth he held an advantage over his own people—how derisory an advantage!—of a body intimately bound to the earth, to plants and to trees, to all animals inoffensive or dangerous, including those who bear the name of man.

In those early times, each new farm called for a brawl, but as he circulated around Zemyock his reputation as a "tough Jew" won him prestige. As for the gentle Jewish souls of Zemyock, they looked askance at him, with the compassionate respect due a fallen Levy and the secretly jealous scorn one feels for a great pirate. The Levys watched him suspiciously; his crude, unshapely hands drew their dismayed glances and his posture, alas, no longer expressed the traditional hunch or the required detachment. They murmured—supreme scandal—that he had become stiff from neck to heels.

Seeing this, he gradually fell into the habit of returning to

Zemyock only on Friday night, at the exquisite approach of the Sabbath. Saturday was given over altogether to contrition, and Sunday at dawn, his books and prayer shawl carefully stowed away in his knapsack, he lost himself again in nature.

One day on his way to a farm at some distance from Zemyock, he ran into an old Israelite seated at the edge of the road on his peddler's pack, with his eyes full of pain and weariness. He carried the load as far as a nearby town where the old man had, as he put it, "a crumb" of family. The pack contained popular Yiddish novels, multicolored ribbons, some glassware; as a game, Mordecai sold a little of everything in the villages they passed through. The old peddler watched him, smiling. But when they reached his home town three days later, he said to Mordecai, "My career is ended, I can walk no more. Take this pack and go. I give you my capital, my jobbers, my itinerary; you are a Levy of Zemyock and I risk nothing. When you have a few zlotys in hand, you can come back here and reimburse me. Go, I tell you. Go on."

Mordecai slung the pack slowly on his shoulders.

A peddler finds lodgings easily in villages; he brings a breath of fresh air into those settlements, withdrawn into themselves the year round.

Mordecai affected nonchalance, laughed loudly, ate as much as he could, and argued with whoever looked dubious about his merchandise, but when he was within sight of Zemyock he banked the lively fire of his eyes and felt himself invaded by a slow and peaceful tide of anguish. And it was with a sort of confused discretion that he deposited his profits on a corner of the table, amid the glacial silence of the Levys.

"So you're back?" his father said dryly. *"They* have let you go again?" And as Mordecai bowed his head in shame: "Come a little closer, good-for-nothing. Let me see how you're made, if you still have a Jewish face. Well, come here to my arms— what are you waiting for, yesterday?" Mordecai trembled like a leaf.

When he was back on the narrow country road, leaving behind the crumbling walls of Zemyock, singular questions came
into his mind. One day, as a friendly gesture, a colleague
offered him a date. Everyone had hurried to contemplate this
rarest of fruits. Hastily they scanned the Pentateuch to savor
in it the word *"tawar,"* which means date, and Mordecai himself, though he was by then an old, experienced businessman,
seemed to see the whole land of Israel in looking at that unique
date. Now he was crossing the Jordan, reaching the tomb of
Rachel and the Wailing Wall in Jerusalem, now bathing in the
delicious waters of the Sea of Tiberias, where the carp play in
the sun. . . . And each time he came to himself by the side of
the road, his little date gray and wrinkled in his fingers, Mordecai wondered, "My Lord, what does all this mean—a peddler
lost on the plain, a Levy far from Zemyock, a date, a tough
Jew, the Sea of Tiberias, a young man facing life?"
     And a thousand other questions.
     One day as he approached the town of Krichovnick, more
than twenty days from Zemyock, he even wondered why God
had created Mordecai Levy. For several years there had been
no reigning fool in Zemyock, and as it is written, "Every city
has its wise man and its fool." But what could be done, he wondered suddenly, sadly, with an animal like Mordecai, striped at
random with one virtue and another?
     He was surely tired at that moment. He had been walking
since dawn, and now his fatigue made the hills of Krichovnick
dance far off in the shifting light of dusk. Every few seconds he
searched the sky in anguish, afraid of finding that first star
which announces that the Sabbath has descended upon the
world. Once, surprised by the first star of a Friday night, he had
abandoned his "capital" in a field beneath the tall grass.
     At the gate of the city a young woman was filling a water
bucket from the communal well with a slow, almost animal
grace that made light of the rope saturated with cold water.
Her attire was Sabbatical: flat slippers with pearly buttons, a
long dress of black-and-green velvet, and the traditional ruffs
of lace at her throat and wrists. From a distance Mordecai felt

that there was in her an incipient animal; the supple beauty of her gestures suggested a restrained menace.

Approaching quietly on the grass, he saw that she was a true Jewish beauty, almost as tall and slender as he. Within three paces of her, he was arrested by her catlike profile—short nose, slanted eyes, small brow pulled back by the heavy tresses that gripped her nape. "God forgive me," he said to himself, "I like her."

Flinging his pack to the grass almost at the woman's feet, he cried out in the tones of a hardened peddler, "Ho, my dove! Can you show me the way to the synagogue?"

He had a cavernous, stentorian voice; the young woman started from head to foot, dropped the rope, caught it up and finally, setting the wooden bucket on the lip of the well, "What a devil of a peasant!" she cried, tossing her head. Almost immediately her frown softened at the sight of the skinny, smiling young man, white with the dust of the road. "Am I a horse?" she asked deliberately in a pungent, sweet Yiddish. "A donkey, a bull, a camel? It seems so."

Steadying the wooden bucket on the stone lip, she threw her hair back with a quick motion of her head. Her eyes, jet, bored into Mordecai with a burning, gluttonous curiosity, but the lower part of her face was tightened fastidiously, the lips pursed; she had resolved to show the utmost disdain for him. "Besides," she said, "I don't speak to strangers, but if you will follow me at ten paces I can point out the synagogue as we pass."

And measuring him with a haughty glance, her back arched proudly, she started off through the village, paying no further attention to "the stranger."

Mordecai whistled, a long, slow hiss between his teeth. "God forgive me," he sighed as he hoisted the sack painfully to his shoulder, "I like her. I like her a lot, even, but . . . I'd beat her with pleasure."

Moved by this contradictory sentiment, he concentrated (keeping his distance of ten paces) on verbal barbs, which had the effect of hastening her step and provoking angry tosses of

her head. Her hair swept her lovely shoulders side to side, like
the ruffled mane of a mare, and its heavy motion, primitively
seductive, incited Mordecai to new sarcasms. "So that's
how you greet strangers in this town?" he bellowed. "At ten
paces? Do you know that God chose Abraham for having
granted hospitality to beggars? Think a minute, maybe I'm a
messenger from the Lord."

But striding straight and firm down the middle of the road,
the woman pretended to have heard nothing, and Mordecai
did not dare diminish the ridiculous distance between them.
As he broke into a forced laugh, overloud, he was astonished to
hear, from the cool silhouette tripping along at ten paces,
these words, of a dryness sweetened by the breeze that
bore them: "To listen to you, my fine gentleman, one would
think you rather a messenger from the Devil!"

Mordecai could hardly believe his ears, and while he wondered if it would be proper to be angry, a smothered laugh
reached him and the black mane shook triumphantly.

"And the Devil," she went on, "is saying a lot."

An odd sadness fell upon Mordecai; he decided to take offense and was silent, suddenly aware of the pack rubbing
against his spine. After which, probably for the first time in his
life, he resented his lambskin tunic, the lining of which was un-
raveling, and his boots, worn and scuffed, and even the uncom-
mon form of his velours hat, owing to its use as a recipient for
solids and certain liquids. "What difference does that make?"
he suddenly decided. "Am I a gold mark, to please everybody?"

At that instant he saw that the girl had set down her bucket
and, turning her face to him with a smile, was shrugging ironically, as if to say, "Come on now, don't be angry; you started it,
after all." Shaking her head then, she again walked off
brusquely, the wooden bucket, once more at her side, bobbing
more quickly in time to her springy step. She seemed to carry
it as lightly as a bouquet, but now the nervous spray was spattering the velvet of her dress, beading it with evanescent
drops of light. The young man felt that the moment was sweet.

Behind the town church appeared the first Jewish homes,

shabby and dilapidated, huddled together like frightened old women. Here and there a bearded figure in a caftan of moire glided along a wall. Night came down suddenly in a fine drizzle; the woman dancing along before Mordecai was no more than a shadow. Suddenly the shadow halted and a thin white finger pointed out the entrance to an alley; the synagogue was there, said that finger. Then it, too, disappeared.

"Who does she think I am?" Mordecai raged at himself. "I'm not a dog that . . . who——" Dropping his pack he marched forward with the flame, the impulse that rises from a feeling of righteousness.

The girl, alerted by the sound of his advance, had fallen back into the shadow of a doorway. But when he saw her at ten feet, so beautiful in the shadow, he thought gently, Come now, it isn't she who owes thanks. . . .

Scarcely tense, she watched him, one hand on the latch, ready for what might come.

"Would you," he stammered suddenly, "that is, would you allow—may I carry the bucket for you?"

"You're a peddler, aren't you?" she whispered breathlessly. "Here today, gone tomorrow—how dare you talk to me that way?"

And with a wide, mocking smile (in which nevertheless he seemed to see a fine shadow of regret) she swung the bucket, more than half empty, let it rest against her calf, saluted the young man with a brief bob of her mane and, breaking into an abrupt trot, disappeared in a splashing of water. He could not tell which street she had taken.

Lifting his pack wearily, Mordecai turned to the synagogue. One star twinkled in the sky between the suddenly black houses. But that star did not evoke the transparent glow of the Sabbath, for the patch of sky in which it winked—like a gold-headed pin—seemed to him cut from the nocturnal velvet of a Jewish girl's dress.

·4·

AFTER THE EVENING SERVICE, the faithful—coughing, chirping, gesticulating in the smoke of the small synagogical stove—debated to whom would fall the signal grace of exercising hospitality. Generally, reacting to his appearance, they offered Mordecai to some notable known for his immoderate taste for the external world, but on this night, far from ranging Mordecai in the category of "happy peddlers," the rabbi assigned him to that of "pilgrims living by trade," and invited him to his own table.

"Rabbi, good rabbi," Mordecai said, "my place is not at your table. I'm not a good Jew, I'm just a little sad this evening. You understand?"

"And why are you sad?" asked the rabbi, surprised.

"Why am I sad?" Mordecai smiled. "Because I'm not a good Jew. . . ."

The rabbi was a little round man, goggle-eyed, with a tiny mouth that seemed to cheep from within his beard. "Come along," he shrilled suddenly, "and don't say another word!"

The repast was regal. Mordecai could not have imagined a better: a spicy, winy fish soup, a roast of beef, and an exquisite dish of sugared carrots. Though delighted to be so well received, Mordecai did not speak out, behaving himself with as much austerity as if he had been in Zemyock at the meditative table of the Levys. But when the hostess passed a platter of carob beans, he could not help saying, as he tapped his belly with a comic air, "Ah, brethren, brethren, a bit of carob is of a paradisiacal savor; it evokes the land of Israel. When we eat it we become languorous, and we sigh, 'Return us, O Lord, to our own land, to the land where even the goats graze on teeming carob!' "

On these words the gathering came to life, and the eternal interrogation began: When would the Messiah come? Would he come on a cloud? Will the dead accompany him? And on what would we nourish ourselves, since it is written, "On that day I will make an alliance for you with the beasts of the field." And how, my gentle lambs, can we hasten his arrival? This concluding question was offered by the rabbi with a brief, desolate sweep of his arms.

Here, and each of them knew it, the discussion of two millenniums reached its crest, the redoubtable summit from which all of creation was visible.

"By suffering," began an old man to the rabbi's right, hollow-eyed, with a pendent pink lower lip, his head never ceasing its tremulous wagging, "suffering, and more suffering, and suffering always, for——"

"Mr. Grynszpan," his hostess interrupted angrily, "and what do you think we're doing now? Isn't it enough for you?"

"Tut-tut," the rabbi said timidly.

"For it is written," the old man went on with no change of expression, "for it is written: 'Suffering becomes Israel like a red ribbon on the head of a white horse.' For it is written: 'We shall bear the sufferings of the world, we shall take its grief upon ourselves, and we shall be considered as punished, stricken by the Lord and humiliated. And then only, when Israel is suffering from head to foot, in all its bones and all its flesh and all its nerves, prostrate at the crossing of the roads, then only will God send the Messiah!' Alas," Mr. Grynszpan finished, his eyes protruding as if in a vision of the terrible things to come, "then only, not before."

"Mr. Grynszpan," the rabbi chirped sadly, "I ask you—what pleasure do you take in terrifying us? Are we Just Men, to live with the knife before our eyes? I'll tell you what, dear Mr. Grynszpan—let us rather speak of something gay. What's new about the war?"

Having said which, and though the ancient joke was known to all of them, the rabbi fell into such a coughing and sputtering and gasping that they were afraid for him. But after the customary exorcisms the crisis of laughter passed as it had come, and he reseated himself at the common table. "We were saying?" he murmured, annoyed.

Then, noting the general disapproval, he composed a serious

face. "I am not unaware," he orated finally, "dear Mr. Grynszpan, how shocking, even painful, my demonstration may
have seemed to you. But I must point out that it was not directed at you or at what you said, and that this outburst was
due solely to the joy I feel on such a beautiful Sabbath. Do
you believe that?"

"Of course I believe you," the old man said with emotion,
"but allow me to bring this to your attention—according to
the school of the Rabbi Khennina . . ."

The conversation turned to the subject of laughter: its nature, its laws, its human and divine significance, and finally, by
an insidious route, its relation to the coming of the Messiah.

Faithful to his role as a peddler, Mordecai had kept silence
until then. From time to time a black-and-green dress flitted before his melancholy eyes. How could he see her again? Staking
everything on one throw, he leaned forward. "For myself," he
offered gravely in the tone his father adopted for such occasions, "for myself, if I note that 'Yitz'hak,' which is Isaac,
means, above all, 'He will laugh in the future,' and if I observe
that Sarah had seen the son of Hagar, Ishmael, when he was
'Metza'hek,' which is to say 'laughing,' I conclude humbly
that the sons of Abraham—Ishmael and Isaac—are distinguished by the fact that the first knew how to laugh in the present, while it was reserved for Isaac, our father, to weep until
the coming of the Messiah—blessed be he!—who will grant
eternal laughter to all. And tell me, brethren, how a truly
Jewish heart could laugh in this world if not at the thought of
the world to come!"

On this noble envoy, Mordecai raised his glass of liquor to
his mouth, and throwing his head back swallowed its contents
in one gulp, like a peasant, to the great stupefaction of all the
guests. Then, clacking his tongue against the roof of his mouth,
he added, not without finesse, "Happily, our own hearts are not
entirely Jewish; otherwise how could we feel such placid happiness this evening?"

His last remark was much appreciated. The rabbi found a
Hasidic flavor in it. Yet he was astonished at such marvels

from a simple peddler, and it was then that Mordecai climaxed his subtle work. Bowing his head almost coquettishly, he said that he was a Levy of Zemyock.

"I would have sworn to it!" cried the little rabbi.

"But I am far from being a Just Man," Mordecai qualified modestly, even as he offered an ingratiating smile to the company. "God forgive me if he can," he said to himself at that moment. "She is really too beautiful!"

The next morning, waking in the master bed (where the rabbi and his wife had insisted he sleep), Mordecai was prey to an uneasiness, a strange torpor, a difficulty in moving—all symptoms of the tertian fever. Equipped with a new jug and supported by his distressed hosts, he went immediately to the nearby river and said to it, "River, river, grant me a jug of water for the trip that I must take!"

Then amid total silence on the part of the many spectators, he brandished the jug seven times about his head, and pouring the water behind him cried, "River, river, take back the water you granted me, and with it the fever that burns me. I beg this of you, river, in the name of our common creator."

This was said with artistry, truly in the style of Zemyock.

Then the sick man and his attendants returned to the dwelling of the rabbi, where Mordecai took to his bed immediately. Many villagers appeared at his bedside, attracted by the renown of the Lamed-Vovnik. They found him doleful, his expression cadaverous, and the fact is that he had spent a sleepless night of anticipated remorse.

Bit by bit, and from tertian fever to quartan, he agreed that to take up his journey would be madness, and as the fever persisted, he even condescended to take up his winter quarters in Krichovnick as a replacement for the beadle. This arrangement delighted everyone, beginning with the beautiful young mane, whom he saw a few days later as he was loafing casually around the well. "You know," she laughed, "your sickness didn't upset me at all."

"Is it possible?" he cried, lost.

"Then you were—" she stammered, "you were *really*——"

Saying this she retreated a stride, backing against the lip of the well with so much pity in her eyes that all her feline expression disappeared, replaced at once by the ready tenderness of her woman's flesh. Mordecai felt a sweet twinge in his breast; with a peddler's gesture, he smoothed back his mustache. "I was really sick," he said, smiling slyly, "and I still am, more than ever," he finished in a hoarse tone laden with emotion.

She left in endless laughter and Mordecai could follow her that day at five paces, which became three the following day, and then zero; happy as a child, he clutched half the glacial handle of the bucket.

This last fever intoxicated him. He let himself speak unchecked sweet words, and grave, and melancholy, such words as he thought would please a young woman of Zemyock or Krichovnick or any place. But she shortly made him understand that she preferred him as the "happy peddler" and, sick at heart, Mordecai complied. That marionette which Judith loved in him and whose strings he manipulated to please her— how he wished now to smash it!

"Why do you have to bay the moon?" she said. "When you love, it seems to me, the greater merit is in making yourself lovable. Am I a moon? I am Judith."

One fine day she admitted as if in a joke that she had never seen a peddler as big, strong, sweet and amusing as he. And doubtless, she went on in the same tone, it was an honor for her to be noticed by a Levy of Zemyock. But there it was, she was an idiot, she didn't feel it, she would have preferred a plain ordinary Levy. What did all those fearful, bloody stories mean that they told about his family? Brrrr, they made her shiver!

And as he had begun to look prim, she exploded. "I don't want any of *that,* do you hear? I want to live! Live! Live! What do I want with a Just Man?"

"But I'm not a Just Man!" Mordecai protested in accents of despair.

"We know you, we know all about your kind," she answered.

"Whoever says he isn't one, that's the one who is. And why do you have to suffer for the world? How does it happen to come to you? And tell me this—does the world suffer for you? Does it?"

"But I'm not suffering, I swear it!"

But Judith was no longer listening. She was wringing her hands and rolling her wild eyes, her small nose quivered and a fine spray of saliva had formed on her lips, as happens to cats. She brought a strange look to bear upon the young man. "And why," she demanded, "of all the showers of men that God rains on the earth, why must it happen to idiot me, Judith Ackerman, that I fall on the one bad drop? There aren't a thousand Lamed-Vov on earth, not even a hundred, only thirty-six, thirty-six! And me, the queen of all fools, no sooner do I catch a glimpse of one of them than I fall in love with him, you hear?" She sighed, with a gentleness all the more poignant in a tall, fierce woman.

And as Mordecai stood dumfounded: "Do you hear me, assassin?" she shouted to his face.

At this, Mordecai took on an expression so submissive, so unhappy, that flinging herself against her executioner and covering his eyes with her hands, the girl suddenly kissed him on the lips for the first time. Demented, grinning, vaguely uneasy, Mordecai knew that there was such a breath of life in her that all the reason in the world came to grief against her lips, shattered and flew off like chaff, far off, high off in the gray, unmoving sky of ideas. Pressing her against him, he murmured, "I'll do— I'll even be your marionette. All right?"

The spirit of Zemyock, smoldering secretly within him, burst into flame after the betrothal, which was a decisive turning point to him. Already subdued, radiant, the fierce animal obviously wanted nothing more than to enter the ready cage, and beneath the tremulous lover the husband suddenly rose, the lord and master, protected by the laws as by so many iron bars. At the first skirmish the husband was victorious. "If you don't understand me," he cried acrimoniously, "it's because you don't want to!" And resigning himself to the truth, he bore a mask of pride that hardened his face, astonishing Judith altogether. "Listen now," he said. "Among *us*, before he marries, a man must recopy the book of our family, the whole history of the Levys, to give it to his children to read, and you want *all that* to end because of your pretty head of hair? I have to go back to Zemyock just once. You can see that."

"Then go ahead," she cried, "but don't come back!"

Mordecai stared at her, hesitated, turned his back in absolute calm.

As he crossed the doorsill two hands fell on his shoulders, and he felt the uneven, excited breath of his betrothed against the back of his neck. "Come back quickly," the proud Judith murmured.

He promised, wept, promised again. If she had known how to turn her defeat to advantage, she could have kept him there. But Judith knew nothing of that weapon, and Mordecai left for Zemyock, mounted on a cart horse that they had loaded down with slices of smoked beef, jars of preserves, a caged chicken with two weeks' feed, and a multitude of cakes, embroidered napkins, spools of thread, buttons, socks and other gifts for the son-in-law's family.

So equipped, he was high and mighty, but on the outskirts of Zemyock three weeks later his enthusiasm disappeared. He found his family at table, surrounding one sole herring. Under the low, cracked ceiling crossed by an eternally bare beam, all those emaciated faces gave him a turn. His father did not deign to rise.

"I thought," the latter offered in majestic sarcasm, "that you would marry without even writing your book."

"I love her," Mordecai said gently.

"Listen to that, he loves her!" exclaimed his elder brother, who raised skinny arms toward the beam, as if calling upon the heavens to bear witness to the enormity.

"And have I not loved also?" his father articulated slowly. "But I thought"—he relapsed into sarcasm—"that the wife must follow her husband. Perhaps you are not of that opinion?"

"But she didn't want to come," the lover said dolefully. In the same instant he bit his lower lip and blushed; a unanimous burst of laughter greeted his confession.

"Peace!"

Dissipating the uproar with that one word, the father rose to his feet, quite tall despite the curvature of age, and, his arms crossed upon his breast—the immemorial symbol of righteousness—his hollow eyes flaming like torches, he pronounced very distinctly these words, perhaps prepared in advance: "Remember, my son: for the man whom women have destroyed, there will be neither judge nor justice."

And seating himself rigidly, he ignored Mordecai's existence.

· 5 ·

JUDITH did not recognize the "happy peddler" who had left her a few weeks before—his beard was longer, his aquiline face had taken on an ivory sheen. He took her distractedly into his arms.

"My flesh and my blood," she whispered against his chest, "how thin you are and how sad. Are you sick?"

"Yes, he's lovesick," Judith's mother said gaily. She was a strong woman with a reddish complexion, and was generally busy in the kitchen preparing ample libations. "It's a good disease," she affirmed peremptorily, "good for the spleen and the shine of the eyes!"

"Is that true?" Judith asked, palpitating with pleasure, and as Mordecai did not answer, she tore herself away from him and cried out, taken by a sudden insight, "You don't love me now!"

Mordecai's gaze fell on her, but without force. His gray irises were hesitant against the pale background of the eyeballs, like clouds wandering against an endless sky. Tears glittered.

"My father did not give me his blessing," he said finally in a dying voice, and then he added heatedly, as his whole face reddened in passion, "But God will see to it, won't he?" And he astonished them all by reverting to his casually cheerful peddler's manner. He grabbed a long-stemmed glass and tinkled it gaily against the bottle of kvass, as one knocks at a door. "Mother-in-law," he thundered with authority, "what's the meaning of this?"

And maliciously citing Scripture, he declaimed, "Give strong drink to him who is dying, and wine to him who has bitterness in his soul!"

He poured the kvass down as if it were nothing; he was laughing! Judith felt better.

But a few days later Mordecai seemed to her to be withdrawing into himself again. As much as he had—before that cursed Zemyock—loved movement and gaiety, so much did he flee all such occasions now, going so far as to mortify himself for hours on end at the synagogue. Judith did not know what to think. It seemed to her that instead of drawing closer to her, instead of intimacy revealing more and more of the man, her lover had wrapped himself tightly within a cloak invisible to the eye and against which her poor heart bruised itself terribly.

She advanced the wedding date. When Mordecai crushed the symbolic glass of the bachelor, she wept. That same evening the ecstatic couple settled into the home of Judith's parents. These latter were bakers of bread; they were hugely pleased by the heavy hands—perfect for kneading—of their son-in-law, which the *"good fortune of the aged"* had brought them.

And Judith breathed easily, for with the passing days and weeks Mordecai never tired of the always accessible body of his wife—always accessible and always distant, secret, woven of innocence. Each night they fell into the same astonishment; it was like a gulf of light, she thought, a heaven upside down. Her mother teased her privately. "Who ever knew love before you? Who else can even talk about it? Nobody."

But for himself Mordecai wondered in shame whether such

delights did not contain a certain excess, a pagan undertone. Did they not cut him off from God?

An uneasiness grew within him which he associated obscurely with his exile from Zemyock. The girls of his village were admirable in one aspect—their will wavered under a simple glance. Any man, were he as timid as a mouse, could keep the reins tight on his wife. Go and try that with Judith!—who not only obeyed neither touch nor glance but even rejected a formal order from her husband as though she were brushing a housefly from her face!

All in all, incontestably the most troublesome problem was her tendency to flirt as before their marriage. For a yes, for a no, she would stubbornly refuse her favors, and in her mania for coquetry she was quite capable of going two or even three days without one tender word, without one sigh. Was this a Jewish heart?

So, though he could never accuse her of shamelessness, Judith had by the use of her charms acquired such power over the poor peddler that he even went so far as to wonder if he hadn't married a demon in the disguise of a marvelous woman. This gulf that they were digging night by night, where would it lead them?

More and more often Mordecai surprised himself by showing a homesickness for Zemyock.

This counteroffensive gathered momentum very slowly.

When Judith saw that her husband was taking on the look of a man of meditation and study, it was too late to revert to their old relationship of ecstasy and stormy argument. The words that Mordecai uttered now seemed marked by the seal of God, his wishes seemed to conform to the divine will; he claimed that his every act was performed in obedience to the commandments of the Eternal, even unto the act of love.

On this last point, Judith reserved her opinion. Yet the day came when Mordecai gave orders, and then the day when his haughty wife obeyed. Shortly afterward, he persuaded her to follow him to Zemyock, for good.

*   *   *

Of a sudden she revolted outrageously. Her looseness of speech, the arrogance of her bearing, were an affliction to both sexes. "Look at that gypsy!" they said. "Oi, what a misfortune! That's what a husband gets when he wanders for a wife." And in the stranger they saw the gap that separated the Judiths from the proper wives of Zemyock.

Early on, it often happened that she would burst into tears and then into a harrowing anger, when she blamed her husband squarely for all her griefs, inscribed one by one on the scutcheon of her rancor, accusing him of having broken her heart and her life by his subtle treasons. "From the first minute, from the first second, you deceived me, you were playing with me! 'Ho, my dove, may I carry your little bucket, my princess?' A peddler, a grenadier, an Alexander devouring the miles! And stupid me, I thought we could enjoy each other and amuse each other every day, all our lives—and what was underneath all that? A sniveling little Levy with a prayer in the morning and a prayer at night and in between—one long prayer!

"But you kept it under cover, you played the part perfectly, you tamed your little dove, oh! 'Today I have to write my book, tomorrow my father didn't give me his blessing,' and then came the last step—Zemyock! Zemyock! Ai, ai, Zemyock—I wouldn't wish it on my worst enemy! What kind of a town is it? Levys, everywhere Levys, nothing but Levys, half the town is Levys. Who could believe there were so many Levys?

"In my father's house you made good bread, and here? My lord trims crystal, aha, the gentleman's trade, the artist's trade, and you turn to crystal yourself, so people can see right through you! But who cares? As long as I babble and gibber prayers at the synagogue and gibber philosophy with all the wise old beards—'Zim-zim-zim, what do you think about heaven? Zom-zom-zom, what do you think about hell?' And what good does that do anybody? Does it help God, maybe? As well as I know him, he feels the same way about it that I do. 'What bug gave them a bite?' he wonders. And he scratches his head.

"But all good things come to an end. I'm leaving. I'm going away, you understand? I'm going back to dear old Krichovnick, where the morons and the illiterates live! And I'll tell them you're dead. I'll go into mourning, and believe me, as your widow—are you listening, Alexander of Zemyock?—I'll be a thousand times happier than I was as your wife! And the plague take me off if——"

Mordecai watched her silently, raising a pained eyebrow, and murmured one word, always the same, with the expert, resigned patience required with animals: "Come . . . come . . . come . . ."

And saying it he ran one hand through that wild head of hair, and musing upon his wife with an infinite tenderness raised his mustache in a smile so young that poor frenzied Judith threw herself into his arms.

All their arguments ended that way. Mordecai never explained himself any further, for the simple reason that he did not understand the reproaches of his poor exiled wife. At night, while she lay beside him, he was taken by an obscure pity for her, for himself, Mordecai, for these two strangers whom the lightning madness of love had thrown into the same bed and who were still unable to address each other like creatures of reason.

"At least," she asked him sometimes in the communion of the marriage bed, "if I knew what was behind all these stories about the Just Men . . . Why do they have to suffer that way?"

Roused from torpor, Mordecai stretched out an arm in the darkness and, encompassing what he could, drew nearer to the good odor of milk spiced with cinnamon that rose from Judith's languid body.

"Marvel of my nights," he exhaled smiling, his lips against his wife's skin, "and who does not suffer? Think," he went on, continuing in his wily way, "of what you make me endure and what you endure because of me. There it is—our suffering is heavy with sin and drags itself on the ground like a worm, like a bad prayer."

"What sin are you talking about?" Judith asked, repulsing him, but with an insidious gentleness.

"But the Lamed-Vovnik takes our suffering upon himself," he went on playfully. "And he raises it to heaven and sets it at the feet of the Lord—who forgives. Which is why the world goes on . . . in spite of all our sins," he concluded tenderly.

Judith loved to change his mood. "Then tell me why the Just Men of Zemyock die in their beds." Thwarted, Mordecai detached himself from the undulating body—a river flowing with life—to find himself suddenly on the sharp, stony bank of reality.

"It's an old question," he said dreamily, to himself more than to his wife. "But to answer it we'd have to know what goes in the heart of a Lamed-Vovnik, and he himself doesn't know, isn't aware that his heart is bleeding away. He thinks it's simply life passing through him. When a Just Man smiles at a baby, there is as much suffering in him, they say, as in a Just Man undergoing martyrdom. And you see, when a Lamed-Vovnik weeps, or whatever he does, even when he's in bed as I am, with the wife he loves, he takes upon himself a thirty-sixth part of all the suffering on earth. But he doesn't know it, and his wife doesn't know it, and half his heart cries out while the other half sings. So what can martyrdom add? Perhaps—who knows?— God wanted the Levys to rest for a bit. Who knows?"

I must be really stupid, Judith decided gently under the blanket. Then she burst into laughter, and in a wild fling threw herself against him, prancing in a rare good humor. "Do you know that I didn't understand a word of that?" she bubbled into his ear, punctuating with little kisses—by which she won pardon for that confession. "Do you know that I'll never understand? You have to tell me about miraculous rabbis who pull evil spirits out of you like thorns in the foot. They make a prayer, it goes up to heaven, and oop! There you are! But the Just Men, where are their miracles?"

The man marveled at her. "A Just Man doesn't have to work miracles; he's like you, he *is* a miracle—a living miracle. Do you understand that at least, little idiot?" In the soft night Judith, for one instant, opened wide, questioning eyes.

One day she went to find the incumbent Lamed-Vovnik.

Rabbi Raphael Levy, with whom she held a long confabulation. A few months later, that Just Man died in strange circumstances. His testimony being the sole basis of an accusation of theft, he was unable to bring himself to offer it and spent the whole of the night before the trial battling with himself—torn, they said later, between the contradictory angels of mercy and of justice. When dawn broke, he lay down on the ground, closed his eyes and died. That end pleased Mordecai prodigiously.

"But why does it make him a martyr?" Judith, intrigued, wanted to know. "At home in Krichovnick, the beadle before you took flight the same way. One day someone made him see what was up between his wife and Heschke of the Golden Tongue. He said, 'Poor little soul, if she knew that I knew—whatever happens, don't tell her, all right?' He went home, he went to bed beside her, and in the morning he was cold. There's your martyrdom! And besides he looked exactly like your Rabbi Raphael—a sharp little man who trimmed his beard sloppily and stuck out his tongue when he talked. You understand? A *sharp* little man who couldn't come to the point!"

Mordecai's penetrating glance fell on her. "And how do you know that the Lamed-Vovnik (may God take him in his hands and breathe gently upon him!), how do you know he was *sharp?* He never appeared in public."

Judith's nostrils twitched, she stormed, whinnied, confessed. "You know how I am," she began tearfully, "but just the same I never wanted to shame you, so I went to him for advice. I've been in Zemyock for two years, I told him, and I haven't changed by a hair. I'm still as crazy as I ever was. What can I do? He stood so well with God, he might have had a little prayer for me, no?"

Mordecai looked away, annoyed. "And what did he answer?"

"Oh, silly stories!" she cried, furious at the memory of the encounter. "At first he couldn't answer at all, he was laughing so hard. Like a chicken, you know, kut-kut-kut. Then he stuck out his tongue and he said, 'You are Judith? Kut-kut, then remain Judith, kut. The camel, kut-kut, who wanted horns, kut-kut-kut, lost his ears, kut.' There!" she finished, tossing her head indignantly.

Abandoning all dignity, Mordecai burst out, "Ah, you! My crazy mare!" And striding toward her he took her nose solidly between his fingers, and laughing in great gusts, he tugged at her curls with his free hand.

Judith arched away and launched one of her marvelous furies, but in her heart she was delighted. She saw that she would remain "stupid" all her life; she made of it first a justification and then a glory. "I, who have the wit of a potato," she took pleasure in saying (thus announcing one of her incursions into the kingdom of the mind), "I, who am not intelligent," she went on in tones so ambiguous that they wondered if perhaps she considered intelligence a flaw from which she was, thank God, exempt, "I, who am nothing at all, *I think* that——"

And yet inexplicably a sense of pride came to her at being allied to the Levys, and with the aid of that subtle balm she ended by feeling as much a native of Zemyock as anyone else.

Judith's dowry had permitted them to move into a small house of two rooms not far from the workshops. But the depression in crystal ran on unchecked, and with unemployment came the misery of another epoch. Newborn babies succumbed to an unknown disease that took them in the second month, fresh and pink, to depose them a few weeks later in the corner of the cemetery reserved for children—but now they were entirely blue, stunted, abominable larvae with extremities twisted like talons. Was it the cold, the hunger, or the blue sickness? The first three fruits of Judith's womb died on the vine—she miscarried. Each time he felt the noble intoxication of progressing by even a hair in his knowledge of the Talmud, Mordecai imagined that it was at the price of innocent blood. When Judith found herself pregnant again he decided—at the risk of cutting himself off from God—to take up peddling again.

It was on an ordinary winter morning. Confused, Judith

added that she had known for two weeks but had not dared to tell him.

The man's first impulse was to press, gratefully but prudently, that belly against his own. "Why didn't you dare?" he asked, smiling. "It's not as though it were the first time."

Judith smiled weakly, in sweet desolation. "I don't know . . . My belly is full of joy, but the joy hasn't reached my heart."

She had stepped away, and now she stood out of her husband's reach, behind the table, wrapped in the great tattered fichu he had once loved. Invaded by his wife's fear, Mordecai turned atrociously pale. And as his own happiness died, a chill of the soul glazed his eyes and he saw with a cruel clarity the changes life had accomplished in the marvelous Judith since their arrival in Zemyock five years before.

Six feet from him, across the table, stood a woman whose face placed her in her thirties and who was not yet twenty-five. If she seemed more, Mordecai understood suddenly, it was not that the years had weighed heavily upon her body but rather that her character had been formed by the misfortunes of the times, and had stamped a sort of premature aging on her features. She had a cat's face now, which would hardly change until her death. Wide and bony at the base, her forehead rose in an ivory curve like a rock of which the peak alone receives the sun. Her brows took root above a firm, short nose, and the arc they traced, rising to mid-temple, was so perfectly designed that one might have thought them the brilliant brush strokes of a copyist of the Torah. Two wrinkles ran from above her nostrils to the bitter corners of her mouth, supporting firmly fleshed cheeks and imposing on the lower part of Judith's new face the alert discontent of an old cat.

She breathed gently, "You're right. We must rejoice."

And coming around the table in her long, dancing stride, she embraced her husband warmly.

Awkward in her emotion, she had slipped her face under the man's beard and left it buried there, like a furry, frightened animal; her hands were clasped at the small of

Mordecai's back. Mordecai barely felt her breathing against his neck, a humid breath, lulled to quietude already, perfectly gentle and regular.

He choked out, "Yes, yes . . . Let us rejoice."

But his heart was petrified with sorrow; he could think only of the cold, the hunger, the blue sickness, of all the misfortunes waiting for that belly blessed by God and which already, like the previous times, he thought he could feel pulsing against his own. As he dared a timid caress, barely sensual, on Judith's white neck, a question crossed his mind: Does God, blessed be his name, wish the death of infants?

All that day, prostrate in the synagogue, he argued with the fathomless heart of God. Toward the end of the afternoon the faithful, surprised, saw him burst into sobs and then rush out of the synagogue like a madman, his face dazzling in its joy. He had come to a decision.

.6.

THE HOUSE nestled at the far end of the village, beside the path that climbed toward the Hill of the Three Wells, but the snow was so thick, so thoroughly drifted over everything, that he had to pick his way in the dark. Judith had been waiting tensely; she opened the bolt the instant he spoke outside the door. She had gathered some dead wood, and the flickering orange of the fireplace battled the yellow halo of the old kerosene lamp that smoked benevolently in the middle of the table. Mordecai was amazed to see Judith wearing her old velveteen dress, the one she reserved for holidays. He had no time to shake the snow from his cloak—already his wife was embracing him with passionate pleasure, and smiling. "Do you see what's on the table? Mother Fink lent me a lump of butter, and I have an idea that the flour comes from Mrs. Blumenkrantz. Now how does that strike you?"

Bringing his gaze back to her, Mordecai found her so desirable that he was momentarily staggered. He leaned toward the face that offered itself to him. "Woman, this holiday is not on the calendar. My crazy mare, oh you . . ." Judith's mouth burned with a flame so bright that everything around her became night.

"Oh, my wife," he sighed finally. "Oh, my mare. And now it's my turn to give you a surprise, isn't it?"

"Don't be silly," Judith said, unbelieving. She laid her index finger on his lips; he nibbled at it.

"Now," he went on, holding her hand against his cheek, "I've just talked to Max Goldbaum. Eh, he had a money order from his brother—you remember him? The redhead with a nose like that, who left for America three years ago? Max is lending me two hundred zlotys, and tomorrow I'm off to Zratow, where I can pick up a little merchandise. I figured everything—with two hundred zlotys I can surely get back on my feet. So, what do you think of that, my own surprise?" he finished, pulling Judith's hair with both hands to bring her beloved face beneath his own, as in the nocturnal embrace. "What? Nothing to say?"

Judith's features were hard, metallic, her expression frozen in pride. "Yes," she said flatly. "I say that you haven't the right."

"But you yourself . . . Four years ago you begged me to think about food for the—you remember—the first one?"

"Yesterday is not today," Judith cut him off. "You know very well that your place is in the synagogue in Zemyock and not on the road like a tramp."

Mordecai cried out, "And the child? The child?" His distress was extreme.

Opening her shawl, the young woman placed her palms naïvely under the velveteen of her bodice, raising her breasts as an offering. "Look at my breasts. Look at them. The trouble with our babies was never hunger; I've always had good mother's milk. And then . . ." She trailed off suddenly.

"And then?"

Now Judith's fingers curved like claws and her feline body, leaning slightly forward, seemed about to spring; abruptly, throwing an angry glance at her husband, she let her fury run. "And what would they say about me if I let you lead the life of a wandering dog? You, you, you, a man so pious now that Mother Fink was saying to me only this afternoon—only this afternoon—that I must feel closer to God since I married you.

"They'd be too happy, those gossips, those women with the tongues of serpents: 'Look,' they'd say, 'the madame eats caviar while he swallows his shame on the road.' And they'd say, 'Ah, too bad he married that doll of a peasant. He might have been a saint with the help of a real Jewish woman of Zemyock. Where will he say his prayers? On a haystack. With whom will he discourse? With the cows!' "

Tossing her head furiously, Judith seemed to be resisting the arrival of a pleasant thought, which suddenly brushed her lips in the form of a moist, thin smile: "And then . . ."

Now Mordecai was altogether upset. "And then?"

Trying to escape his look, Judith threw her arms around his neck, and in a tone of amorous confidence, her strong voice as transparent as a little girl's, she murmured into his lightly hairy ear. "And then me, what would I think of myself?"

Mordecai threw up his arms playfully. "God in heaven: a miracle!"

While a neighbor woman sponged her thighs, heavy with flesh and blood, Judith waited anxiously for the cry of the newborn. It came only at the sixth minute. The midwife slipped a fat finger between the gums of the baby and to the great surprise of the prostrate mother withdrew a clot of blood the size of a hazelnut. Filling her matronly lungs then, she forced her tongue into the creature's mouth and blew in a slow, voluminous mouthful of air. A trembling stirred the little mass of purplish flesh. In their efforts to hold on to the vital breath, the minuscule fingers and toes knotted, clenched, arched like the talons in the blue disease. Finally the mouth opened on a thin cry. . . . "What good is that?" grumbled the skeptical midwife while Judith rolled over on her pillow, soft and moist to her very soul, reconciled with life.

A frail plant, the new arrival offered no scope to disease. Contrary to all expectations, he survived.

In a slender body, host to only a droplet of life, he displayed two round eyes full of a hard malice that, according to Judith, hurt her like touching a pinpoint to her finger. She added immediately, "But will he be a *sharp* one who pricks others, or one who pricks himself?"

"I'm afraid he's like a mosquito," Mordecai murmured unhappily.

Shocked by the small size of his son, the father could not see him as an authentic and veritable descendant of the dynasty. There has been an error in heaven, he told himself in consolation. And then, Judith having presented him with three more Levys, one after another, all richly formed by nature, he forgot his first mortification, thanked a clement heaven, and forgave the mosquito.

This last seemed animated by a frenzy proper to certain insects; he never stopped prowling, investigating, fidgeting in all directions, as if through his gymnastics he would fill all the space that his skinny limbs left gaping about him. Judith was ecstatic. "And how can I stop him?" she asked a furious Mordecai. "If I grab him by an arm it may break off; what would we do with a baby's wing? And you're being unfair to him. He didn't come into the world all by himself; flesh of your flesh, he is."

"Of the flesh only, worse luck." Consequently Mordecai neglected the mosquito's religious instruction, consecrating the greater part of his time to the three later sons, who were already beyond their elder brother in size as well as knowledge. And as soon as Benjamin had reached the age of eight, his father hurried him into an apprenticeship with a tailor, which, if it did not result in a salary, at least economized by one mouth at the noonday meal.

*   *   *

Benjamin was certainly a *sharp one,* as Judith said, but he was of those whose pointed souls are turned inward against themselves. Yielded so young to the caprice of his master, that point was sharpened: he suffered.

Though he applied himself to the work, immobility made him nervous. He contained himself badly, and all the animal spirits dancing incessantly in his body kept him fluttering constantly on the stool that was his prison. Reduced to his own resources and guessing that he was somehow segregated from the profound community of the Levys, he began to examine the world with an eye not Jewish but in some way passionately personal. He knew now, for example, that if the Just Man was the king of Zemyock, there yet existed other powers in the world—and perhaps, he told himself, not without malice, there existed somewhere a Just Man greater than Zemyock's. . . . Who knew?

His doubts were crystallized on the day of his *bar mitzvah* when, according to custom, the young communicant was presented to the incumbent Just Man. The latter had achieved a septuagenarian dignity stiffened by rheumatism. As his infirmities kept him imprisoned in his room, the younger generation knew of him only by hearsay and consequently imagined him so much more solemn and wraithlike. His house was halfway up the Street of the Glass Blowers, at the foot of which the rusty chains of the former ghetto were still visible, wound about two stone markers.

Gliding in the costume borrowed for the occasion, Benjamin, all his senses sharpened, made his entry into a very dim, malodorous hallway. He pointed his nose left and right in the vain hope of descrying some sign characteristic of the presence of a Lamed-Vovnik. But when, flanked by his pale father and poor Judith, he entered a small, dark room, so excited at seeing the "miracle" at close range, Benjamin felt the marvelous thrill of discovering an attic—masses of dark air, bizarre objects and furniture heaped in disorder, a trembling shaft of light as though from a dormer window, the subtle presence of dust. . . .

"Step forward!" Judith cried, shoving him to the center of the room.

"Tut-tut," a disapproving voice said suddenly.

Squinting, Benjamin made out an old man who had been seated in the dark recesses behind a narrow iron bed. A black skullcap on a pink skull, his robe belted by a silvered sash, the old man was stepping forward now with the help of a cane; at each step he twitched it forward like a frail and insufficient prop, while his body curved in the shadows with the panting exhalation of an exhausted animal. When he was quite close to the child, the latter discovered with piquant pleasure that the Lamed-Vovnik was not at all different from the old-timers who mumbled nonsense on the stone bench in front of the synagogue and who, if you passed within reach of their gnarled hands, never failed to caress the back of your neck or to tweak your ears with a greedy little gesture. Entirely reinvigorated, Benjamin grasped the dangling hand of the old man and placed it with an air of complicity on his own head, which it covered altogether, to the ears.

"My God, may the holy man forgive this rascal!" Mordecai cried in terrible alarm. And turning to the child who was smiling beneath the hand, he thundered, "What did I tell you? You *kiss* the holy man's hand!"

"Oh, that's all right, it's all right," bleated the old gentleman, who seemed greatly amused. "Well, well. . . . The child has blessed himself."

And caressing Benjamin's neck (as foreseen), the hand descended to his chin and raised it with a gentleness full of nostalgia. "This is Benjamin, then, son of Mordecai?"

The child confirmed it with a friendly wink.

"This is then the new Jew that God brings us today?"

"Oh, yes," Benjamin answered condescendingly.

Under the shadowed vault of his brows, the old gentleman's gaze sparkled in bluish irony. His eye was clear, unringed by wrinkles, but at the moment when the old man's eyes met the child's, Benjamin felt a slight burning sensation and suddenly lowered his lids, astonished.

"And tell me, Benjamin, tell me now—what do you know of the Pentateuch?"

The child was silent.

"May the holy man forgive us," Mordecai said, "this little fellow doesn't study much. He's a tailor's apprentice."

A thick silence fell upon the room. Judith stared at her husband, who had stepped back a pace or two in shame toward the door. Benjamin released a plaintive sob.

"And I, what do I know of the Pentateuch?" the Just Man asked suddenly in a voice whose softness seemed aimed at the child.

Surprised, Benjamin raised his eyes. Above him the bony white head nodded tremulously, as the old man's mouth opened in a sweet, dark smile.

"Tut-tut-tut. A little tailor, eh?" the Just Man bleated. Slipping his index finger under the boy's palm, he raised the small hand to his lips, sheltered behind the beard, and kissed it.

Then, seeming to come to himself, he sent his visitors away with sweeping gestures that admitted of no reply. The interview was over.

They all wanted to inspect the hand that the Just Man had kissed. A yellow aureole was still visible upon it, a vestige of the old mouth stained with tobacco, and they made the child swear not to wash as long as it was still there. The boy's identity seemed concentrated in that hand; he was spoiled by visitors and his brothers made flat advances to him. The proposal to wrap the hand in a band was dismissed. Only Mordecai shrugged, saying that it was all incomprehensible, that it was doubtless one of those "obvious oddities" that are commonplace in the lives of the Just Men. But Benjamin tended rather to the view of his mother Judith, who had let slip the thought that after all the Just Man seemed to her a "good little old fellow like the rest of us." Secretly Benjamin agreed.

The faint illusions he still entertained of the Just Men were dissipated during his stay in Bialystok, where several years after all this, now become a lackluster, well-bred young man, delicate of eye, the rough edges worn smooth and dull, he had gone to finish his apprenticeship.

Bialystok was a true city with apartment buildings, tricycle carts, horse cabs and drivers identical in every respect to those he had seen in the one copy of a Polish newspaper possessed by his former master.

He remained for two years. They worked fifteen hours at a stretch in a small room drowned in the constant vapor of the steam presser. Five commingled sweats composed a startling variety of perfumes. Benjamin was at once companion, apprentice, delivery boy, handyman, nursemaid and even now and then cook, when the boss's obese wife felt excessively torpid. But he believed that he was living an adventure unique in the annals of the Levys, for everything, even the dim air of the workshop, belonged to a world infinitely more real than Zemyock, that bazaar of dreams. . . .

At noon he ate lunch in the company of the presser, Mr. Goldfaden, an old handyman whom the boss had been threatening to fire ever since his emaciated arms had begun to have trouble raising the enormous steam presser. Benjamin was bound to him in a wordless friendship made up of routine daily activities. One day when the formidable Mr. Rosnek, the boss, had gone out to deliver personally a valuable redingote, Benjamin looked up from his needle and said without thinking, "Pardon me, my dear Mr. Goldfaden, but may I ask what you will do when the day comes you can no longer manage the steam presser?"

The presser dropped the iron to its tripod and his pasty face, as though souffléed by forty years of sluggish, suffocating heat, took on a displeased expression. "What will I do?" he articulated slowly. "With God's permission, my child, I shall starve to death!"

"But you're a good Jew, Mr. Goldfaden. And God will not——"

"I am not a good Jew," the old man cut him short grimly.

On those words his face sagged in fear, and Benjamin recognized the magisterial tread of Mr. Rosnek in the next room.

The next day Goldfaden became bolder and revealed to the adolescent that almost six months before, he had ceased to believe in God. Benjamin stared at him uncomprehending. Mr. Goldfaden, this cosmopolitan gentleman, had shown him more consideration than anyone except the Lamed-Vovnik had ever displayed. Assuredly, he was not an unbeliever; then what could this mean? "What do you mean exactly, dear Mr. Goldfaden, when you tell me that you don't believe in God? I am not entirely sure," he added smiling, "that I grasp the basis of your thought."

The old man turned away; he seemed mysteriously irritated by Benjamin's tone. The boy went on with the same skeptical indulgence, "Am I to deduce, dear Mr. Goldfaden, that you don't believe that God created the heavens and the earth and all that followed?"

As he pronounced those words he was illumined by a sudden insight, and Benjamin understood that the good Mr. Goldfaden quite simply did not believe in God.

"But after all, dear Mr. Goldfaden," he went on, chilled by fear, "if God did not exist, what would you and I be?"

The old man offered a compassionate smile, and his voice sought vainly for the lost tone of gaiety. "Poor little Jewish workingmen, no?"

"And that's all?"

"Alas," said the old presser.

That night on his mattress set directly on the floor Benjamin tried to picture all things as Mr. Goldfaden must see them. Bit by bit he arrived at the terrifying conclusion that if God did not exist, Zemyock was only an absurd fragment of the universe. But then, he wondered, where does all the suffering go? And seeing again Mr. Goldfaden's hopeless expression, he cried out, in a sob that ripped through the darkness of the workshop, "It goes for nothing. Oh, my God, it goes for nothing!"

He could go no further; he wept for a long time and then fell asleep.

Every day the presser became more awkward. When the boss was out, he took to raising the iron with both hands. Finally he dropped it, in an acrid scorch of cloth and dry wood. The fire left only a black smudge on the floor, but the day after that accident, not seeing the old workman at his place, Benjamin came up against the somber silence of Mr. Rosnek.

In the afternoon a young man appeared whose arms were as skinny as Mr. Goldfaden's but who seemed resolved not to drop the iron.

Benjamin did not become at all friendly with him. The young man told racy stories, wore a tie, and expressed scorn for "pinheads" who did not see life as it really was. He was an authentic unbeliever, while Mr. Goldfaden—Benjamin felt this strongly—had lost only the traditional outward aspects of the good Jew. It was nevertheless better not to set this man of the world against him, which is why, caught up in the toils of his own diplomacy, Benjamin found himself one night in an alley where women walked. The unbeliever made all the arrangements. As if in a dream, Benjamin ascended carpeted stairs and followed a corridor worthy of a palace. Then there was a room appointed in frightening luxury, as if tapestried with mirrors, and then a fat woman who transformed herself into a mauve, trembling flesh-and-blood doll. Somewhere beyond the globe of light the Song of Songs glittered: *"Come with me from Lebanon, my spouse. . . ."*

Squatting on the bidet, the flesh-and-blood doll bade him approach. Beckoning, her index finger crooked and straightened, crooked and straightened. Benjamin murmured in Polish, "Pardon me, Miss," opened the bolted door and fled.

·7·

WHEN HE RETURNED to Zemyock, Benjamin had definitively abandoned all search for the truth; all he wanted
was to retrieve those crumbs of daily purity that he had fled
from two years before and that henceforward he would value
above all things. Judith's nose twitched, her fingernails flashed
forward. When Benjamin wormed out from under her still
flapping wing, Mordecai in turn welcomed him. He looked into
his son's eyes, found them clear, and pronouncing the prayer
of welcome rubbed his mustaches solemnly against Benjamin's
forehead. Benjamin decided, in his renewed plenitude, "My
God! If all this is error, I prefer it to the picayune reality of
the unbelievers!"

But the line of demarcation was still fuzzy. If Zemyock was
only a dream, than what was he, Benjamin—no longer even a
part of that dream . . . ?

The year he returned to his home town, a war broke out
somewhere in Europe.

The gentle souls of Zemyock were informed of this only in
the month of February, 1915, by letters arriving from Paris,
Berlin and New York. Strange rumors spread. It was learned
from them that the Jews of France and Germany had been
obliged to don the uniforms of hate and to do battle, just like
those cruel beasts of Christians: they were *forced to!*

These horrendous facts were the subject of scathing dis-
cussions among the elders, some of whom maintained that it
was wrong to cast a stone at the faithful who were constrained
to bear arms for the nations. But all talk gave way to the
blackest mourning, to prayer and affliction, when they learned
by the next mail that boys from the same town, brothers who
had settled in mutually hostile countries, ran the risk in these
faceless massacres of assassinating each other most Christianly.

Moaning, they repeated the gloomy pronouncement of the Just Man: "All this is happening," he said in the Council of Elders, "because Israel is tired of carrying the sacrificial knife in its own throat. The sacrificial lamb has gone out among the Nations, he has knelt before their idols, he knew not contentment, he no longer wished to live with God. Our unfortunate brothers have become Frenchmen, Germans, Turks and perhaps Chinese, imagining that in ceasing to be Jews they would cease to suffer. But behold—the Eternal sees today what has never been seen in the two thousand years of exile. Adorned with strange armors, speaking different tongues, adoring faceless idols, *Jews are killing one another!* Malediction!" And seated on the bare ground, the Just Man heaped his white hair with dust and rocked back and forth with shrill cries, like a wounded animal.

The women retailed a strange story (no one knew who had brought it to Zemyock): "It is night at the front, a shadow, a shot. The Jew who has just fired hears a moan. . . .

"And then, mother, the hair stands up on his head, for only a few feet from him in the darkness the enemy voice is reciting in Hebrew the prayer of the dying. Ai, God, the soldier has cut down a Jewish brother! Ai, misery! He drops his rifle and runs into no man's land, insane with shame and grief. Insane, you understand? The enemy fires at him, his comrades shout at him to come back. But he refuses; he stays in no man's land and dies. Ai, misery, ai . . . !"

The war was not yet over when rumors of revolution reached them and then rumors of pogroms, rumors that rose like a whispering in the fields. The Ukraine was fire and blood. "As the buzzard and the kite share the heavens," the revolutionary bands of Makhno and the white-kepied detachments of the Czarist Petlura came down, turn and turn about, on the Jewish communities of the Great Plain. Even the people of Zemyock, though sheltered behind their hills, no longer knew what to think; several times, led astray by false reports, they fled into the wooded heights. Those who had stayed home in bed made fun of the returning fugitives, so that at the hour of real danger a great many people, become skeptical, were taken in the subtle trap of false alerts preceding the real thing. . . .

The night before the end, they saw a bright glow in the direction of the village of Pzkov. The month of August had been torrid, and they reassured themselves with the thought that it was a forest fire. The first cries echoed at dawn. It all happened very quickly. The Cossacks were already unfurling over Zemyock when many Jews, barely awake, showed themselves at the windows, bewildered, still in night clothes and with the skullcaps askew on their heads, shouting at the panicky fugitives to find out what was happening.

Accompanied only by their son Benjamin, Judith and Mordecai reached the peak of the Hill of the Three Wells safe and sound. Before following his parents into the groves, Benjamin could not resist a look back at the village now in the hands of the Cossacks. He was first struck by the beauty of the countryside. A ring of fog circled the little valley halfway up, and the green slopes trailed off into the shrouding gray to re-emerge fifty yards below. Black figures swarmed over the neighboring hills like so many ants. The pink roofs of the town stood out with a blinding sharpness within the ring of fog. Benjamin was looking for the open space of the church square when he heard the cries. Then he saw many blackish flakes seemingly born of the pink roofs as if by magic; the cries were now (thinned as they were by distance) like the ludicrous cheeping of a nest of baby birds. Above it all the sky remained motionless and blue. Benjamin opened his mouth to scream and then changed his mind. The air was absolutely still.

"What are you waiting for?" Someone had whispered; Benjamin turned and smiled mechanically. A few yards away, floating up out of the underbrush, the pale, hollow face of his mother Judith showed a mouth oddly open in mute appeal, while from the thicket a dreamlike hand rose, its index finger, in beckoning movement, reminding him of a child playing hide-and-seek. I'm stupid to smile, Benjamin thought. Still smiling, he crossed the ten yards of silent earth between him and the underbrush with what seemed to him a springy stride, and found himself suddenly in the crackling shadows of the pines, whose indifferent crests looked out over the smoking pink roofs below, in silent complicity with heaven.

"Did they follow us?" Judith gasped. She was trembling.

"Why should they follow us?" Benjamin said, absurdly. He sniffed at the odor of resin. There was that world down below -—and this one. Which was real? His mother Judith was bundled up in a coat of black cloth, and her feet were bare, and bare the upper part of her chest, which the tightly buttoned coat pressed lightly upward. The massive, square face of his mother Judith was white, and yet as if sprinkled with a fine red powder that had clotted in halos on her cheekbones. Her eyes seemed lidless. Benjamin suddenly understood the reason for his smile; his mother Judith had not had time to snatch up her wig, the wig of a Jewish wife, and her bare skull, recently shaved, displayed only a stubble of white hair, which gave her the look of an aged infant. Averting his eyes, Benjamin hoped that she was unaware of it. "Come on, come on." With a sharp tug Judith had pulled him behind the shrubbery while her heavy face turned scarlet, sweating with fear, with breathlessness and with a profound confusion apparent in her slightly demented gestures, her slightly mad expression.

As he followed the tall, wide, nervous figure of his mother into the underbrush, Benjamin became aware of his father, with the huge body of a woodcutter out of the Torah, well back in hiding, and who was not only fully dressed but had found the time and the wit to bring along his great prayer shawl, draping his chest with it as if with an armor against the evil raging in the air. All through their flight together, Mordecai had made haste slowly, content to lengthen his stride rather than rushing as Benjamin and his mother Judith had. Each time an impatient Benjamin turned toward his father, he believed he saw a delicate, dreaming expression on the majestic, emaciated old man's face, while the huge lumberjack's body accomplished, precisely, reflectively, and serenely, the actions necessary to flight. And halfway up the hill Benjamin had seen his mother Judith turn to Mordecai and say in a curt, breathy voice, "You're holding us up! Are you in such a hurry to die?"

The old man had stopped in the middle of the path, and as peacefully as if he were amid the circle of faithful in the synagogue, he had declared in sententious tones, "Woman, woman, do you think that you can hold back the hour of God?"

Then he had set forward slowly through the fog, like a stone column moved by a clumsy laborer. Piqued by the pity so apparent in her husband's voice, Judith had answered angrily, "And you, do you insist on setting it forward?" Panicky, Benjamin felt that she wanted to launch an immediate argument, but a shot from the bottom of the valley made her leap forward in confusion. And now his father was moving tranquilly through the shadows of the underbrush, seemingly undistressed by the branches scratching across his face or by the shrill wails that reached them from the floor of the valley, or even by the hate-filled glances that poor Judith threw his way when she stopped every ten steps to wait for him and suddenly set off again like an arrow, straight ahead, indifferent to her feet, bloody now, and to her breasts, one of which had pressed up out of the coat. After a time she stopped short and whispered, "Let's hide in the brush." The lines of her face had been distorted by terror, and Benjamin thought that she was frightful to look upon. Suddenly she seemed to notice the white pear of her breast, trembling outside the open cleft of her coat. Slowly she turned a wild look on the two men, and raising the collar of her coat held it tight from then on with two fists clenched in shame. Then she wept. Mordecai sat back against a pine. His heavy gray eyes stared aloft at the open patches of white and blue shifting against the upper branches, and his beard stirred lightly, as though he were muttering a prayer. Benjamin sat down and remained motionless. All three were so deeply plunged in thought that none heard the Cossack approach. Each of them was alone. Now and then Judith let her haunting fear escape between her teeth: "My God, what have you done with my other children? My God, only my sons and I . . . only us . . .

It was learned later that individual Cossacks had searched for the girls hidden away in the woods surrounding the valley of Zemyock. With no warning, Benjamin saw a fair-haired man in cavalry boots come into his field of vision. A thin ray of sunlight projected the Cossack's shadow almost to Benjamin's feet. He held his saber straight before him like a jib. The triangle of his chest was hairy, his moist yellow eyes glistened slyly and his square face was that of a Ukrainian peasant. He moved forward raising each booted foot in infinite caution. . . . His head still bowed against his knees, Benjamin wondered if his parents were pretending not to hear the snapping of twigs just behind them or if they were truly aware only of their disquieting thoughts. In that same instant Benjamin felt astonishment that his own heart was beating no more quickly, that no sound escaped his lips, that no tremor seized his members. Immediately the reassuring thought came to him that all of this was merely a spectacle in which he had no role except a contemplative one. Mordecai was still sitting back against his pine and Judith was still erect in the middle of the clearing, her eyes closed, trembling in all her opulent flesh, her fists clutching the collar of her coat. Benjamin noticed that on his retina the image of the Cossack made a sort of sparkling leap, landing with his feet together between Judith and Mordecai, who started in terror. The Cossack looked over his three victims scornfully, disappointed. Then, choosing Mordecai, he directed the point of the saber slowly toward the old man's throat. Until then Mordecai had not broken out of his relative calm. But when the point of the saber was a few inches from his throat, he threw his head back, flattened his hands firmly against the pine behind him and rolled furious eyes toward heaven as he shouted the first words of the prayer of the dying: *"Shema Yisrael!"*

In his voice was a tone so dark, so desperate, that Benjamin marveled at such an attachment to life.

The Cossack suddenly pointed at Mordecai's terrified face, seemed struck by an extremely comic idea, withdrew his saber in a convulsive gesture and burst into a horrifying whinny of laughter. He was doubled over, shaken by spasms and clutching at his belly with his left hand, the hilt of the saber in his right hand, its point stuck in the ground. No word had been spoken. Benjamin noticed that his mother Judith had come to life and guessed that her temper was rising. Suddenly he saw her raging, her patience scattered, angry as she was so often at home. What followed was unclear. Taking a step forward, his mother Judith had swung her left fist (or perhaps simply the powerful flat of her hand) against the Cossack's face, and when he went over immediately on his back, she snatched up the saber and struck blow after blow on the man's head and shoulders, as she might have with a meat cleaver. The Cossack's hands went to his head. Distinctly, Benjamin saw the wide blade of the saber cut through a wrist, which dropped away from the forearm with the passivity of a piece of kitchen meat. . . . When his father Mordecai rushed to his mother Judith, it seemed to Benjamin that a layer of skin had been peeled from his eyes. Was all that real? He could not yet believe it.

When darkness fell Benjamin took a chance at the edge of the wood. Deep in the valley all was silent, but a bad smell was rising and so were black spirals writhing through the deep blue of the night.

As he descended the slope, tiny sparks of light appeared here and there. He crossed the field where the washing and drying were done and slipped into the shadows behind a house. A Jewish silhouette crossed the street—beard and caftan, in its hand a candle. Trembling, Benjamin set out through the deserted streets of Zemyock. A sort of murmur rose from the center of town. It came from the church square, where dozens of figures, candles in hand, were identifying their dead among the indistinct heaps of corpses. At dawn, Benjamin discovered his three brothers under a portico. The whole day was given over to gravedigging. They improvised a new cemetery beside the old one. Benjamin and his father made several trips there to tear Judith away from the mound under which her three sons were buried. For a week Mordecai shut himself into a room with her. She believed that God had punished her for the murder of the fair-haired young man; she saw herself a criminal both to her sons and to their assassin. Her hand plunged an imaginary saber into her own breast. Then the fever fell.

They learned that the pogromists were White Guards who had come through that lost town of Zemyock entirely by accident. They were on their way to the Ukraine under the command of German, French, English and American officers for the common purpose of destroying the new materialist regime. They were led by Kozyr Zyrko, a celebrated hetman. Many of the Jews of Zemyock had reached the hills. Kozyr Zyrko had assembled the others in the church square, and by way of encouragement to his men had hoisted an infant on the point of his lance. "This is a nothing!" he shouted. "A nothing! This is the seed of revolution!"

A singular thing: while families knotted together in bloody clusters and died embracing, the old incumbent Lamed-Vovnik trotted among the corpses, begging vainly, "Pierce, pierce, kill me too!"—to the great happiness of the soldiers who, finding him comical, confined themselves to slicing off his beard. And several times they simulated his execution. Kneeling, his eyes closed, the old Jew submitted himself in a kind of ecstasy; but constantly disappointed in his human despair and in his legitimate hopes as a Just Man, he remained the only survivor in the church square.

The pogrom at Zemyock passed unremarked among hundreds of others. Little by little, help came. The Jews of Europe and America banded together once more. But when peace was restored after the decade of the twenties, the survivors of the pogrom discussed the miraculous survival of the Just Man. Some saw in it a measure of the celestial meekness, others scented out a mysterious and terrifying irony of God, hinted at in the sacred texts. A rancor stole into the hearts of certain inhabitants of Zemyock. The young ones were joining the

Jewish General Union of Russian and Polish Workers, and the desire to live and die in the forbidden land of Canaan suddenly flooded the Jewish soul like a powerful, voracious ground swell. Judith announced openly and sarcastically that the survival of the Just Man was an event so ridiculous that henceforth the Levys could abandon their pretensions. Benjamin agreed silently. Mordecai flashed them a glance compounded of astonishment and a nameless bitterness. He felt betrayed, but he could not have said whether by his own family or by God. His sons were dead and the Lamed-Vovnik was alive. Perhaps in that there was some particularly occult intention of the Most High?

In his doubt, he allowed Benjamin to exile himself abroad. And if he had not permitted it, his declining authority could never have stood up against the thenceforth inflexible will of Judith.

III

STILLENSTADT

. 1 .

Benjamin dallied for several days in Warsaw, undecided about his choice of exile. He felt as though it were a game, a childish fairy tale. The names of the countries proposed seemed as little serious, as altogether fantastic as the squares traced out by children in the Jewish version of hopscotch, which stood for a loaf of white bread, a sigh, a pound of chick-peas, an insult, a chicken in the pot, a Polish slap, a million zlotys, typhus, a week among the angels and finally a pogrom. The ball rolled about in his mind, crossing one by one the squares established by the Committee of Rescue and Emigration and returning sadly to its starting point, nothing settled.

Generally the ball rolled very quickly past the word "England": how could he flee from an island in an emergency? But it lingered pleasurably on the word "America"—that vocable first of all suggested the furious ocean that would separate Benjamin from his family; then it recalled the Biblical dance about the Golden Calf, to which his tailor master in Zemyock had once compared the life of American Jews; and finally it evoked the fatted calf, salacious, rolling blind orbs over the Creation. As for the word "France," it suffered the inconvenience of association with the word "Dreyfus," which Benjamin had heard often. They said that the French had sent this Jew to Devil's Island; if the name alone stimulated a shudder, what must the thing itself be like?

At last, after this painful tour of the world Benjamin decided in favor of the word "Germany." For the German Jews, he had heard, were so pleasantly established in that country that a number of them considered themselves "almost" more

German than Jewish. This was doubtless very strange, if not praiseworthy, but it demonstrated all the better the warmth and gentleness of the German character. Immediately, in a transport of enthusiasm Benjamin imagined a German personality so exquisite, so refined, in short so noble that the Jews, conscience-stricken and lost in admiration, became German to the depths of their souls.

Berlin disappointed him immediately. The city had no beginning and no end. He had been there hardly twenty-four hours when he felt the desire to flee—but where this time, O Lord? The Committee had quartered him in an abandoned synagogue with hundreds of refugees from the East. Whole families lived in a great hall divided into apartments by chalk lines. Cutting the hall in two, an aisle barely two feet wide gave the tenants access to the door. Each resident feigned unawareness of his neighbor's existence. To cross a chalk circle was to straddle the wall of a private life. To pay a visit one said with a forced smile, "Knock-knock," and waited politely until the host invited one to enter. It was as though they had all been driven crazy by homelessness. Some of them attached cords to the ceiling and hung up a mirror, a painting, a family photograph. Only the children obstinately refused to honor the "walls" drawn by the adults, which occasioned constant squalling and squabbling.

"They're all waiting for an apartment," said a young man standing in the chalk aisle on Benjamin's first day. "They still have hope!"

"And what are you waiting for?" Benjamin asked smiling.

A face loomed out of the shadow above Benjamin, who raised his eyes uneasily. The young man had just left his bed. His unruly red hair seemed to slash at the surface of his forehead, where Benjamin saw a swollen wrinkle like a scar, twisted vertically. The young man snickered, "I'm waiting for the Messiah, but he's in no hurry. He has all eternity, no? Greetings."

Such was Benjamin's first meeting with the young man from Galicia, whom he was to see often in the weeks to come, forever reclining or seated on the edge of his bed, plunged in a dream, his hands trembling like an old man's. Benjamin suspected that he was dying of hunger. When he received a package from the Committee, he invited the young man to share the soul-stirring omelet, the kosher frankfurters that inevitably made him think of home, or some other most rare viand that he stewed over the flame of the spirit lamp. Depending on his mood, the young Galician followed him with a constrained smile or insulted him obliquely.

"When are you going to leave me alone?" he said one day.

"Excuse me," Benjamin stammered, "I've just found work, so I allowed myself to prepare a little banquet. . . . You understand?"

"Go on," the other said more calmly, almost indulgently. "I know, I know how much you wanted to find a job, how hard you'll work, how happy you'll be working. I congratulate you. What more do you want?"

Benjamin lamented sadly in the ancient words, "And who will not eat this night?"

A gentle Jewish gleam rose to the flat eyes of the Galician. Then the gleam wavered and became a flash of incomprehensible nastiness. "Never mind. You eat for me."

The words struck Benjamin like a slap. Benjamin retreated prudently, followed by the hostile comments of the "tenants," all of whom were ashamed of the Galician and seemed incensed by Benjamin's kindness to him, in which they saw an implied repudiation of their judgment of good men.

Back in his own room, Benjamin turned and noticed that the young redhead had fallen into his habitual attitude, head between his hands, prisoner of some unknowable dream that isolated him as thoroughly as if he had been truly alone and not at the continual mercy of two hundred hostile glances. "What can he be thinking about?" Benjamin wondered, not without the sharp uneasiness that the Galician's presence, or even the simple mental image of him, always brought on.

He probed into his pot and bit into a kosher sausage without pleasure. "Of course I embarrassed him, the poor sad young man, but he will never know what miserable pleasure I took in his company. . . ." And ceasing to chew for a moment, he wondered for perhaps the thousandth time, "Is he a sharp one who only pricks others or does he prick himself too? There's the question."

Nevertheless, and though he reproached himself for it, he was much relieved the next morning as he walked down the chalked aisle on his way to work to notice that the young Galician barely glanced his way. Already dressed, he lay on his bed, his bare, blackened feet splayed shamelessly at eye level of the tiny children who played near him, knocking at the invisible doors along the corridor. He never even blinked. He had cut the last thread of the frail mooring that united him with the synagogue, and it seemed to Benjamin from then on that every day the young man receded farther from the shore line of his own people, lying on his bed, gliding toward a high sea known only to himself and reflected in the gloomy roll of his eyes.

But the young Galician, of whom Benjamin now considered himself free, reappeared to him cunningly in the persons of his fellow workers, who were all victims, though to a lesser degree, of the same disease—the "Berlin madness," as he called it when he had painfully come to know it better.

Herr Flambaum's employees were all fugitives from the pogroms and bore some trace of the upheaval, but the workshop was suffused with an atmosphere of snarling mockery, ironic deprecation of the old life in Russia and in Poland. A demoniac spirit breathed in all of them, changing clear water to blood, killing off the delectable roots of goodness, showering rain and hail on each shoot of Jewish thought bursting up from the soul. Benjamin offered a hand and seemed to see a bloody scratch rise across it. Though, bent cautiously over his stitching, he contradicted no one, all those lances, all those knives, all those needles shaped by their eyes seemed to turn against him. They took the form of ridicule. One day when the boss was out, Lembke Davidovicz jumped up on the cutting table with the "Berlin rictus" twisting his lower lip. "Listen," he proceeded in a voice now grave, now modulated to a sort of tart sob, "listen, if the little rabbi keeps his virginity too long he'll grow wings from his shoulder blades. And then what? He'll be edible, delicious. The whole world can feed on him— you, me, the last little German half-wit can reach out a hand and tear off a wing or a leg. They'll all want a bite," he laughed. "And better than that—when there's nothing left but his little angelic delectable rabbi's heart (and who, fellow citizens, would want it, the soft, flabby part with no future on the market, not even listed on the Berlin exchange?), then we'll sit him down on a train and sound the trumpets! Sound the trumpets of God—a little Jewish heart is going home!"

This discourse evoked delirious enthusiasm. The orator, grimacing appropriately, took several bows, jumped from the table and shook the proffered hands with mock greediness. They forgot about the victim.

"Look," someone called, "he's stuck himself. He's bleeding."

Struck dumb, Benjamin contemplated the disaster of his thumb bleeding onto the pale cloth. The workshop was silent.

"We're the ones who cut him," Lembke Davidovicz said softly.

"We did it," another said.

"Have we forgotten everything?" Lembke, looking at Benjamin as if he had never really seen him, went on as his obese body sagged under the weight of the sudden discovery his own eyes had made—eyes almost feminine, with long lashes fluttering now over an entirely disarmed look, sad and naked. "Have we become such perfect German gentlemen?" he asked finally, with a disgust on his face that was immediately reproduced on the faces of all of Flambaum's employees.

"At least it didn't hit the bone?" a worried voice asked.

Lembke approached Benjamin and gestured suddenly. "Go ahead, talk!" he cried. "Insult us but say something—one word! Just one!"

But Benjamin, his eyes still glittering with suppressed tears, could only nod pensively, his thumb deep in his mouth, his appearance at once pathetic and comic while, mixed with the bitter taste of his blood, he had already tasted the startling thought that they would never "prick" him again.

. 2 .

BENJAMIN stopped before the synagogue, and thinking that one brain was not enough in this world below, he scraped his boots vigorously on the mat crusted with snow and mud.

Within, beneath the high nave of shadow that failed to repel the cones of light from the candles, the stripping bare of all these lives upset him once again—here an old man groaning under his blanket, farther along the young couple restricted to the motionless embrace of statues before the obviously interested eyes of a pale urchin whose mother was squatting before a tiny spirit lamp, her shaky hands sheltering a finger of flame that seemed to flee along the icy stone of the floor. . . . And as for the uproar, as for the ghastly screaming of children, he could not be sure whether his ears had become more sensitive or the young throats, cloistered for so many months in this vast, airless, lightless dormitory, had become only more piercing.

"Home so soon, Herr Benjamin?"

Halting in the chalk aisle, Benjamin, who had recognized the voice perfectly, pretended to be investigating the darkness of the bed from which it had come.

"My dear sir, do you no longer wish to recognize me?"

Benjamin was upset. "Forgive me—can't see a thing in here. So, Yankel, what can you tell me that's good since——"

The sickly face, the red hair, came out of the shadows. "Nothing," the face said. "You keep alive."

His adolescent slimness accented the incisive character of his nervous mouth, his long, melancholy, hooked nose, his flat

eyes so cold that Benjamin had difficulty meeting them. "But
come in," Yankel said quietly, as if it were the normal thing
to do. "No admission fee. My word of honor."

Immediately Benjamin sensed a "suffering in the soul" in
the boy's unusual behavior, and raising a foot modestly, he set
it down on the other side of the chalk circle. "Well, Yankel,
how does life suit you?"

"It doesn't suit me at all," the young Galician said. "Several
sizes too big for me. Or maybe too small—I don't even know
any more. But you must be wondering, 'How come this
young fellow who hasn't said a word to me for two months is
suddenly talking to me again? Surely he must want a good
omelet or——' "

"No!" Benjamin cried. "A thought like that would never
have occurred to me."

"Forgive me," said the young Galician. "I don't know how I
get along. It's my tongue. I can feel it like a knife in my mouth.
And when I use it, it has to cut someone. But it wasn't always
like that, my tongue——"

"No?"

The young man laughed loudly. "No, I swear it, once I had a
velvet tongue. Once. But please sit down, and if you don't
mind, not just on one buttock. Good. And now let me look at
you, let me admire the new man! Ah, look, you've kept your
fur cap, your bootees, your Hasidic caftan, and my God, you
haven't even had those rabbinical curls cut! How can that be?
Don't you know yet that you're in Berlin?"

"Do you think I don't know it?"

The young man smiled vaguely.

"That I don't *really* know it?" Benjamin went on emotionally.

At these words the fine hands of the young Jew rose before
Benjamin's face, twisted in a brief, nervous, desperate dance.
"But then," he whispered in extreme amazement, glancing
at the neighboring beds, *"if you know it,* then how do you get
along, even just walking in the street, for example? Yes,
frankly, when you walk down the street *like that,* don't you feel

a kind of weight on your shoulders, like a cloak that gets heavier every day?"

Benjamin started, alarmed to be so easily found out. "Yes, yes, it's just like that—a cloak. And . . . I can't even hurry along, because of the street lights."

"What?"

"Oh, yes," Benjamin said with a touch of derision. "In the beginning I walked right down the middle of the sidewalk— you know, the way the Germans do, in a military stride? But they all looked at me, so I began to hug the walls along the shop fronts. But even then there was always somebody coming out of a doorway, or else it was a street light."

"So what do you do?"

"God forgive me," Benjamin said, swept up in the humor of the situation, "what do you suppose? I hug the walls quietly, and the shopwindows, with a good little Jewish shuffle."

"Ai, ai, a *good little Jewish shuffle!* But the people, do you think you can escape them that way?"

"Oh, the people," Benjamin murmured, "there's the real cloak, as you called it. And I can never take that off, that cloak —no, not even here, and not even when I think very hard for a long time about my home town, in Poland. . . . The people are really terrible here, worse than the cars," he laughed. "And even the Jews," he added dreamily, *"they weigh on me.* So what can I do? Rip out my insides?"

Seated on the edge of the next bed, a wrinkled man with a beard all ringlets was gazing down at a Bible open on his knees, lighting his way with a candle he held at the height of his temple, in the hieratic position of the nocturnal vigil. Benjamin felt that he was listening to their conversation. Intercepting his glance, young Yankel said scornfully, "My dear Jewish colleague, pay no attention to that old fool. He thinks he's meditating, and he doesn't know that he's only an owl. At night he leans over to see if I'm asleep. . . ." The man with the book, without removing his gaze from the text, started slightly as the candle, suddenly tilted by his emotion, released a drop of molten wax that fell to the parchment—a fantastic, mute teardrop.

Yankel chortled wickedly. "You see? We're all in the same soup."

His voice had become shriller again, and his arm sliced through the dark air, snatching away in one quick gesture the thick shawl that had muffled his throat. Beneath his chin was a laceration. A thread of dried black blood ran down toward the thin growth on his bare chest. "Aha! The latest gift from Berlin!"

Uneasy, Benjamin understood—the young man was forcing himself to hold back the heavy, venomous secret coiled in his throat. He whispered gently, "Brother, please, tell me what they did to you. . . ."

A high-pitched laugh spilled into the shadows. "Ah, what a pleasure to tell you secrets. Nothing is lost, everything finds a home in your heart—ai, my God, ai, ai, ai, the heart!—because you're a little Jew from the old home town, do you know that? A little angel of blood," he tittered. Then, noticing Benjamin's humble expression, the young Galician suppressed a shiver, and as his features softened, his back rounded to a hunch. "Forgive me, forgive me," he said tonelessly. "And forgive my tongue, if you will. For two years it hasn't been able to keep still in my mouth. It moves. It does contortions. You'd think it wanted to get out!"

The hump rounded even more, and the young man's eyes were larger, glassier in the shadow. His voice took on a childish inflection. "Two years already," he said. "Is it possible? And in my mind everything happened just yesterday. Yes— every morning when I open my eyes it seems to me that the pogrom came last night. Is it the same with you, *dear brother?* Strange, really strange, the way time stops like that. Myself, you see, I'm always down in the well where I'd hidden. I have the same water right up to my mouth, and I still see the same circle of blue sky—that hasn't changed either. And then I hear the silence. No shouts—silence. Because in my town, when I came up out of the well there wasn't a soul alive in the whole village. There was no more synagogue; there was nothing. Only me, of course. . . ."

The young man winked maliciously, as though that had been a prodigious joke they played on him. "Oh yes, oh yes," he whispered smiling. "And I buried them all, you know, the whole village without exception—didn't miss a fingernail. And for each one of them, even for that dirty little liar Moshele —he lived next door—for each one of them, I swear it, I said all the prayers from A to Z, because in those days I was a famous praying man before the Eternal, ai-i-i-i! It lasted eight days. And nobody came. The peasants were afraid. And when it was done, I felt queer all over, you know? It was in the cemetery. I woke up and I grabbed a handful of rocks and began to throw them at the sky. And at a certain moment the sky *shattered*. You understand?"

"Oh, yes," Benjamin murmured. He had been weeping silently. "I see, I know, I understand."

"Shattered like a simple mirror, and all the shards spread out on the ground! Then I said to myself, 'Yankel, if God is in little pieces, what can it mean to be a Jew?' Let's take a closer look at that, my friend. But then, as closely as I could look I couldn't see anything but blood, and more blood, and blood again. But meaning?—none. So what place does Jewish blood have in the universe? There it was. And what should a Jew do—who is no longer a Jew? Hey?"

Now, in the half-light of the synagogue, the hallucinated gaze of the young man of Galicia seemed to spill out over his whole emaciated face, the face that fever had splotched with livid patches and reddish patches and patches dampened by a sweat that now and then reflected the yellowish light of the candles flaming near him.

Benjamin asked fearfully, "And why had you never looked for a nice little wife at home? You're handsome and strong . . ." The young Galician, dumfounded momentarily, shook his head as if to throw off that incongruous change of subject. Then, grasping Benjamin's elbow as the latter cried out, softly and moistly, he rapped out, "Do you want to listen to me or not?" And without transition, as if plunged along by his mad confidences, "All right, listen—they held a rally this afternoon! No, no, not the Jews. What would the Jews rally around—their nakedness, their weakness? Can you picture that, an army of little frayed bleeding hearts marching hup-toop, hup-toop, along Unter der Linden? Ha!—you're delicious, and you know it, don't you?

"No," he went on in a kind of contained fury, "it was the Spartacists, the hammer and sickle. And when I saw them coming forward in the street, calmly, the way a river moves, and . . . Ah, that red flag above the tallest of them! I—I don't know why, even now!—I ran out to join them! And believe it or not, at first they didn't *recognize* me. I was marching. I saw the flag in front. It was crazy. . . . Do you understand? I was drowned in it for a minute," he laughed, "and then the man next to me turned to me and said, 'Jew, what the hell are you doing here? There's going to be a brawl, you know?' He said it gaily, with a look of amazement. But the one who was marching behind me started to yell, 'He's a provocateur, it's the only explanation!' And . . . they shoved me toward the sidewalk, and . . . and . . . I'll get them for it, I'll get them!" he finished in a sudden shout, bombastic and shrill, which, rousing the people in the dormitory, immediately surrounded that strange conversation with a high wall of silence.

"But what did they do to you?"

"Nothing. Exactly nothing. They stomp on you without seeing you. They're marching and you're on the ground, so they march right over you—what could be more natural? And all this time I was saying to myself, 'Yankel, dear heart, do me the great favor of never putting yourself into such a ridiculous position again!' But there was the question, 'What can a Jew do, who is no longer a Jew, to avoid spending his life on all fours?' I've thought about it all afternoon, and I think I have

the answer—simple as hello and goodbye, and it's enough:
*'You want to make a calf of me. Then I'll make myself a
butcher!'* "

"What? Whom do you want to kill?"

Yankel twisted his mouth into a knowing smile. "Who said
anything about killing? There's nobody to kill. Or maybe yes.
You might fill the bill, but I'm not sure yet. I'll have to think
about it!

"But what's the good of talking?" he said suddenly in a
distraught tone.

He had sat up tall on his bed and was examining Benjamin curiously with his piercing glance, like a bird of prey, as if
he had suddenly realized the extreme distance separating him
from this wan, sly, fluttering little nestling. His attentive stare
seemed to say, "Now look at that—I gave my secrets to this
shadow!" "Never mind," he said. "Don't torture yourself trying to understand. You can't, you still have one foot in the old
days. In the . . . dream, hey? Like all these poor fools," he
added, sweeping the dark air with a lordly gesture. "Go on, go
on, grandpa, leave me alone now. . . ."

Benjamin objected weakly, "But you were the one who
wanted to talk."

"I know. Thank you. Because I still have in me a little—
Benjamin who flaps his wings. Ai-i-i, he doesn't want to die;
ai-i-i, look how he struggles. But sh-h-h, sh-h-h, let us sleep
now, him and me, will you?"

And taking note of the hostile gathering grouped closely
about his bed, the young man offered a wide salute to the
world at large, tapped Benjamin's cheek, smiling, then, raising his long arms above his head—as free and easy in his
movements as if he had been within four walls—he peacefully
peeled off his old sweater, under which he was nude, his torso
barred with bones and dirtied with blood.

Benjamin stared silently at him for a moment. What had
happened? Scratching his head in confusion he rose and
went to his "room" without a word. With a kind of easy
relief, he crossed the circle of chalk that marked the limits of

his lair, and began to cook meatballs. He ate practically nothing. Stretching out on his mattress, he wondered if the bedbugs would bite as much as usual. Indignant murmurings persisted in the synagogue, and with night came the wailing insomnia of the small fry. Benjamin closed his eyes and imagined that the chalk circle was rising as a wall all the way to the ceiling. The wall seemed so solid, so marvelously thick, that soon he felt sheltered from the whole world.

Yankel's bed was empty the next morning. When he got back from the workshop, Benjamin found it occupied by a little old woman caparisoned in black who looked like a turtle. As soon as he spoke to her, she withdrew her head between her shoulders as if to take protection as quickly as possible under the shell of her age. Benjamin laughed to see it.

Three months later the young Galician made a last appearance. He was seated on the edge of Benjamin's bed, with a distant expression, indifferent to everything and looking at no one. His hand fidgeted with a spool of thread lying on the blanket. He played with it gently. And his long, ungainly body was crimped into a suit of English cloth. A stiff collar rose to the middle of his scrawny neck, from which hung a flabbergasting necktie. Slowing down, Benjamin noticed that what had once been an adolescent mop of red hair now covered the skull in a thin, iridescent film, carefully parted in the middle. The face seemed still unhealthily hollow and discolored, but his mouth had hardened, thickened, and his lips thrust forward greedily.

The young man rose and proffered a well-kept hand. "Pardon me. I took the liberty of coming into your room." His eyes remained sad and cold, but the thickness about his lips trembled in irony.

"Plague take me," Benjamin said, "if you haven't turned into a real 'gentleman'!"

Immediately he regretted his admiring tone.

"I have *become*, did you say?" Yankel asked bitterly.

"But how? By what miracle?"

"Rest easy, little Jew. I haven't killed anyone. It may be worse. I'm a merchant. I buy and I sell."

"What? What do you sell?"

The young Galician offered the smile of an old fox, but the upper part of his face, distressed, contradicted the slyness of his mouth. "My dear little Jewish colleague," he enunciated with boyish affectation, "in Berlin everything is bought and sold."

At that instant Benjamin felt a deep surge of pity for the young Galician. His hand rose unwilled, and like a frightened bird came to rest on Yankel's shoulder as his mouth opened to release words whose origin he never knew. "Brother," Benjamin's mouth pronounced gravely, "why all this shame and unhappiness? Awake, I beg you. . . ."

The young man did not seem to have heard, and Benjamin withdrew his hand hurriedly, surprised by the audacity of his gesture. But suddenly, moved by some terrible impulse, the redhead rose to his full height, and pasting that indefinable smile on his sickly face, he murmured in a dragging, exhausted voice, "Jew, little Jew from the old home town, you're very sweet, do you know? So sweet that a man would like to bust your teeth in, one by one."

And turning, the young man of Galicia found the chalk-lined aisle, crossed the synagogue in long, nervously jerky strides, disappeared forever.

An hour later, slipping under the blankets, Benjamin found the envelope hidden between the mattress and the bolster. He guessed that it contained a small fortune. A few lines were traced in Yiddish, in the elegant hand of a scholar: "Dear little man, this money is the legitimate profit of a legal transaction. It was thieved honestly, according to the laws of commerce—with license and soon, I hope, with a respectable thief's place of business. Leave this huge Berlin for the countryside and send for your family, if you still have one. For in Poland, my friend, a Jew can hold out all alone, with a herring and a synagogue. But here, believe me, if all you have in the way of roots is two feet, life ceases to rise as far as your heart. Even yours, dear little man. Don't judge me. Thank you. Yankel."

· 3 ·

B ENJAMIN set one foot on the platform of the little Rhenish station, pulled down the bound crate that served him as baggage, and found himself face to face with an individual, dressed in the German manner, who claimed to be the rabbi of Stillenstadt. Suspicious, Benjamin refused to let him carry the "valise," maintaining against all evidence that it was light as a feather. As they walked along, the rabbi told him what a godsend the little shop on the Riggenstrasse would be. "Herr Goldfuss—that's the owner—preferred to offer it to a victim of the Slavic persecutions, of which you are one, are you not, my dear coreligionist? A pressing iron, a sewing machine and several pieces of aged furniture are included in the, shall we say, 'more than charitable' rent."

All this proved true, with the slight reservation that Benjamin had not imagined the furnishings, or the place itself, in so advanced a "state of age," as the rabbi had put it. "But then," the latter replied smiling, "we don't look a gift horse in the mouth!"

As they chatted, the shop was invaded by eight or ten Germans who seemed to lunge forward, hands outstretched, toward Benjamin. He uttered a cry of fear, thought he would faint, and then recognized with relief two or three Jewish beards in the gallery of Germanic faces that surrounded him, bickering over him as over a piece of merchandise.

"Aren't you ashamed?" cried a woman's manly voice. "You're crushing him, crushing him, squeezing the kernel out of him as if he were a piece of fruit!"

And cutting a path through to the "victim of Slavic persecutions," a buxom Jewish woman in a flower-print dress and a plumed hat displayed before Benjamin two smiling outrageously rouged lips. "If it comes to that," she went on in the uncontradictable tones of a chatelaine, *"he belongs to me!"*

"What do you mean?" Benjamin breathed as his hands flattened cautiously on the "valise" over which he maintained an anguished guard.

"But leave your crate here," said the astonished goodwife. "Are you afraid that these gentlmen will run off with it?"

Benjamin felt his resistance rising again. "It's nothing, it's nothing," he stammered. "You see? Light as a feather."

But as he had practically disappeared under the huge crate, gasping and panting beneath it, the excellent lady could not resist asking him, "My fellow Jew, what have you got in there that's so valuable?"

"Everything," Benjamin said, dying of exhaustion.

Since his departure from Berlin the previous night, figuring from that moment when the train had plunged into the tunnel —foreshadowing for him this new plunge into the dark night of exile—Benjamin had not for one instant lost physical contact with that crate, which indeed contained everything he owned in this world—the few rolls of remaindered cloth, the three or four flatirons, the mannequin and its one unscrewed foot, the presser's bench and all the accessories he had managed to assemble, thanks to the incomprehensible gift of the young Galician. Trusting more to the crate, an object difficult to make off with, than to his own sensitivity to pickpockets, he had sewn the rest of his "fortune" into one of the dummy's buttocks. On the train his fear and anguish, the acute distrust that squeezed at his heart, were mysteriously transformed on the level of thought into resolves whose fiercely sentimental heroism forced him into attitudes of defiance, and at moments into brief interjections that startled his fellow passengers—provincials fascinated by this little man dressed in the "Russian style," rubbing his fists desperately against his scraggly goatee while his eyes, moist and glassy, seemed to throw off incessant sparks of suffering.

He even imagined in the middle of the night that henceforth he would look upon all things as did the young Galician.

"Yes," he blurted suddenly in Yiddish, to the great excitement of his neighbors, "I say it and I proclaim it—in this world of iron the sword is the best answer to the sword!"

An old lady smothered a cry and left the compartment. Had she actually cried out, Benjamin, roused from his "Berliner" fantasies, might have fainted outright.

Thus armored against the worst, terrorized, haggard, broken by exhaustion and inanition, all he saw of the Jews of Stillenstadt was their German manners and their strange preoccupation with his crate. He never even wondered where she was taking him, this imposing woman who had assumed possession of him. "It's nothing, light as a feather" was all he managed when she mentioned the burden he struggled under.

He did not want to leave it even in the living room, where Herr Feigelbaum, husband of the elegant plumed lady, tried vainly to dupe him with a hearty welcome—certainly hearty but not good enough to fool our "Berliner," wise in the ways of life—nor even in the dining room, which he entered lugging his "valise" behind him obstinately. Nevertheless, when he discovered right under his nose the steaming savor of a certain Jewish marrow soup that he had believed the exclusive prerogative of his mother Judith, his nostrils suddenly began to prickle with "the joy of living."

And as he lowered the spoon into the plate dreamily, a strange phenomenon occurred—first a light, seemingly elastic bubble was born in his breast and, rising, obstructed his throat exquisitely. And then, on the foaming yellowish ripples of soup, appeared the face of his mother Judith, the skull shaven and the eyes flashing in shame. Then there appeared in the soup the imperial profile of his father Mordecai, whose beard suddenly disappeared; the bloodless face of the poor young man from Galicia, whose red hair twisted and died like flames; and finally the three faces embracing in the bloody doorway at dawn after the pogrom in Zemyock. . . . And all that, coming to life and dying again as if miraculously on the shining film of soup, generated a beneficent warmth in Benjamin, hunched over the plate, fascinated. . . .

"My God, he's crying!" Frau Feigelbaum said.

Benjamin blushed, grimaced, sketched a smile. "Tut-tut-tut," he managed in a shrill voice, "this soup is hot!"

As he sensed rather than felt the intoxicating tear slipping along his nose, he brought the spoon close to his lips and blew on it at great length, with a kind of expert, though blind, application. Then he introduced it into his mouth.

Straightaway Herr Feigelbaum, who until then had manifested himself only by bearded and malicious smiles, set about insulting his wife while his cheeks turned an incendiary purple. "Don't you see that the soup is too hot? No? You don't see that? Animal, stupid animal that you are! A hundred times I told you don't serve the soup too hot! Oh, you stupid animal! A hundred times . . ." Changing his mood again, Herr Feigelbaum began yelling loudly for his bottle, punctuating each of his demonic cries with a shake of the fist, as drinkers do. But his wife was already repeating with him, "The bottle, yes, the bottle," and sat smiling, bursting with love. Finally, with one last oath Herr Feigelbaum bolted to the buffet and came up with a green swanneck bottle that contained, he said, some authentic and veritable Palestinian wine.

"It's been asleep too long," he cried, raising its round mouth with a swashbuckling air. "Ah, my children, I promise you that it will be drunk before the coming of the Messiah! Ah," he declared emphatically, "I'll swear to that!"

Surprised, Benjamin noticed that the bold Herr Feigelbaum was fidgeting terribly and that his hand, so solid, nevertheless trembled in pouring the liquor of Carmel. But already his host had raised his glass at arm's length (a bit like a hussar, it seemed to Benjamin) and was fiercely thundering an old Yiddish couplet:

> *Sing, oh my Jewish brother,*
> *Sing, I beg you, sing. . . .*

As Benjamin marveled at such *brio,* at such vehemence brought to this rather sentimental plaint, he observed that at the end of each verse a brilliant gleam appeared in the corner of Herr Feigelbaum's eye, disappearing as soon as he had begun the next.

The singer interrupted himself suddenly. "Good heavens, I'm stuffing you with sweets and gorging you with flat notes!"

"Oh, but—" said Benjamin.

"Not a word!" Herr Feigelbaum said.

After that, each course was an exquisite dessert to Benjamin. But before the end of this love feast, some Jews erupted helter-skelter into the dining room. Insisting that no one bother about them, they arranged themselves silently all about the table and more specially opposite Benjamin, whom they watched chew, shaking their heads in approval, as if he were there accomplishing a rite—holy, adorable and full of mystery, and which had the effect of incarnating the invisible, the suffering and the death of the Polish Jews who were visible through him, as though he were in filigree. The discussion burst out just before an attack on the fairyland strudel that reigned in the middle of table, and it became immediately impassioned. After two hours of arguments, concessions, and counter-concessions, Frau Feigelbaum, who intended to keep an iron hand on Benjamin's nutrition, arrived at the following compromise with him: All the noonday meals with her, and the evening meals to be shared among the other Jewish tables of Stillenstadt—"if, of course," she said, with gentle treachery, "our dear brother really wishes to go elsewhere. . . ."

All aquiver with "the joy of being alive," his nose low over his plate, Benjamin realized that every noon, every night, his place would be set at a Jewish table where he might, under cover of the traditional cuisine, gorge himself on tenderness. Unable to restrain himself, he rose suddenly and undertook to tell "a good old Jewish joke from my home town," as he put it, "that would make a corpse shake with laughter."

But he was a terrible raconteur: He gasped nervously at each word, lost the thread of the story wherever possible, picked it up and twined it with another of a different color and, excusing himself a thousand times, took up his story from the beginning with "This time I have it. . . . This time I have it. . . .."—which finally trailed off into "Well, there it is, I've lost it," said plaintively, while with his right hand beating like a wing he pictured sadly for them the definitive flight of his good old Jewish story.

And yet—it mortified him a bit—they laughed throughout his strange narrative, and some of them, including Herr Feigelbaum, went at it so boisterously that the laughter dribbled down into their beards.

·4·

STILLENSTADT was one of those charming German cities of an age gone by. With its thousands of doll houses, pink-tiled, bedecked with potted flowers, it seemed a living manifestation of that old Germanic sentimentality which penetrated and bound all things intimately—even as the spittle of the swallow by an invisible thread holds together the twigs that make its nest. But there was nothing aerial about Stillenstadt. Simply set down on the plain, it lay in the fork of a river that divided at the entrance to town. The principal arm of the river fed the shoe factories ranged on its banks, as well as the industrial-dye factories where female workers faded slowly. Too thin and fragile, the secondary arm threaded its way delicately through the fields. The Schlosse—that was its name —was good only for fishing and summertime pleasures.

The tiny window of Benjamin's shop was boarded over by ineptly nailed planks; from the hallway he could enter the shop or go upstairs to his second-floor apartment. Hoping to win back the former clientele quickly, he began with a summary overhaul of the "emporium," as he already enjoyed calling it And first of all, a moving moment, a sign awkwardly traced in German announced the coming inauguration of the establishment: "The Gentleman of Berlin."

For the first three months he slept on a mattress spread out on the floor of this retreat. Then, as his anxieties diminished, he began to think of touching up the "apartment." At the beginning, he saw himself established in the style of an American millionaire—a sewing machine and an ostentatious shop front. But business being slack, he decided to alter his campaign. It was a workingman's quarter, the aftermath of a lost war lay heavily upon the German people, and no one foresaw a quick end to the depression. Considering all this carefully, Benjamin thought it out so well that he became inspired. And one fine morning the astonished neighbors were greeted by the new shingle of the little immigrant—an immense poster, blocking off half the shopwindow and rising like a bower up to the second-story windows, bore these words, drawn in handsome and noble Gothic lettering (a soft blue against a pink background): "Specialist in Patching and Repairing Old Clothes—Fantastic Prices—It's Old, Presto, It's New!!!"

In his desire to bring in business, he had set ridiculously low prices, which bordered on unfair competition. On that first day he had more work than he could handle. The next day he plied his needle for sixteen hours and considered himself a happy man. He had seen himself on the edge of failure; this one stroke of genius established him in Stillenstadt. The days passed and the weeks, and he forgot the cheap origins of this public infatuation with the Gentleman of Berlin, and even yielded to a dream—a soft blue against a pink background— that his sewing machine had won the unanimous friendship of the town.

As he worked at the local language, modulating each syllable with care, the day came when his customers understood a few snatches of his jargon. So he loved to engage them in conversation on any subject compatible with their German brains, with his dignity as a Jew and with his extraordinary difficulty in pronouncing certain words. Fittings particularly favored these idyllic relations between the church and the synagogue. Inserting a pin, hemming a lapel, Benjamin eddied about his Christian like a fly, and to win that heart used all the politeness, all the grace, all the refinements he might have employed in the seduction of a woman.

Receiving his customers called for a slow and painful elab-
oration. "My dear sir," he articulated, shaking the hand of the
newcomer tenderly, "may I know to what happy circumstance
I owe your visit?"

Whether they were in janitor's blue or a peasant's tunic or
even dignified by a necktie, his customers all had a right to
this same treatment, which nevertheless managed to disquiet several of them. But Benjamin, immersed in his ur-
banities, never saw the eyebrow raised—interrogative, suspicious, or frankly acerb. He liked to think that these little
people were renouncing their anti-Semitism for his sake, that
they had been able to detect under its Jewish envelope a
universal human nature that expressed itself with less enthusiasm, perhaps, among the other Israelites of the town.
"You have to set an example," he jubilated secretly. "The
esteem they feel for me profits all Jews. Through me they have
been exposed to the simple truth!"

Even better, after several weeks he attempted certain popular expressions that established his familiarity with the workers of the town—not, of course, that he would pronounce the
impious phrase "God damn" or oaths at that level, but he let
himself go so roundly with expressions like "Well I'll be!" or
even "You don't mean to tell me!" or even "Don't make me
laugh!"—he put so much weighty conviction into these words,
using his whole body as he spoke, in the German style—that it
seemed to him, although he could see all its advantages, that
he might honestly pass up the phrase "God damn." From
time to time, however, after making sure that no Jewish ear
was lingering in the neighborhood, he condescended so far as
to take the holy name of God, in German, altogether like a
man of the people. "Eh, my God!" he cried timidly, to the
amazement of his customer. Then he muttered a prayer to
himself. A similar sentiment led him to express modernistic
ideas discreetly. He enjoyed referring to "the big industrialists,
sir, our common enemy," without suspecting at all that certain
workmen—particularly the unemployed—considered him
among the blackest capitalists of the street. And so it hap-

pened, after a fitting during which he had bathed in "the milk of human kindness," that he wondered how far his fearful sympathy for the workingman would lead him. But on the next day a cold eye, a mocking smile, an outstretched forefinger in the middle of the street reminded him happily that he was a Yiddl and nothing more.

In truth he found true "human kindness" only in the sweet company of the Jews of Stillenstadt, who had not only adopted him but, even more, seemed to revere in him some secret property attached to his puny person and clothing it, like the cloak of suffering in which the faithful of Zemyock clothed the Lamed-Vovnik. Was it possible, Benjamin wondered occasionally, uneasy. But no overture was ever made to him, and if it happened that the conversation bore on the thirty-six Just Men who haunted the world, he was at least able to convince himself that the German Jews had no knowledge of the mystery surrounding the Levys of Zemyock. Only once did the rabbi allude to a legend according to which, yes, one of the thirty-six Just Men had been chosen by God from the descendants of the famous Yom Tov Levy—"You know, of course, the one who died for the Sacred Name in York?" But few of them had heard about it, and Benjamin reassured himself with the idea that these "Saturday Jews," as they called themselves regretfully, revered in him only the burning flame of Polish Judaism and their great pity for it.

At the end of six months they disclosed to him, as they might a shameful fault, that several Jewish converts to Catholicism were thriving in the town. They inhabited the upper-class residential sections, in those white six-story structures that gleamed behind the church. They were described to him as wicked, perverse, more patriotic than monkeys, detesting especially the immigrants from Poland and the Ukraine, whom they referred to as "an Asiatic horde, the scum of the earth, foreigners," and so on, and when one of them was pointed out to him crossing the street stolidly, as stocky and impenetrable as a German, Benjamin was unable to repress a shudder.

The second apostate who was shown to him lived in the Riggenstrasse, a few houses away from the shop. Now and then Benjamin saw him crossing in front of the shopwindow, a discriminating look flashing from his bent head. But depending on the day, the apostate's chin jutted forward like a prow or drooped humbly toward his chest. His whole attitude was that of an incorruptible German burgher, morose and well established in his undistinguished and dull clothing, of military cut and aggressively buttoned across his stomach. He worked in a municipal office and had been converted, he said, by patriotism and by grace. Benjamin heard very soon that the apostate was spreading rumors about him, accusing him of eating the bread of German workers. "He said," a neighbor-woman reported slyly, "that you didn't even know the colors of the German flag!"

"Me?" Benjamin cried indignantly, and then, unable to prove the contrary, he hastened back into his shop overwhelmed by shame.

He waited for the next appearance of the apostate in order to reproach him forcefully, but he had barely approached the man when that notable released an icy breath of contempt from the side of his mouth and went on his way, chin high, cane scornful, as though some cheap and ignoble public spectacle had been imposed upon him.

Now, it happened that one day that apostate, named Meyer, appeared at the synagogue and threw himself at the rabbi's feet, kissing his knees avidly. "I can't do it any longer, take me back, my heart has remained Jewish," and so on. Great agitation on the part of the rabbi, who chases the man away wrathfully, and urgently convokes an extraordinary assembly of the faithful of Stillenstadt. Stationed at the doorway of the synagogue, the apostate salutes each arrival with a humble bow and scrape; he has set a skullcap upon his head, his hair is full of earth and ashes and his clothes are rent. No one responds to his greeting. Not knowing which side to take, Benjamin enters the synagogue with his head held high, but

obliquely addresses the man an absurdly conspiratorial wink.
The trial began.

Ensconced in the last row of the faithful, Benjamin was
fascinated by the bizarre figure of the apostate, standing
out against the central pulpit before the ark of the holy
of holies, where two lions squatting on their golden haunches
seemed, at either side of the unfortunate, to watch over him
like policemen in a trial court. In his white face, almost
flour-white, two red caverns lent him a terrible expression,
and his sweat, diluting the ashes on his hair, drew black
bars down his forehead, which gave his tortured face the ab-
errant character of a carnival mask. At each insult he bent his
knees slightly and ducked his head to witness that he admitted all evil; with his right fist he thumped his heart like a
metronome. His lips were pursed.

His eyes fixed grimly on the apostate, Benjamin was remembering that once in Berlin, unable to see any way out of his
sadness, he had thought of yielding himself once and for all to
the Christians (he did not know to whom, exactly—the Pope,
a priest or some mysterious dignitary of the church) *so that it
would be all over for him.* Thus he could see himself now in the
apostate's place, and each phrase of invective made him withdraw his head further into his shoulders in a convulsive movement, as if he had been stunned by a blow. Suddenly Herr
Feigelbaum, livid with rage, climbed onto the pulpit and announced that as a childhood friend of the guilty man he had
been present at the psychological martyrdom of the latter's
parents. "Not content with conversion, this mouthpiece of
Satan lacerated his mother and father in their shop, calling
them 'dirty Jews' and other names that I do not wish to pronounce in this holy house. Is he an apostate? That's the least of
it! He is first of all, he is above all, an assassin!"

At this point in the debate, one of the faithful expressed the
idea that, having been sincerely converted to Christianity, the
apostate had become sincerely anti-Semitic—"since it is, alas,
in the nature of that religion not to tolerate us, is that not so?"

"Do you think so?" Herr Feigelbaum cried and, turning

toward the apostate, whom he blasted with a look: "Herr Hein-rich Meyer, formerly Isaac, can he be so bold as to claim that excuse?"

Here occurred an event that escaped Benjamin's under-standing, for instead of seizing upon this providential justifica-tion through faith, the apostate rose slowly, with an unfeigned pride and with sarcasm on his suddenly heavy lips. "But how do you believe," he declared, hammering out the words, "how can you think that I believed for one instant in a God who, to bring relief to poor mankind, found nothing better than to be born from the body of a virgin, to become man, to suffer a thousand tortures and then death. . . . And all that without any appreciable result?"

And once again with a look of submission: "My former friend Feigelbaum is right. I *transfixed* my father and my mother because I wanted to live as the Christians do. I was ashamed to be a Jew, very simply ashamed."

"And what have you gained?" Herr Feigelbaum asked scornfully.

"A greater shame."

After that admission, they deliberated the penalty. They competed in suggesting infamies. In the end, they decided that the apostate would lie at the entrance to the synagogue so that the entire community could step over him. The apostate beat his breast and begged a greater penance; he declared himself "resolved to suffer." Suddenly someone pronounced Ben-jamin's name. "Our brother who has come from Poland, per-haps he can give us a useful opinion, point out a precedent. Why has he not spoken?"

Benjamin sank back upon his bench and tilted the skullcap down over his eyes, as if to protect himself from the unanimous gaze converging on his small figure, piercing it as with a single ray of flame.

"Listen," he stammered finally, "I do not know much, really. Back home in Ze— At any rate, back home nothing of this kind has ever happened. But I remember, yes, in the fifteenth century, Rabbi Israel Isserlein . . . he said that he who returns to Judaism—you follow me, don't you?—that one imposes upon himself a continual penance. Yes, that was it—a continual penance."

"And so?" cried one of Benjamin's neighbors, a solid, rubicund man whose pince-nez joggled suddenly on his fidgety flesh.

"And so?" Benjamin repeated in a thin voice. And carried away suddenly: "But don't you understand?" he cheeped, pointing in despair to the apostate. "Look at him, he has turned his back on the advantages and felicities of Christianity, and he has taken upon his shoulders the . . . all the suffering of . . . is that not so? And therefore he is expiating his sin, by the simple fact that he has come back. . . . No? Then why add a stone to his burden?" He finished in a painful tremolo that surprised the faithful more than all the rest.

Then, glancing about the assembly now reduced to silence, the little man seemed to remember his true size. Trembled. Twisted his frail shoulders. Put his arms back under the prayer shawl and sat down again so abruptly that his skullcap fell forward over his forehead.

Nevertheless a thread of trembling voice soon made its way out from under the skullcap. "Ah, yes . . . it was the Rabbi Israel Isserlein . . . Rabbi Israel Isserlein said it. . . . I swear it to you. . . . And is there one among us who never thought about it? One?"

An incredulous stupor greeted these words, followed immediately by a fairground tumult from the heart of which, sunk back on his bench, Benjamin vaguely heard astonishing phrases—"That's what it means to talk like a Jew!" "Have we already forgotten everything?" and so on. And rising from the elders grouped about the oratory stove, a piercing voice came like an arrow. "Is there one of us who has never thought of it? One?" With calm finally restored, the rabbi of Stillenstadt gently begged the apostate to take his place among the faithful. "As before," he said.

It was then that the event occurred.

The apostate, who had until then remained somber and

silent, suddenly released a vast burst of mocking laughter, even
demonic, according to certain listeners, and from the eminence
of the pulpit deserted by the rabbi, he set about insulting the
whole assembly, already terrified by this theatrical reversal.
His face was convulsed with rage. He set a curse on Benjamin.
In a blasphemous flight, he took his skullcap and flung it to
the floor with scorn, stamping on it, hammering at it as if it
were a thing to be killed. Now laughing himself breathless,
now flinging out a stream of obscene insults—"I suppose you
don't notice that it stinks of Jews here?"—he pushed through
the dumfounded gathering and left them.

· 5 ·

THEY LEARNED the next morning that he had left the city.
Tongues wagged freely. The rabbi went so far as to say
that Benjamin should not have stopped the apostate from
expiating, and our good apostle saw himself examined with
suspicion. They accused him of flights of fancy, of manias.
Only the Feigelbaums admired him, admitting that strange
circumstances were involved which escaped human understanding.

Banned from the best tables, looked upon as a bird of evil
omen, Benjamin bought a sumptuous sheet of paper and composed the letter he had been thinking about since his departure
from Zemyock.

That letter, which is still in the annals, began this way:
"My very dear and very venerable father, and you, oh my so
dear and so venerable mother, Now it is two years since your
obedient son left you to search for a nest somewhere in the
world. Today it is with a heart overflowing with joy that he
tells you, 'Come, oh my loved ones,' for the moment is finally
here when the bird, with the blessings of the Most High . . ."

When she was able, under the flow of images and Biblical comparisons, to discern the immediate and precise meaning of that invitation, Judith cried out ecstatically, "And now Zemyock is over!"

"Which makes you very happy, doesn't it?" Mordecai answered bitterly. "All right, what are you waiting for? Why aren't we already on the train?"

He remained silent and impassive throughout the trip. Judith was less preoccupied by the absurdities that the windows of the iron monster offered her than by those wrinkles of gray resignation, that helpless prostration that weighed so heavily upon Mordecai's hook-nosed mask, dissolving the majesty of his features. Now and then the old man shook his head as if he were unable to believe what was happening, and Judith heard him mutter feebly into his beard, "But how can that be—a Levy from Zemyock?"

Benjamin was waiting for them in the little station at Stillenstadt. Two years before, he had been a young man whose features were entirely dominated by an amusing little goatee, a rather nimble person, although tiny—in any case, certainly Jewish. Judith had expected to find a similar Benjamin, drowned in the traditional habiliments—Polish boots, a black cloak, a velours hat with a flat brim. To tell the truth, she could hardly remember his features, and when she evoked his image, it was primarily through his small size, which was easy enough to hold in the imagination. Stepping down from the train, she found herself facing a small German gentleman who had long ears, a curved nose like a rabbit's, fine and bony jaws and the facial expression of Benjamin. That apparition impressed itself painfully upon her. Was it perhaps this beardless face . . . ? But she had the distressing feeling that Benjamin was a kind of skinned rabbit still grazing and jumping about as if nothing had happened, all his muscles and nerves exposed but with a constant grimace on his face. What could have gone wrong? "Ah, I've been lucky," Benjamin repeated miserably. She could get nothing more out of him and was suddenly aware that she did not know him, that she had never known him.

Coldly, Mordecai pressed this parcel of Levy to his breast, and allowed himself to be guided to "the house," as Judith was already calling it.

The old couple made a sensation in the streets of Stillenstadt. Both seemed to have sprung from another age. Black from head to foot, girded with the naïve majesty of figures in old prints, they moved forward with slow, assured steps, entirely self-sufficient and looking at nothing but the small figure of Benjamin, who pranced about three paces from them, his frail arms embracing the many small bags Judith had insisted on keeping with her. Mordecai was carrying a small fur-covered trunk on his right shoulder, and his left hand lay gently on the back of Judith's neck. Both were still handsome, with that hieratic splendor of strong beings that accompanies them to the end of their lives.

Benjamin had planned the reunion dinner in detail. In his fear that Judith would be exhausted by the trip, he had begged Frau Feigelbaum to prepare a banquet for them. "What's all this, what's all this?" Judith cried as she entered the kitchen gleaming like a new penny. "You no longer trust your own mother, and you have to have your meals fixed by I don't know what local imitation Jewess?" Suspiciously she sniffed the dishes at length, finding one a bit overcooked, another composed of badly kneaded dough, and so on. Benjamin noted excitedly that his mother examined everything up to and including the fruit.

It was just after the soup that the mysterious bout of fever began.

Sitting at the foot of the table, Benjamin had Judith to his right and Mordecai to his left, as it had been during those last days in Zemyock after the emptiness of the pogrom. Bracketed by these two black pillars, he felt more at home in his own kitchen. The walls whitewashed by his own hands, the tile floor he had almost licked clean, the utensils bought one by one —all these products of his own sweat became slowly a part of him now; he delighted in them suddenly, finding in them a thousand unsuspected virtues. Something simmered softly on the three-legged stove, but Benjamin, ashamed, dared not lean forward to identify the odoriferous contents of the pot. His father was sucking at the end of his mustache; he set his spoon across the plate and grumbled with lassitude, "So that's how it is. No one in Stillenstadt knows who we *really* are?"

To Judith's great surprise, Benjamin was not in the least upset. "No," he said with authority, "no one knows. And no one will know," he finished in a somewhat tart tone of command.

Mordecai said simply, "Good, good." His arms crossed on the tablecloth, he attested a profound and dignified sadness. Across from him Judith took a bit of soup, clacked her tongue with an expression half approving, half disgusted, and then, turning to the ecstatic Benjamin, "Not too bad for a German woman, but myself, I always put a little parsley in it. So this Frau Feigelbaum, you were saying . . . ?"

As poor Benjamin considered the peaceful rectangle of the table, itself inscribed in that of the kitchen which, without a possible doubt, was encompassed within the strictly enclosed volume of the house, he seemed suddenly and finally to shake off the nightmare he had shouldered in Berlin, in the narrow and fragile rectangle of chalk. To fortify himself, he began to fiddle with an infinitesimal crumb of bread. At the same instant he felt the beat of heavy blood awakening in his veins after a long, cold sleep. . . .

"But it's impossible! He's covered with sweat!"

"Me?" Benjamin asked disbelieving. But bringing his hand to his forehead, he felt his whole arm shiver.

A few minutes later, a grumbling Judith tucked him into bed.

On the third day of that curious fever, he awoke enthusiastically and began work immediately. His eye was lively, his complexion fresh, and he brought to all things a sort of loving gaiety that rejuvenated his features and made him more perky than ever. Judith concluded that there had been "a change of blood."

*　*　*

Since the pogrom in Zemyock, Mordecai had taken on the appearance that would be his until his death. His hair would whiten, his body would bow, he would become more wrinkled, but his essence would remain intact—the tall, brooding mass of his body, whose rather slow displacements expressed a predilection for quietude, which he broke only with an effort, with that kind of heavy regret expressed in the slow tread of an old elephant, each step seemingly torn from a vast, inert immobility. On that enormous structure was grafted, in Stillenstadt, a thickening of the waist that reinforced the impression Mordecai gave of a huge animal or a massive, bleached tree. But his face remained innocent of fat, as if the exercise of the spirit continually redeemed his threatened features, preserving the long curved crest of the nose and the hard shelf of the cheekbones beneath the slightly staring gaze of his heavy gray eyes which, without the slightest vagueness or distraction, always seemed to look and see beyond visible things.

If Judith adapted rapidly to her third existence, it was not the same for Mordecai, who was no longer more than half alive now, rolled up within the shell of his piety, which hardened a bit more each day. Even back in Zemyock she had noticed that the death of his three "real" sons had been a more than mortal wound to him, destroying in him all hope of seeing the line of Just Men perpetuated by his blood. Taking no further part in the world, Mordecai trusted himself to her advice like a child who takes refuge in obedience.

Shortly after Benjamin's exile, she believed nevertheless that she was witnessing a rebirth. Mordecai watched her with a dreaming eye, declared smiling that she was still as beautiful as ever, and also began to show such mad ardor that Judith, torn between her so recent mourning and the joy of seeing a man return to life, could reserve her judgment only by the use of ambiguous phrases like "the noontime demon," "the swan song," and the like. But soon Mordecai put ever more searching questions to her, going so far as to ask outright if she felt nothing "on the way"; poor Judith understood that her old tree of a husband was hoping for a last fruit. She reminded him that she was fifty years old. Nevertheless, she added, all is possible with the aid of the Most High. Who would have said to Abraham, "Sarah will suckle a child"? And yet she bore him a son in his old age, and so on.

It was in Stillenstadt that they ceased altogether to be husband and wife.

One night as he was embracing her fervently, she felt herself flung back by the shoulders, and sensed that her rude lover, changing his mind, had turned heavily toward the wall of the alcove.

"Good night to you, my wife," said Mordecai's voice in the blackness.

Judith's surprise was extreme; she could hardly understand the abruptness of that decision, and yet upon reflection she had to admit that Mordecai's withdrawal had not taken her entirely by surprise. For in the always strong passion of her husband she had many times felt something like a secret rancor, a secret reproach to her for being so beautiful and so desirable. The further he aged, the more it seemed that his effusions were forced by desire and not freely consented to, joyfully called forth, as during the first years of their union. But from that night when he ceased to express his desire for her, she noted that in exchange he showed her a deeper friendship in daily life, a better and softer indulgence, a manner of new respect.

Certainly he became more distant each day, a cold star orbiting relentlessly in the peaceful heaven of his prayers and acts of contrition, but Judith sensed that at that distance from which henceforth he looked upon his wife with his gray eyes, heavy and slow like clouds in winter, there was now only love for her. And although she was still a woman, that voluntary detachment pleased her; she saw in it secret homage to her beauty, a last bouquet laid upon her body.

The last thread that tied Mordecai to daily life was broken insidiously by Benjamin's nimble and delicate little fingers.

From the day of his arrival in Stillenstadt, Mordecai had undertaken to find work, for he did not wish to be, he said in a singular tone, a charge upon his son. He was in the habit, was he not, of earning his own living.

But the unemployment that had devastated Germany offered no hope to an old man, an alien and, even more, a Jew. After humiliating attempts, seeing himself thrown out upon the sands of life, he came to rest one day in his son's shop, filling it altogether with his cumbersome carcass. He wished to learn to sew buttons, to iron, to remove basting stitches, and so on— all tasks within the capacities of a ten-year-old apprentice.

But the work of his fingers—"stiff as wood," he said in excuse—had to be redone by Benjamin's nimble hands. The son complained to himself at the old man's mania for usefulness, and then protested out loud. At that, Mordecai gave up earning his living.

"Not to abandon a world that has abandoned you," he said to himself, "is to add madness to your misfortune. Should I be a laughingstock?" He left the shop and retreated to the small room on the second story, behind his sacred parchments.

Benjamin reassured him, cajoled him, sprinkled him with unctuous little phrases, saying that in a Jewish home it was necessary to have a man of purity who would intercede with God for everyone. And willingly, at table, Benjamin emphasized the pre-eminence of prayer over basely material activity (meaning by that his daily work as "a trimmer of paper," as they had said in Zemyock, in distinction to the noble work of trimming crystal).

Thus cradled in words, and burying himself deeper each day in his interior world, old Mordecai finished by slowly forgetting the open wound in his manhood. His son plied the needle, his wife held the purse strings, and he labored for the souls of men.

And yet one day, while he was dreaming between two verses on the obscure path of his life and on its inglorious conclusion, he resolved, as a last resort, to have grandchildren. That thought rejuvenated him. Rapidly he investigated the marriageable girls of Stillenstadt. A tiny Fräulein Blumenthal was among them, who seemed made to order for the little twenty-five-year-old tailor. Mordecai hardly investigated more than the size of his future daughter-in-law or hoped for more than the promise hidden in her rounded haunches. Benjamin was frantic, but then understood that his father wanted to console himself for the loss of his three "real" sons. He accepted the meeting that had been arranged for him with little Fräulein Blumenthal.

She did not displease him. She seemed so impressed by him that he considered her rather long face sympathetically, and her dress, which was well filled, and above all her eyes, unmalicious eyes where on a background of bluish fear, almost terror, the multiple mischievous sparks of childish curiosity danced. When she began to blush, he found her desirable.

"Well?" Mordecai asked when he returned. Benjamin stared at him in silence.

"No?" the old man asked, uneasy.

Benjamin smiled thinly. "Yes."

And without waiting for compliments, he plunged once more into the daily course of his life, running upstairs to change and dashing into the shop afterward, where he could only fidget, nervous and indecisive about choosing the most urgent task. "All of this doesn't put any butter in the soup, does it?" he asked himself aloud, with an affectation of importance that surprised him. But when he least expected it, something in him fell apart and he burst into laughter.

.6.

A N HOUR LATER, Benjamin was sitting cross-legged on the cutting table, a vest across his knees. Vigorously he pushed his bent thumb and index finger against an invisible needle. The bulb, lowered close to his head, enveloped him in an aureole of harsh light.

"Why don't you wear glasses?" his father asked him affectionately. Benjamin raised his reddened eyelids, their lashes thinned by the work of the needle. "So you're happy?"

"I'm happy," Mordecai said. "I'm only sorry they don't know about it. We'll have to tell them soon!"

"Oh, they saw right away that I liked the lady. . . ."

"It isn't that, my son," Mordecai said in an oppressed tone.

He was breathing noisily, and his mustache lifted with the passage of his breath as he emerged timidly from a long and suffocating descent into himself, begun the day of his arrival in Stillenstadt. "We shall have to tell them who we are. Who we *really* are, do you understand?"

At that dizzying word "really," Benjamin had interrupted his needlework, and his hand remained hanging in the air, as if floating in the electric light. Finally he declared, "I'm sorry, but we will tell them nothing at all." His eyes were blinking with fatigue, as well as with the old fear that his father inspired in him.

"Nothing at all?"

"Nothing at all," Benjamin confirmed dryly.

"And her, you won't tell her either?"

Benjamin pursed his lips.

"I was afraid of it," Mordecai growled low. "You are an abominable pagan but . . . and the children?"

"What children?" the little tailor asked coldly while Mordecai's mouth opened in a grimace over the shattered yellow stones of his teeth, as if to make way for the torrential rumbling that suddenly roared out at a terrified Benjamin. "When there is a marriage, children are a possibility, aren't they?"

Two curious figures froze into immobility in front of the shopwindow.

Benjamin hunched his shoulders and with a discreet pressure of his heels retreated a bit from the wave of fury that was breaking over him. Then, in a voice as thin as thread, he answered humbly, "The children will know later, if they become men. I will not bother them with stories in which, I must tell you, my venerable father, I no longer believe. . . ." He added immediately, on a note of bitterness, "In which I no longer want to believe! Oh, papa!"

As Benjamin, prudently withdrawn to the end of the cutting table, ended that strange confession of faith, his head so low that it almost touched his knees, his father Mordecai began to cry out so piercingly that Judith ran in from the kitchen, a casserole in her hand.

She got the gist right away, and swinging her casserole with fiery gestures plunged into the discussion, immediately speaking of the future Levy as if he were already present on her breast in place of the casserole she embraced lovingly. "Who's going to tell whom?" she cried indignantly. "If the good Lord, blessed be he, has made a decision one way or another about his little bird (and what shall we name him?), the little one will know about it when the time comes, soon enough, alas. But may God spare us," she finished shrilly, "from having a Just Man!"

"Oh, papa, papa," Benjamin went on emotionally. "You know very well that to be a Lamed-Vovnik is worth hardly anything in this world—and maybe not even in the next."

Outnumbered, Mordecai retreated slowly toward the door. Having opened it, he pointed a thick, accusing finger out of the shadow, and on a tone of supreme derision, "For the good life, to lose all your reasons for living?" Then he withdrew, cut off from his son for good.

On the wedding day he barely acknowledged the presence of the bride's parents. As for little Fräulein Blumenthal, he pretended not to see her—she was no longer any use to him, she no longer played a part in the dream of his life. This time he had retreated altogether into the pit of his age.

That old elephant, Judith always said of her husband from then on, that old solitary, that rock.

Although tiny and quite thin, Fräulein Leah Blumenthal was well made, but no one noticed that until her wedding day, a neighbor woman having helped her to emphasize all her beauty. She seemed totally lacking in natural coquetry. Her face was always clean but not engaging, her hair always in order but not truly coiffed, and her appearance constantly well-groomed but neutral.

Herr Benjamin Levy, her husband, wondered how it came about that she had such slender white hands, with the fingers of a rich woman. He never suspected that that virgin whiteness required an unheard-of amount of daily attention, of meticulous care so subtle that no one noticed, watching her peel a vegetable, with what precautions she surrounded herself in order not to chip a fingernail or scratch the precious ermine of a patch of skin.

Judith announced that her daughter-in-law handled all things with tweezers. But Benjamin was delighted with her hands. While his wife was asleep he loved to play with one of those bony mechanisms that took on in his palm, in the blackness, all the forms his imagination might give it—animal, vegetable, and even the almost intoxicating form of five thick hairs that he combed against the supple skin of the pillowcase.

Still, in those first days of marriage he was astonished at the amount of time she spent indefatigably "licking herself like a cat." After each embrace, she went down to the kitchen to make her complete toilette. That might have ended by annoying him if each time she had not touched a drop of perfume to her armpits, which lent balm to all her freshly soaked body. And then when she reappeared, draped in her nightgown and holding the candle as far as possible from her hair, the childlike, confused freshness of her person suddenly illuminated the room with a quivering clarity, bounded by shadows, and caused Herr Benjamin Levy's heart to beat rapidly.

"Ah, Fräulein Blumenthal," he said to her, smiling agitatedly. "Have you had a nice walk?"

"I wanted to bring you a surprise," she said submissively, and sitting at the edge of the bed, she pushed toward her modest sovereign's mouth an apple, a slice of bread and

butter and a lump of sugar with which she earned pardon for
her desertion of the conjugal bed.

One day he surprised her undulating and simpering, all
alone in the middle of the room, like a siren at a hairdresser's.
She had gathered her nightdress around her waist; her hair was
spread wildly over her shoulders, giving her an air of animal
luxury that at once aged her girl's face and restored to it the
coquettish expression of childhood. Benjamin burst into laughter. . . . From the one example of his own wife, he knew
now that all women are little girls getting on in years, each
endowed with a body greater and more important than her
mind, and all of whom adore surrounding themselves with
meaningless mysteries. It was only much later that he learned
that Fräulein Blumenthal lived in a narrow universe haunted
by fear and by two or three sentiments equally terrible in
their simplicity—the love of a few beings, the repressed
pleasure of having a body.

The fear came to her in a direct line from her mother, a
woman of imperial aspect and character who had made herself a perfect slave to Herr Blumenthal. She suffered accesses
of cruelty, she found a voluptuousness in such things. But
when Frau Blumenthal died of the disease that had made her
so shrewish and cruel, Herr Blumenthal saw nothing more fit
than to marry immediately a person of equal wickedness. Miss
Blumenthal then suffered the yoke of the stranger until her
own marriage, toward which her stepmother had labored
frantically.

Soon afterward, the latter discovered that Berlin was a
city with a future, and Fräulein Blumenthal was abandoned
to the Levys. She watched her father leave the way one de-
parts this life—this time she was altogether lost.

Naturally the one person in the world whom she feared
from now on more than any other was Judith. An order from
the latter made her tremble, and even though "Mother
Judith's" violence was distributed solely in words, little Frau
Levy always hunched over and raised an elbow gently, as if
one day or another she might get a real slap. And yet she

stared directly into Judith's eyes, to the point where Judith
was occasionally upset by this gentle gaze focused on her
violence like a beacon on an absurdly agitated sea. But until
her first child arrived Fräulein Blumenthal bowed to the
slightest frown of those terrible brows. Mother Judith alone
was mistress of the house, and in the fear that someone might
encroach upon her territory, she preferred two precautions to
one, assigning a task to her daughter-in-law only with reluctance, and she never hid her opinion that she would have performed it better herself. It was that way until Miss Blumenthal's first confinement.

Already during her pregnancy (which was immediate),
the new Mama Levy was offended that Mother Judith should
treat her simply as the repository of a precious object belong-
ing primarily to the Levys, and more exactly like a simple
perfume jar ignorant of the value of its contents. Mother
Judith watched over the infant being nurtured in the young
woman, ordered her to lie down, to drink a maximum of
beer and to be aware at all times of the unmerited honor of
being the vessel of a Levy.

"Be careful of the child," she would say in a tone that meant
almost "Remember that you are carrying our posterity."

In a movement of instinctive revolt, little Frau Levy turned
the trembling but stubborn beam of her eyes (the eyes of a
domesticated bird) upon Mother Judith, and leaning forward
she surrounded her enormous belly with both arms in the
solemn gesture of a gravid woman, a gesture that had become
familiar since the child had taken root in her.

Open warfare broke out in the hospital. The mother, thin
and pale, lay back on her pillow. At the foot of the bed, the
swaddled thing in her arms, Mother Judith received the congratulations of visitors. They admired the infant, they listened
to the sage comments of Mother Judith. Now and then one
turned toward the exhausted mother as if to say, "Ah, that's
true, a bit of the credit goes to her."

Suddenly little Fräulein Blumenthal half sat up and gave

out a piercing cry. "Give him back to me, he belongs to me!" There was a moment of embarrassment. From the nearby beds in the ward a murmur arose. Mother Judith had reddened, and she frowned at her daughter-in-law—white, gasping, her body arched on her forearms, entirely hardened by her new hate and her new love. And yet when they yielded the baby to her, setting it in the hollow of her breast, she lay beside it and fell asleep almost instantly, so much had that exceptional explosion of energy exhausted her.

Herr Benjamin Levy secretly exulted, while Mordecai declared in a tone of tender respect, "May God protect us, we have a she-wolf in the house." Mother Judith was silent; until they were weaned, Fräulein Blumenthal would remain the mother of her children.

The drama was revived later on. Children respect only the supreme authority. Mordecai was always wise enough to efface himself before Herr Benjamin Levy in their presence, but it was not so with Mother Judith, who became mother-in-chief as soon as the children were old enough to obey her. Fräulein Blumenthal found herself relegated to nourishment. In the end she became accustomed to the successive abandonments—she saw in it an ineluctable destiny, Mother Judith representing in her eyes only the first step toward the final detachment of the adult, which was, to her mother's heart, an ascent into nothingness. She even borrowed her authority from that of Mother Judith, and when she was not obeyed quickly enough, she went to fetch the mother superior in person. She never suspected that she nevertheless remained the true spring, the sole well of maternity, hollowed out in a mysterious fashion in the heart of each of her children. It was in the kitchen, close to her skirts, that the ingrates came to sit when they were seized by a sadness without reason, or by one of those impalpable agonies that come from the depths of being and are appeased only by the sound of a certain voice.

Her husband was no different from the rest of humanity.

Manifestly he took her for a negligible quantity, speaking to her only to tease her as if she were a child.

Once, a foolish young girl, she had dreamed of a man for whom she would be important, beside whom she would play a role, however slight. But Herr Benjamin Levy felt about her as he did about a length of thread, and several times she bit back the desire to ask him suddenly, point-blank, what was the color of her eyes. She thought he would be unable to answer, she imagined desperately his nonchalant manner. "Ah, yes, your eyes, they're . . . and will you please go away and not bother me with these children's games?" She was quite sure that he had never really looked at them.

In which she was mistaken, as in the rest, for not only was the tender Benjamin aware of the color of her eyes but even more, quizzed on that chapter he could have expatiated endlessly on the slightest particularity of the lashes, of the white of the right eye, slightly whiter than that of the left, on the infinitesimal grains of pink that rose against the grayish background of the irises and that he was doubtless the only one in the world to have noticed. But could a man say these things? Fräulein Blumenthal had brought herself to his bed by duty, and in all decency it was a bit late to subject her to a courtship that she seemed not to solicit at all. So for a long time after the marriage Benjamin continued to call his wife "Fräulein Blumenthal," half in affectionate mockery and half in that insane inhibition which kept him from acknowledging the deep, definitive bond that united him to that accidental wife. Their lovemaking was deaf and mute, but at times from those great nocturnal depths of silence a crest of foam and cries arose out of an embrace, and both tasted an extraordinary heightening—to which they never referred, for there was obviously something in it that did not belong to this world. Later, it required old age and, above all, the approach of violent death in the concentration camp to make Benjamin decide to express his love to his wife. She did not grasp his meaning.

*   *   *

Hurried by all the members of the Levy family, she had given birth to her first prematurely. Nevertheless he weighed nine sumptuous pounds at birth. Whom did he resemble? The question was never even asked. It went without saying that here was the traditional form of the Levys, which little Herr Levy, the father, had transmitted in self-defense. Mother Judith wasted no time in examining the eyes, the nose, the mouth, as she might have if the least doubt existed as to the "resemblance" of the newborn. Addressing herself to the old man, she delivered a résumé of the situation in these words: "He resembles *us*." Fräulein Blumenthal might recall the strong personality of her dead mother, trace a lip formed in tiny symptomatic points, emphasize a short nose that obviously came from the Blumenthal side—nothing made any difference. The child was not of her blood. And although the history of the Just Men seemed to Mother Judith to include an unhealthy element, she found herself almost tempted to throw it in her daughter-in-law's face to stop her mouth finally of these supposed rights to the child. In her fierce desire to claim the scion for herself, she went so far as to identify herself with that illustrious line. She labored over certain domestic details of the cult; she made herself more than ever a Levy.

As he grew up, the living enigma set them at it again. It became obvious that he was neither Levy nor Blumenthal but some indeterminate human creature dotted by a touch of Germanic brute. The new arrival, Moritz, seemed above all eager not to let himself down among the little hoodlums who were his comrades—and moreover succeeded quite well, aided by an appropriate physique. From the day of his birth he sported a good round belly that was like an expression of his animal joy in living, and the quickly formed structure of his body testified to the real strength beneath the cheerful *bon vivant's* exterior. For years his face was like a doll's— regular teeth, a short nose with thick nostrils, and luminous, avid brown eyes always beaming forward, outward toward the world, like a hand extended happily.

At first Mordecai thought that in the child he could see

again the scandalous young man he himself had been in Zemyock, and his indulgence was exaggerated by the conviction that sooner or later the young devil would also lay aside his horns. He nourished the child discreetly on anecdotes of the Just Men and secretly reckoned the young one's chances of measuring up to that honor. But as soon as Moritz was old enough to get about by himself, they never saw him at the house. The street attracted him. There he joined a gang of urchins among whom—a painful thing!—not one even slightly Jewish nose could be seen.

Moritz was a ringleader—he invented games and loved nothing so much as mock warfare on the banks of the Schlosse. When he prowled among the reeds, a half-drawn bow against his thigh, he knew that his destiny was not what they thought it at home. And when they undressed to dive into the river, the clothes of the presumed Moritz Levy disappeared, revealing a naked savage in a menacing forest of reeds. He attacked the enemy enthusiastically. And when the two of them slid into the mud, he could have wished their shouts genuine, the knives real metal. . . . He came home with his face afire, his knees and clothes in tatters, and undid his suspenders, waiting patiently while Mother Judith finished rousing herself to anger. There was an immanent justice. They played at "killing each other," as Mother Judith said weakly; then they got a good spanking. After which they could consider themselves even with God.

School finished the job of dividing Moritz's life into two irreducible halves. They never saw him except at mealtimes. Invariably he arrived late, sat down contritely, performed the necessary motions of grace and then leaned forward over his plate and forgot heaven and earth until it was emptied, the last stains mopped up with bread. Only then, raising his disheveled head, did he become a presence in the world of the Levys.

"Has our pagan finished his soup?" Mother Judith asked sadly.

"And when will you find a moment for the study of the

Talmud?" the old man asked him in a resigned voice. "At your age I was already into the Midrash up to my ears. Aren't you Jewish?" Moritz, annoyed, mumbled incomprehensibly, "—my fault—homework—school."

Benjamin, altogether astonished at having fathered such a scoundrel, came to his defense immediately. "It's true, you know, in Zemyock there was no Christian school. But here, how can they become good Jews?"

"But you were the one who wanted to leave!" cried the old man, angered by so much bad faith.

Benjamin smiled imperceptibly. "Ah, don't I know it! But it's too late now, and as the Talmud says, 'In the home of a hanged man, don't even say, "Go hang up this fish for me." ' "

"No," Mother Judith then said, "I can't see this child 'sweating,' either for us or for the Christians." And she concluded with the strange comment, "God has punished us. Our little ones won't even be Saturday Jews; they'll be Sunday Jews."

A reflective silence fell over the room. Then little Frau Levy served the next course, and conversation rose again on another subject, grave or mockingly sentimental, as if the problem were solved. A slow feeling invaded Moritz, who burrowed delightedly into the warmly reassuring atmosphere of the family meal. What they were saying passed far over his head, birds tracing indecipherable signs in the sky, but which he loved to watch.

An abyss separated this little world of grace from the vast universe that Moritz sniffed as soon as he set foot in the street. Occasionally it made him dizzy, like holding on to the very top of the big chestnut tree at school, standing between two branches with an insupportable emptiness between them. Why weren't all the Christians Jews? And why weren't all Jews Jews? Couldn't everybody enjoy this kind of happiness together? And what did the old man want of him, what was he scheming behind his bloody anecdotes, his tragic expression, his constant allusions to the Lamed-Vov? When he set out on these disconcerting paths, Moritz's brain was in a whirl soon enough, and his heart, it seemed to him, split horribly with a dry ripping sound. He therefore risked it very rarely.

· 7 ·

ERNIE was Fräulein Blumenthal's second fruit. He arrived within exactly nine months. But when she saw that he was even more ridiculously puny than Moritz had been, Fräulein Blumenthal repressed a cry of happiness in her childbed. This one would not be claimed by Mother Judith; this little nestling was hers alone.

It was easy to see that Mother Judith was in trouble. Several months after the delivery, Fräulein Blumenthal again surprised her examining the baby minutely. "It's funny," Fräulein Blumenthal offered, "I can't tell whom he resembles. . . ."

And Mother Judith looked her up and down before admitting deviously, "He's built like his father, but his head—the head comes from nobody. All this will be decided later," she said almost menacingly.

Indeed, Ernie Levy's head offered no clue. When he emerged from the maternal fluids, his skull bore a fine sheath of curly black down descending to the nape of his neck, and his eyes, which were blue for three weeks, soon shifted to a midnight blue sprinkled with brilliant stellar sparks.

Mother Judith did not understand whence came that thin straight nose, wings swept back to expose the open nostrils, that long white dome of the forehead, and particularly the length of the neck, "no thicker than a finger," which supported the whole edifice with the inimitable grace of a bird. But when she embraced the marvel, Mother Judith smiled indeterminately, wholly admiring, and her richly sensual gaze tightly enfolded that mysterious living thing, the baby in whom ran at least a drop of her blood and who yet seemed to her so different from all known flesh that she called him only "little angel."

Forewarned by Moritz's example, the grandfather took Ernie in hand when he was less than four. From Poland he had sent for a Hebrew alphabet in relief. He initiated the little angel by the ancestral method, which is sweet and attractive —smeared with honey, the rosewood characters were given to the young student of the Law simply to suck on. Later on, when Ernie was capable of reading brief phrases, Mordecai offered them molded on cakes, in the making of which Judith displayed all her cleverness.

Ernie began to trot along behind the old man. Their relations became so intimate that Fräulein Blumenthal was moved. They held long conversations in the room upstairs. When she put her ear to the door, Fräulein Blumenthal heard only whispering, now solemn, now so fine and lyrical that her breast tightened fearfully. One day she heard, "So then will you lend me your beard?" There followed a long and solemn whispering.

But more than anything, the way they had of being together affected her strongly. From her kitchen she watched them now and then in the dining room during those awful Hebrew lessons. The old man's attitude seemed as reverent as that of the child. When Ernie asked a question, the patriarch nodded thoughtfully before answering, as if this were a learned Talmudic discussion. And once in a while his hand came to rest on the curly hair, straightening a lock.

Fräulein Blumenthal did not understand. She sensed a kind of umbilical cord between the old man and the child but was unable to visualize the nourishing substance that ran through it. One day, peeking through the kitchen window, she saw the child hunched over a spelling book and stroking an imaginary beard with great dignity. An unexpected truth struck her— Ernie was *imitating* the old man. Alerted, she noticed other details. When he believed himself alone, the little one clasped his hands behind his back, his eyes became heavier, his head drooped forward, and with the slow tread of an old man, he paced about the table as if plunged in rabbinical meditation. And other times, seated before his spelling book, he began to sing psalms with an inspired air, as do the angels and the pious Jews. She also surprised him in the act of trapping a pinch of wind, which he introduced delicately into his right nostril, sniffing it then in slow concentration and lifting his head in the old man's manner.

One Friday night after the Sabbath service, the old man climbed to his room and came down with an enormous volume bound in calfskin. Fräulein Blumenthal knew about this book through her husband, whose lips opened during certain moments of calm intimacy. She knew by hearsay a bit about the Just Men, about Zemyock and about the money orders in varying amounts that took the road to Poland every month. She might have been able to learn more, but she was not really curious about the subterranean world of the Levys' daily life. She never spoke of it to her husband, pretending to have forgotten. So she was as surprised as Judith and Benjamin when the old man slowly opened the book and began to read the first chapter. A heavy silence fell. The children saw Mother Judith pale, majestically angry. Suddenly she gave vent to a raucous, guttural exclamation. The old man raised his eyes and blasted her with a look.

His voice was icy. "These children don't know what a real Jew is." And pounding the tabletop with a stiffened hand, he added, "And you, you don't even know that I'm still a man." Then he went on with his reading in the same slow, harsh, occasionally tremulous voice. It was the same on the following Friday.

Fräulein Blumenthal knew enough Hebrew to understand the dedicated lives of these martyrs. She made an effort to exclude the horror of them from her thoughts. And she was grieved to see that the little angel, leaning toward the reader, his eyes terribly wide, was "imitating" the bloody characters of the book with all his heart. And then on the fourth Friday, when the old man had finished his reading, Ernie raised an obedient finger and asked him, *"If all these stories are true——"*

A shrill, unpleasant laugh escaped Herr Benjamin Levy.

And then Mother Judith seemed to swell with fury while her eyes turned in supplication toward the old man, who hesitated and chewed on his mustaches. Finally he murmured in a dry, truly broken voice, "Well, what do you think, my little fledgling, can such things really happen?" A fine line appeared between the child's brows. "No, of course not," he answered bitterly.

On those words the old man closed the book and left the dining room. Late at night Fräulein Blumenthal heard the echoes of the argument between him and Mother Judith. He never again brought down the book of the fabulous house of Levy.

Mother Judith had always cast a gloomy eye on Ernie's diligence in learning from the patriarch. "That one doesn't even need honey to chew up his ABC's, but where's the good of it all?" She was fearful that by plunging that vulnerable consciousness into the "old stories" Mordecai might insidiously communicate the virus of Zemyockism, as Benjamin called it. But the cure was close behind the disease, for soon attendance at school would lead little Ernie to the games of his own age—that, at least, was what the old lady hoped.

Events proved that the study of the Law had created a mechanism no less sensitive to pagan programs than to the divine Torah and the Prophets. And Mother Judith found consolation in the fact that Ernie was wearying visibly of Mordecai's teaching, and devoting himself to profane studies.

He preferred to work in the kitchen, on a corner of the table set aside for him by Fräulein Blumenthal. Mother Judith would find some pretext for an intrusion, and while the distracted scholar chewed on his tongue, the two rivals, spying on each other, subjected him to the gamut of their uneasily curious glances.

On one fatal day he came home with an armful of prizes. Neither Mordecai nor Mother Judith congratulated him disproportionately. Although it was for diametrically opposed reasons, both evinced serious (and in certain respects dramatic) reservations about what was to Benjamin cause for a thousand embraces. Fräulein Blumenthal, torn between panic and admiration, could only clasp her hands and supplicate, "I hope only good comes of it. My God, I hope only good comes of it."

As Ernie moved solemnly to the stairway, Mother Judith followed him on tiptoe. Watching him mysteriously enter the young couple's room, she approached stealthily and heard the sound of voices. Gluing one ear to the keyhole, she heard these astounding words, pronounced by the little angel in a professorial tone, his German curiously modulated by Yiddish inflections: "You again? Congratulations, my boy, congratulations, my young man. You again?" Then she heard a mouselike laugh and understood that the little angel was strutting ironically before the mirror, at which she could not help bursting out with a huge laugh of happiness herself—producing immediate silence behind the door.

Until that day the only books around the house had been prayer books, Talmudic texts or some schoolbook forgotten by the children. In the beginning, when she saw Ernie deep in one of the prize volumes, Mother Judith suspected nothing, accepted this as inherent to the custom of the country. But one night, in an excess of scruple, she asked Benjamin to tell her something about the little angel's latest reading. Her son's answer surprised her—two collections of fairy tales, an adventure novel set in China, and three tales of old German chivalry! After half an hour of confused explanations, she lost her temper. "I don't understand a thing you've told me. What I want to know is yes or no, did everything written in those books happen?"

"No," Benjamin said resolutely.

"Then it's all lies," Mother Judith declared with marked repugnance.

"It's not lies, it's stories."

Judith's eyelids fluttered, the breath hissed between her pursed lips. "Why don't you tell me right out that I'm crazy?"

The conversation was over.

But Mother Judith had formed her conviction, and on that same day she noticed for the first time that if Ernie was suddenly interrupted in his reading, he raised toward her a blank expression swollen by dream and delirium, and recognized her only reluctantly.

"Where are you?" she asked him gently. And as the child watched her without pleasure, she was sorry not to be able to follow him into that sphere where things invisible to the naked eye are so beautiful to one who knows how to read that he has no further desire to return to this world.

Shortly afterward, without her knowing how, new books appeared between the child's hands, each more disquieting than the others. Some of them were illustrated, and horsemen could be seen, and women in long gowns bedecked with diamonds, and curious beings and plants that doubtless came from China. But the volumes that Judith feared most were those that gave no hint of their content. When he emerged from them, the child seemed completely lost. After a few weeks, the rims of his eyes took on an unhealthy pink flush and his tiny blue veins stood out clearly against the exquisite white of his skin. One night at table, Ernie's eyes began to water with fatigue. In great agitation Judith called upon the whole family to witness this. No, no, things could not go on this way. "Those awful books are eating out his eyes, and I wouldn't be surprised one of these mornings if they ate out his whole insides!"

Severe measures were voted that evening. As soon as she had rallied unanimous support, Mother Judith stalked into his room and expropriated all the volumes of "lies," without exception.

In the next few days the battle became more bitter. It transpired that the child was smuggling books home in the seat of his pants.

With that ruse exposed, he redoubled his ingenuity and did so well that Mother Judith, as she put it, "surrendered." Still, though defeated as a censor she became a spy, keeping track of the little angel's activities and gestures, seeing to it that he did not succumb to his vice in the attic or in the cellar or even in the little corner of the room that now served him as a study. Driven out of his last line of trenches, Ernie tried to profit by the adult conversations that took place every night in the living room. Slipping barefoot into the hallway, he managed to take advantage of the ray of light that gleamed from the doorway of the room—with the door left artfully ajar. They discovered him behind the door after midnight, haggard, his eyes wild, too tired to know what was happening to him.

But from then on, at the slightest signal of approach, if he gave so much as a gentle, understanding sigh Mother Judith's voice came to him from the other side. "Ernie, my lamb of suffering, go to bed."

.8.

HAVING WON the battle of the books, Mother Judith went so far as to hope that the little angel would follow the example of his pagan elder brother.

But soon enough, alas, she had to admit that in driving out one devil she had admitted another in its place, even more dangerous because totally elusive. Whether he was at table or doing his homework (and even during his rare frolics with the younger children), the little angel would suddenly freeze up, his features immobilized. A fine pink blur rose to his eyes, and he became as distant from all of them as though he were off in the land of books. She suspected that he was telling himself tales of chivalry. For—an astonishing thing—when he came out of those reveries he adopted an air of martial dignity, the detached, abstracted bearing of a hero.

She decided to use strong methods. If there was the slightest hint of sunshine, she expelled the child into the street without ceremony, and one day it was finally learned that the little angel was forgathering with the other youngsters of the neighborhood. She had won.

The headquarters of the gang was some way up the Riggenstrasse, in the back yard of an abandoned, dilapidated house. The grass and the rubble, the heaps of garbage and the unused well, composed a landscape rich in magic possibilities. Two of Ernie's classmates were also in the "gang by the well." One of them was a delicate little blond girl named Ilse Bruckner, to whom Ernie never dared speak because her eyes were two lakes and her golden hair cascaded with discipline and majesty onto her shoulders, giving her the look of a medieval fairy princess. She wore a knitted sweater with red and white checks. Around her neck was an iron chain from which hung a cross, and when they asked her to, she sang senseless little counting rhymes in a voice that made them lightheaded and giddy.

There was something miraculous about Ernie's admission to the gang. Once Mother Judith had chased him out of the house, he had fallen into the habit of wandering about, following the thread of his reverie, hands in his pockets, his body erect and his head held high on his long neck, springing like a stem from the open collar of his white shirt. Paying no attention at all to what went on in the street, he stumbled against pedestrians, crates, anything set out on the sidewalk, so that finally, made prudent, he directed his steps outside the town, along the edges of the lush fields that bounded the Schlosse. But one day, alerted by a voice recognizable among thousands, he slipped into the ruins of the old house, and huddled in the shadow, he watched Ilse sing in the middle of the group, her face drawing every gaze and the sun sparkling in a cone of light on her corn-silk blond hair. The next day he came forward openly, his hands deliberately crossed behind his back, showing by his whole attitude that he was only a delighted little spectator of the gang's activities and laughter. They grew accustomed to his mute presence. They assigned small parts to him. He guarded the rock piles, refereed tournaments, was a professional prisoner, was page to King Tristan—duties that scarcely demanded the wearing of a sword. When the game proved too violent, he cautiously left the field—the simple sight of bruises wounded him. And when they were swept up in the game and whacked away at each other with wooden swords, Ernie wondered why they had to dream with their bodies when it was so sweet to dream with the soul alone. One day Wilhelm Knöpfer, a chubby little boy with laughing eyes and a double chin, suggested that they play the trial of Jesus.

"But who'll be the Jews?" asked Hans Schliemann, who was their undisputed leader.

They all protested. Finally they discovered Ernie Levy squatting behind a nearby wall, white with terror. Amid loud bursts of laughter, he was dragged to the well against which Ilse Bruckner was already leaning, her arms wide above the mossy rim of rock, her head hanging in agony. She was on tiptoe, in imitation of the nailed Christ. Wilhelm Knöpfer immediately improvised a potbellied, hilarious Pontius Pilate, who now and then rubbed his palms together significantly and shot a sly look at all of them. "You get it? I'm washing my hands of it." Now and then he slipped a hand into his shirt in an inexplicably Napoleonic gesture.

"Aha!" he puffed at Ernie. "You're our only Jew, you're our only Jew, so you have to do it—otherwise who else do you want to be *them?*" And imposing silence on the excited gang, he frowned, raised a majestic lower lip and announced gravely, "Ho, Jews! What do you want me to do with Our Lord? Do I let him go?"

"It isn't like that," interrupted a neatly braided little girl in a professorial manner and an incontrovertible tone. "In the catechism, first it's Barabbas."

Wilhelm Knöpfer trumpeted, "Leave us alone with your catechism! Here *I'm* the priest. . . . All right, then," he began again, upset by the interruption, trying to win back his shaken prestige. "Do I let him go, yes or no?"

A veiled sharpness shone cruelly in Wilhelm's good-little-boy gaze from pupils dilated by an interior vision, vindictive and heavy with reminiscence. Ernie blinked his long lashes sadly. Bound by the solid clasp of two boys and suffering the corrosive action of all those glances, it seemed to him that his fleshly self was dissolving into the air, to be reborn in some mysterious way in the spirits of his playmates—but concealed now behind a mask, wearing cheap and bloody finery, as in those nightmares where one sees oneself reduced to some sort of abject vermin. He threw a defeated glance toward Ilse, whose golden head hung loosely against one shoulder, with an abandon as coquettish as it was moving. And when the cross, swinging against the girl's sweater, awakened the fabled memory of Christian atrocities, a weakness softened Ernie's knees. "Oh, let him go," he breathed.

Which evoked an immediate concert of protests. "Ah, no, it wasn't like that, not like that, not like that! You said to crucify him! 'Crucify him!' you said. So say it, go ahead and say it, say it, say it!" They all took it up in chorus while Ernie hung his head sadly, his lower lip already bleeding between the teeth that refused to part for the word of death.

"For God's sake!" Hans Schliemann cried furiously. "Did you say it or didn't you?"

In the deferent silence that followed the leader's intervention, the melodious voice of the crucified girl was heard. "Ah! The nails, the nails, how I suffer!"

"Oh, my God, have pity," said a little girl in a miserable tone that pierced the hearts of her strange audience, freezing their blood, cutting their breath, agitating the girls' eyes, the long luminous lashes now fluttering, or trembling, or closing over shameful tears.

"But no, I didn't say it," Ernie offered, upset.

"Yes, you did say it!" Hans Schliemann growled in the voice he used for distributing justice, while his arm of iron came down mercilessly on Ernie's shoulder. Ernie sighed.

"And," the little girl with braids took it up, "you even said, 'Let Barabbas go, and crucify Jesus.' Didn't he say that?"

"He said it! He said it!"

"I didn't—I didn't!" the accused stammered, a tear streaking one cheek.

"You said it, you said it," the children repeated more violently while Ernie Levy, hiding his face between his hands, murmured in a more and more hesitant voice, as if the others were convincing him, "I didn't say it. I didn't, no, I didn't."

A little girl's voice exploded against his ear. "You dirty Jew!"

At the same time the viscid weight of a gob of spit trickled down his ear.

And then Wilhelm Knöpfer screamed indignantly, "Murderer!"

And grabbing one of Ernie's hands, he smacked him in the belly so hard that the child spun about, lost, in air turgid with shouts, with fantastic fists and with the sharp fingernails the little girls were digging into the flesh of his shoulders and thighs as they fired plaintive insults at him. "Wicked, wicked—you killed God!"

A hand stopped him in his dizzying fall, and he saw close to his own the face of Hans Schliemann, gray and unrecognizable in a concentrated fury. "Look what you did to her!" Hans Schliemann cried, pointing to little Ilse, who was weeping by herself, still leaning back against the rim of the well, her arms spread wide, her dying head twisted painfully as, in her pious imitation of Jesus Christ, she let a thin thread of spittle drip from the corner of her pink mouth, twisted in pain. When she realized that they were watching her, she breathed in a touching voice, "Oh, my God, what did I ever do to you, you Jews? Oh, my God, the nails, the nails . . ."

At which, no longer able to restrain himself, Wilhelm Knöpfer picked up a rock and, slipping behind Ernie, hit him hard on the back of the neck, crying out, "For Jesus!" The Jewish boy fell in a heap on the grass, his eyes rolled back, his arms crossed. A red flower bloomed on his black curly hair. After a few moments of contemplation, the gang scattered silently. Only Wilhelm Knöpfer stayed behind, with a little boy of about ten who kept murmuring, "Oh, oh," and stared in fascination at the red flower spreading on Ernie Levy's neck.

"He's dead," Wilhelm Knöpfer said, dropping his bloody rock to the ground.

"We ought to make sure," the other one said, terrified.

"I don't dare."

"I don't either."

"He never did anything to us," Wilhelm said in a strange voice.

"No, he didn't," the second boy agreed.

"He was nice," Wilhelm admitted suddenly, shaking his head as if unable to retrace the obscure road that had led to his act.

"Yes, he was," the other one said with surprise.

"Shall we carry him back?" Wilhelm asked.

"We have to," said the other one, who was already kneeling.

He took Ernie by the shoulders, and Wilhelm, between his legs, raised the body by the thighs. "He doesn't weigh much more than a bird," Wilhelm remarked in a tearful sigh. Then he began to weep silently, and went on weeping all the way down the Riggenstrasse, staring at Ernie's bloody neck, which jiggled at each step, while a small group of curious bystanders formed a strange cortege to this even stranger hearse. Mother Judith was the first to know. With a shattering cry, she gathered up the child and carried him to a room on the second floor, followed by a silent Wilhelm. No one paid any attention to Wilhelm. When the doctor, called immediately, passed a smelling bottle under the little victim's nostrils, Wilhelm made the sign of the cross mechanically, and stricken by the memory of their play-acting, he thought that he had made a sign of death. But the Jewish child, his head back on a pillow already red, suddenly gave a long sigh and murmured, "I didn't say that, I didn't say that. . . ." Wilhelm slipped outside unnoticed. Once on the sidewalk, he ran as fast as he could.

Although its origin would always remain mysterious, in time

the act of aggression against Ernie took its place in the series
of anti-Semitic acts that announced Adolf Hitler's rise to power.
Communists being scarce in Stillenstadt and democrats being
altogether lacking, it followed naturally that the local section of
the Nazi Party directed the full fire of its propaganda against
the few Jewish families that "were rife" in the town. After
Adolf Hitler's accession to the supreme office of Chancellor of
the Reich, German Jews felt trapped, like rats condemned to
run in circles while waiting for the worst. "We should never
have left Poland," Mother Judith admitted one day. "I ask forgiveness. It was my fault, mine. . . ."

"Come, come," the patriarch answered her gently. "If evil is
everywhere, how can you hope to escape it?"

It was the year 1933 after the coming of Jesus, the beautiful
herald of impossible love.

IV

THE JUST MAN
OF THE FLIES

. 1 .

I T WAS Ernie's father who gave the alarm. They had hardly
left the Riggenstrasse when Ernie sensed that his father was
tense and alert. It was that way every Saturday on the way to
the synagogue. As soon as they set foot outside the Riggenstrasse, Herr Levy no longer felt secure. Twisting his head in all
directions, he raised his rabbit's-head, and Ernie thought he
could see the ears quiver, tall and projecting. But today the
street was so calm and empty, the red tiles of the roofs gleamed
so gaily in the sun, that the child could not help feeling an ir-
reverent delight at his father's agitation. Looking up sideways,
he noticed that Herr Levy's thin lips were also trembling, closing and opening silently like the mouth of a suffocating fish.
Suddenly Herr Levy's lips closed altogether and opened only to
hiss.

"Sh-h-h . . ." said Herr Levy's mouth. He froze in the middle of the street.

"What's the matter?" said Mordecai.

Once more Ernie was astonished at the calm of the patriarch,
who never seemed to be upset about anything that did not bear
on the observance of the Law. The old man took two steps
backward, and raising a hand slowly to his beard, he pulled deliberately at one of its curls. "Well, what's the matter?" he repeated with a slight nuance of impatience. But his heavy gray
eyes remained calm and did not seem to share the nervousness
of the younger Herr Levy. The latter brought a hand behind his
right ear and said, "Do you hear?"

"I don't hear a thing," said Mother Judith, who had just arrived, out of breath, gleaming and plump in her eternal black
taffeta dress.

143

"I hear . . ." Fräulein Blumenthal said feebly.

"I do too," said Moritz.

"They're coming by the Rundgasse," Herr Levy continued. His right ear, carefully aimed, was still concentrating on the music, which came closer by the moment.

The Levy family remained immobile with fright beneath the sun, bathed in the yellow, suddenly cool light that delivered them up to public attention.

"All right!" Mother Judith cried. "Everybody to Frau Braunberger's house, quick!"

With those words, snatching up a child under each arm, she crossed the street and the sidewalk like an arrow and was already plunging into a nearby house, followed by the rest of the family. The patriarch was at the end of the line. His body moved forward heavily, and his spirit was remembering a former flight.

Ernie had reached the rear of the entrance hall when Mother Judith rushed down from the second floor, flustered, calling that Frau Braunberger's door was locked. "She's already left for the synagogue," said the patriarch, who was leaning calmly against the wall.

"What's to become of us?" Mother Judith cried. She stretched an arm toward the yellow rectangle of the street and then dropped it gently around Jacob, her youngest grandson, who was pressed against her thigh.

"Come now," said the patriarch, smiling in the semi-darkness. "Don't make a second hell for yourself. . . . Of course, if they catch you in the street they knock you about. But they don't come into houses to look for you. They won't come here especially for you, will they?"

"Listen to him!" Mother Judith cried grimly. Ernie saw her teeth flash suddenly in a brief, mirthless smile. Then she made her decision. "All right! Upstairs!"

She was already moving forward, followed by the whole silent troop. Even the old man, Ernie noticed, took each step on cautious tiptoe.

On the third-floor landing a closed window looked out over

the street. Ernie managed to slip between the old man's bowed legs just in time to see the S.A. patrol appear at the street corner. Their song struck suddenly at the windows, and the thunder of their steps echoed on the wooden floor of the landing. Seen from so high, with their leather boots, their wide military belts whose buckles glinted at random in the sunlight, and above all their small close-cropped heads, they seemed a kind of inoffensive, clanking insect crawling beneath the bright sun. When they reached the level of the building, their song died on a sudden beat and then a new song rose through the warm air, a song very familiar to the Levys but which made them all shiver nevertheless.

"When Jewish blood flows under the knife . . ."

"One-two-three!" cried the platoon leader.

"That does our hearts good, that does us good!"

"One-two-three!"

Then the platoon slanted off into the Magistratstrasse, leaving behind only a distant rumble that seemed unreal.

"How wicked they are," Fräulein Blumenthal said plaintively.

"All right, all right," Mother Judith interrupted her. "Let's not talk about it any more. We have to hurry now. We're a little late."

Jacob groaned, "I don't want to go!"

"Go where?" Judith asked distractedly.

"To the synagogue."

In answer the old woman grabbed his shoulder with one hand and jolted his head with an authoritative slap. Then, appeased, her body well balanced on the double column of her legs, she decreed, "Today they're out for Jewish blood, so we go to the synagogue in small groups. Each group will take a different road—there's no sense in being noticeable on a Saturday. You, Ernie, take Jacob and go around behind the Gymnasium. . . . Yes, right now, go on!" And turning her back on the two little boys, who had already clasped hands, she detailed orders to the others.

Ernie squeezed "little" Jacob's hand, and as he found it

wider across the palm than his own, he tightened his fingers for a better grip. With each step downward, Jacob's snufflings diminished. When they reached the ground floor, Jacob was silent. "All right?" cried Mother Judith from the stair well.

"All right," Ernie cried as quietly as he could.

But already, separated from his own by three dim flights of stone steps, he was discovering his solitude, and when he emerged at a hesitant pace into the dazzling sunlight of the street, his right hand tugging at Jacob's stubby, trembling paw (and he could guess at the kind, chubby face behind him, a bit swollen with fear beneath the odd note of a blue cap that Jacob always liked to tilt down over his forehead like a jockey—a face on which he could sense the fear, expressed in a light, wild sniffling), Ernie was shaken by an anguish so piercing that he wanted only to go back upstairs, back to the first-floor landing, to return to that haven so precarious and yet sheltered by the shadow of Mother Judith.

"Come on," he said gently. "I can't pull you all the way."

Jacob stared at him without understanding, thrust his chest forward slightly, and hooking on to Ernie's hand at arm's length as if harnessed in team with him, he followed heavily in his elder brother's footsteps. In almost the same moment he complained, "You're walking too fast. . . ."

Ernie became impatient. "You're bigger than I am," he said dryly.

"Yes, but I'm smaller," Jacob answered, meaning "I'm younger."

The one pulling the other in the sunlight, the two children set forth through narrow, darkened alleyways. All went well as far as the Street of Sparrows. Ernie had taken off that enormous, ornate purple handkerchief (a gift from Mother Judith, therefore obligatory on Saturday), which was obviously attracting glances from passers-by. Little by little the streets widened, the sun shone more brightly on the façades. They were approaching the better neighborhood. The boys reassured each other—no one seemed to be showing evil intent. Though he knew the way well and could ordinarily orient himself easily, Ernie had more and more trouble keeping his course among those beautiful homes, each so much like the others, though they were all different, while in the neighborhood of the Riggenstrasse the houses, short, squatty, truly identical, each had, like a face, some distinctive sign by which he recognized it at first glance. Ernie thought that the houses in the better neighborhoods had no odor—they were like water.

Jacob gasped, "Is it still far?"

"We have to get to the Gymnasium first," Ernie said deliberately. "I'll know the way better from there."

"I don't know these streets. I never saw them before. Maybe we ought to ask somebody?"

"We can't ask anybody," Ernie said after brief reflection.

"Why not?"

"Because of our voices," Ernie said, worried. "We have Yiddish voices."

Jacob waxed sarcastic. "And you think that the people don't see that we're Jewish? We wouldn't have to open our mouths— they know it already, don't they?"

In a long, slow look around, Ernie compared the blond children playing in everyday clothes on the sidewalks nearby with the short, polished figure of Jacob, his shoes carefully shined, his clothes carefully pressed, his skin carefully washed, his thick black hair strangely covered by his checked blue cap, his Jewish eye, the Jewish curve of his nose hooked fearfully over his upper lip. "It's true," he said. "It's Saturday and we've got our Sunday clothes on. . . ."

"And then we're wearing hats," Jacob added in a meaningful tone.

"That's true too," Ernie said. "In the summertime 'they' don't wear hats."

"All right, all right then, will you ask somebody?"

Ernie did not answer. He was looking around, gauging the Christian world. Finally, after endless hesitations he spied a tiny housewife sweeping her doorstep. Pulling Jacob behind him, he raised his beret and asked in his prettiest German accent "if the Gymnasium might be along here. . . ."

"Oh, it's straight ahead," said the surprised little woman.

Then, taking a better look at Ernie she laid her chin against the broom handle and smiled a bit with her mouth but even more with her small, light eyes. "You're right, little ones," she said understandingly. "It's better to go this way because the main streets are bad for 'you others' now that 'they' never stop marching around. But listen, it might be even better not to go at all to the synagogue. . . ."

Suddenly a second housewife emerged from the corridor. "Ah, those!" she exclaimed. "Talking to them won't do you any good!" And then turning to the two children she added for their benefit, "Cocorico, you Jews—watch out for trouble today!" And arching her back complacently, she set her hands against her comfortably swollen apron and sighed with ease. Immediately the faces of several curious children appeared surrounding the small group. Ernie and Jacob walked away hastily. They heard shrill cries and the sound of a chase at their heels. Tightening his grip on Jacob's hand, Ernie began to run full speed. At the corner, amazed that they had not been overtaken, he turned and saw in the distance a group of children laughing uncontrollably with gestures of hilarity. A small figure crossed the sidewalk, a broom in one hand and a child in the other. At a doorway the figure slapped the child and dragged it into the house. Ernie and his brother Jacob went on walking. Jacob was breathing heavily. He said in his sharp, changing, slightly shrill voice, "When I'm bigger I won't go to the synagogue any more."

"When you're bigger," Ernie said, "we'll all be dead."

After a few moments Jacob went on innocently, "If I take off my cap, they won't see that I'm a Jew, right?" And in a frightened tone, "Oh, Ernie, my cap—I could put it back on just before we got to the synagogue, couldn't I?"

Ernie halted. Jacob's face approached his own. The wide black eyes gleamed in supplicating fervor while Jacob's fleshy lower lip began to tremble so wildly that Ernie felt an extraordinary suffering rise within him. He raised his left hand and set it against his brother's cheek. "But what about me? They'll still know that I'm Jewish," he said as gently as possible.

"Yes," Jacob said in his shrill voice, "you look a lot more Jewish than I do. But . . ."

Meanwhile frowning, Ernie was thinking. "Anyway," he remarked suddenly, "if you take off your cap you die. So?"

"That's not true," Jacob said. "I've already done it many times."

Ernie thought a bit more. "God didn't want it, but he could do it to you any time."

"You think so?" Jacob cried in fear.

"I'm sure of it," Ernie said in a dream. "But you know . . . if you're so afraid . . . maybe you could . . . Oh, my God, why are you so afraid? Am I afraid?"

Jacob stared at him attentively. "Of course not," he said, *"You never feel anything."*

At that instant Ernie felt his back hunch, his head tilt slightly over onto his right shoulder, and as his eyes filmed over with a dull anxiety, he murmured in his ordinary soft, indifferent voice, "All right then, give me your cap. I'll walk on ahead and you follow along behind me. That way they won't know you're with me."

And as Jacob removed his cap hastily, Ernie took it from his hands and, his eyes turned to a heaven that he felt quite close, alert, listening in, he murmured solemnly, "Oh God, let his sin fall upon me." And then to the surprised Jacob, "That way," he said indifferently, "you won't die."

"But you?"

Ernie smiled with an annoyed expression. "Me? Me?" And then casually, "Oh, me—God can't do anything to me because I didn't take off my cap. You understand?"

And holding Jacob's cap under his arm as if it were a schoolboy's notebook, Ernie thrust forward his left leg, then his right, then the left again in a thin, fragile, mechanical motion that did not leave him with the impression that he was truly walking. So when he turned after having counted exactly twenty steps, he was surprised to see Jacob trotting along behind at some distance, his bare head erect on his stocky shoulders, his eye calm, his face beaming. He threw a discreet wink at him, about-faced and went on walking, his head tilted and his thin back still bowed in an arc of distress.

As he looked about him, seeing the finest details of the sidewalk, the anonymous façades and the sky, which like an immense blue arrow tapered to an acute angle at the end of the street, Ernie felt fear coming to life in his belly and then slipping upward into his chest, icy, boring into his heart like an earthworm. He was so alone in the street, so small, so slight, so unimportant, no one would care if an S.A. gang beat him black and blue—which had happened the week before to poor Herr Katzman—or even if they chopped his head off.

As he walked, he began to listen closely. At first he concentrated on his right ear, which told him nothing in particular, but when he turned his attention to his left ear, a disquieting patter vibrated against his tympanum for an instant and then became feeble music punctuated by an infinitesimal hammering of feet. Finally the right ear also vibrated. After that he tried to pinpoint the songs but he was unable to. Now they came from in front of him, now from behind him, from the left, from the right, and at times it even seemed that the music originated above him, in the heavens. At a crossing he slipped along a wall, moved forward as far as the corner of the house, and peering around it with one eye examined the side street. It was calm and almost deserted. "Then where did all that noise come from?" the child wondered before starting for the other side. As he stepped out, a hand struck his own. He cried out sharply and turning saw Jacob, white with fear.

"I'd rather stay with you," Jacob said, sobbing.

Jacob's hand was crushing his own, but its palm was wet.

Ernie did not know why, but that liquid between their palms terrified him. And as Jacob panted beside him, he made an effort to quit the present moment, as he had at other times, playing on his imaginative soul. Therefore he widened his eyes as strenuously as he could in the thin hope that the houses, the sky, the bystanders and Jacob and even he himself—everything, the whole moment—would begin to shimmer on its base as it had so often before, and then to sway peacefully and pour itself into the fog of his eyes, into the gulf that was his throat. But it was no use. Today neither the houses nor the sky nor the people blurred before his wide eyes. All things remained clear, gleaming, of a cruel visibility, and still he felt that stickiness in Jacob's palm.

"You're sweating," a voice said.

"*You're* sweating," Jacob insisted sadly.

Ernie glared impatiently. "I don't sweat!" he declared forcefully, and at the same moment he realized that the heavy annoyance spreading over his face was sweat. Then he became aware of the yellow light flowing slowly in the street, bathing in its soft waters a cyclist, two hurrying housewives, baskets in hand, a young ruddy-faced man whose shirt collar was open. Above the houses, the dancing eddies of light threw off a fine blue mist. He turned toward Jacob and said, "It's hot."

Jacob was silent and then spoke up in a thin voice. "You're sweating because you're afraid." As Ernie turned to him, furious, he saw Jacob's face soften in fear.

The two children were motionless on the sidewalk.

Suddenly Jacob's tearful eyes, his despondent mouth, the fist that he was rubbing vigorously against one eye, his fine head now pathetic beneath that strange checked cap, and the plump jolting of his chest beneath the white shirt, his helpless attitude, feet spread wide and arms dangling—all that entered swiftly in a single flash into Ernie Levy's widened eyes, and at that moment he became unaware of his fear and his sweat. A group of Hitler Youth marched out of his mind. . . . They were booted, helmeted, armed with long black-bone-hilted knives, and they came screaming after little Jacob, who had no idea where to hide, where to curl up the round and fragile flesh of his body. . . . And now he saw the knight Ernie Levy flinging himself before those wicked men and smashing skulls while little Jacob fled into the distance, safe and smiling. And from his gentle mind a phrase sprang out like a sword, a white, vital, stinging phrase—"If they come, I'll spring at them." And as he set his trembling hand against Jacob's moist cheek, strong, hard words burst from his tightened lips: *"Oh, Jacob! If they come I shall spring at them!"*

Stunned, Jacob stared at his elder brother, and measuring him from head to foot with one look, he broke into laughter. Between two bursts of mirth, lively and merry, he said, "Even me, if I push you, you go down like a feather!" And with a gentle thump, he shoved Ernie away.

Ernie's neck swelled, and he cried between his teeth, "I tell you I'll spring at them!" But Jacob was nodding as he smiled, and it was with a kind of mocking condescension that he put his hand into Ernie's. Reassured now, his face pleased and shining, he walked beside his brother with a springy step. His free arm swung cheerfully, and now and then he chuckled, bantering.

Ernie had trouble breathing. His hand lay in Jacob's as if dead. For the first minute he tried to repeat mentally, "I'll spring at them, I'll spring at them. . . ." But the phrase no longer awoke any conviction in him. Then, returning to a more objective appreciation, he imagined that in flinging himself at the legs of the Hitler Youth like a poodle he would give Jacob time to flee. Finally, hopelessly, he admitted that he could do nothing, and raising his eyes regarded with calm the heavens beneath which he was so small. Once upon a time he had seen himself easily in heroic attitudes, either with a sword in his hand or naked to the waist and with beautiful, pious Jewish words adorning his lips. But he had finished with all that a long time ago, and now he felt bitterly that if a noble occasion presented itself, not only would his slight body prohibit him the least movement but even more, his courage would be strictly in proportion to his size. What could he do against all that? He was nothing, nothing at all, a little butt end of nothing at all. And doubtless he did not even exist entirely.

Jacob's high voice pulled him away from those reflections. *"Just like that, you'll spring at them?"* And without transition

Jacob shouted aloud, "Idiot, here we are!" And dropping his protector's hand he shot forward along the wall, a little ball of joy flung through space.

Surprised, Ernie made out the gray worm-eaten spire of the synagogue, fifty yards from the street corner, above the gay German roofs that surrounded the paved courtyard. A second later he recognized the stocky black figure of Mother Judith, dominating a group at the entrance to the alleyway. He was inundated with joy. The little ball reached the group and was lost in it. Ernie felt a crazy desire to run, but restraining himself, he hunched his back again, bobbed his head heavily in the manner of the patriarch, and lowering his eyelids over the uneasy fire of his eyes, he moved forward again with a deliberate, grave, pensive step, as became a true Jew impassive before death.

Mother Judith greeted him with no more emotion than as if he were returning from a short walk. "You took enough time," she grumbled. "All right, come here. What were you doing, dawdling along like a cabinet minister?"

Ernie reddened and tilted his head toward one shoulder.

"And he lost *my* handkerchief!" the huge woman exclaimed. Confused, the little boy pulled the purple square from his pants pocket and transferred it, slowly and sadly, to the pocket of his jacket over his heart.

"Hurry, hurry," the patriarch enunciated clearly as if nothing had happened that deserved the slightest comment by a Jew. "I tell you the services are about to begin!"

"I can't," Moritz announced with an air of importance. And with a gesture of his chin toward the menacing street, "I'm on guard today."

The crowd was already drifting into the courtyard of the synagogue, where the traditional separation of the two sexes took place. Ernie slipped behind the patriarch, whose hand suddenly lay across his shoulders like a gigantic necklace of tenderness. For one instant, one short instant, he closed his eyes in pure pleasure, and then the fabulous paw passed on, abandoned him distractedly, and the tall figure of the "elephant" crossed the doorsill. Retracing his steps suddenly, Ernie went to the mouth of the alleyway where the three weekly guards stood, hands against their brows as visors against the sunlight, scrutinizing the street, eyes gleaming in the shadow. With his index finger he poked Moritz's elbow. Moritz, alert, started in fright.

"I'm staying with you," Ernie said to him with some compunction.

. 2 .

"THEY WON'T COME any more now," said Paulus Vishniac. "They may take the trouble," Moritz said. "Still, I forgot—we never sent them an invitation. . . ."

He spoke distractedly as he traced out with his shoe a six-pointed star at the foot of the post he was sitting on. The three other boys were squatting in the shadow behind the two posts at the entrance to the dead-end alleyway. Drifting over the high wall, snatches of Hebrew melody dropped into the alley. The sentries' ears were dangerously lulled by these chants, which seemed to Ernie to be in some mysterious and final harmony with the blue of the sky, the dazzling yellow of the house fronts and the shadowed verdure of the avenue—as if nothing could ever disturb the dreams of things beneath the sun, as if God were there outside watching over the prayers of the synagogue, and not four glum and nervous boys breathing uneasily.

Paulus Vishniac wiped his forehead and attacked again. "If the bastards were going to come, they'd be here by now. It isn't right. I don't see why they'd wait any longer. If they were planning to come today . . ." And then turning to Moritz, who from the top of his post continued to trace meticulous stars in the dust, "At least don't stay up there," he begged. "You know they can see you from the avenue!"

Moritz's square, fleshy face tightened. He murmured coldly, "So what? They see us, we see them, we run back into the court like rats. I say it's all pretty stupid—especially that part about the gates. . . ." He spat out his disgust in a long, furious gob and discovered Ernie, who had been huddled behind the post from the beginning of their vigil, petrified. "You still there, little bean?" Moritz's thick lips, barred by a bandage that crossed his face, sketched the shadow of a smile. "One more hero!"

Ernie contemplated his brother's bruised face.

"You know very well that we're all heroes these days," Paulus said superciliously. "God will remember us. It's guaranteed—the rabbi swore it."

"And I say that the whole thing is stupid, stupid, stupid," Moritz answered with marked lassitude. "What good is it to be stubborn when we don't even have the right to close the gates any more? Why don't we let it go—abandon the synagogue, say our prayers in our homes . . . ? But no, that would be too easy, that wouldn't be worthy of Jews, hey?" And swelling his cheeks in a burlesque of the rabbi's luxuriant, bland expression, he murmured, *"My dear brothers, the persecutions are increasing, but our hearts do not weaken. They may chase us from the House of God, but they cannot expect us to abandon it!"*

The third sentry, almost a young man, had not ceased sucking at a corner of his sweaty mustache. Interrupting his pastime, he said, "It's nothing to laugh about. With all the kids and the women, it could end up like Berlin. . . ."

"Like Berlin?" Ernie cried in a voice shrill with fear while his eyes leaped from one to another of the three suddenly embarrassed young men. "What happened in Berlin?"

"Nothing, nothing," Moritz said placidly.

But the next instant, to Ernie's great surprise, his brother jumped off the post, his belligerent features swollen and fierce with anger, and firm and sturdy on his strong legs in magnificent trousers of navy-blue serge, he drove his right fist into his left palm like a sledge hammer. "Ah!" he shouted furiously. "If I only had a pistol!"

"Me," Paulus Vishniac said slyly, his eyes squinting with contained malice, "if I only had a million, a little million, you understand?" Raising his eyeglasses, he savored the mute pause of his three listeners, and suddenly he was doubled over, laugh-

ing. "I'd *buy* them!" He got the words out with difficulty, "I'd
buy them *all!*"

"That's pretty smart," the third sentry said slowly. Then he
swung back toward the avenue, turning his back deliberately on
that "feckless youth, feckless, feckless . . ."

Moritz vaulted up onto the post again and sat with his stubby
hands on his trousers, which he had carefully hitched up. Two
cyclists crossed the avenue without a glance at the chanting synagogue. The steel of their vehicles glittered outside the shadow
of the plane trees. Very high in the sky crows glided. They too
seemed to be waiting, enjoying the spectacle in advance, the
event Ernie feared wildly all of a sudden, closing his eyes on the
world, thinking in despair, "God is not here, he's forgotten us. . . ."

Moritz's guttural voice snapped him out of it. "And you," he
was saying with heavy good humor, "what do you wish for? A
pair of scissors to cut them all in two, to bring them down to
your size? You're damned lucky to be so small," Moritz added.
"Me, I have to fight, and I have to fight, and then I have to
fight again. There are times when I'd be glad to make peace
with them, believe me!"

"You mean they don't want it?" said Paulus Vishniac. He
went up to Moritz and slapped him jovially on the shoulder
like a fellow conspirator.

"Ai, no, they don't want it! And," Moritz added in a sud-
enly solemn voice, "I'm beginning to have enough of fighting,
no kidding."

"You mean you're still going to the school?" the third sentry
cried in amazement.

Moritz strutted naïvely. "It's my last year. I'm going on four-
teen—you'd think I was older, wouldn't you? Remember, in the
beginning I liked it, I enjoyed fighting. . . ."

The third sentry commiserated, "But the guys in your gang,
did they let you down?"

And as Moritz averted a face stitched with scars, the third
sentry went on rapidly, "Oh, I remember it, I remember it too,
in the beginning—a long time ago. . . . Yes, it was in the *old*

days. Two years ago it must have been! We had real brawls then, even right here when services let out. I was part of Arnold's group, you remember—the one who left for Israel? But whether we bled or made them bleed, we couldn't hold out, I swear! They brought big guys, at least eighteen years old. Then it was the Steel Helmets, and one fine day we saw some S.A. men. You understand."

Paulus Vishniac said, "They won't be coming any more today."

"You're absolutely right," Moritz said bitterly. "But take a look at the street corner, old pal. . . ."

At that moment the nightmare burst upon them.

Moritz was still sitting on the post. Ernie saw Paulus Vishniac lean over his shoulder and suddenly fling himself backward as if the sunlit air had burned his face. And then the first notes of a Nazi melody came through to him, as if in counterpoint to the terminal pleading of the Sabbath service—nostalgic Hebrew and rococo German mingling above the alleyway, which seemed to sway under the shock. "And now the rats to the rathole," came Moritz's guttural voice. He was suddenly erect, his teeth open over a flash of pointed tongue as he grasped his younger brother by the shoulder and pulled him with a jolt into the shadow of the alleyway.

Paulus Vishniac and the third sentry were giant crows, wings flapping against the narrow walls of the alley. Moritz, in his magnificent trousers and his pearl-gray jacket, had the heavy flight of a partridge, shuffling at each step against the paving stones of the alley, which suddenly began to clatter under Ernie's well-shined shoes while the walls swayed first one way and then the other, as if they too were drunk with the fear that intoxicated Ernie, as if their hearts too were spinning. "Come on, snail!" With a sharp flap of one wing, Moritz had thrown him between the folding doors, and now Ernie was quaking in the courtyard of the synagogue, in the midst of the faithful, who fluttered about him for a few moments and then fell back one by one against the rear wall, where the largest families were already huddled, paralyzed by fear. "No, no, don't go back into

the synagogue. Everything has to happen in broad daylight!"
rose the rabbi's strident voice. His thick arms blocked access to
the doorway, halting several fat women who were jabbering in
their finery and who suddenly, enthusiastically, cried out,
"Broad daylight! Broad daylight! Broad daylight!" Then there
fell a great silence, things took on their normal summertime colors, the floor of the courtyard oscillated a bit more, as if in a
last burst of malice, and was finally still. Everything became
strangely clear. A few steps from him, in the front rank of the
faithful, his mother, dead white and sweating, her cheek
against little Rachel, the last-born female Levy, swathed in
pink, was whining timidly, "Ernie . . . Ernie . . . Ernie . . ."

He took the three suffering steps that separated him from her
and buried his head in the silky warmth of a palpitating belly.
Then he grasped his mother's hand and set it against his wet
cheek. And as he became calmer in spite of himself, a vast sigh
surging from the breasts of the faithful enveloped him. It was
followed by a general gasp of anguish. No sound came now
from the crowd, no breath, not even a baby's whimper. Turning immediately, he saw that the Nazis had arrived. They were
blocking the gate, cutting off the alleyway.

Stunned, Ernie thought he recognized the old grocer from
the Friedrichstrasse in an S.A. uniform, in front of the others,
planted solidly on his black boots. Behind him, closing the trap,
his men constituted a wall across the gateway, but dominating
the scene was the sky, empty now of crows, unreasonably blue,
and Ernie had a staggering intuition—that God was hovering
above the synagogue courtyard, vigilant and ready to intervene.
One, two, three urchins slipped among the Nazi boots, armed
with stones they were already flinging at the congested mass of
Jews. Fräulein Blumenthal shook; the shudder brought her thin
hip against Ernie's cheek. Lifting himself on tiptoe, the little
boy brought his mouth close to his mother's ear and wild-eyed,
the shadow of a smile flitting over his lips, in his crystalline
voice: "Don't be afraid, Mama," he said, suddenly imploring.
"God will come down in a minute. . . ."

*   *   *

The windows opened and a few jeers rose from the high, crannied façade overlooking the courtyard.

Ernie had the feeling that the twenty yards of torrid space between the Jewish ranks and the Nazi wall—stabilized before the gate as if hesitating at the silence of its victims—were now reduced to a thread.

Then he realized that the jeers were directed at the S.A. men, who were looking up in annoyance, their hands swinging sharply to their clubs, while in Ernie's mind the thread expanded dizzyingly, like a rope that would hold the Nazi flood back against the doorway. *"The windows bother them,"* he understood with an exaltation and hope that made him raise his own head toward the adjacent building; it seemed ivied by the heads of men and women and even children, whose lively eyes shimmered under the parapets in the white, saving light of the sun falling brightly on the stones of the façade and on their faces. "How can it be?" he wondered in a joyful flash. Until now, those windows had never opened except for arms that tossed out garbage as the Jews came and went in the courtyard, so what could have changed up there? And then he saw way up at the crest of the façade, like a bird on the platform of a pigeon house, the familiar mustached face of Herr Julius Kremer, his teacher at the public school.

From that face came a shrill exclamation. "Have you no shame?" Herr Kremer shouted at the petrified Nazis while his index finger (Ernie noticed it in a kind of bitter happiness) rose against the blue of the sky, as if to rebuke faltering students.

Around Ernie, not a whisper from the Jewish ranks. A thin whine rose in his mother's throat, but her lips remained tight. Ernie felt that God was there, so close that with a little boldness he might have touched him. "Stop! Don't touch my people!" he murmured as if the divine voice had found expression in his own frail throat. And closing his eyes, he imagined that the mass of the faithful was rising rapidly into the blue, with both the impetuous elegance of a stone flung into space and, paradoxically, the ceremonious dignity of a carriage, rising now to such fantastic heights, becoming a mere point in the slack, naked blue, that Ernie could distinguish only his mother's nose, as fine and precise, though infinitesimal, as the alert proboscis of a mosquito. And perhaps even now, he told himself smiling, his eyes still closed, the carriage of the Jews was whirling above the miraculous land of Palestine, bathed in honey and in the delectable milk of asses.

"You up there!"

Shocked awake, chilled, the scales fallen from his eyes, Ernie saw that the Nazi officer had taken a step to one side toward the façade and that his strong-man torso was trembling in rage.

"Close those windows!" he added, raising his knotty fists above his fat, shaved head. And with his arms still stiffened toward the windows, he turned in a circle, the grave, gyrating motion of a drunkard. But Ernie, terrified, saw clearly that the Nazi was drunk on his own anger, on his own blood, which gleamed in the ruddy skin of his face as his mouth opened and closed, spraying spume, searching for the words of release.

"Tell me, up there," the man went on suddenly, whirling a furious arm in circles, "tell me, don't you know these pigs of Jews yet? Don't you know all the harm they've done? Comrades, wasn't it they who wanted to destroy our country? Our country, the land of our ancestors," he finished in a tearful voice that surprised the child more than all the rest.

The Nazi's mouth twisted momentarily; he was speechless. Then his hairy arm fell toward the frightened flock of faithful as a reddish index finger sprang like an arrow from the fist.

"Tell me up there!" he screamed in a voice Ernie did not recognize, a muddy voice spurting in heavy floods from his belly. "Ladies, gentlemen, if you want to make them welcome, these pigs with their droppings, these flyspecks from hell—if you want to let this filth piss on your heads, all right! What are you waiting for? Come on down here, and if that isn't enough you can crawl up their assholes and worship at that shrine!"

During the fiery diatribe he shook his fist at the windows, which closed, almost all of them, prudently, abandoning the

Jews to the bare house front. But perhaps ten German witnesses remained leaning upon their sills, saying nothing, looking out over the courtyard as if they felt the pleading gaze of the faithful, who now, one by one, the women and the children first and then a few adult males, raised their trembling arms toward the compassionate windows. Caught up in the contagion of movement, Ernie set his heart's anguish in the cuplike hollow of his open hand. "O God," he prayed fervently, "O Lord, look this way just for a moment, please. . . ."

At that moment old Frau Tuszynski stepped out of the Jewish ranks.

She was in a rage. Her long, emaciated arms writhed about her head like a nest of snakes, and she flung imprecations at the suddenly paralyzed Nazi wall. "Ah, what do you want with us!" she screamed in her bastard German-Yiddish, "what do you want with us, what have we ever done to you? Don't you even know how to talk, are you only animals? The Day of the Lord is coming, hear me. He'll take you in his hands, he'll crush you like that!" she finished with a pulverizing gesture while Ernie, suddenly sobered out of his fear, out of his mysteriously dissipated anguish, even out of any religious feeling, was no more than a pair of popping eyes fastened on the old woman who step by step, swearing and gesticulating, approached the menacing wall of brown shirts and gleaming, nervous, sharp boots.

When she was an arm's length from the Nazi leader, she flung at his face, weighing each word in perfect German, "You'll all burn for eternity! Yes, yes, yes, you'll burn!"

There was an endless pause. Then the Nazi took a step forward, restrained his men with a gesture and smiled visibly at Frau Tuszynski. "But you," he said, "you will burn right now. . . ." And as he slapped her brutally, and as the old lady's wig spun in the sunlight, and as Frau Tuszynski fell backward, hands covering the public shame of her carefully polished skull, Ernie took two short steps forward, giddy. "No, no, no," he repeated to himself while his eyes registered the suffering of Frau Tuszynski, prone at the feet of the Nazi, her face against the earth, sheltering that strange eggshell with both hands. At the

same moment he realized that he was shrieking. Fräulein
Blumenthal, who had moved forward with him, clapped a hand
over his mouth, but the boy freed himself almost immediately
and continued forward, keening shrilly. The thing happened so
quickly that no one had time to react. The child was already six
feet from the Nazi officer, his bare arms dangling beside his
shorts. He was in the grip of an agitation so violent that despite
the distance Fräulein Blumenthal, petrified, distinctly saw
Ernie's reddish legs trembling at the knees and heard his cry as
though he had been standing beside her.

Two Jews stepped out in front of the group; their eyes were
hard and yet dreamy. . . .

When the service ended, Mordecai had been carried along
by the violent jostling of the crowd, separated from his own
family, pushed irresistibly back into the angle between the outside wall and the small sacramental poultry abattoir just beneath the roof. In the triangle of shadow his head touched the
eaves. The crowd's every motion eddied in upon him like a sad
human undertow, crushing him against the stones as he tried
vainly to hold it back, while his gaze skimmed the tide of hats,
skullcaps, headdresses, disheveled hairdos, trying to make out
in the hollow of a wave some sign of the presence of his own
family. But only the Medusa's face of Judith, her curls unkempt, was visible in the flood sweeping her along like a
ground swell. Resigned, Mordecai awaited the worst. An ancient voice in his heart of hearts recalled the holocaust since the
beginning of time, since Zemyock, most of all since a year ago,
when Christian barbarism had burned its brand into the German Jews. But this, the madness of these women and all these
children, come with trepidation to stand against the Nazis—he
had not wished for that. He had even opposed it, and it had required the unanimous delirium of Stillenstadt's faithful to
make him, following their example, accept the need to offer
his own family to the synagogue. What mysterious instinct im-
pelled them, he wondered, while under his amazed eyes their

faces, at the appearance of the S.A., took on a more dignified look—even those of the most gossipy chatterboxes, even those of the skinniest children, who also seemed to be discovering a grandeur in the present moment. What harsh ancestral fire had ignited in the breasts of these tepid Jewish souls of Stillenstadt, lulled for a hundred years in that calm Rhenish province, who were discovering abruptly, through persecution, the dizzying significance of being Jewish? They who had forgotten all but the simplest memories of yesterday's martyrs, they who seemed entirely disarmed, naked before suffering—the event found them suddenly ready, stiffened.

Thus meditating, Mordecai had witnessed the unhoped-for opening of windows and had wondered, while an ebb softened the pressure of the wave, "What will happen, my God, on the day when German windows no longer open upon Jewish suffering?" Then he had coldly analyzed the growing fury of the Nazi and had seen, not without melancholy, the casements close one by one and the Jewish hands rise one by one toward heaven, as if they had abruptly discovered their signal feebleness.

And as the crazy old woman flung herself forward into no man's land, Mordecai had suddenly tried to clear a passage through the heads bobbing at the level of his shoulders, through the sweaty cheeks of the women, through the bowed foreheads of the men and the uplifted eyes of the children, who were crying now, drowning in the adults' agonies while above them the same reflection leaped from mouth to mouth: "O Lord, O Lord, let not Frau Tuszynski's madness fall upon the heads of the children!"

When he was almost at the edge of the burning gap that separated the two worlds, Ernie's cry reached him.

The child was already standing before the terrible "brown shirt," so small that he seemed servile at the man's feet, so puny that in the cruel splendor of sunlight on the stones of the courtyard the man's shadow covered him entirely.

And suddenly, as Mordecai saw the trembling figure more clearly, as in his heavy Jewish soul Ernie's frail bleat of horror (a bleat that seemed to come from those thin, quaking legs, from those tiny black curls badly covered by the ridiculous German beret) vibrated and throbbed, the old man had a sort of vision: "He is the lamb of suffering; he is our scapegoat," he said to himself, despairing, while tears clouded his eyes.

What followed took place far away, in one of those dream-worlds of ancient legend to which the sparkling sunlight, beaming its mysteries on each detail of the scene, added the lively color of an old illuminated manuscript. First of all the Nazi broke into laughter, pointing at the child, while behind him the other uniforms joined the party, whinnying and slapping each other in delight. "Look at the defender of the Jews!" they shouted. The sky, almost white-hot above the hilarity, expanded the laughter to infinity. Mordecai understood that this happy wave surrounded the child with a protective veneer. Ernie seemed to know it too. He stooped suddenly, picked up the wig at his feet and set it on Frau Tuszynski's head. She grasped it avidly before falling to her side again, her knees brought forward and touching her elbows—a long, bony body swathed in mourning clothes, the plumage of a dead crow. But as the child stood up, the Nazi stopped laughing and with a sharp blow set him rolling against Frau Tuszynski's body. Her skirt rode up on a whitish, wrinkled thigh. The Nazi blinked several times and stepped back in annoyance, his men surging back behind him into the alleyway. It was over for this day. The crowd breathed.

· 3 ·

Frau Tuszynski had broken her collarbone when she fell, but the child was intact. Nevertheless Mordecai, slipping an arm under the barely scuffed knees, raised Ernie to shoulder height and set off without a word into the alleyway, indifferent to the prudent advice offered by the faithful lingering in the courtyard. Though he forbade her sharply, Fräulein Blumenthal came stubbornly along behind him, bleak, tiny, mumbling, prey to a vague religious fear.

A bead of sweat trickled down Ernie's temple. He protested that he could walk by himself. . . .

Meanwhile the patriarch moved silently forward in the sun-whitened streets, and the Germans stopped to watch the passage of that enormous old man bearing a little boy perhaps wounded at the synagogue. They had no trouble, only a few children following them down a street with a refrain to which their limpid voices gave the unexpected grace of a nursery rhyme:

> *Jews, Jews, matzo eaters,*
> *Tomorrow come the knives,*
> *Next day the stake and fagots*
> *And afterward—hear this well—*
> *You'll all be sent to Hell.*

But with his eyes looking inward at his own dream, already planning the phrases of his "revelation," Mordecai did not hear the thin shouts of the urchins, who finally became tired of his indifference. Only now and then, reminded of the lamb who lay in his flesh-and-blood arms, he lowered a distraught mustache to the curly, dusty, sweaty head of hair. Back at No. 8 Riggenstrasse, he carried the child to his room and undressed him with unaccustomed, awkward gestures. The boy opened terrified eyes and Mordecai repeated hollowly, "Don't be afraid, my little love, don't be afraid. . . ." Then the child found himself tucked in bed up to the neck, like an infant. Bolting the door, Mordecai went to the straight chair beside the bed and in a hoarse voice, as if strangled by all the years of silence he had imposed upon it, told the prodigious history of the Levys from beginning to end.

He interrupted himself often, trying to read on the child's face some sign of intelligent comprehension. Then, adapting his words to the passionate blush of a cheek, to an attentive tongue peeking between baby teeth, to the midnight-blue flash of a half-open eye, he dropped another step in order to reach and raise, to lift Ernie's level of understanding toward himself. But at each of his attempts and all through that strange monologue, it seemed to him that nothing more than the memory of a thousand classic legends of the Lamed-Vov was awakened in the child lying between two sheets in the half-shadow thrown through the tulle curtains by the afternoon sun. Only when he observed that the last Just Man of Zemyock had died three years ago without designating a successor (so that the Levy Lamed-Vov were submerged now in the indistinct night of the unknown Lamed-Vov), he thought he saw in the depths of those blue eyes a small, disquieting gleam that flickered and vanished immediately.

"And why," he asked unexpectedly, "did you do what you did a while ago in the courtyard at the synagogue?"

The child reddened. "I don't know, Grandfather. It— It hurt me, so"—and lying back on the pillow he laughed like a mouse, laid two fingers politely against his mouth—"so I *sprang upon him!* You understand, Grandfather?"

"Don't laugh. Oh, don't laugh!" Mordecai murmured desperately, already regretting his foolish confidence, already sensing a shadow of remorse, the feeling of a crime no less invisible than subtle but, like any crime of the soul, irreparable.

The "old elephant" leaned over the bed and kissed the astonished Ernie on the forehead silently and moved toward the door, which he opened slowly as if in guilt. A gentle call made him turn at once: "Tell me, Grandfather!"

Mordecai returned with dragging steps, heavy with lassitude, to the narrow, shadowed bed. "What is it, my soul?"

Ernie first smiled to reassure him, and then an unwonted red enlivened his cheeks. "Tell me, Grandfather," he whispered, barely audible. "What should a Just Man do in this life?"

Immediately prey to a terrible trembling, the patriarch had no idea what to answer. The child's face slowly became bloodless, pallid in the shadow, but his wide, dark eyes, spangled with points of light, glowed passionately against the dim background of the pillow, in the manner of Jewish eyes long ago, of the ecstatic eyes of Zemyock. Mordecai's hand fell to the oblong skull and sheltered it in a sheath of flesh. And as his fingers played among the young curls: "The sun, my little love," he murmured hesitantly, "do you ask it to do anything? It rises, it sets—it rejoices your soul."

"But the Just Men?" Ernie insisted.

His insistence softened the patriarch, who sighed, "It's the same thing. The Just Man rises, the Just Man goes to bed, and *all is well*." And seeing that Ernie's eyes remained upon his own, he continued uneasily, "Ernie, my little rabbi, what are you asking me? I don't know much, and what I do know is nothing, for wisdom has kept its distance from me. Listen, if you are a Just Man a day will come when all by yourself you will begin to . . . *glow*. Do you understand?"

The child was amazed. "And in the meantime?"

Mordecai suppressed a smile. "In the meantime be a good little boy."

No sooner had the patriarch left him, no sooner had his slow, cautious tread faded on the stairway, than Ernie seriously undertook the dream of his own martyrdom.

The late-afternoon shadows softened the rays of sunlight that traced uncertain forms, sashes and scrolls, around the bed and the chair and on the gossamer fringe of the curtains. A skillful narrowing of the eyes blurred it all, leaving only a pretty yellow filament that danced against the chair and then in turn dissolved in the surrounding night. Sounds from the living room died discreetly against Ernie's ears while phantom personalities, here and now, undulated at the foot of his bed. He tripped another switch—this time deep within his brain—and the desired figure rose before him in the lunar clarity his eyes had distilled.

Sitting back against the pillow, Ernie was pleased to recognize dear Frau Tuszynski, whose spider fingers were steadying a column of wigs on the gleaming point of her skull. Then the column fell apart, there was a confused flight of wigs, and Ernie suddenly recognized the bruised oval of Frau Tuszynski's skull, set like a strange eggshell above her wrinkled face, above her angry open mouth. "All right, don't be upset," he said to the apparition. "And first of all blow your nose calmly, Frau Tuszynski. Because I am a Just Man, a Lamed-Vovnik, you understand?"

"It's unbelievable," she said, smiling.

"It is as I tell you," Ernie announced gravely.

Then, without waiting any longer, sitting squarely back against his pillow now and frowning severely, he gave birth to a troop of knights who until then had been hiding in the closet. Waving maces studded with sharp points, the plumed knights line up against the door and jostle each other with a kind of metallic pleasure and a very serious air. "And now," says the grocer from the Friedrichstrasse, well protected by his iron mask, "shall we avenge the Christ?" At each end of the cross on his shield is the cruel mark of the swastika.

Obliged to reveal his secret voice, which he knows to be rolling and magisterial like a swollen river and not jumpy and timid like a small brook, Ernie fills his lungs with air. "My dear sir," he answers the grocer, "I shall be at your service immediately." And on a sigh that would rend the soul, he raised the blankets, came to his feet in a dignified manner on the floor where, in the measured tread of a parade, he started toward the door, toward his martyrdom.

The faithful remain motionless as a sign of respect.

But Mother Judith's inflexible arm stretches above the heads, and her greedy hand clutches at Ernie. And—the height of annoyance—Fräulein Blumenthal has deliberately flung herself to the floor, blocking the Just Man's way. Pushing away Mother Judith's hand gently, Ernie sets the extreme point of his bare foot on the highest point of Fräulein Blumenthal's belly and with a delicate spring leaps across the grieving obstacle.

"So you're the Just Man?" the astonished grocer mocks him. "So you're the defender of the Jews?"

"I am," Ernie Levy replies dryly. "Go to it, savage," he adds in a choked voice. "Kill me."

"Crack!" goes the grocer.

His gauntlet flashes out against Ernie Levy's neck. Ernie staggers under the blue sky of the synagogue, and with him, in the disquieting shadows that were registering upon his narrowed eyes even as he dreamed, staggered the sparse furnishings of the bedroom in the middle of which he was spinning, a small white phantom in a nightshirt. Finally making up his mind to die, he stretched out in romantic fashion near the closet, his eyes still half closed, his face turned toward the ceiling, where the figure of his executioner disintegrated suddenly and then disappeared, conjured away by a violent irruption of light.

"Little angel of heaven," cried Fräulein Blumenthal in a trembling voice, "what are you doing like that in the dark? Are you sick?"

Aware of Mother Judith's vigilance, Ernie feigned drowsiness. Finally, in a burst of audacity he let a faint whistle escape his lips. "Are you asleep?" whispered Mother Judith after fifteen minutes. "Bzzzz," Ernie's mouth replied subtly. Immediately the old woman rose, sighing and stretching her back. Across the screen of his lashes, amused, he saw her go toward the door on tiptoe in her slippers with the halting gestures of a conspirator. The ignoble light bulb finally darkened, the stairway squeaked, then a door closed on the third floor and the silence was complete. The whole house was asleep but him.

Having learned to be cautious, he waited about an hour in the black and suffocating air of his first night as a Lamed-Vovnik. The lightest breath, the least rustling plucked at the tightened strings of his body. But with discipline and penetration his thoughts followed the fantastic road that his Just Man's consciousness laid out for them and, his eyes wide in the night, twisting and turning on the rack of certain memories, he even managed to classify the marked differences among the diverse destinies of his predecessors. For example, he arrived at the conclusion that having been dragged by the tail of a Mongol pony, like Rabbi Jonathan, was of less merit than being plunged directly into the flames by burning at the stake, as had happened to other, more meritorious Lamed-Vov. The flesh and the fat broiling horribly around the bone and falling away in drops, in flaming shreds—oh, my God! Although he forced himself toward it with all his heart, he did not succeed in tolerating even the idea of that last agony. Suddenly, resigning himself to the test, he slipped quietly out of bed.

He began modestly, by holding his breath.

In the beginning that torture seemed to him derisory. But when his ears started to ring, and he felt a reddish wrenching deep in his chest, he wondered in a triumphant flash if the thing was not comparable to the full martyrdom of a Just Man. Then he found himself on the floor—he had held his breath too long.

"That's about enough," said a small voice inside him.

"O God," he answered immediately, "pay no attention to what I just said. It was only a joke."

Feeling his way in the darkness, he then went to the corner where he knew he would find Moritz's box of treasures.

With one hand, like a woman, he raised the long nightshirt in which his bare feet got tangled, while the other hand came and went in the dark, waving its fly's antennae. He knelt near the table, undid the lid of the box, tapped the strings, the lead soldiers, the six-bladed knife, and finally discovered the box of sulphur matches.

The point of the flame was blue.

"Now show us what you really are," he murmured to give himself courage, and loosing a sigh, he guided the match to the palm of his left hand.

While the delicate sizzle of flesh and the strong odor uplifted his soul, he was amazed at the slight reality of pain. The match burned out at the end of his fingers, and with the return of darkness tears flowed from his eyes, but they were tears of joy, lively, clear, sweet as honey to the tongue.

"It's not possible," he thought suddenly in a flash of desolation. "I couldn't have brought the match close enough!"

And when he wanted to strike a second match, he realized that the fingers of his left hand no longer obeyed him, were rigid, splayed like a fan about his burned palm.

Opening his eyes, he saw that all was dark; he replaced Moritz's paraphernalia and went back to his bed. When he was stretched out, he set his left arm with great precaution above the blankets, for the wounded palm gave off a furnacelike heat against his thin nightshirt. An immense joy wrung his heart. If he trained himself methodically, perhaps later God would grant him, at the hour of sacrifice, the strength to suffer an authentic martyrdom. Yes, if he hardened his body perhaps he would be ready when the day came to offer it heroically to the holocaust, so that God would take pity on Mother Judith, the patriarch, Fräulein Blumenthal and Herr Levy, and Moritz and the smaller children and the other Jews of Stillenstadt and also—who knows?—all the threatened Jews everywhere in the world! And as he wondered again at the ease of the operation, Ernie suddenly felt an extravagant shock at the end of his left arm while his palm contracted convulsively and split wide open like water running over. "All the same," he said to himself delightedly, "I won't cry."

Then he unclenched his teeth, and only then did he begin to feel raw, naked pain.

· 4 ·

IN THE MORNING his palm displayed a splendid stigma, gaping open as far as the wrist. No explanations were forthcoming from the little Just Man, feverish and half delirious with insomnia. A burn from a red-hot iron, according to the doctor, that wound sent down in the night offered matter for exorcism. Mother Judith hastened to slip under the patient's pillow a certain red sachet, comprising seven grains of ash from seven ovens, seven grains of dust from seven door hinges, seven pea seeds, seven seeds from seven cumins and finally, oddly enough, a single hair. Then she lost herself in conjecture.

"I don't understand," she said later in the kitchen before the assembled family. "Yesterday the little angel jumped at the Nazis like a heroic flea and this morning here he is maimed. But it isn't enough to make us suffer with his wound—the little gentleman lies in state in his bed and stuffs himself and looks like a general who's just won a battle. And if I, his poor grandmother, ask him, 'Little angel, what happened to you last night?' he laughs in my face and drapes himself in some kind of mysterious silence. Listen, I almost have the feeling that he's watching us—from up there!"

"Impossible," Benjamin said.

"From *up there*," Mother Judith repeated. And rubbing her hands in despair, she cried to heaven, "Good Lord, who could have brought that kind of bad luck on him?"

"It may be," Fräulein Blumenthal interrupted, "that he fell down fairly hard yesterday, couldn't it?" Equally frightened herself, she did not dare go on to finish her thought, which was that the child was indulging in some new and highly extraordinary "imitation."

As for the patriarch, who said not a word, he was suffering tortures. On the pretext of feeling queasy, he slipped discreetly into the bedroom of the possessed, who greeted him with a triumphant smile and admitted, not without vainglory, that he had begun training himself. His hollow eyes, his cheekbones radiating fever and that enormous bandage that he held up like a pennant marked his confession with the obvious seal of madness.

"But training yourself for what?" Mordecai asked trembling.

Despite the early hour, the curtains maintained an artificial shadow in the room, against which the sun's rays played. The patriarch's nose took a ray right along its crest, and two or three spangles of gold skipped about on his beard. Ernie smiled reassuringly.

"To die," he announced gaily. And he accented his smile to show the patriarch that everything was going beautifully.

The old man bristled. "Little Jew, what are you telling me?" he cried out as Ernie, suddenly conscious of a monstrous error, doubled up and disappeared in the wink of an eye under the blankets, which he wrapped quickly around his body as if to lose himself in the very fiber of things, a frightened little animal. But suddenly, softened by the night of the blankets, a gentle caress fell upon his shoulders. The patriarch's hand rose along his neck, searched for his head, found it. "All right, peace be with you, peace be with you. I could hardly believe my ears, that's all. But all the same, can you explain why you did that? Did I say anything to you about dying?"

From the depths of his little night, Ernie hesitated. "No," he said, surprised.

"By the beard of Moses," the old man grumbled while his fantastic fingers became even softer, their touch almost sweet, "by the miraculous rod of Aaron, what's the meaning of this story of training? Men," he finished in a sigh, "who among you has ever heard of a thing so strange?" The thin voice beneath the blankets was broken. "I thought, oh my grandfather, that if I died, you would live."

"If you die, we live?"

"That's right," Ernie breathed.

Mordecai fell into a long meditation. His paw remained upon Ernie's hidden head in a somewhat savage pose that the moist reverie of his eyes belied. "But then," he began finally in a very gentle voice, "when I explained to you last night that the death of a Just Man changes nothing in the order of the world, didn't you understand what I meant?"

"No, that I didn't understand."

"And when I told you that nobody in the world, not even a Just Man, has any need to run after suffering, that it comes without being called . . . ?"

"Or that either," Ernie said uneasily.

"And that a Just Man is the heart of the world?"

"Oh no, oh no," the child repeated.

"And now do you understand?"

"That . . . that if I die . . ."

"That's all?"

Ernie wailed in earnest, "Oi, I think I do!"

"All right then, listen to me," Mordecai said after a bit more reflection. "Open both ears: If a man suffers all alone, it is clear his suffering remains within him. Right?"

"Right," Ernie said.

"But if another looks at him and says to him, 'You're in trouble, my Jewish brother,' what happens then?"

The blanket stirred and revealed the sharp point of Ernie Levy's nose. "I understand that too," he said politely. "He takes the suffering of his friend into his own eyes."

Mordecai sighed, smiled, sighed again. "And if he is blind, do you think that he can take it in?"

"Of course, through his ears!"

"And if he is deaf?"

"Then through his hands," Ernie said gravely.

"And if the other is far away, if he can neither hear him nor see him and not even touch him—do you believe then that he can take in his pain?"

"Maybe he could guess at it," Ernie said with a cautious expression.

Mordecai went into ecstasies. "You've said it, my love— that is exactly what the Just Man does! He senses all the evil rampant on earth, and he takes it into his heart!"

A finger against the corner of his mouth, Ernie followed the course of a thought. He exhaled sadly, "But what good does it do to sense it if nothing is changed?"

"It changes for God, don't you see?"

And as the child frowned skeptically, Mordecai suddenly became terribly pensive. "That which is far off," he murmured as if to himself, "that which is profound, profound, who can reach it?"

Meanwhile Ernie was following his own idea, fascinated by his own discovery. "If it's only for God, then I don't understand anything. Is it he then who asks the Germans to *persecute* us? Oh, Grandfather, then we aren't like other men! We must have done something to him, to God, otherwise he wouldn't be angry at us that way, at just us, the Jews. Right?"

In his exaltation, he had sat up and raised his heavily bandaged hand high above his head. Suddenly he cried in a bitter voice, "Oh, Grandfather, tell me the truth! We aren't like other men, are we?"

"Are we men?" Mordecai said.

Leaning over the bed, he regarded the child with marked melancholy. His shoulders slumped. His skullcap slipped to one side, giving him the grotesque look of a schoolboy. And then a strange smile lifted his mustache and buried his eyes even deeper in their sockets—a smile of terrifying sadness.

"That's how it is," the old man said finally.

Bending over, he embraced the child strongly, pushed him away with violence, kissed him again and with a sudden, incomprehensible start fled. Ernie noticed that the old man's steps halted for an instant on the stairway. Finally the door to the living room slammed. "Poor Grandfather," Ernie said to himself. "Ai-i-i . . . Poor Grandfather."

Seated on the edge of the bed, he brought his good hand to his neck; his spirits rose slowly. On his knee lay that enormous bandage which he suddenly found ludicrous. The old man's smile hung trembling before his haggard, sleepless eyes. There were millions of words in that smile, but Ernie could not decipher them. They were written in a foreign language.

Bewildered, he considered his bandage again, examined it carefully in the hope of finding some legitimate satisfaction in it. But his grandfather's smile blotted it out, and soon it seemed to him that as grandiose as he might imagine them, all his exercises in suffering would never be more than child's play. How had he dared to cause so much excitement about his own little person? To bring on so many worries? Two fine needles pierced his eyes, opening the way to two sandy tears.

"I am nothing more than an ant," Ernie said gently.

The old man's nose appeared first. It seemed woven on the moisture in Ernie's eye, and its bony curve expressed a nameless rending. Then there was the majestic hill of the patriarch's forehead, topped by his black silk skullcap. And finally the indescribable smile of his old eyes and his old beard: *That which is far away, that which is profound, profound, who can reach it?*

"You know," Ernie said immediately, "I'll never touch matches again. And tomorrow I'll go back to school. And holding my breath too—that's over." But the patriarch seemed in no mood to console him, and the sadness of his smile so far exceeded the bounds of Ernie's universe that the latter found himself once again become small, even more ridiculous than before the "revelation," diminished to the point of being nothing, not even an ant.

At that moment, when he had yielded to the idea that Ernie Levy did not exist, suddenly the patriarch rose full length before his awe-stricken eyes, metamorphosed into some ordinary old man, with all the marks of age inscribed upon his face, engraved in every wrinkle of his great elephant's body.

"So you're an old elephant?" Ernie said pityingly.

The patriarch agreed gravely. "That is what I am."

"I'll take your suffering upon myself. Is that all right?" Ernie asked supplicatingly, his good hand clasping his bandaged hand. Then he closed his eyes, reopened them and delicately extracted Mother Judith from his brain. . . .

When he had finished with her, he was sobbing at the surprising idea that she was a simple old woman, and bathed in his own tears he brought forward the person of his father, then that of his mother, who smiled at him with her timid mouth for one second before slipping back into his brain. But when he tried to evoke Moritz, his interior vision fogged over so completely that he found himself sitting stupidly at the edge of the bed, before the window open on a torrent of sunlight.

"I'm not *small* enough before Moritz."

"Still, you're nothing more than an ant." At that moment, in a slow exhalation, he succeeded in evicting all that remained of Ernie Levy from his own breast.

Then appeared a chubby boy whose hair was cut short over a plump, doll-like face and whose brown eyes, set wide on either side of the nose, radiated a kind of joyful electricity.

Dumfounded, Ernie recognized his brother Moritz. But as he rejoiced to see him so alive, in those blue serge trousers, that pearl-gray jacket, with his round belly, with his wide mouth open on magnificently regular teeth, he suddenly discovered the scars on Moritz's cheek, his lacerated knees and his trousers in tatters. Moritz took a step forward.

"You see," he growled, "I'm not the leader of my gang any more. They didn't like being led by a Jew. To tell you the truth, I'm not even in the gang any more. And tell me this, Ernie, why do the Germans hate us like that? Aren't we men like everybody else, aren't we?"

Ernie was flustered. "I . . . I don't know." He added abruptly, "Oh, Moritz, Moritz, Moritz, that which is far away, that which is profound, profound, who can reach it?"

"A little fish," Moritz said.

At that, the vision of Moritz winked conspiratorially, saluted him with an expert flip of the hand and vanished, leaving behind it the impassioned smoke of a wink.

Ernie realized then that his soul truly contained the faces of the patriarch and Mother Judith, of his father and mother, of Moritz and perhaps also the faces of all the Jews in Stillenstadt. Glowing with enthusiasm, he ran to the window, which he opened wide on the chestnut tree in the yard, the neighboring roofs, the swallows in the almost tactile flight of bats, the blue of the sky, so close. And stretching his neck toward the laughing face of the sun, "Let me stay tiny!" he cried, imploring, inarticulate. "Oh, my God, be good to me! Let me stay tiny!"

Like that legendary idiot who one day discovered the keys to paradise beside the road, so Ernie Levy, admitted to the banal yet extraordinary world of the soul and sniffing out its secret miseries, trusted blindly to that small, ridiculous key that the patriarch had passed on to him—compassion.

The heart starts to shake with laughter at the thought of him brimming with joy at his discovery, his cheeks still sparkling with tears, dressing and going downstairs with a smile to meet those souls whom he had taken under his charge.

The first one he met was that of Mother Judith, sitting plumply in an armchair in the living room, bending all her flesh to a minuscule job of sewing. She had not heard him approach. Watchful, he stood still on the last step. And while he forced himself to become "tiny," his dilated eyes became slowly intoxicated at the spectacle of the old Jewish woman, crouching on her years, whose multiple wrinkles and crevices suddenly seemed to him scars of suffering. An idea struck him: Against all likelihood, Mother Judith had once had the body and soul of a girl. What evil then had come crashing in upon her? What immense dolor, he wondered while he glided toward the armchair with tiny steps.

When he was close enough he reached a completely unprepared Mother Judith in one light leap, and grasping her heavy hand, freckled like a dead leaf, he kissed it with fear and trembling, as one touches upon a forbidden mystery.

"What, what's going on!" cried the old woman. "What are you doing here?"

Meanwhile an electrifying sweetness tingled in her bleak and blind blood, and it was with more surprise than anger that she went on, "What new fantasy is this? What's got into you to come downstairs and lick my hand? It's enough to drive a body crazy in this house since yesterday! Back to bed, now, hop to it!"

Her shrieks drew Mordecai's attention. One way and another he managed to separate her from her benumbed little prey. And while he held the old woman back with his arms spread wide, barring the way, "Please, please," he repeated, "don't be a stone on the heart of a child. You know very well he's been half out of his mind since yesterday, don't you?" And then turning to Ernie, who had been panting and clutching at his coattails, "The anger of Mother Judith," he announced emphatically, "is like the roaring of the lion. But her favor is like the dew upon the grass. Stop trembling; look— the lion is smiling."

"I am not smiling!"

"And I cannot believe you," Mordecai said twirling his mustache in an affectionate manner. "But you, you prankster, can you explain why you have to go around licking hands?"

"I don't know," Ernie stammered, red-faced. "I . . . *it just happened.*"

"Just like that?" Mother Judith asked him. She laughed behind her hand.

"Just like that, yes," Ernie said solemnly.

At that Mordecai pulled at his beard forcefully to keep a straight face, but suddenly unable to hold out, he burst into his proud laughter of the old days. Judith followed him with a whinny. Altogether sheepish, Ernie slipped between the old man's legs and beat a retreat toward the kitchen.

Fräulein Blumenthal welcomed him all aflutter. First he had to calm her down. "I was bored in bed," he said smiling, half jesting, half in earnest while his greedy eyes were already off in search of his mother's secret face—the face he knew to be cowering under her drawn features, as if grayed by timidity, under her maidservant's appearance and even under the finicking and precautionary way she had of grasping objects, feeling for them with her long hands whose mysterious, sharp whiteness he noticed for the first time.

"Why are you looking at me that way?" she asked in surprise. "Have I done anything to you?" As she spoke, she continued to stir the soup with a hand raised high above the smoking pot while with her free elbow she went on expertly rocking the cradle that sheltered Rachel, the last-born. Woebegone, Ernie's eyes drank in his mother's features, unable to find in them a reflection of her interior face. But suddenly he had a dazzling insight into Fräulein Blumenthal's soul: it was a delicate fish, silvery and fearful, in perpetual flight under the exhausted wavelets of shallow gray water that made up her face.

Still worried, she repeated, "Have I done anything to you?"

"Oh, no," Ernie said, upset. "You haven't done anything."

"Then it's your hand that hurts?"

"Oh, no, it's not my hand," Ernie said. Fascinated by the uneasy mimicry of Fräulein Blumenthal, he did not take his eyes off her, discovering in her abysses of virtue an insignificance worthy of a Just Man. So he admired her when she let the wooden ladle drop into the pot, cried out plaintively, and as if to disguise the unrest she felt under the steady gaze of her son's wide moist eyes, said to him abruptly, with a smile, "You know, we need more bread. I'd love you a lot if you'd run and fetch me a loaf. But maybe you don't feel like it?"

Ernie jumped at the chance. "Oh, yes! I do feel like it, I do!"

And as she handed him the money, bewildered, Fräulein Blumenthal noticed that the little man held on to her fingers and squeezed them with the expression of a bashful lover; then he seemed to resign himself to the worst, rose on tiptoe, and pulling the money toward him set his lips and the point of his nose against the white palm.

He scurried off quickly, hunching his shoulders in confusion.

The street was so fresh and alive that Ernie wondered if it too was not concealing a soul somewhere, beneath the paving stones round as cheeks. The idea sent him into a transport of joy. "And all that because now I know the secret—tiny, tiny-tiny, tiny!" Forcing himself then to be more serious, he moved along, his steps now solemn and majestic, now brisk and gay, toward Frau Hartman's bakery, beyond the Hindenburgplatz, where the Jews of the Riggenstrasse had bought their bread since Herr Kraus too had set that strange announcement in his window: "Forbidden to Jews and Dogs."

When he arrived cheerfully at the corner of the Hindenburgplatz, Herr Half Man surged up like a figure from a nightmare. Nothing but a torso set upon its base, like a sculpture on its pedestal, Herr Half Man propelled himself by the motion of his fists, with knuckles horned over like shoe soles. His misshapen skull was no higher than Ernie's; a pointed helmet, lying pitted in the bottom of his wagon, served him as beggar's bowl. And his ragged clothes were speckled with particolored ribbons and medals.

"Pity for a poor hero," Herr Half Man psalmed while a bitter smile made clear what meaning should be given to his chant. Moved by a sudden inspiration, Ernie stepped to one side, and taking an unceremonious stand directly before the cripple, he contemplated him with a sad expression—the proper expression, he judged, to indicate what part of Herr Half Man's "trouble" he was taking upon himself.

And as he felt himself become "tiny," an infinitesimal bubble, Herr Half Man's flaccid face swelled to fantastic proportions. The black cavity of his mouth came closer to Ernie. Then the blue marbles set in red flesh leaped out of Herr Half Man's face to take their place in Ernie's sockets, from which now trickled two thin threads of blood, clear and hot and terrifyingly soulless.

"You all through staring at me or not?"

Ernie jumped backward. The little blue marbles radiated hate in short flashes, followed by bleak, cold eclipses. The little boy discovered, amazed, that the cripple's flattened fist was being brandished in his direction. He retreated a few steps more and, terribly upset, explained, "I didn't do it on purpose, Herr Half Man. I only wanted to show you . . . I only wanted to tell you . . . I mean I really like you, Herr Half Man, I do."

The veteran shrank further into his crate. His feeble head tilted to one side, tilted to the other, dropped to his chest. His features wavered between grimace and ingratiation. Ernie knew then that Half Man's soul was a kind of moon gleaming with despair in the middle of the night.

Abruptly, in a single flight, the man reached a peak of rage. "I always have my fists!"

And as Ernie hurried off fearfully, his bandage tucked under his elbow in a thief's gesture, the cripple pivoted suddenly on the seat of his trunk, distorted his mouth, and savor-

ing in advance the word he had chosen, "Spawn of a Jew!"
he spat out voluptuously in a supreme tone of Christian
scorn.

Racing, Ernie turned the corner of the Hindenburgplatz.
Then he paused with his back to the wall, for his heart was
beating very strongly. His legs too seemed to be throbbing in
painful pulsations, like a saw at the level of his knees. Despite
Herr Half Man's bad nature, it was terribly difficult not to
visualize the place where his thighs had been ripped away by
the French shell—that immense scar which supported the
whole weight of his body. How were such awful wounds
possible? And yet the sky was its ordinary blue; automobiles
lined the curbs; here and there human beings stirred their
intact limbs, and the fountain in the Hindenburgplatz was
covered by a cloud of doves. Some of them, perched on the
rim, were pecking at the water. And what had happened?

Ernie murmured remorsefully, "It all happened because
maybe I looked at him too long. In that case, do I have to
take up people's troubles without their noticing it? Yes, that's
the way I have to do it."

But as the child praised himself for that new discovery,
he noticed with some bewilderment that instead of remaining
"tiny" he was suddenly growing at such a rate that the whole
world now came no higher than his ankle, and that all things,
from the height of the compliment he had just paid himself,
were disappearing at a prodigious rate from his own view.
"And now look—I am not a Just Man any more," he said to
himself in alarm.

· 5 ·

W HAT ELSE HAPPENED during that day when Ernie found
himself plunged, as if into a bath swarming with marvels,
into the once unsuspected world of souls? The many twists

and turns that he imposed upon his heart; that magic key revealed to him by the patriarch for opening each of the doors and arriving at each of the hidden faces that surrounded him; his efforts to comprehend in one and the same affliction all the chickens, all the ducks, calves, cows, rabbits, sheep, fresh-water fish and salt-water fish, poultry or feathered beauties, including nightingales and birds of paradise, which he knew by hearsay were daily assassinated for the stomach; the elastic balance of his being between the delicacy of crystal, the glori-fication of his tininess, and his irrepressible urge toward the shrouded peaks of pride; the mass of domestic incidents occasioned by his desire to take in evil through his eyes and ears, and by his inexplicable need to touch it with lip or finger —all those things, if they were reported in detail, would make too many jaws drop. Let us point out in any case that toward the end of the afternoon, Ernie's oddity became intolerable and that, scolded by everyone, discreetly threatened by the patriarch, he beat a strategic retreat to his father's shop, where the latter welcomed him with unfeigned wariness. "What are you doing here?" he asked sharply. "Come to see if I prick myself?"

As if in the grip of a strange panic, the child picked up the heavy tailor's magnet and busied himself about the shop, his frail shoulders suddenly hunched, a thin black wrinkle between his brows, his eye wild, investigating, poking and ferreting even under the cutting table in search of some problematical pin. When with his magnet he had prospected one by one the planks of the floor, he deposited a small heap of pins at the feet of his father, who was sitting cross-legged on the pressing stand. Then with his jaw hanging, his eyes rolling, Ernie took up a station near the window and pretended to contemplate the traffic in the street. A strange fatigue weighed upon his heart. His hand, a prisoner within the bandage, throbbed ever more sharply. And while he forced himself not to break into tears, his thoughts galloped along his temples in a harrowing hammer of hoofs. But each time that he believed them on the point of consolidating in one simple truth, they rushed headlong like desperate wild horses toward a huge black pit which gaped in the middle of his mind, and seized by anguish, terrified that he would understand nothing of the day's events, the little man shot a furtive look toward the figure of his father, toward his rabbit's face with lips that seemed to be sucking at the needle, not now in order to discover Benjamin's soul or to share his "evil" but with the obscure desire to attach his own soul, which seemed to be floating and lost, to him—with the unreasonable hope of slaking his own misery, that inexplicable "evil" that was aching in his brand-new consciousness as a Just Man. Thinking himself observed, Benjamin responded to those timid advances by a look bristling with a multitude of pins which came to rest, as if upon a magnet, against Ernie's tearful eyes. Then he released a disapproving sigh, with a nuance of tribulation, and Ernie blushed to his ears.

So passed an hour. In the middle of this intrigue, the door squeaked and a customer broke in, a worker who asked humbly to have a patch put on his trousers. After a thousand preparatory courtesies, Benjamin let it be understood that he could not perform the operation on living flesh. The honorable customer agreed, accepted the artist's suggestion and installed himself behind the cutting table with a blanket across his hairy knees, much amused.

When the patch was completed, it appeared that the man's feet refused to take their proper place in his shoes. Benjamin offered him a soupspoon, which did not have the desired effect. The unfortunate panted and struggled and hammered the floor strenuously with his heels.

Benjamin said, "All things considered, it's been so long since I first started to agitate for a shoehorn that I ought to have a whole collection of them by now. But you can't depend on a woman's promise! Here, Ernie, instead of sitting there looking at me like a china dog take this and go buy me a shoehorn. But be careful, no more foolishness, or we'll all choke on our own bile and you'll be alone in the world. No, keep quiet and go ahead."

The workman interrupted triumphantly, "Don't go to all

that trouble, Herr Levy. I've already got one foot into one of these damned boats. The other one can't hold out much longer!"

"Go along just the same," Benjamin went on. With a sudden sweep of both arms he flapped the air in front of him sharply. "At least I'll be rid of you for a while."

Ernie felt strangely empty. He went out without saying a word and found the Riggenstrasse plunged in twilight—blue, with purple streaks on the roofs and a confetti of yellow light floating against the bed of houses. The confetti thickened in halos around the street lights and in the rectangles of the windows. Above this carnival a sheet of glossy, dark paper undulated in the wind. He sensed its silky fragility; it was the sky.

Lingering at the lighted window of the grocery, he enjoyed a long, satisfying look at a can of preserves imprinted with palm trees against a background of dancing monkeys. The label bore this mysterious word—"Pineapple."

Lost in reverie, Ernie opened the door mechanically and discovered the grocer's daughter, a skinny little thing nine years old who often took care of the shop in the absence of her mother, who loved to absent herself. And as he recalled that shoehorns were purchased at the hardware store, he cried out, "Oh, pardon me!" and saw the alarmed little girl slip quickly back behind the counter. Full of remorse, crestfallen, he closed the door with the same gentleness, the same excessive precaution he would have exercised for a dying man. The grocery being next to Herr Levy's shop, on certain evenings they heard the cries of the little girl distinctly, shrill and continuous, when she found herself under the grocer's fist —the latter was a fat man who was moved to such music by drunkenness on beer—and more sharp and shrill but springing out of interminable silences when caused by the girl's mother, who had sensitive ears. So Ernie, before walking away, threw a languid look back into the grocery.

Only the little girl's head was visible above the marble counter, as if sliced off at the neck. A thick tongue emerged from her small, thin-lipped mouth, and when she saw herself observed, the little girl rolled white eyes, a bit crossed, as tadpoles did in the Schlosse, and with that eternally uneasy expression that characterizes those little creatures.

"I have to explain to her," Ernie said to himself immediately. "I have to tell her everything—the shoehorn, the can of preserves, the latch. She'll understand." And reopening the door unctuously, he stepped forward amiably into the shop, his bandaged hand discreetly hidden behind his back. "It was nothing. I only wanted to buy a shoehorn."

"A what?"

He stared sadly at her, in seventh heaven at finding her so close and in such perfect communion with his soul. And yet she had not attracted him at all until this day. She had not even the grace of a fly, although she had its industrious and fearful flight—always leaping at a piece of merchandise, crawling beneath a crate or losing herself at the top of the ladder, glued to the ceiling. In a brief flash, he imagined her skin striped with welts and admitted with emotion that anything might make her suffer—a sharp voice, a too insistent glance, perhaps simple contact with the air.

"It's nothing at all," he went on, smiling tenderly. "I only wanted to buy a shoehorn." He had lowered his voice to an almost inaudible whisper.

"We don't have any," she said resolutely.

"I know that very well," Ernie said, smiling even more. "It was for exactly that reason . . ."

"Ah! All right."

"Because shoehorns," he went on prudently, "are found in the hardware store."

"That may be. But we don't have any here."

And she offered him a vague smile that fear reduced to so puny a thing that Ernie, already badly off, tipsy, almost drunk with compassion, managed to lose his head entirely. "It's for a customer," he stammered. "He wanted a pair of pants . . . uh . . . so I opened the door . . . uh . . . uh . . . uh . . ." Then, raising his voice to a more melodious level, "I swear it to you," he said, smiling tearfully.

Resolved to reassure the little girl, he frightened her. *She knew nothing about shoehorns; she had never heard of them.* Meanwhile she retreated behind the counter, making herself smaller and smaller in the shadow of the shelf. Did she take him for a madman, a criminal? All those painful suppositions crossed the impressionable mind of the Just Man, who resigned himself to beating a retreat.

Taking a few steps backward away from her, he tried to explain clearly to her what a shoehorn was and what were its normal uses, but swept up in his explanation, obliged, he believed, to amplify it by example, the little angel suddenly let himself go so far as to take off one of his sandals, insert, under the wide eyes of his public, two fingers into the proper place, and in a most convincing manner imitate scrupulously the "normal" use of a shoehorn. "And there you are," he said in conclusion, straightening up with good humor. "A shoehorn is nothing more than that!"

The little girl's reaction chilled him. Terrified by his unusual behavior, she had half buried herself in the sugar bin. She plucked at her cheeks nervously with thin fingers.

"I'm on my way," Ernie said. With the sandal and his bandage, he went hastily back to the counter intending to explain to the unfortunate little girl that he wished no more than to leave immediately. But as he approached the small mass of terrified flesh, it seemed to him that he was growing fantastically. His arms and legs were stretching to all four corners of the shop while his head was splitting the ceiling. "Oh, no," he said in supplication, "it's just that I didn't want . . ."

At that moment the little girl set her hands flat against her cheeks, opened the circle of her mouth, took in a breath of air and launched her shriek.

A spine-chilling creature surged up from the trap door in back. Two streaks of red stretched her mouth; her eyebrows fled in arches above her temples, which pressed down on the polished stone of her eyes and seemed to drive them into her cheeks; an infinity of curlers and dozens of pink ribbons divided her hair into rolls that fell heavily on her cheeks, which were sweating some thick cream. Surprised at her toilette, she took in the scene with one furious glance and advanced upon Ernie. He closed his eyes philosophically.

When he was able to open them, stunned by the shock, his good hand was still holding the sandal but all he could see of the grocer's wife was the imposing contour of a huge rump.

"What did he do to you?" she shouted shrilly.

Still huddled behind the counter, the little girl stared for some time at the hideous face of the little Jew, but it was useless. She no longer saw in it whatever it was that had frightened her. Finally, raising her eyes to the maternal wrath she was gripped by a legitimate fear and . . . began to shriek even more loudly.

"I see," announced the grocer's wife solemnly, pivoting on her high heels, grasping Ernie by the back of the neck and shouting in triumphant tones. "You dirty little fiend!" She dragged him outside as easily as a cat by the skin of his neck.

Drowning in a painful dream, Ernie had only one care—not to drop his sandal. For the rest, it was henceforth in the hands of adults: he felt extremely, unsuspectedly, tiny.

Fräulein Blumenthal was leaning out the window on the second floor. On the sidewalk, in the halo of the street light, a group of agitated housewives appeared. One of them, in curlers and a flowered peignoir, was screaming at the top of her lungs, "The Jew! The Jew! The Jew!" It was the grocer's wife. She was shaking an inert object violently against the sidewalk. The pale cone of light bounded the scene. Between two contorted figures Fräulein Blumenthal recognized a familiar curl of hair that disappeared immediately, like a graceful fish in a cluster of seaweed. On the instant she lost all awareness of herself, of her timidity, of her signal weakness. She had always seen herself as a little female good-for-nothing, and yet she was out in the street in less than a moment, her sharp elbows brought together like a jib cutting irresistibly through the brawling, tumultuous tide.

When she was within reach of Ernie, she tore him from the hands of the grocer's wife with one silent motion and then fled without asking for more. She had clutched the child to her thin breast; her whole attitude revealed an emotion so desperate and yet so resolute that no woman had the heart to impede her retreat.

A minute later Mother Judith made her appearance. They spread out to make way for her; her volume inspired respect. The women of the Riggenstrasse did not always confine themselves to fighting with their tongues, so that the course of any argument, even the most banal, was set by the opponents' physical makeup, by one's robust stockiness or another's dry female ferocity. The grocer's wife was numbered among the best hair-pullers of the street. Taking her stand, Mother Judith was an enigma. But her tough corpulence, her chiseled cat's mask and the mortal fixity of the look she flashed upon the grocer's wife augured well for her.

The circle closed about these two noted adversaries.

"What? What? What?" Mother Judith bayed in her German, narrowly reduced to the most simple expressions.

And crossing her arms majestically, she waited.

There was a pause.

"Look at them, they're admiring each other!"

"Jesus Mary, and my soup on the stove! All right, ladies, is it going to be today or tomorrow?"

A third, disillusioned, offered, "What do you want? *It's an even match.*"

Then the grocer's wife shuddered from head to foot while her shoulders shifted an invisible burden. Manifestly, only a thread separated the battlers.

"Be careful," Mother Judith said coldly.

The grocer's wife seemed fascinated by the big Jewish woman's nostrils, which were flaring in almost a calculated rhythm.

"My—my little girl," she stammered wildly.

Then she retreated in disorder, seeking the door of the shop behind her. But ten seconds later she surged out, transformed, her child dragging behind her.

"What? What? What?" Mother Judith repeated, with a barely perceptible hesitation.

"All right, tell her what he did to you. . . ."

The crowd drew together again. Terrified by this wait for her first words, the little girl sighed, sniffled, and—was silent.

"Good God, will you tell them or do I trounce you?"

And rigid with impatience, the grocer's wife tapped the child's cheek. The little one crossed her arms and hastily bowed her head on her chest, in the posture of a penitent.

"He—he was bothering me."

"Tell them, tell them what he did!"

"I can't."

"It was dirty. It was dirty, wasn't it?"

". . . yes . . ."

"Not possible," Mother Judith declared. "He's not nasty."

But in the pitying look she gave the skinny, weeping victim, all the housewives read her true thoughts clearly, and amid a hostile murmur she retired silently, heavily, all arrogance dead, thinking sadly, "Still, he isn't very wicked ordinarily. . . ."

She found Ernie in the kitchen, in Fräulein Blumenthal's arms. The interrogation ended with two majestic slaps into which Mother Judith put all her former adoration and the obscure repulsion henceforth inspired in her by the boy, who had come indirectly from her own womb, but in whom she no longer recognized herself.

Ernie's head pivoted gracefully toward one shoulder. He was a bit pale. His eyes, lost beneath the long black curls on his forehead, were half closed. He shook his head, once to the right, once to the left, and then walked out of the kitchen slowly with ceremonial steps.

The door closed. The two women listened attentively; they were astonished to hear no footfalls in the living room. Suddenly the door swung silently on its hinges and the tiny profile of Ernie Levy appeared in the opening. Directing his attention toward Fräulein Blumenthal, he took her in pensively. His eyes were two wide puddles of scintillating black water. Suddenly the puddles broke into motion, and there remained only the narrow face of a child whose cheeks were running with tears.

"I'm leaving for good," he said in a firm voice.

"That's right, run away," Mother Judith agreed scornfully. "But be careful not to be late for dinner!"

The head disappeared and the door closed, this time with finality.

Mother Judith declared, "My daughter, that child has no heart."

Fräulein Blumenthal thought it over. "And yet," she said, "he's so pretty."

.6.

JUST BEYOND the bridge over the Schlosse, Ernie tripped against a rock, stretched out his arms and closed his eyes, realized that his body was lying in the grass of a ditch beside the road. It seemed to him that the darkness outside and the night within himself were one. Turning over onto his stomach he opened his mouth wide and let his last tears flow, for it was obvious to him that he would never catch his breath again nor would this vast rolling motion of earth and sky ever cease, though his arms, spread wide like oars, were trying to slow it down. He had run too fast, and perhaps he was going to die.

"So, are you all right like that, Ernie? All right like that?"

"Well, Ernie?" he went on aloud.

There was a moist rustling against his palate. Round and light, transparent as bubbles, the words came out of his mouth and flew off toward the moon, arousing in him nothing more than a feeling of dazzled surprise.

Concentrating hard, he tried a different phrase. "Hey, Ernie!" he murmured in some delight.

And immediately the person hailed turned and addressed

to him an obsequious salute. "What? What do you want?"

Rising carefully to his elbows, he knelt, sat down and raised his knees, circling them with his arms. It all happened as if two little men were chatting inside his head, like two gossips over a cup of tea. He thought again, "Hey, Ernie . . ." But a third Ernie appeared, hopping up on a finger, and all was confusion.

He heard a gust in the distance, and the squalling wind whipped the treetops like a wave. On the ground, dead leaves fluttered. Beyond the meadows the waters of the Schlosse lapped against the little stone bridge.

The wind fell as quickly as it had risen, and the countryside became silent again. Motionless, the moon waited. Far off at the end of the road, dim lights flickered alive, not at all menacing. On the contrary, they winked timidly, set out like a row of candles against the deep line of the horizon; they gave off a whispering sound. It was Stillenstadt.

"That dirty child!"

Mother Judith's face was truly like an old cat's face. She had arched her fingers like claws, and her imposing body, leaning forward slightly, seemed prepared to pounce. Choking back a sob, Ernie turned away from the town and took up his travels again. Later on, after many years he would return to Stillenstadt. He would know a great number of words, and the whole world would weep to hear the Just Man. Mother Judith's heart would open. There would be the yellow tablecloth with the great seven-branched candelabrum. And there would be . . .

Ernie had been walking for so long that he could not be far from a great city. The green wheat he had nibbled at in his hunger was stuck in his throat. When sweat began to run down his feverish body, he tucked his bad arm into the opening of his shirt as into a sling. But though his thirst became sharper by the minute, the little fugitive continued to avoid the villages. They were infested with dogs, and nothing was more disagreeable than their barking and howling at night.

Nevertheless his thirst bordered on delirium, and the little boy slipped foot by foot into a farmyard where he reached the trough without difficulty. The water flowed from a long pipe shaped like a cane. Ernie leaned over the trough and offered his tongue to the flow.

"You don't drink it that way. I'll show you."

A boy of Ernie's age, in Tyrolean shorts and barefoot, was standing in the moonlit clarity of the yard. His face was masked by the visor of an enormous helmet propped on his ears, but his helpful attitude implied peaceful intentions. He slipped toward the frightened Ernie silently, and telling him with a gesture to observe carefully, drank demonstratively from the hollow of his hand. Ernie imitated him immediately, in ecstasy.

"The trouble is that I always drink from glasses," Ernie said, wiping his mouth.

The boy's helmet nodded discreetly. "I understand," he said solemnly.

He seemed not the least bit surprised by the fugitive's astonishing adventures. At first their conversation took place under conditions of perfect equality, but little by little, impressed by the significant silence of the helmet, Ernie unconsciously admitted its ascendancy. He went so far as to admit his fears of the farmyard dogs. "Wait a second," the helmet cried, "I'll show you!" And clutching at an imaginary stick, he embarked on a very complicated pantomime at the end of which, with one masterful blow, he broke both of the hostile dog's forelegs. Then without transition he ran toward the lighted building, from which he returned a minute later, his arms laden with carrots, a chunk of wheat bread, and a splendid hazelwood stick.

He hesitated, then pulled a rusty jackknife from his pocket. "If you're ever attacked by a wolf . . ."

Ernie smiled. "What do I do then?"

"For a wolf, it's exactly like for a leopard." And wrapping his shirt around his forearm—for the claws, he said—this strange boy began another warrior's dance, this time with the jackknife playing the role previously played by the stick. Although the figure of the wolf did not cease worrying him, Ernie was above all aware of the nonchalance with which the peasant boy's bare feet came down on the rocks, whose points glittered in the moonlight.

The boy accompanied him to the outskirts of the village. Approaching the road of tribulation, he slowed and murmured with annoyance, "Now I have to go back. Because of the old man and the old lady, you understand?"

"You did a lot for me," Ernie said.

The other, suddenly melancholy: "I'm going to go away too one of these days." The helmet's visor fell.

"You mean they don't love you at home?" Ernie cried in an explosion of pity.

"Oh, you know how they are—all the same." Lugubriously, "They don't know . . ."

Then the boy raised one hand and waved his fingers sadly in farewell. His arms loaded with provisions, Ernie imitated the gesture as well as he could, touched by the pathos of the ceremony. The children turned away from each other simultaneously. Ernie covered a hundred yards or so very quickly. The peasant boy had disappeared, and his village was entirely drowned in the night; it no longer seemed to be a human agglomeration. The countryside itself had melted mysteriously into the sky; trees floated in the soft air. He felt that he was miles and miles from Stillenstadt, which after all was only an insignificant idea, no larger than the point of a needle, and which Ernie could very well do without.

A nearby field of alfalfa welcomed him for his first night as a vagabond. As he chose his bed, a mosquito buzzed about his ear and lighted upon a marigold growing at his feet. A ray of moonlight fell suddenly on the marigold, disclosing a tiny fly on the yellow center of the flower. Ernie held his breath, bent forward, and realized that it was a young fly, apparently feminine—that was obvious in the delicacy of its figure, in the slender juncture of its minuscule wings and most of all in the dainty grace with which it rubbed its feet one against the other, sketching out a delightful, motionless dance step.

Without hurrying, at the careful pace of a punctilious clerk, the fly began to climb along one petal.

Ernie felt a slight twinge near his heart. How his arm executed the gesture, he did not know. A cloud passed before his eyes, and the young female threw herself stupidly into the hollow of his hand, which he closed immediately. "That's it, I have her," he said to himself half regretfully.

The rustling of the wings attracted his attention, frenetic prickling against the end of his finger like the point of a needle. He felt sympathy for the jolts and jerks convulsing that small particle of existence. The glimmering of moonlight on the animal's wings produced two blue sparks. Bringing the miserable jewel closer to his eyes, the child was ravished by the minute arrangement of the antennae, which he was noticing for the first time. Those fine filaments, they too were trembling in the gusts of the interior storm. Ernie shivered in grief. It seemed to him that the antennae were chopping the air in terror. Anguished, he wondered if the feeling that made the fly between his fingers flutter its wings was as important as the feeling of the grocer's daughter. At that moment a part of his own being slipped insidiously into the fly, and he realized something about this tiny insect—were it even infinitely tinier, invisible to the naked eye, its fear of death would not diminish. He opened his fingers then like a fan and for a second followed the fly's flight. The fly was a bit of Ernie Levy, a bit of the grocer's daughter, a bit of who knew what. . . . A fly. "She didn't waste any time, she got away fast," he said to himself, amused. But immediately he missed her company, for he found himself only more alone in the middle of a field of alfalfa.

A stalk snapped somewhere in the night.

Kneeling on the ground, the child sniffed the ambient odors. Then he stretched out on his back and closed his body's

eyelids immediately, commanding it to fall asleep as quickly
as possible to escape the circles of fear that were knotting
more and more tightly about his soul. But it was strange—much
as he might tighten his eyelids, slowly, strongly, enough to hurt
the eye within, it seemed to him that they did not separate him
at all from the moon, from the stars, from the road, from the
field of wheat he sensed at a distance, or from the alfalfa obvious by its thin salad smell, or from the fly or from the little
waves of wind that drifted across his cheeks. Two transparent,
porous partitions, his eyelids closed off only his own emptiness.
Gripped by fear then, the child called himself at length, as if
hailing someone far off: "Ernie Lee-ee-vy-y-y, Ernie Lee-ee-
vy-y-y . . ." But within his head there was no answer, and the
pocket of emptiness remained as transparent and black as the
sky. He opened his mouth and muttered very quickly, "Ernie!
Ernie!"

He waited a brief moment.

Then he felt himself glow with a sudden light, and as his
limbs melted deliciously into the alfalfa, an idea marvelous
in its simplicity came to him: If the whole world rejected him,
he would be a Just Man for the flies. A stalk of alfalfa stroked
his left nostril affectionately. The earth became softer. Soon
both nostrils flared, enormous, gaping, quivering with pleasure,
and began to inhale the night slowly. When the night had
flowed altogether into his chest, he repeated with much relief,
"Yes, a Just Man for the flies." Then the pocket of emptiness
was full of grass, and he slept.

"Hey, there, little fellow! Are you playing dead?"

Ernie saw a yellow wooden shoe right up against his nose,
then gray pants, a circle of black hat surrounding a bloated
red face round as an apple. There was no menace in the voice.

With an easy pull, the peasant raised Ernie from the ground
and set him on his feet in the alfalfa. Then he measured him for

IV *The Just Man of the Flies*

a moment, sniffed severely and loosed a great burst of laughter
in the child's face. As Ernie retreated under the avalanche,
the peasant stopped abruptly and said, "You look like a fish
that got caught by the tail."

Then, obviously considering it justified, he bent his knees,
threw his head back, and slapping his thighs heavily flung his
laughter this time against the sky.

"What fish?" Ernie asked, interested.

"What?"

"Yes, what fish?"

The gray eyes wrapped him in a cloak of suspicion. "First
off, what are you doing here?"

Only ten yards away, a team of two horses stood patiently
at the edge of the road. The peasant followed Ernie's gaze.
"Yes, that's mine," he said less harshly. "I'm going into town,
and I'll bet that's where you come from. You came all the way
on your knees, it looks like. They've got a shine that isn't
normal. And your arm . . . Your folks beat you, right? You
poor little shrimp, you did right to run away."

Ernie shook his head, smiling. "Oh, no, sir, it wasn't that."

"What was it then? Did you do something real bad this
time? Stole money, broke something valuable?"

"Oh, no," Ernie said, smiling once more.

The peasant put on a solicitous expression. "I know—you
wanted to see the world. Tell me, did you run away very long
ago?"

"Last night," the child said after a moment's reflection.

The peasant hesitated, his hand fell heavily on the curly
head and rubbed it with a kind of awkward delicacy. "You
know, pal, they must be pretty worried back home. So what
about it—do you want to tell me where you come from?"

Something stirred in Ernie's breast. There was that adult's
hand set upon his head, and that mountain of flesh casting its
shadow upon him.

"You don't look like a bad boy," the peasant growled with
good humor.

"Stillen—stadt," the fugitive stammered. At the same mo-

ment he glimpsed the full extent of his sin and foundered in
sobs.

The cart rolled along at a good pace. From the fantastic
height of his perch, Ernie witnessed the transformations of
the countryside. When his eyes tired, he came back to the
solemn, swaying stride of the work horses, their manes undulating like white waves against the rock of their necks and
withers, rising and falling endlessly. "Not that these vegetables
are very heavy," the farmer had said, "but I hitched these
horses up together because they get along well, they don't like
to be separated. But maybe you'd eat an apple, hey? And how
do you like my apple? Like velvet, isn't it? Ah, my friend, I'm
bringing a fancy load of vegetables to market this morning,
yes, sir." Now and then the man traced an arabesque with his
whip above the dappled-gray rumps. When this failed to
produce a sharp, handsome snapping, he simply clucked his
tongue against the roof of his mouth, which was hardly as
satisfactory to Ernie.

But more than anything the parade of landscape claimed
Ernie's attention. Twisting to the four points of the compass, he
tried vainly to recognize some detail dimly viewed the night
before. Already, a little while ago, awakening in the alfalfa
he had lost the curious impressions of the previous night. The
sky and the trees and the road and even the least blade of grass
seemed diminished or impoverished in bright daylight. And the
villages they passed through recalled nothing of the masses of
shadow crumbling in the moonlight. Now the houses had pink
roofs and he could count the tiles clearly.

"So," the peasant repeated, "you're a son of the Levys in the
Riggenstrasse?"

Ernie affirmed it with a sober nod.

"Not that I regret doing it," the man went on in a tone of
annoyance. "There are good people and bad people every-

where—or so they say. But just the same you have to admit it's funny. . . . What do you think of that, my friends!" He shot a quick glance at his passenger, and then turning away, still annoyed, said in an impersonal voice, "I should have guessed because . . . little dark heads are all over the place in this part of the world."

A question was burning on Ernie's lips. Frowning, he risked it in a voice that was deferent though marked by a friendly undertone of sorrow. "You mean you're against *us?*"

From brick red the peasant's jowls turned to rawest purple. A neigh escaped his lips, and his fleshy carcass jiggled so happily on the seat that Ernie was afraid of seeing him fall overboard. "What a little shrimp!" he exclaimed several times. "What a nervy little shrimp!"

More than anything, that odd epithet "little shrimp" cut Ernie to the quick. Resolved to show no emotion, he huddled in his seat, leaning back against a crate of potatoes. Then he attempted a detached whistling. But after a minute the peasant's left hand dropped the rein, approached him like a huge blind bird covered with hair and came to light gently upon his head. The man's tone was teasing. "Don't be afraid, little shrimp. Levy or not, we'll be there in five minutes. And after all you don't suppose that I'd make you get out and walk? I'm not smart enough for that. You take a man who's really smart—it's pretty rare he turns out to be a good guy."

Nevertheless, doubtless sobered, he did not speak again until they reached the Riggenstrasse. The horses snorted in front of the Levys' shop. Ernie discovered in astonishment that the narrow window had been replaced in his absence by badly squared-off planks. But he had no time to say anything. The peasant had grabbed him by the shoulder, and without moving from the seat raised him in a strong hand and deposited him gracefully on the sidewalk. Then he flung out a cheerful "So long, shrimp," and with a single snap of his whip started his team off at a fast trot, as if he were afraid to linger in the region of the Levys.

*   *   *

At the evening meal the night before, Mother Judith, point-ing at Ernie's empty chair, had judged Ernie guilty *in absentia*. Two hours later, the child absolved of all sins, she had loosed a volley of accusations against the rest of the universe.

Suddenly wrapping herself in a shawl, she had erupted into the streets of Stillenstadt, raising the alarm among Jews and Gentiles as she went, and when she was quite sure that the lit-tle angel was not in the town, she had begun to plow through the surrounding fields. They found her three days later in a quite distant farm where she had come to rest, sick, barefoot, her dress shredded by the brambles.

For his part, Mordecai had spent the night seated in a chair. At the first gleam of dawn, the shopwindow was shattered by a paving stone. The grocer's wife had given her husband's racial passions free rein. Mordecai hastily put together a few planks as a precaution against looters. Then he released a long sigh, lit the oil lamp and awaited the coming of day through the luminous interstices that separated the badly joined boards of the panel. "I hope it doesn't all end in another ghetto," he med-itated secretly. Afterward, for a thousand reasons of which one alone would have been enough—namely, money—the wooden panel remained nailed to the shop front—a frontier for the Ger-mans and a symbolic prison for the Levys.

At the sound of the cart he rushed outside. Already the horses were trotting away, but on the sidewalk, crowned with grass, filthy with earth and blood, his arms full of carrots, the bandage hanging down to his feet, the prodigal son stood dreamily. He did not budge when the old man came rushing at him with wild gestures and a tremulous expression, as if fear-ing to see him disappear again.

"Don't talk about it, don't be afraid any more," Mordecai stammered. "You understand me? Nothing happened. Oh, God is good, good, good!" he repeated furiously, clasping the boy tightly.

Ernie seemed to have kept his calm entirely. When his mouth was free again, he asked, intrigued, "Why is the window boarded over?"

The milkman's delivery tricycle moved away from the corner of the Hindenburgplatz like a twitching insect. Except for that, the Riggenstrasse was still deserted in the morning mists. Mordecai squatted on the sidewalk, laid his cheek against the child's forehead to check the temperature and then, finding in his expression a placid divinity, explained after certain oratorical precautions what had happened since the night before.

"You understand," he said tenderly, "if you were a true Just Man, things would certainly not have come to pass this way. . . ."

"I understand everything," Ernie said.

"So you must become as you were before," the patriarch said glibly, "behave as you did before."

The wide dark eyes dimmed in reflection, and then filled with tears that gleamed at their pearly rims.

"Why are you weeping?"

"Because now I think that I'll always have trouble with everything—even if I'm not a Just Man!"

"Shema Yisrael!"

And lifting the child against him, Mordecai rose to his full height, his head full of sunlight, thinking, "O Lord, the heavens in their elevation, the earth in its depths and the heart of a child are equally . . . impenetrable."

V

HERR KREMER
AND
FRÄULEIN ILSE

. 1 .

AFTER THIRTY-TWO YEARS of service, Herr Kremer's entire personality bore the serene marks, the contemplative hues of democratic learning—professorial, with a tall, almost elongated figure that seemed to undulate at the slightest movement, to modulate, like the shadow of a flute, some solemn, secret harmony. And that rectangular mask springing up from his detachable collar like a strange flower from its pot—professorial.

By the same token, his smile comprised an infinity of instructional nuances—half-smile, quarter-smile, an eighth, and so on. In periods of scholastic calm, he generally displayed a cautious half-smile, circumspect, halfway between the sweetness of life and the polar rigors of duty.

From the beginning of his career, he had distinguished himself by a troublesome alliance of natural suavity and superannuated pedagogical theory. The venerable Hofmeister did not mince words with him. "Don't be leaning over your students so much," he shouted at a full-dress teachers' meeting. "It's the ideal position for getting a kick in the behind!"

Turning purple, the young pedagogue had meditated for some thirty seconds and then answered with much dignity, "Despite its discourteous form, I must acknowledge that the rector's opinion seems to me quite authoritative."

And yet, though from then on he carried a pointer, he had continued to believe secretly in the purity of childhood, which he contrasted to human imperfections. "The child," he said to his friend Hartung, "is descended from the man, yes—in the same way that the latter is descended from the monkey!" He judged that instruction in civics and the teaching of poetry, extended to the whole human race, would erect an eternal dike against barbarity. In that respect the German romantic poets seemed to him an ideal nourishment—particularly Schiller, whose slightest verses radiated civic consciousness. The day when Schiller was known to the entire population of the world would be a fine day. Then there would be no more troubles about politics or money or fallen women. On that blessed day, Herr Kremer imagined, childhood would no longer be a minority on earth. Every adult would remain a child, every child would become a true adult, and—and so forth.

These reflections caused him to neglect the reality of current politics to the point where suddenly he was unable to remember if Germany was a republic or still under the rule of the Hohenzollerns. He had known several regimes—none had had any profound consequences for the teaching of Schiller. Besides, these governmental quarrels always came down to a question of words—"republic," "empire," ad infinitum. He would never have dreamed of allowing himself to be caught up in it, feeling that one day all words would fade to silence before poetry. Doubtless he had had his love affair, like any other man, of which there must remain a memory as painful as that of the wound he had received during the war—in the lower part of his belly, to be precise. "Oh, my dear Hildegarde," he had said blushing, "I assure you that this . . . that that . . . at least . . . has not made me unfit for marriage. And here is proof. . . ."

The years having covered the incident with the cynical patina of time, Herr Kremer wondered if it would not have been better to offer his fiancée a proof somewhat more convincing than that ridiculous medical certificate. Their meetings had become rather less frequent. In the end Herr Kremer had been annoyed that the girl considered his infirmity—"partial, my darling, only partial"—the result of a vicious action in which he had been obscurely an accomplice. With the help of an Iron Cross, he had been able to end his war in an administrative armchair, but the memory of another cross, unmentionable, which he carried in his flesh had unfortunately cooled his patriotic ardor. They suspected him of defeatism. And his casual indifference to being German finally convinced the young lady that his noble parts had been reduced to nothing. As a woman of heart, she married a one-legged hero whose patriotism was rigorously intact.

As time went on his war memories melted so intimately into his sentimental reminiscences that soon Herr Kremer looked upon them both with the same wide wounded eye, confusing in a single bitterness the hole opened in his flesh by men and the emptiness of his existence. And although his high opinion of love kept him from carrying the thought too far, at times it seemed to him that one and the same blow had struck him in the heart and in the left testicle.

"Fascism," he judged at the beginning, "is the rule of the tavern in the streets and in the government. Soon they will all be sent back to their bars or prisons. Soon the old Germany will punish her bad boys."

He greeted the first measures with the foolproof philosophy, prudence, and tact of an old humanist. The decree on corporal punishment made him smile, but when he learned that his colleagues, for greater convenience, were applying this decree to the backs of Jewish children, a small weed sprang up on his forehead, so pure of any hint of evil. . . . And the burning of the synagogue did the rest.

That fire broke out late at night. By dawn there remained only blackened panels. The dead synagogue smoked over Stillenstadt for two days. From his sixth-floor apartment on the courtyard, Herr Kremer noticed that a long beam amid the tiles and the rubble pointed like an accusing arm toward the Christian house front. Happily, the Jews had gathered in their temple only episodically since the irruption of the brown shirts, so there was only one victim, a belated believer whom the fire suffocated as he prayed. But for a week afterward the people of the neighborhood complained of a subtle odor floating about the ruins, which they believed that of the old Jew who had gone up in smoke into the peaceful sky of Stillenstadt.

That funereal incense irritated Herr Kremer's nostrils disagreeably. To his colleague and friend Herr Hartung, who took him to task regularly on the subject of the Jews, he remarked that his words were "quite fiery." The other pretended not to understand. But the spell was broken, and as they left school the two friends went each his own way, walking along the avenue fifteen yards apart when morning and evening since the first of October, 1919, they had paced it together.

Still, the mechanism had not yet been set in motion by which our delicate humanist would be led into a concentration camp. And when the wheel of death began to turn, its initial motion was so slight that Herr Kremer was not even aware of it. . . .

The school comprised perhaps fifteen "Jewish guests," as people affected to call them now, and about the same number of Pimpfe—pioneers in the Hitler Youth. But by an unexpected trick of the childish soul, when the latter launched their attack on the Jewish platoon in the corner of the playground near the chestnut tree, many "apolitical" students joined them for that small, so recreational war. When the Jewish lines broke, they dragged their prisoners to the middle of the playground where, under the prudently detached eyes of the teachers, they amused themselves with them.

These Roman games left Herr Kremer thoughtful, but fearful of attracting some imperial lightning to his own head, he confined himself to pacing up and down along the wall opposite the Jews' chestnut tree. And yet at times, unable to plug his ears, he retreated to the office reserved for teaching personnel and blew his nose loudly in the darkness. Each time he felt the lump in his throat about to burst, he blew strenuously into his handkerchief. When he came out again, his nose was red and painful. That reaction of his did not pass unobserved.

One day, in the middle of the play period Ernie Levy came rolling in the dust at Herr Kremer's feet. There were two Pimpfe at his heels. Hans Schliemann drove a knee into the small of the Jewish child's back. Ernie's arms lay limply on the ground and his palms were bleeding; his eyes were closed. Grabbing Ernie by the hair, Hans tilted his thin face toward the sky in the posture of a beggar. "What's the matter, don't you want to play any more?" Hans Schliemann's mouth was wide open and his teeth sparkled. He seemed indifferent to Herr Kremer's proximity. The teacher brought a hand to his bald head in an absent manner, then sighed, squatted on his long legs, murmured between his long yellow teeth, "Now, now, my child," and grasping the Pimpf suddenly by the collar raised him to the height of a man and flung him several feet through the air! At that sacrilegious sight, the entire playground fell motionless.

Herr Kremer continued pacing slowly, in a dragging, harassed step, bringing his foot forward awkwardly and setting it to earth carefully, like an old nag too heavily loaded, who verifies each step before raising the next hoof. But as he reached the corner of the wall, he sensed a light step behind him. The Jewish child was walking in his wake, arms crossed, expression delighted, placing himself overtly under his protection. What to do? Herr Kremer resigned himself, and at the end of the play period it was two small boys and one little girl, in seventh heaven, who trotted along behind him quite well behaved, hand in hand, constituting for him a cortege as compromising as possible. The next day there were fifteen of them. Finally, three days later Marcus Rosenberg—the great Marcus, ultimate defender of the Jewish colors—took his place in turn under the banner of Herr Kremer, a steel ruler under his arm. It was done.

That day, when he returned to his classroom a childish inscription was sprawled all the way across the blackboard: "Out with the Jew-lover!"

He approached the blackboard, picked up the eraser and, changing his mind, dropped it negligently back into its box. He stood for one full minute with his back to his pupils. When he finally turned toward the forty hostile gazes, his face was geometric and cold. And suddenly larger, harder, his jaw set forward like the desperate muzzle of an old carriage horse (to which the shafts and a blanket flung superbly over his withers lend an illusion of vigor), Herr Kremer advanced toward his lectern solemnly, girded about by thirty-two years of everyday respectability. And as a disorderly murmur rose in the classroom, the teacher squeezed his pointer between thumb and index finger, raised it vertically and tapped it against his ear in a light, graceful movement while his features maintained a superior impassivity. Dead silence fell immediately.

"Very good," he articulated with a miserable smile. "And to go on with our day's work, I propose"—he rubbed his glasses with one hand as if to clean away a few grains of dust; behind the metallic frames, his wide, gentle blue eyes blinked incessantly—"a pretty little exercise in dictation," he went on finally. "Take up your pens and your paper. This applies to you also, Fräulein Leuchner. Ready? I shall begin—one, two, three! How-sweet-it-is-comma-the-song-of-the-tomtit-comma . . ."

Leaning over their papers, the pupils applied themselves. In the first row he glimpsed the face of his favorite, Ilse Bruckner, whose green eyes flashed toward his lectern each time he began a new verse. All he could see of Ernie Levy was a curly tuft of hair and the meditative point of a nose far to the back of the classroom. "All these heads are full of life," the old man thought, "and yet a very special threat hangs over the four little Jewish heads. . . ." And as he compared the destiny of those four to that of the other pupils, Herr Kremer abruptly had the strange feeling that an unnamable monster, a kind of octopus settling down upon his class, was devouring them indiscriminately. . . .

On the evening of that final defeat, Herr Kremer was weak enough to hold back the two elect spirits of the current year—Ernie Levy, first in German, and Ilse Bruckner, first in singing. On a vague scholarly pretext, he invited them both to tea—"tomorrow, Thursday, at precisely three o'clock," he announced, in order to stress, by that artificial exactitude, the official character of his invitation. "Don't forget," he said as he dismissed them, "precisely three o'clock," and he flashed them a singular smile in an attempt to combine a trace of good fellowship, which would make their coming pleasant, with that professorial distance which would make it an obligation.

When the two students were gone, Herr Kremer realized suddenly that they composed his entire circle of friends. Still, an instant later the thought of tomorrow made him chuckle with pleasure. He had always known his children from far off, separated from them by the distance that his function imposed upon him. But he could not die without seeing them at close range at least once, without speaking to them, without smiling at them as if they were his own flesh. He mused that they both had the same thin legs, the same stemlike necks, the same tiny, graceful waists. Turning his gaze to the open window, he discovered the blue of the sky like a promise. The tip of the chestnut tree was blossoming. He approached the window and plucked a leaf which he inspected in his palm; it was glistening in all its fresh green pith. He leaned out the window and received the revelation of the chestnut tree, whose myriads of leaves rustled in the wind like a head of wild hair. He had lost everything, but some things went on without him—the sky, the earth, the trees, little children. "And if I die," he thought tenderly, "all that will not depart the earth." It seemed to him that he had just invented the world. Of a sudden he felt extraordinarily happy—he did not know why.

. 2 .

HERR KREMER's was not the house of a man of poetry. It resembled all those apartment buildings in the neighborhood of the old synagogue, about which Mother Judith, sketching a doubtful grimace, had once commented with distaste, "You can see right away that the best people live there."

But the apartment was on the sixth floor, and this detail gave Ernie's imagination scope (no one in the Riggenstrasse lived so high up, since the houses lacked sufficient stories). For him it was precisely the number of stories that marked a kind of elevation of the soul. His pleasure was increased by the fact that the fifth-floor landing offered a spiral staircase as narrow, as ambiguous, as dark, as gilded with the dust of mysterious events as the one that led to the Levys' attic. The idea that Herr Kremer had carved his apartment out of an attic seemed full of poetry, and the thing itself worthy of such a man.

As he rang the bell, the thought of Ilse Bruckner made him hesitate. He had not addressed a word to a little girl for a year now. In the neighborhood of the Riggenstrasse, tongues were still wagging. Some stated positively that the "Jew boy" had pulled his little sex out of his fly, and saw in that fact a brilliant confirmation of all that had been reported of the sexual and financial devilishness of the Jews. Several Nazis had demanded an investigation, but they had been able to extract no information from the little girl about Ernie Levy's fly. . . .

"So you have come?" asked a somewhat choked voice. Herr Kremer, in a swallowtail coat and with a festive look, leaned forward in the darkish rectangle of the doorway. A gray hand fluttered and came down to caress Ernie's cheek, which it chucked in a gesture of infinite lightness. Then the old teacher pointed, feigning terror, to the hatbox Ernie was clutching gracefully to his chest. "But what in the world can that be? I hope that you haven't brought us a bomb, at any rate?"

Ernie hesitated, understood, smiled. "My grandmother, she doesn't make bombs."

In the foyer he felt frustrated, but the living room astonished him. Four tiny stained-glass windows diffused a bluish light upon the armchairs, the lace antimacassars, and the golden squares checkering the rug like dead leaves. "I shall leave you for a moment," Herr Kremer said, and it was only then that Ernie noticed Ilse's quiet head of blond hair, set like a butterfly above the grassy plush of an armchair. Then he made out the girl herself, who rose with a quick movement and took three steps toward him, her hand outstretched at the end of a smooth arm so white that it seemed to be springing freshly from the short sleeve puffed at the elbow, like the disproportionately long pistil of a flower.

"Very pleased to meet you, Herr First-in-German."

Ernie took her hand ceremoniously, reddened, and said with much gravity, "Very pleased, Fräulein First-in-Music."

He could not have said exactly what it was that bothered him in those formal phrases—perhaps that they seemed to him disproportionate to his own person; perhaps that they sounded strange in the girl's mouth; perhaps, finally, that they dampened some of the timid, vivacious pleasure he felt at gazing into Ilse's sea-blue eyes. Still, he was rather pleased with the way he had extricated himself—with a step both delicate and surprising.

Ilse Bruckner burst into laughter.

"You had me going," Ernie said smiling.

Ilse wondered, "Really?" And as Ernie Levy's eyes continued to smile into her own she blushed, pirouetted on the elastic tip of a toe and flung herself into the lime-green armchair, which she filled by laying her hands on its arms. "It's nice here," she said firmly.

At that moment Herr Kremer crossed to the middle of the room. On a small iron table he set a tray covered with small porcelain cups and with other objects, no less preposterous in his hands—a sugar bowl, a teapot and the like. Opening the hatbox, he seemed surprised to find in it the cake to which Mother Judith had added some finishing touches late at night. The way in which he frowned seemed to indicate that this special attention was not to his taste. "But what is this? No! But this is madness, pure and simple. . . ." And turning suddenly toward a dumfounded Ernie, his frown deepened while his pale eyes sparkled brightly. "It looks delicious! It's real madness! Ah, my God!"

Then he cut the thrilling madness in slices and poured the tea.

"What splendor!" Ilse Bruckner simpered, her mouth full. She was holding her teacup in three fingers, her little finger vertical and her lips, rounded as if to whistle, produced a warbling.

"What do *you people* call that?" Herr Kremer asked.

Ernie Levy was jubilant. "That's a *lekach!* A honey cake."

And Herr Kremer repeated the word over and over, saying that it was madness but that it was delicious.

Suddenly he set his cup on the table, extracted a vast checkered handkerchief from his pocket, plunged his face into it and blew his nose strenuously. The two children were appalled. A heart-rending singsong issued from Herr Kremer's nostrils. His pale, lifeless eyes once again displayed a brilliant sparkle. "Nothing, nothing," he stammered as he rushed out, handkerchief to his nose.

"He's really funny," said Ilse Bruckner, who had raised herself on her elbows to slide deeper into the chair.

"Funny," Ernie Levy agreed.

"But he's awfully nice!"

"Nice," Ernie said circumspectly.

His misadventure of the previous year danced before his eyes.

"Listen," Ilse said suddenly, "you aren't too mad at me, are you?"

The boy choked in fear. "Why?"

"For what happened three years ago, when we were playing Christ. . . ."

"Oh, no, oh, no," Ernie said warmly.

"And you're not mad at me because of my cousin Hans either?"

"A cousin's a cousin."

"And you," the girl concluded, "are not very talkative."

And with a thin, throaty laugh, she huddled up, disappearing into the depths of the armchair.

Ilse's chair squeaked. A choked laugh rose from it. Ernie felt a silky ripping in his chest. Everything was happening as if the girl were putting herself out to make him want to share her little blond happiness, even as she deprived him of any real possibility of it. For Ilse was not an animal, or a ray of sunlight in which one could bask without asking consent, and yet she was not altogether a person who could deliberately forbid one entrée to her soul. In her face and hands there was a kind of animal or bird, in her voice and expression a kind of person. Anything could be expected with Ilse, Ernie thought dreamily, for she was this thing and that thing and perhaps much more than he could even imagine. . . .

"What do you see?" she asked.

"I see that you're hidden," Ernie Levy said.

And as he finished his phrase, he burst into a laugh whose freshness surprised him, like a brook swirling about the stones of his mouth, and the source of which, within himself, he had never guessed at—that strange joy Ilse had awakened.

"You laugh like a crazy man," Ilse said, huddled in the armchair. And with no transition she began to warble sweetly— "laaaa, liiii, laaa," as if the laughter in her had followed a delicately etched groove in her throat, very slowly and with much precision, without overflowing its banks by a drop. An extension of that crystal groove, Ernie lowered his eyelids and murmured very politely, "You sing well."

When he opened his eyes again, the little girl's head was peeking up over the lace antimacassar, and she was making a face at Ernie Levy. But in the shadow where the eyelashes began, lashes curved back like petals, Ernie made out quite clearly the ironic and tender sparkle in an expression like a swelling, gilded, dusty pistil, expressing the naïve subtlety of a flower.

"How goes it?" Ilse said then in a velvet voice.

"I don't know," Ernie said. At the sound of his voice, Ilse was moved. The Jewish boy's eyes were like two black cherries set into the white flesh of his cheeks; she thought that if she bit lightly at them, delicate red juice would flow, the delectable blood of cherries. "You know," she said confidentially, "I want to be a singer."

The next morning, in the name of some formal courtesy that had never entered his head until then, Herr Kremer seated Ernie Levy solemnly in the first rank, right next to Ilse. The laureate took his place with an unhappy air and did not move thereafter. She could barely hear him breathe—light, rapid, well-spaced gasps. Coquettishly she leaned forward and saw that her sweet idiot's forehead was covered by a thin sweat. She was amazed. "Jesus, how scared he is," she said to herself. "Yes, it's that way, that way, that way that I like him!"

But during the play period she could not escape Hans Schliemann's interrogation. "So," he said, "you're sitting next to a Jew now?" Leaning back against the bathroom door, he crossed one ankle over the other negligently. His fine blond hair hung at either side of his forehead; he was shaking his head furiously; he was handsome.

Ilse smiled scornfully. "What's it to you? Just because Papa Kremer put us in the same row? You're not jealous of him?" she laughed. She brushed a fleck of dust from his hair, and he quivered. "What do you want me to do about it, with that stupid little Yid? He's not a man like you. Stupid Hansi," she simpered, making a face at him that he loved, her lower lip offering itself moist with saliva.

"Be careful," Hans said, "I'm a Pimpf. I'll bust you in the mouth, both of you. . . ."

"Go ahead and try," Ilse said. Frigid, she offered her cheek. "Well?"

Hans wailed, "You know I couldn't do that!"

"All right," she said coldly. "But remember that I'm not Sophie. I'm Ilse, and I do what I want to. And that Jew is the biggest idiot in the world. If you touch him, then—you won't touch me any more. And go away now. Hurry up, the bell is going to ring. . . ."

The little girl leaned forward in annoyance. With his fingers Hans Schliemann searched for the curved flesh barely visible under her smock; then closing his eyes suddenly, he pinched quickly, simultaneously, the points of Ilse's budding breasts.

"Today it's free," she said pushing him away. "But remember . . ."

When the school day was over she took Ernie familiarly by the arm, under Hans Schliemann's helpless gaze. Silently they walked around the block; silently, with a timid handshake, they parted. Ilse was already arguing with herself. "What do you see in that idiot?" the first Ilse said in exasperation. But immediately the Ilse below became tender at the memory of a detail. "Jesus, Jesus, Jesus, he let you drag him off like a baby. He didn't ask you a single question, did he? He's not the least bit curious, that one. No, not the least bit," she repeated to herself drunkenly. "But what is he thinking about all the time?"

She enjoyed their walks along the Schlosse more every day, but the schoolboy community vexed her, denouncing her openly as the "concubine," as Hans said, of the Jew. Ilse suffered brief but violent attacks of shame.

As for their Thursday visits, now ritual, they were the honey of her week. The ceremonial tea, the short recitals with which she regaled the party afterward, the waxed parquet, the knickknacks and the upholstered armchairs—all placed at her fingertips a world that floated a hundred cubits above her family's tenement. Herr Kremer varied his dress, going so far as to try a top hat, and Ernie too was invariably comical, with his flapping navy-blue pants—donned for the occasion—which, riding up almost to his armpits, nevertheless dragged along the floor, constraining him to a cautious tread whose effect was highly amusing. Sometimes Herr Kremer disappeared briefly, sometimes he blew his nose without leaving them. And on the stroke of four o'clock (Ilse reveled in it beforehand), the old gentleman took on an artificially detached manner.

"Listen," he said, "if you haven't got it settled today, put it off until next Thursday. For myself, I must admit that it leaves me completely indifferent."

"You don't want to play?" Ilse said, baiting him.

"But see here, my poor child," he cried shrilly, "I am only a silent partner!"

"Shall we?" the girl asked calmly.

Ernie nodded indulgently. "Let's," he said.

They were playing dominoes.

One day Ernie took the silver tray back to the kitchen. His absence seemed long to her, and Ilse slipped into the hallway to surprise him. Raising a corner of the curtain, she saw Ernie hunched over the table, lost in contemplation of a black speck in the middle of a puddle of milk. He seized the black speck, which was a fly, and approached the red-hot oven with his arm extended. Ilse had the sudden feeling that Ernie was performing a malevolent rite of the Jews, and everything about him suddenly disgusted her—his thin white wrists and ankles, the curve of his neck, even the graceful movement of his round arm above the gaping oven. . . . But immediately abashed, she saw the fly hopping about on the end of Ernie's thumb, then trotting peacefully on the palm of his hand. Finally, chasing a last wisp of steam, the fly was on the ceiling in one light hop!

When Ernie moved to follow the insect's flight, Ilse caught his expression, and if not for the risk of pimples she would cheerfully have kissed him. It was the same beatific, flabbergasted expression he had when he listened to her sing. . . .

As soon as she saw her mother that night, Ilse guessed that her charming cousin Hans had spilled the beans. In anticipation of the inevitable marriage, Frau Bruckner held it a principle not to risk her child's beauty. Nevertheless she used the poker. After this operation, she explained, "From now on and beginning today, no more Thursday, no more teacher, no more Jew. If he comes here to ask for you, I'll take care of him! Let me see your face—do you have any pimples yet?"

"We don't kiss." Stretched out on her belly, Ilse hiccuped.

"That's not true," Frau Bruckner retorted. "You smell of Jewish filth ten feet away! Ah, Jesus, Jesus, Jesus—so you had to go there, and with that one especially! I know all about it, Hans told me everything. That's the one who attacked her, the little girl in the Riggenstrasse that made all those stories in the newspaper. And I suppose you didn't know it, you little whore?"

"*Yes, I knew it!*" Ilse screamed. "But he'll never do anything to me. . . ." And in a delicate whisper, "He loves me."

Herr Kremer listened to her in profound melancholy and said that it was of no importance. Friends, he added a bit ironically, could be separated by nothing in the world. "And our little band will survive at school, won't it?" he murmured in an engaging tone. But the next day Herr Julius Kremer arrived unshaven, and the following day drunk.

It was Hans Schliemann who sounded the death note. Hostile scrawls covered the blackboards, augmented by obscene drawings. They also knew that neither the teachers nor the Hofmeister were speaking to Herr Kremer at all. The latter's manner was distraught, absent. One day he delivered a brief discourse on government. The following day Hans Schliemann put a lump of dry ice on the cushion of his magisterial chair.

Not the jokes or the excesses of language or even the sly projectiles persuaded Herr Kremer to give up the defense of the Jews in the playground. On the contrary, he assembled them in ranks himself, in order of size, and as he convoyed them he threw furious, provoking glances at the others. When Hans Schliemann told her that Herr Kremer's replacement was imminent, Ilse offered her chest once more to her cousin. Unable to persuade her to quit her Jew, he promised (in exchange for an incursion under her dress) that he would do all he could to hold back the ardor of his *men*. "But soon," he added, "that will be impossible. And for you it will be too late."

One fine morning the students found the Hofmeister in Herr Kremer's place. The latter, he explained, being no longer worthy of his position, had been obliged to leave the city at dawn. He passed over Herr Kremer very quickly, and then announced the arrival of a replacement the next day, straight from Berlin. "Then," he said with an ambiguous smile, "order will be restored in all things."

In a protective gesture, Ilse gripped Ernie's arm. Outside, their steps led them quite naturally to the banks of the Schlosse, where Ilse suddenly sat down on the grass and broke into sobs. Then she smiled through her tears to reassure the boy, who also sat down, a bit uneasy in spite of everything. Indecisively she picked a daisy, and still smiling plucked a petal from it delicately.

"I pluck out one eye," she says, hardly realizing what words she speaks. For an instant, the daisy's white ligula spins; it falls into the shadowy hollow of Ilse's smock.

"I pluck out both your eyes," she continues slowly, while her own eyes, still smiling, narrow to threads of green light. And her voice becomes hurried, her gesture of mutilation becomes jerky, quick, dry.

"I cut off one paw—both!

"I eat up one hand—both!

"I pluck out your eye again. . . .

"I pluck out . . ." she began feverishly, but that time her thumb and index finger came together on emptiness. Not a single petal remained on the yellow, innocent heart of the daisy.

Panicky, Ilse raised her head to see what effect her words had on Ernie. But he seemed to have guessed nothing, and leaning toward her, his wide, dark eyes shining with compassion, he set the ends of his fingers against Ilse's palm, on the limp daisy. "What's bothering you so much?" asked the gentle idiot in a trembling voice.

Ilse was in absolute despair. She said very quickly, "It's nothing, I've already forgotten. . . ."

Then she raised the little finger of her right hand and made it dance gracefully in the air to the beat of a Viennese waltz she began to whistle with mock solemnity. Ernie burst into light, throaty laughter as his eyes followed the dancing fingers. "He has no memory, not a penny's worth," she said to herself, her heart horribly contracted. No, no, no, she could not tell him that it was all over, she hadn't the courage. All right, she would wait for a better time. Let him wrong her just once. If she had to, yes, she would create the situation herself, for, oh God, it couldn't go on, oh Jesus. Truly, she had been miserable for some time now. And under Ernie Levy's bewildered gaze, there she was sobbing again, in the middle of her song, which trailed off for an instant and then died.

· 3 ·

THE NEW TEACHER burst in without ceremony. At five minutes after eight the door blew open and a short, square man sprang in like a jack-in-the-box. Paying no attention to the students, he went to the desk immediately and sat down, keeping a stiff attitude in order to lose nothing of the little height he had. The abruptness of his entrance was almost funny, but Ernie restrained himself because everyone seemed extremely serious. Herr Geek had a face of dried clay. Crevices lined it in all directions. The loose skin of his neck slightly overflowed his starched detachable collar. A strange smudge of mustache widened the yellow wings of his nostrils. "A peasant in his Sunday best," Ernie thought dryly.

But his joy lasted only a moment. Herr Geek was already pushing back his chair, standing at attention and proclaiming in an angry voice, "Attention! One, two, three, all rise!"

The tone was so aggressive, the voice so resolved to make itself heard that Ernie felt something like the bite of a whip at the base of his spine. He rose with a wild abruptness that surprised him, and as he stuck out his chest he noticed that Herr Geek's eyes were shining with a strange pallid glow under the heavy eyelids that bound them like dried cement.

At that moment Herr Geek clacked his heels, and his arm rose obliquely into the air in a single sudden motion, with the rigidity of a beam. "Heil Hitler!" he cried furiously.

Herr Geek's gesture was so sudden that the students responded without exception. Ernie himself, somewhere in the obscurity of his being, found the inspiration and the technique for a perfect clicking of heels. At the same moment he realized that he was crying at the top of his voice "Heil Hitler! Heil Hitler!" His voice was lost in the roaring of the whole class. Dumfounded, he discovered his arm pointed at the ceiling. Slowly, he brought it down and let it lie discreetly at his side, like a branch alien to his body.

"It is truly unbelievable," Herr Geek declared. His rural

accent struck Ernie again. The thin lips stretched like leather thongs opened on a blackish mouth, and the words that escaped them were as if carved from some hard material, from wood— and brutally, by a machete. Ernie thought that neither the lips nor the teeth nor the shrubbery that served him for eyebrows nor the curious lawn of mustache nor the bumpy, rutted relief of wrinkles nor even, finally, the eyes, stagnant amid all that, like two shallow puddles of gray water—nothing of Herr Geek marked a teacher. One would have said, rather, a peasant come to barter in the church square, whose expression, depending on his mood, might be watery or earthy or cold, crushing, stony.

Suddenly Herr Geek's face tightened altogether, some eddy blurred his expression while his mouth twisted to form a hole at the right side of his nose. A thin stream of trembling, icy voice trickled out of the hole. "I thought—yes—they told me there were Jews in this class." And gesturing briefly at all the arms raised in the Hitlerite salute, "But I see only brave Germans who adore their Führer. Right, my boys?"

The triumphant laugh shook the ranks of Pimpfe in brown shirts. Hans Schliemann applauded enthusiastically. Herr Geek muttered in satisfaction, turned his glance toward Hans Schliemann and seemed to reflect for a moment. Then, spreading his enormous, blackish hand on the edge of the desk, he stepped calmly off the platform. At each step half his body sagged heavily to one side. His gait was that of a man carrying a burden. Ernie noted that he seemed to tap the ground with his foot first and then to place the full weight of his body upon it before swinging the other leg forward. But his left shoulder sloped lower than his right.

When Herr Geek had reached Hans Schliemann, he stood still and looked sympathetically at the boy's uniform. "There are only three Hitler Youth in this class?" he asked in a tone of pained astonishment. And then, as Hans Schliemann came to attention, he went on in a voice informed by severity, "The Hitler Youth must set an example of discipline." And without changing his benevolent expression, he slapped Hans Schlie-

mann twice. The second slap drove the child's head against his
desk and knocked him under his chair. Ernie was surprised to
hear him shouting enthusiastically, "Yes, Herr Professor! Yes,
Herr Professor!"

"That's what I like," Mr. Geek declared suddenly.

In his heavy, slow step, his fat hands swinging against his
thighs, he walked peacefully back to his desk. When he was on
the platform again, he stiffened his neck, and taking up the
pointer, he thrust it forward in a gesture of command. "And
now," he cried in a raging tone, *"die Hunde, die Neger und
die Juden, austreten!* Dogs, Negroes and Jews, step forward!"

For a moment Ernie Levy attributed those words to Herr
Geek's incomprehensible sense of humor, but when the students did not laugh as the teacher stared furiously at Ernie's
dark curls, the boy understood that the phrase was directed
solely at the Jews. Immediately, he slipped to the side to take
up his position as a Jew in the center of the aisle. Behind him,
fat Simon Kotkowski was already sniffling.

"Jews!" Herr Geek cried. "When I give an order to the class
in general, it means that I am addressing myself to the German
students and not to their guests."

Rigid in his military posture, only his lower jaw moving, Herr
Geek launched a confused, menacing diatribe at the "Jewish
guests." These last, among others, were to know that Herr Geek
would always find a way to make himself understood when he
wished to address himself to them—for example, by beginning
the phrase with the name of an animal.

When the guests, at the order of the master of the house, had
retired to the last row in the classroom (isolated from the pure
Aryans by a row of empty desks), Herr Geek relaxed and
loosed a vast sigh of relief, answered by a vast burst of laughter
from the Pimpfe. Finally, solemn again, he directed the rude
language of truth to the German students—they had all been
Jewified by their former professor, so all of them were to some
degree suspect. He personally judged that Herr Kremer had
some drops of Jewish blood in his veins, "or somewhere else,"
for a thoroughbred German would never have committed him-

self to such repugnant promiscuity. The hour of the Jews had struck—it was a funeral bell. The hour of authentic and pure Germans was beginning to sound in the heavens, and it was a victory bell, rung by him to whom we owe everything—Adolf Hitler. Finally, the students were not here *to play at learning* but to prepare the true grandeur of the Fatherland, for a day would come when the pen, transformed into a sword . . .

Here Herr Geek stopped suddenly. In the first row it was noticed that the new teacher's face was pale. "Uh . . . on that day"—he continued with an effort—"you will all be men!"

Then a thin smile brushed his lips and a sudden gleam appeared in his small white eyes. "Hey, fat boy, back there," he called brutally, his arm stretched toward the back of the room. "Yes, you, what's your name?"

"Simon Kotkowski, sir," answered a fearful voice.

Herr Geek's sparkling steel ruler described a slashing orbit in space, finishing at the precise point where he wished to see the Jew take his position. "The Jew Simon Kotkowski, right here!"

Placid, resigned, huddled in his cheerful fat, the amiable Simon Kotkowski approached the blackboard. The singularly Jewish shape of his nose had struck Herr Geek, who made it the subject of his first lesson. But sarcasms and comparisons, "typological" analyses and "biopolitical" commentaries seemed to bounce off Simon Kotkowski's elastic epidermis, lending a clear, lively pink tone to his expression.

"Jew," Herr Geek murmured, "you and your people, you're fighting for the domination of the universe, right?"

"I don't know, sir," the accused answered straightforwardly.

His arms crossed, his paunch cheerful, the hair frizzy on his low forehead, he presented a picture of the most total incomprehension. The bridge of his nose, like a carp's (like a vulture's beak, Herr Geek had said), rose and fell hesitantly. He seemed much intrigued.

"Do you hear?" Herr Geek said softly. "He says that he doesn't know. . . ." And leaning toward the child as if to underline the confidential character of the interview, "Jew, Jew," he exhaled, "isn't Germany your mortal enemy?"

"No . . . no . . ."

"Jew, little Jew of my heart, how can I believe you, will you tell me?"

"It's true, sir," Simon answered, terrified.

"The strength of the Jews," Herr Geek went on without seeming to have heard him, "do you mean to say that it no longer lies in the suppleness of their spinal column?"

At that, Simon Kotkowski remained silent and Herr Geek took on an expression of extreme solemnity. In a voice that all the students guessed was broken by emotion, "Jew. Ah, little Jew, you who are still a child—tell us what fate you have reserved for us if"—here the tone of Herr Geek's voice thinned in terror—"if—ah, my God!—if we should emerge defeated from this fight to the death? *Von der Totenschlacht?* What will you do to us?"

And the Jewish child, fascinated, caught in the play of collective fear swirling about his person, the titanic struggle of the Jews and the poor Germans finishing as a sketch upon his eyeballs—Simon answered, with frightened good will, "We won't do anything to you, Herr Professor, we won't do anything to you. . . ."

Geek would have loved to take that incorrigible peon of a Kremer and cleave him in two before the whole class. A noncommissioned officer in the Imperial Army, recently promoted to the position of shock-instructor, Geek saw the purification of the class as a work worthy of the former leader of a mopping-up squad. From eight to ten in the morning he offered brilliant solutions to all pending problems, but the question of singing proved to be infinitely more delicate. . . .

Judging that the Jews would inevitably sing off key, he decided that they would not sing at all, "except," he added, "if they feel an irresistible urge. In that case, since cats meow, since dogs bark, and since pigs grunt, why shouldn't the Jews sing?"

That query split the class in two with the precision of a razor —those who laughed, and the Jews. But soon the teacher noticed that the Jews were not singing, that the Aryan pupils were, and that the result was a ridiculous double injustice. Four flat zeros in the record book did not console him for it, nor four seated interrogations, nor four kneeling punishments, lined up along the blackboard. The fact was unchallengeable—they were not singing.

The students launched the march of the Pimpfe, "Strike, pierce and kill"—the girls soprano, and the boys tenor in order to accelerate their change of voice—when the solution appeared to Herr Geek, simple, clear and natural.

"Halt!" he commanded, his arms scissoring the air. The chorus broke off cleanly.

Then Herr Geek, smiling: "It seems, my friends, that our guests are taking life a bit too easy. While you sing, what do they do? They listen tranquilly. They think themselves at a concert." Herr Geek was unable to resist pursing his lips at his little joke, and several students laughed boisterously. And yet he had to follow up on that felicitous phrase. Herr Geek wiped his eyes slowly, blew his nose into a handkerchief, took in a great breath and, thwarted, realized that the rest of his discourse was being awaited.

There was a considerable pause.

Twisting their heads in his direction, the four Jews themselves seemed crushed by the silence flowing from his lips, still half open, like lava immediately frozen into heavy, soft sheets on his face. And yet the suddenness of his attack surprised them. "Let the Jews sing," he growled, purple with indignation. "Let them give us a serenade!"

At which there was a new pause, but this was the pause of victory, the silence of the great German eagle, wings spread majestically, and already all were applauding but the Jews. . . .

* * *

Simon Kotkowski stood up, shook a cramped ankle and then stepped forward miserably to stand before the instructional pulpit. As soon as he had received the order, he rounded his mouth to a heart shape and with great good nature broke into the celebrated lament "There is no more beautiful death on earth," dedicated to the memory of the hero Horst Wessel. His eyes upon heaven and his pudgy hands lying delicately on his paunch, he had barely whispered "Unfurl the blood-soaked flag" when an atrocious laugh swept the class, sparing none of them, not even the three Jewish souls still on their knees.

The terrible interpreter serenely launched the second verse, "Arise! That which God made German . . ." Herr Geek suddenly leaned across the lectern, screaming in Simon's ear to stop him, and striking him with the pointer to make his meaning clear. Himself in the grip of a nervous twitch, the teacher seemed highly shocked by such an interpretation, which was not a Jew's and yet not a German's. Simon Kotkowski went back to the blackboard, and immediately seeking the ideal position let himself fall backward, so as to rest his buttocks on his heels, then clasped his hands below his chubby abdomen as if to support himself better in his trial.

At a curt gesture, Moses Finkelstein rose with a fully submissive air. He stepped forward, repressing a birdlike hiccup. When he had arrived before the large lectern, a tear rolled from under his glasses, a tear of shame, of suppressed hilarity and of terror. No one really knew Moses Finkelstein—his father had abandoned his mother, who did housekeeping and breathed through the nostrils of her son, which is to say barely at all. Placing his hands flat against his chest in a vague gesture of defense, he broke into singsong in a sighing, nasal voice, almost a murmur. He was then sent back to his knees, broken, fearful, licking at his tears, tasting the dregs of shame.

"I don't want to sing," Marcus Rosenberg then said.

Standing, his back against the blackboard, he swaggered defiantly.

"Who is forcing you to sing?" Geek answered coldly.

Rather tall, with the thin, prominent neck of a young stag,

Marcus Rosenberg could not bear humiliation. Often in the evening the Pimpfe organized a pack to bring him to earth. The scars all over his face announced the score of old defeats.

"No, I won't sing," he went on in a voice choked by his own surprise.

And as Geek limped heavily toward him, bending his adult back in order to bring his soothing gaze better to bear on Marcus Rosenberg's eyes, the latter retreated against the blackboard, which stopped him.

"But who is forcing you to sing, my friend?" Herr Geek repeated in a smooth, insinuating voice. "Where I come from people only sing for pleasure. Ask Moses Finkelstein . . ." Then, taking him from behind, Geek threw the Jewish child to his knees, twisting his wrist in a hammer lock.

The aptness of the conception and the great good taste of his execution enchanted the Pimpfe, who applauded in silence.

"So it's that way? We have our pride?" Geek murmured affectionately, and he increased the pressure to force the child to groan. "But the pride of the Jew is made to be broken. And this is how," he added, and Marcus Rosenberg released a wail within himself without opening his tightened lips.

Geek's voice was syrupy sweet. "Come now, come now—*'wenn Judenblut'*, when Jewish blood . . . ? When Jewish blood . . . ?" At the end of five minutes, Marcus's lips were opening imperceptibly. When his mouth was wide open, a sudden drowned scream of music escaped it. The proof of Jewish ignominy was achieved. Herr Geek breathed delightedly, and flinging the child to the floor, he said, "Filth!"

And noticing a livid Ernie—"And that one, I almost forgot him."

Marcus Rosenberg stayed as he was—his face to the floor, hands over his skull, mute. The Pimpfe were rejoicing that his pride had been broken.

Two tears hung on Ernie's lashes. He managed nevertheless to make out his friend Ilse in the first row; her face, frozen in stony attention, implored him to sing.

"And when will this imbecile deign to begin?"

The child turned toward the teacher's desk, a thin wrinkle between his brows, his nose pink with grief. "Excuse me, sir," he stammered, rolling his eyes wildly. "I don't know yet if I ought to . . . oh . . ." Then he brought an arm behind his back, offering himself without resistance to the extraordinary hold of the teacher. The class was silent. Intrigued, the pupils in the first row took in the snatches of speech escaping Ernie Levy's lips: "I don't know. . . . I don't know. . . ."

Geek suspected a trap. He advanced one hand cautiously, guarding his face with the other, but when the child did not stir, he grabbed his wrist quickly and twisted it with such vigor that the boy gave a brief fishlike jump before falling back to his knees, imprisoned.

"You still don't know?"

But Ernie had taken his final stand right there. While Herr Geek went on with the cruel lesson, while the Aryans appreciated its clarity and the Jews its rigor, Ernie Levy was gliding at the height of a dove, crowned by the faces he would not assassinate in song—Mother Judith, the patriarch, Papa, Mama, Moritz and the little ones.

· 4 ·

HERR GEEK'S comments bluntly confirmed the fact that Ernie had not sung.

But when the cruel excitement of the moment had passed, an immense majority of the students secretly refused to admit that he had not *wished* to sing, so that it was impossible to go on seeing an offense in Ernie's silence, and even more impossible to see a personal triumph or—as Geek had complained —the triumph of Jews in general. According to that secret majority, neither defeat nor victory was possible for the idiot. They felt that he had no wish to conquer anyone, and not being engaged in any combat, he could not undergo any defeat comparable to Marcus Rosenberg's. And yet deep within themselves that secret majority felt a hate for "the idiot" all the more lively in that it found no nourishment in his silence. The hatred of Marcus was a response to his permanent defiance, and Marcus vanquished inspired nothing more than the scorn he had wished to escape. But Ernie's silence had none of these motives, and several children suspected that he would willingly have sung if he had *been able to*. From then on their hatred of Ernie Levy was immeasurable, for it was aimed at the very gentleness that emanated from his person and that each of the children felt within himself, confusedly, buried like a taproot.

The Jews remained on their knees until the last Aryan had left, so that each might admire them in passing and express that admiration by word and deed. But there was not a glance for Ernie; the students turned away as they brushed by, as if they had been exposed to a subtle danger. Ilse could not help glancing sidewise at him. Surprised, she saw only a tangle of disheveled hair, for Ernie was staring at the floor, not in fear, but ashamed and grieving to have been irremediably separated from both the Aryans and the Jews.

The children dispersed with all the bustle and grace of a flight of sparrows. No group was formed to speed the departing Jews on their way. The Pimpfe themselves looked at the cripples joylessly. Simon Kotkowski swore never to come back to school—even if his father had to suffer harshly for that infraction of the law. Marcus Rosenberg sharpened an absolute revenge. Moses Finkelstein ran home. And with dragging steps, intoxicated by the afternoon sun, Ernie Levy went to meet his friend Ilse, who was waiting for him, as she did every day, beside the Schlosse, beyond the great block of houses, her blond hair sparkling in the sun. That day when he saw the beloved figure, the pain in his shoulder blinded him suddenly and tears leaped to his eyes. Ilse was standing in the middle of the street not far from the riverbank, motionless, her head set like a pretty apple above her black smock. Without the aching shoulder and the tears and that interminable approach over which each step increased his feeling of aloneness, he would doubtless never even have dreamed of kissing Ilse Bruckner on the cheek. He would doubtless not have dared. But had he only dreamed it? It seemed to him as he approached that Ilse shared his solitude and was offering her cheek, and he could not have said if he had kissed it before she offered it or if, on the contrary, Ilse had initiated that kiss—it all happened as if the two things were only one.

"You pig!" was the first shout from Hans Schliemann, camouflaged in the shrubbery on the bank. At that signal Hans's "men," surging out of the nearby houses or springing up from the reeds of the Schlosse, disclosed the ambush.

Ilse's eyes, gentle, blue, green, yellow, shone peacefully at him.

"Run!" Ernie cried, surrounded by the Pimpfe, smacked in the face, dragged against the naked wall of an apartment building. And as he worried about Ilse, he glimpsed her for a brief instant still in the middle of the street, in the sunlight, her arms hanging against her short pleated skirt, observing it all with a curious eye.

He heard a sharp voice, felt a tickling breath against the back of his neck. "That's the second time today he's sullied the honor of Germany," the voice announced in an extraordinarily solemn tone.

Yet Ernie felt that Hans Schliemann's voice was hollow, as empty as the display dumbbells the hardware man's children played with, the ones they lifted contorting themselves and turning red in a thousand imaginary tortures. So he decided that Hans Schliemann's voice merited a secret smile.

"Pig!" a Pimpf belched against Ernie's face. "I bet you've already kissed her on the mouth!"

"And maybe rubbed a titty or two!"

"Or stuck his hand in the little basket!"

Trembling in anger, the invisible voice of Hans Schliemann echoed against Ernie's neck. "Or maybe this little pig has already 'knocked her off'?"

Falling to his knees, Ernie felt the pain in his shoulder more acutely than ever. He was beaten without a fight by a single twist from Hans Schliemann.

The pain in his shoulder became sharper. Moisture blurred his eyes, then his forehead too was moist, and the little boy imagined confusedly (as the fire in his shoulder raged hotter) that all that abundant liquid leaking from his eyes and his skull, his neck and his trunk, and congealing in his throat, filtering through his lips drawn back by the mechanical pressure of his jaws and teeth, at the breaking point—the child imagined that all the liquid in his body was leaking away, fleeing the white-hot bar of his right shoulder.

"Schweinhund!" Hans Schliemann shouted, almost out of breath. "Have you decided to sing yet?"

Drunk on indignation, Hans Schliemann could only repeat incessantly, *"Hund,* dog, dog, dog," while the other Pimpfe spat in Ernie's face, stooping each in turn, bringing their rounded mouths to within an inch of him, spewing phlegm at him. His eyes closed, the little boy imagined that the sweat, the saliva, the tears and the phlegm in which he was bathing were simply one and the same substance, welling up from some spring deep within his being, splitting its envelope now and flowing in the sunlight. All those liquids emanated from his own interior substance, blue-green, shadowy, viscous, not composed normally of flesh and bone, as he had once thought. . . .

Time now seemed to him a bottomless sea.

Strangely, the floodgates opened and all the waters disappeared.

Opening his eyes, Ernie found himself kneeling on the hard, dry sidewalk. Some distance away, the Pimpfe were in a huddle. They seemed to be arguing a serious point, but Ernie was more aware of their expressions, concentrated and discouraged, than of the mysterious words they were exchanging, glaring at him sidewise from time to time. Between Wolfgang Oelendorff's solidly bowed legs Ernie discovered with delight the placid figure of his friend Ilse Bruckner, who seemed to be frozen in the same spot. Soon she directed her smooth, blue-

green gaze between Oelendorff's legs, apparently without seeing Ernie, although her delicate features had contracted for a
second, he thought he noticed, when their eyes met briefly.

"That Jew there," the redhead said, "he looks more Jewish
than the others to me."

"I think we ought to strip him in front of Bruckner," Wolfgang Oelendorff said. "I hear their pricks are trimmed."

"No, no, not that!" the terrified redhead cried.

"Why not?" Hans Schliemann inquired calmly. *"We can
pull the Devil by his tail."*

The group burst into strained laughter, every head turning
toward Ilse, who seemed to have heard nothing—though her
cheeks had colored—and whose eyes were taking on the light
opacity of blind eyes, though she still stared in the direction of
the boys, alternately at the Pimpfe, now silent, and at Ernie,
still on his knees, accepting the caress of the sun between
Wolfgang's legs. The heat comforted his shoulder.

All these things seen and heard seemed so unnatural that
Ernie Levy believed the sun was approaching him, spinning
on its axis like a wheel of fireworks only a few inches from his
half-closed eyes. Yet a part of him was aware of the threat.
Half rising, he propped himself sidewise against the wall of the
house and opened his eyes still clogged by the sun, tears, the
sweat running down his forehead, saliva and phlegm. Truly
all these things were without precedent, and slowly becoming
aware of the words spoken, the little boy took his eyes off Ilse
Bruckner in vexation; she was still motionless in her black
smock, and her face had become a pair of huge green eyes.

The Pimpfe surrounded him in silence. The little boy did
not budge, staring at the spinning disc of the sun. These events
concerned someone else. Nothing like them had ever happened to anyone. There was not the slightest allusion to any
such phantasmagoria in the Legend of the Just Men. Desperately tense, Ernie searched his memories, hoping to find a
clear path, a road to help him through that forest of strange circumstances, which did not seem entirely real though they bore
a certain appearance of reality. . . . He found no road.

Hans Schliemann's arms bound him nonchalantly. Hans proceeded as if he had Ernie's complete agreement. The latter moved an elbow out of the way, allowing Hans to take a firm grip comfortably.

The redhead knelt and undid Ernie's suspenders.

Ernie Levy lowered his eyes and saw a head of red hair at the height of his belly.

With a sharp jerk, the redhead pulled Ernie's pants halfway down his thighs. Ernie noticed that his own legs were shaking violently, and as the redhead slipped two fingers between the skin and the elastic of the underwear, the little boy freed himself from Hans Schliemann's embrace in one jerk and raised his hands as high as he could. They fluttered in the air, up against the wheel of the sun, as if he did not know what to do with them and wished simply to testify to his own impotence.

Disturbed, the Pimpfe looked at those naked hands fluttering in the sunlight. But the redhead got back into the spirit of things immediately and pulled down the underwear, uncovering Ernie's sex, and it was at that moment that the beast a-borning rose to the little boy's throat, and he howled for the first time. He had already dropped to the redhead's feet, digging his teeth into the flesh of a calf and keeping them there. A flux of saliva rose to his mouth; his nails dug into the redhead's ankles.

Immediately Hans Schliemann set his knee against Ernie Levy's back and pulled the little boy backward violently, his hands reversed and his thumbs dug into the boy's eyes. Ernie let go, screamed again and hung by his teeth from one of Hans Schliemann's hands. Hans freed himself only after dragging the child for ten feet along the sidewalk. Hans Schliemann took a few steps more, as if he wanted to lengthen the distance between his hands and Ernie Levy's mouth. Then changing his mind, he saw that all the Pimpfe had suffered the same reflex and were on the defensive now, in a compact group, out of reach of Ernie Levy's teeth. Ernie had risen quickly to his feet and was standing, his back to the wall, facing them and growling in his throat like a dog while the tears sprang from his eyes like so many tiny, sharp knives.

"Dog shit," said the redhead.

"Jewish shit," said a Pimpf.

"Jewish dog," Hans Schliemann went on without conviction, and as he drew closer, he added in a forced tone, "Be careful, he may have rabies." The Pimpfe spread out even more, but smiling to show that they did not take the remark seriously. They could not let Ernie Levy off, and yet no one felt like breaking the evil Jewish spell they had just witnessed. Hans Schliemann's little joke seemed to offer a way out.

"We'll take him to the furrier's," a Pimpf said. "He'll take him off our hands."

"How do they slaughter them?" a Pimpf asked.

"They give them injections," Hans Schliemann said, "and they die with their mouths open."

"Where do they do it?" a Pimpf laughed. "In the ass?"

"That depends," Hans answered in the manner of an expert, "that depends. . . . With Jewish dogs, they say it's in the prick."

And as if they had been waiting for that signal, the Pimpfe roared with laughter, shoving each other enthusiastically, slapping their thighs in such an excess of hilarity that they were suddenly conscious of evading the principal question and fell silent again. The redhead picked up a stone and threw it at Ernie Levy; several others followed him. In their anger, they aimed badly. Soon Hans Schliemann gave the signal to disperse.

"You coming?" he asked Ilse.

"You in a hurry?" she said dryly.

"You looking after your sweetie? Watch out, he's crazy."

"I'm not afraid of him," Ilse Bruckner said.

Turning toward Hans, she winked conspiratorially and whispered, "Go on, I'll catch up with you right away."

"At the corner by the school?" Hans asked.

And at her nod, he glanced strangely at her and turned his back slowly. Soon the gang reached the end of the street. A song rose in the distance. Their voices were fresh and cheerful.

* * *

The tears had dried. Slowly the spinning sun slipped back into its natural orbit. Finally it ceased spinning and was still, infinitely far away, like a candle in an enormous room. In the meadows a blackbird took up its song, and the Schlosse lapped among the reeds. Ernie noticed that his friend Ilse had not moved away. Her shoes had buttons instead of laces. She was wearing her pretty black smock, and her notebooks were on the ground, propped between her ankles. Ernie noticed that her moist eyes and all the glossiness in her hair and face gave her the look of a fish. At the school masquerade she had worn a long dress; she made it undulate like the tail of a little Chinese fish. There had also been many pretty things adorning her face and hands, with their marvelously pink fingers, but no one knew what all those things meant, no one knew what to call them. Ernie smiled at her in delight; her eyes were dilated in fascination and in a curiosity greater than herself. Abruptly all the green sparkle left her expression, the shadow of a smile passed fleetingly, raised her lip, reached a dimple, faded, disappeared. Now the little girl was staring at him from far off, as if at a stranger to be scorned and feared. Ernie started forward; she paled, stooped, picked up her notebooks and fled like a graceful arrow in the track of the Pimpfe; twenty yards away she turned and applauded three times. The sun was so low that her silhouette, made sharper by her black smock, was like a sparkling insect in the path of its rays. And then there was nothing.

The sun began to spin again, faster and faster. Sparks leaped from the flaming wheel, shooting through the sky in multicolored spangles. Blond hairs too shot away. Ernie pulled up his pants. The beast in his heart was roaring so horribly that he was afraid he would die on the spot. As he mentally dug his teeth into the Pimpfe, he understood that he was feeling hate for the first time.

· 5 ·

WHEN HE reached the bridge over the Schlosse, Ernie turned and saw that he was alone.

Quite small, chipped, humped, the stone bridge crossed the Schlosse with the rustic good nature of an old peasant. Tendrils of ivy gave it a flowered beard straggling down as far as the water. Now and then Ilse and Ernie had leaned upon it to watch time pass interminably between the banks. Carp and gudgeon followed the trail of the hours, and Ilse claimed that all fish disappeared into the sea—otherwise where would they go? Ernie never contradicted her, though he knew that certain delicate species—the bleaks, for example—stopped just at the border, at the frontier between fresh and salt water.

Today the Schlosse seemed frozen in its bed and the water as transparent and empty as air.

The little boy crossed the bridge and took the path that dropped to the river's edge to the left of the parapet, among the brambles, nettles and soft green tufts of grass on the bank, and the bouquets of yellow flowers blooming in the shadow of the reeds. Halfway down, the pass curved around the famous Rock of Woden, the Germanic god of war, of storm, of lords and kings. The boulder thrust upward from the bank ten or twelve feet high, like a cliff. Once, during the time of the republic, it was said that workingmen had dived from its summit every Sunday in summertime. It seemed so profoundly rooted in the earth that it was impossible to imagine it alone, isolated, reduced to itself like a simple huge stone; it was a granite tree, the stump of an oak, one might have said, still living with all its roots, decapitated but indestructible. Yet Herr Kremer had been positive: the ancestors of the Gentiles had brought it from the mountains, trimmed and chiseled it where it was, and used it as a slaughtering table where the throats of beasts and men were cut. The blood ran off into the Schlosse, which carried it as far as Taunus, where the witches of the Brocken came on Walpurgis Night and lapped it up—it was a *sacrificial altar.* . . . Some nights the Pimpfe and the adult members of the party burned tree trunks on it. People in the Riggenstrasse no longer said "the Stone" but "Woden's Rock"—with much respect. A professor from Berlin had found a swastika under the moss. The newspapers insisted that it was several thousand years old, and Ernie's father, shrewdly, that it was barely the age of a child in the cradle.

Ernie Levy stretched forth his arm and touched the rock with his index finger prudently, as if it were a sleeping animal. Then he went on down the slope and walked off ten yards or so in the late sunlight, out of reach of the fantastic shadow cast by the boulder. The rows of reeds thinned out along a tiny sandy beach. Ernie Levy dropped to one knee and noticed that the shadow of the rock extended onto the surface of the Schlosse, carried along by the movement of the water so that threads of shadow were cast up on the beach. With one knee dug into the sand, he leaned gently to the left so that the two shadows, his and the rock's, became one. Leaning over the liquid shadow, from which muddy bubbles rose, he spread out his handkerchief like a raft. It drifted for a few seconds and then sank.

The ripples swirled. Ernie Levy wrung out his handkerchief slowly and proceeded to wipe off his forehead.

The slashing metal ruler had opened a gash; its lips were caked with dried blood. Ernie Levy swabbed it out with his handkerchief and then covered it with a nettle leaf. The wound seemed absolutely painless. Running his fingers over his skull, he noted with surprise that it was covered with swollen bumps. Yet he felt none of those bumps, nor even his jaw, simply numbed by Herr Geek's fist. If he was not suffering, it was because he would never again suffer; it was because the organs of suffering were abolished in him. Out of curiosity he bit into his palm, a deep bite that left toothmarks. In one of the depressions was a drop of blood, which caused him no perceptible pain. He could admire it as something pretty. "But the

Just Men suffer," Ernie Levy murmured suddenly.

He cupped his hands and dipped up a little water with which he softened the blood dried on his face and on his naked chest. Then he scrubbed it with the wet handkerchief, rinsing it out afterward. The joint shadow of his body and the rock kept him from seeing the water redden; the tint was drowned quickly in the current. He rose and wiped off his sandy knee. Absolutely nothing stirred within him.

It was shortly afterward that Ernie had his first intuition of emptiness. Not wanting to go back along Woden's Trail, he pushed his way through the nettles on the bank, and from the height of the slope he contemplated the meadows for a moment before setting out across them calmly, in a ceremonious tread. . . . Some of the grass rose higher than his chin; the farther he pushed into the green, stagnant, infinitely divisible water of the meadow, the more it seemed to him that the waves of grass were rising about him as if they intended to drown him, or at least to imprison him by closing about him instantly, obliterating the wake of his random steps. He could not have said if the advancing waves were swelling to drown him or if, on the contrary, he was plunging step by step into that sea like someone deliberately abandoning the shore.

When the shore seemed far enough away, he stopped and saw by the immensity of the sky that Ernie Levy was a mote lost in the grass. At that moment he experienced emptiness, as if the earth had split beneath his feet, and while his eyes rejoiced in the immensity of the heavens, these words came sweetly to his lips: "I am nothing." The earth around him gave off its odors. All things were fixed, enveloped in the smells of the earth. The silence had that smell, and the exhalations of the sun, and the immutable blue of the sky. A grain of dust struck his cheek and stuck to it; he took it between index finger and thumb and submitted it to examination. It was a red ladybug dotted with black, its legs vibrating like tiny hairs. It might have been a jewel, a pinhead cut out of a ruby with tiny black dots inked in. With infinite gentleness, Ernie Levy set the ladybug on the end of his vertical thumb:

Ladybug, ladybug, fly away home,
Your house is on fire, your children will burn.
One,
Two,
Three!

The childhood tradition demanded that when the word
"three" was pronounced, one blew on the ladybug from behind.
The little boy had rounded his lips, but changing his mind
suddenly, he raised his index finger and squeezed it violently
against his thumb. The insect's pulp crackled between his
fingers. Ernie rolled the pulp into a soft, thin twist. Then, with
a circular movement of his index finger, he transformed the
ladybug into a tiny ball, the consistency of a bread crumb. It
seemed to him that all the emptiness in his heart was there,
pinched between those two fingers. But that was not enough:
setting this atom of matter in the hollow of his hand, he rubbed
it between his palms at great length until the ladybug was
annihilated, leaving only a grayish stain.

Then, raising his head, he realized that the silence had just
died.

The meadow was alive with the rustling of wings, with the
movement of grass, with that invisible, heavy quivering of life.
The earth itself was seething defiantly. Ernie Levy noticed first
a fragile grasshopper, perched on a sod, twitching its legs
gently in a ray of sunlight. He leaned forward cautiously but
the grasshopper seemed not at all upset by the menace, and
the child saw that its mandibles recalled the industrious
nibbling of a rabbit—even better, the alert tightening of an
old woman's jaws. With that thought he shot a hand forward
and caught what he could; the insect found himself imprisoned by a paw, between the palm and the index finger.
Ernie Levy bent his thumb and crushed the grasshopper against
his palm. Then he made a ball of it, a greenish color, abundant
this time, which stained his fingers altogether.

The next victim proved to be a butterfly. . . . Rare are
those who appreciate the butterfly at its true value. What

generally lowers the butterfly in the eyes of the profane was for Ernie another reason to respect it—that it was born of the caterpillar and that its beauty was as dust. . . . Balthazar Klotz collected butterflies. He ran through the fields tilting the lance of his net, anesthetized the victim with a flagon of ether, executed it at home, in his own good time, with a pin driven through the geometric heart of the thorax. Balthazar Klotz's room was covered with fragile trophies. Examined with a magnifying glass, each of them proved to be a cathedral, and the beauty of the wings gave them a lifelike character, the illusion of being not yet dead. Ernie would have liked to hunt butterflies for pleasure, the pleasure of seeing them, but even if they were released it cost them a broken wing, a golden antenna forever extinguished, a radiance forever dead. So he settled for a silent approach to the wonder, stalking it cleverly, like an Indian, then contemplating it at leisure. He was rigid as stone; some of the butterflies fluttered about him, settling on his head or on a finger, like a ring—marvelous.

The martyr was a tiger swallowtail with wings like stained glass. The popular name swallowtail derives from the hind points of its wings, half an inch long—the immensity of its wingspread gives it the noble flight of a bird of prey.

The swallowtail landed on a violet. Ernie Levy enveloped the flower and the insect in his still moist handkerchief, and slipping a hand beneath it, he snatched at both things together, the butterfly and the violet, and then kneaded them between his already sticky palms. After the swallowtail came a dragonfly, a giant cricket, a beetle, a small butterfly with pearly-blue wings, other butterflies, other dragonflies, other grasshoppers. Ernie Levy ran through the meadow, arms spread wide, flapping his hands, gummy with vermin. . . .

Still, he was tired. Each insect death cost him more. Each death added its cortege of soft ordure, and now they were filling his stomach—viscid liquors on his palms but dismembered insects, seething and suffering, in his own belly. His heart heavy with these things, he stretched out and closed his eyes, his hands flat against the grass. His belly seemed to sprawl in all directions. In the imperfect night of his eyelids, its victims growled and swarmed. Profiting by the darkness, the thousand chitterings of the outside world entered his ears, flowing insidiously into that pouch where the butterflies and other insects were still suffering. His flattened hands were dead.

Ernie raised his eyelids and drowned in the fallen sky.

Soon the high grass formed a frame in the middle of which birds were gliding. The sky was swollen with them.

He tried to follow a bird with his eyes, hoping to reach it and to fly off with it. But the birds maneuvered scornfully, indifferent to his gaze, and the distance between him and them did not diminish. How could he have pretended to those heights, to the even greater heights of the Just Man—he, a puny, rapacious insect; he, crawling on a heavy, enormous belly swarming with its insect nourishment . . . ? *I was not a Just Man, I was nothing.*

As he thought, "I was nothing," the little boy buried his face against the earth and intoned his first cries. At the same instant he felt astonishment that his eyes should be empty of tears. For half an hour he cried out, his mouth against the earth. He seemed to be hailing someone far off, a being buried deep in the earth from whom he wanted only an echo. But his cries only exaggerated the silence, and the vermin remained lively in his belly. His mouth was full of grass and dirt. Finally he knew that nothing would answer his call, for that call was born of nothing: God could not hear it. It was precisely here that Ernie Levy, the little boy, felt burdened by his body and decided to let that burden fall.

In a heavy, slow step, shuffling through the grass, he went back to the riverside to perform his funeral ablutions. The song of nature no longer disturbed him, and crossing through the grass his only battle was against Ilse's face. With no emotion whatever he walked by Woden's Rock. The mixture of insects was so adhesive that he had to fall back on sand to clean it from his hands, his fingers, his fingernails darkened by a greenish ring. A head was stuck to the sleeve of his smock. Examining it carefully, he recognized the saltlike eyes and the noble antennae of the swallowtail. "You too," he thought, "God has taken you between his hands." When the water was still, he leaned over it to see his own reflection. A few lines were visible, shimmering, but as his features became clear in the mirror, two drops fell from his eyelids, spreading concentric ripples over his face, which disappeared. "My tears fall *all by themselves,*" Ernie Levy decided, "but I am not weeping." And when his legs trembled beneath him after he had crossed the bridge and was on the road to town, "My legs are trembling, but I am not afraid."

He barely recognized the Riggenstrasse. It was a street, and its living creatures all walked on two feet. The people (certain people, particularly women) stopped to watch him pass, but he did not look at their faces. In the same fashion, as he entered the house by the door on the courtyard he barely addressed a thought to the creatures from whom, through the veil of the corridor leading to the kitchen, he heard only the taut, volatile filaments of human speech. His separation from the members of the Levy family—the kernel of his dead universe—was so complete that he never even dreamed of saying goodbye: Far, far away were all farewells.

And yet as he went up the stairs his legs trembled so shamefully that he clutched the railing, repeating half aloud, "Who would dare to say that you're afraid? Who would dare to say that you're afraid?"

But facing him already, like a living danger, was the heavy iron-barred door to the attic.

The hinges squeaked. Ernie feared that their bitter lament would reach the kitchen along the treacherous path of the partitions. When he pushed open the worm-eaten door, the pressure of the darkness forced him backward a step, bringing his feet together back on the landing. Then his body trembled in a vague movement of retreat, for the darkness, suddenly fluid, was advancing toward him like a tidal wave. Finally the gray and black of the attic resolved into a middling dimness compounded of the ambiguous light from the landing and the night, which was gathering slowly now, revealing the skylight, from which a thin rope hung, supporting an entirely naked celluloid doll by the neck, two or three feet above the floor. (It was a game; Moritz and his friends had hanged it by the neck until dead. The doll was Adolf Hitler, thanks to two smears of black crayon beneath the nostrils. Nevertheless Ernie thought that there was something of Ilse's face in it, and felt a distant satisfaction, like the caress of a breeze within him.)

Then he made out the rows of curved tiles on the lower roof, their crests gleaming like so many black teeth; made out the rubble, the pieces of string, the broken chairs, the old dining-room table (too small since the birth of Ernie's sisters and brothers), the Teddy bear, decapitated, the shallow pan full of dishes reserved for Passover. Then he made out the whole attic, and he stepped forward to set a chair beneath the sky-light. . . .

At that moment a halo became visible in the center of the window, and the place was invaded by a lightlike dust, yellow, tepid, flowing into his throat, irritating it. The little boy took the chair squarely by its back, and raising it he had the feeling that it had come to life at his touch: One of the thing's feet had just struck his knee. Climbing up on it hesitantly, Ernie stood at his full height and managed to raise the skylight until it locked open. Then, gripping the edge of the frame, he attempted a classic pull-up—which means that the athlete raises his body purely by the strength of his wrists; that he takes a firm grip with both hands on the obstacle to be surmounted, and with a simple pull of his forearms consolidates his position gracefully, swinging a knee high enough to catch hold. Although Ernie hardly believed himself made for such physical triumphs, it seemed reasonable and just to him that today his body, because of the altogether exceptional circumstances, would submit naïvely to his will. But as soon as he was hanging by his hands the frame of the skylight slammed down on his fingers.

Pinched to the ceiling, his legs kicking aimlessly, he was happy enough to settle for the shock of a fall, after which, sitting in the dust, he acknowledged that the order of the universe would not yield to his misfortune.

Generally people in his situation hang themselves. Ernie had never wondered why people hang themselves in those circumstances, but now he understood that it was the most practical way. Or else they drowned themselves—that too is a natural method, requiring few things. It is, in short, available to anyone. He might have done better to throw himself directly into the Schlosse a little while before. It could not have been so disagreeable, particularly on a fine warm day. He would have been swept along in the current like a piece of wood or a tangle of branches. So he was reduced to hanging himself, since he was unable to get up onto the roof. But to hang yourself you need a rope, a chair, and a hangman's knot. He had no hangman's knot. If you don't use the hangman's knot, you risk dangling at the end of the rope and hurting yourself badly. Feverish again, Ernie untied the doll and noticed that Moritz and his pals had simply bound the rope around its neck; they had not hanged it correctly. Though affliction had numbed his fingers, he tried several varieties of hangman's knot, but either the knot fell apart when he pulled at it, so that when he jumped from the chair he would run the risk of smashing to the floor brutally, or else the cursed knot squeezed tight when he slipped his wrist through the noose, and became dangerously rigid. If he had stayed with it he might have managed to construct a good hangman's noose, but all things considered it was not a very pleasant method. He had retained from his picture books the memory of a hanged man with a thick tongue flapping out over his chin. Doubtless it was no more agreeable to fling oneself from the roof, but at least there was the jump beforehand, while in a hanging there was nothing. He was no longer in a hurry, so Ernie sat down on the chair to think things over. This was a solemn occasion and deserved meditation.

The beings and things he loved and knew paraded slowly

through the window open in his breast—Mother Judith, the patriarch, Papa, Mama, the second-floor room, Herr Kremer, Moritz, the infants, and the high sun floating above the trees and houses, and Ilse, who was dead. Why were all these things leaving him today? And why did he feel heavier and not lighter as they abandoned him? It was truly as if he were falling from the heavens at a great speed and nothing would cut short his vertigo better than a real fall. It was therefore eminently regrettable that jumping off the roof was impossible for him because of his inability to execute a classic pull-up.

Lowering his glance, he saw again the Teddy bear of his childhood, the pan full of dishes, the ropes, the heaps of rags, the old dining-room table. A broken chair caught his eye—it lay on its back, waving its one foot in the air. Ernie Levy recognized it and remembered the manner of its death, in one of Mother Judith's heady furies. One could not become part of a piece of wood, yet Ernie had the inexplicable feeling that he and the broken chair were one.

Perhaps people ended as objects ended? No, certainly not, for one never knew how people contrived to die, one never had the slightest idea. Many times, generally at the evening meal, Mother Judith had announced that So-and-So "had passed on this afternoon," and then sententiously she had offered the name of a disease, as if pointing out a villain. According to Ernie, all those pretexts of sickness were more or less fallacious. A simple look showed clearly that all those people had been *carried off*. You could tell by the noses and beards of the mourners, for besides their sorrow, a very natural thing (although Ernie had often been intrigued by the extreme desolation of adults in mourning, since they themselves, not being immortal, would inevitably find their loved ones in heaven), the relatives of dead men always, rather characteristically, had a slight air of annoyance.

Only the Just Men did not die in such a hasty, disobliging manner. The day came when the Just Man bore witness to his justness, and the entire universe cooperated in preparing his deathbed—kings fomented invasions, noblemen pogroms. The

Just Men were not obliged to lift a finger—all had been fore-seen, organized in its slightest detail since the martyrdom of the holy Rabbi Yom Tov. No lessons were to be learned from that, since none of them had, like Ernie, anticipated the will of God.

And in any case neither the Just Men nor the dead and dying of the neighborhood had ever been in a situation com-parable to his own. There was no tuberculosis, no torture, no massacre, there was only Ernie in the attic.

Bird song filtered through the skylight. Ernie Levy stood up and flexed his cramped ankles. His last chance was to jump out of the small bathroom window, which also overlooked the courtyard. As he took a step toward the doorway, the sun dis-appeared. The wound on his forehead and the sharp laceration of his fingers by the frame of the skylight had suddenly blinded him with such pain—harsh and dark, wilder than a storm at night—that he was not at all surprised to find himself coming to on the floor. He also noticed a cutting pressure at his temples, which had suffered no violence at all. It all came from a devil-ish crumb of candy he had found shortly before in the lining of his pants. He had set it on his tongue and had felt sorrow flow-ing through his veins immediately, under the mawkish mask of pleasure. Rising to his feet, he felt that he had grown to such proportions that his head was wobbling, too heavy for the elastic frailty of his limbs.

Gripping the banister, he could go down the stairs confi-dently. The bathroom was on the floor beneath, across from his parents' room. He wondered why tears had begun to streak his cheeks again—"My tears are falling all by themselves, but I'm not really crying." And when he reached the bathroom door he sensed with an almost visual precision the spasmodic trembling of his legs—"My legs are trembling, but I'm not at all afraid."

The toilet was at the end of the small room, just beneath the small square window through which the setting sun beamed like a river immobilized in its rectilinear bed, the myriads of dust motes hanging gracefully like an infinity of dancing fish. Ernie raised the cover so as not to dirty it and then climbed up onto the porcelain to find himself at the height of the small casement. The opening was wide enough for his shoulders, but the project required that he hoist himself outside headfirst, let his body swing, and with the help of his own weight plunge to earth, so that he would not truly be leaping into space but would simply let himself be sucked out the window. Imagining that he would certainly fracture his skull (which would break like an egg, leaving no trace of his face), he again began to feel sorry that he could not leap from the roof, as was normal.

His legs were trembling so badly that he was afraid of falling from the bowl on which he was balanced. For several moments an evil genius had been at his legs simply to shatter the calm of his soul. No tears flowed from his eyes now. All the hostile malaise was in his legs, ordering them to do as they wished. The independent will of his legs was so far beneath his own superior will that he barely bothered to look down at their trembling. But fearing that his legs would betray him into a fall, he took the wiser course and stepped down cautiously in order to give the sudden disorder of his soul time to calm down.

After a minute or so he noticed that he was mechanically counting the toilet articles on the shelf. The bar of sunlight did not reach the basin, and all those objects were dim in the shadow, composing a single silhouette that the little boy's eye altered, climbing peaks, skimming nonchalantly down their slopes as if it were a mountain range. Shaving tackle caught his eye. It was on the far edge of the shelf, a large part of it hanging out over the precipice. Abruptly the little boy's mind was empty of all disquiet, his heart of all anguish, and he knew that his legs and eyes were once more his own.

Rising quickly, he moved to the shelf. In the box was a packet of unused blades. Each of them was wrapped in a protective sheath. On his palm the naked white blade gleamed like a gem, a cameo. It was too bad that neither the patriarch nor Ernie's father used a straight razor to trim the contours of their beards. Even in just shaving, certain people managed to cut their throats with an overhasty gesture. Some claimed that straight razors were so keen that setting the edge of the blade directly upon the skin was sufficient to cleave the flesh. The ease of the operation implied that a man could cut his throat without feeling even a tickle.

Ernie Levy set his left wrist on the edge of the basin, and piercing the fragile bluish skin with a corner of the rectangle of steel, he cut as deep a groove as he could. Pulling the blade away, he noted in surprise that a drop of blood had beaded on its corner. Yet he had felt no pain and his wrist was barely marked by a pinkish thread—a fly bite, they would say. He thought mockingly, "A fly bite," and suddenly the groove separated into two threads even thinner, which, spreading a few millimeters apart, opened the way to a continuous flow of blood. So the operation had been a success.

As the blood was staining the tiles, Ernie went back to the toilet and let his arm drain above the water tank, so as not to make unnecessary work for his mother. His left hand hung down, absolutely red, and the flow of blood cascaded from the end of his little finger by the same witchcraft that makes the blood of chickens slaughtered in the ritual abattoir flow through their beaks. Once, Ernie remembered, he had taken a chicken to be killed. When the razor had done its work, the chicken struggled savagely, then with a kind of bleak despair that shook its wings in floppy jerks, then it ceased to fight, thus showing that it was still alive, since blood is life, no? Ernie had eaten nothing of that chicken nor of any later chickens or fowl, because from that moment on he had known how they came to his plate. . . . And doubtless a part of his own being would continue to fight, like the chicken; perhaps that was why his legs were trembling again. . . .

Now his cramped hand took on the shape of a bloody beak, the open wound in his wrist indicating the chicken's neck. Agitating his thumb against his four clenched fingers, he saw the chicken's beak chop through the air in terror, saw its round eye gleam.

At what point would life quit his body? That was a most interesting question, and Ernie waited in delicious anguish for the moment at which the passage would take place. All people were considerably terrified by death, for they thought that one saw nothing more afterward, that it was total silence and that nothing ever again happened. But Ernie knew very well that that kind of death was impossible. Everything went on as before, with the sole difference that one was no longer bothered by a painful desire to die. It was not so unpleasant, death, and to begin a new existence Ernie Levy imagined himself in the form of a bubble, so transparent that, spinning in the sunlight, it reflected all visible things. But when a pin drove immediately into the bubble, it was annihilated in his thoughts. . . . Then, in his desire to avoid the pin he decided that death resulted rather in one's becoming invisible.

"My children," said the patriarch, standing at the head of the table in all the pomp of religious occasions, "my children, our beloved Ernie has left us for a better world. He did not wish to cause us grief. He left us because of the ladybugs and all the things you know of. Where he is now, he is happy, and I am sure that he is looking down upon us. Let us sing, so he will not be sad."

"I can't sing," Mother Judith said.

"Neither can I," said Ernie's father.

"Nor I," said Fräulein Blumenthal.

"I loved him," Moritz said, sobbing so pitifully that Ernie Levy, seated but invisible on the sofa in the dining room, felt invisible tears flow from his new eyes and fall to the floor with a splat-splat-splat inaudible to all ears but his own.

Opening his real eyes, he discovered that the sound was really caused by his blood, falling drop by drop, slowly, as if the reserve stored in his veins was at the point of exhaustion. An intoxicating sweetness radiated from his wrist—his whole organism was made languorous by it. There was nothing to compare with that sensation except the pleasure of strolling along the Schlosse with Ilse and glancing sidewise at her face.

Ernie imagined that once he was dead he would go to visit his grieving, repentant, inconsolable friend. "I ask you to forgive me," Ilse said. "You're dreaming, my little friend," Ernie said aloud while the dripping of his blood slowed down—splat . . . splat . . . splat . . . That morning Herr Geek had said that after the Battle of Verdun the spirits of the dead continued to fight in the air. In the same way Ilse's applause would echo eternally behind the row of houses and nothing, neither Ilse's regrets nor Ernie's death, could silence that applause. It echoed now in Ernie's ears.

Each drop of blood was a caress to him. And if, yielding to that delicious desire to sleep, he awakened more alive than ever? Gripped by an insane anguish, the little boy opened his eyes and so realized that his lids had closed without his knowledge, even as he had insidiously slid to the floor and was sitting back against the wall, his naked legs gleaming in a swamp of blood. Ilse's applause modulated to an ironic, light music, a music of quick black insects shining malignantly, each note buzzing about his ears and swooping in suddenly to sting.

In his efforts to rise, he sprayed blood. He managed to set one foot on the edge of the bowl, and pulling with one hand on the frame of the window raised himself high enough to set the other foot beside it. Bringing his arms together in the attitude of a diver, he wriggled half his body through the gaping square of the window and found himself suspended between heaven and earth. His left arm, dangling against the wall, had already trailed blood down to the second floor. Huge birds glided above the chestnut tree. Their butterfly wings—yellow, blue, green— reflected the sun like mirrors. The bird-butterflies swooped by so quickly that his eyes could not follow them. They rose so high above the roofs, above the chestnut tree and the little boy, that he made fun of himself gently. . . . Suddenly the harsh odor of blood disappeared, his arm ceased to bleed, the butter-flies thinned out and singsong, dreamlike words could be heard as the sun took Ernie's face in its gentle hands. They were the words the patriarch pronounced every Friday night at the solemn meal that opened the Sabbath of glory and peace—the words of the poet: "Come, my beloved, to meet your betrothed."

. . . Ernie was already slipping down the wall, his hands high and his head raised as if he wanted to bind himself for one moment to a vision of heaven, or as if he were refusing to see the earth rushing toward him more than he melted toward it, the earth flying up toward him—oh, high-diver; oh, dying swan—his skinny arms spread wide like wings. . . . Ernie had already taken flight when his feet caught on the window sill, holding him back for an instant by a ridiculous reflex, as if all his will to live had taken refuge *in extremis* in that part of his body, though uselessly, or as if, anesthetized by suffering and absolute self-abnegation, the fear of death had awakened suddenly in his heart of hearts, pulling him back toward life when it was already too late.

VI

THE DOG

. 1 .

STATISTICS SHOW that the percentage of suicides among the German Jews was practically nil during the years before the end. So it was in the prisons, in the ghettos, in all the caves of darkness where the beast's muzzle sniffed up from the abyss, and even at the entrance to the crematorium—"anus of the world," in the words of a learned Nazi eyewitness. But back in 1934, hundreds and hundreds of little German-Jewish schoolboys came up for their examinations in suicide, and hundreds of them passed.

So the first death of Ernie Levy takes its place among the statistics beside hundreds of similar (though more irrevocable) deaths. It is admirable that during a period when they were teaching murder to their Aryan scholars, the instructors taught the Jewish children suicide. This point illuminates German technique—its extreme rigor and simplicity, from which no departures are tolerated even in pedagogy.

When Mordecai discovered the lifeless body of the child at the foot of the wall in the courtyard—a bird blasted in flight, in a spattering of feathers and blood—he felt himself going mad. His heavy gray eyes remained dry; they hung like stones in their sockets. As he approached the body his teeth dug deeper into his lower lip—one red thread, then two, then three fell along his squarish beard. He saw that Ernie was lying cheek to the ground like a hunting dog, his long curls covering his face discreetly. Death had overtaken him in a position of sleep. *"O Lord, did you not pour him forth like milk? Did you not make him firm like cheese? Hear me, you covered him with flesh and skin, you wove him of bone and nerves, and now you have destroyed him. . . ."* Falling to his knees, Mordecai was shocked at the buzzing of flies circling about the thin corpse. One of them, enormous and greenish, landed greedily on the point of a bone that had ripped through the skin of the elbow. Mordecai slipped his arm under the broken body and raised it from its bed of stone and blood. "Here," he said to the child in a calm voice, "I cry out at the violence and nothing answers." At that moment the schoolboy's smock lifted, fell, lifted again with the miraculous regularity of living organisms. Mordecai was immediately moved to gratitude toward a God so good. Just as he was, in his old tan wool bathrobe, the child clutched to him like a bloody prey, he crossed through the living room and ran through the streets—with all the terrified Levys at his heels. That evening Ernie lay delirious in the hospital at Mainz —the Jewish section. They had made a little plaster doll of him. Mordecai thanked God, who had been kind. He thanked him for six months, a year, but when Ernie returned to Stillenstadt, he was obliged to admit that if the Eternal, in his infinite pity, had restored life to the little angel, he had not restored his soul.

Ernie knew very soon that death had set its hand upon his spirit. Of all the outraged suffering that shocked each cell of his body, imprisoned by a scaffolding of straps and buckles, metal supports, multiple tubes distilling life through openings cut in the plaster, the most agonizing came from his one eye, rediscovering not only the forms and colors of the world but also its eminent cruelty. In his initial surprise, Ernie thought that God had withdrawn himself from things, all of which now stood colorless, dimensionless, like castoff clothing thrown at random into the halls of the hospital. Then he understood that he was no longer seeing them with the lying eyes of the soul. And, though he could feel his tongue moving normally in his mouth, he decided not to respond to any overtures from this graceless world. "He's not really awake yet," Mordecai's voice said. Mother Judith's enormous face floated above Ernie's round eye, tears glittered on her lashes like diamonds. "*Are you awake, my love?*" Ernie's only answer was to raise and lower his one eyelid. . . .

So it went through an incalculable number of days and nights. No words passed through the orifice contrived in his mask, for Ernie held them all back. Only at night, amid the snoring and wailing of his neighbors, he prayed God to change the government. But his prayer was overheard by a nurse, and as the living tried to turn it to good account, tormenting him eternally for more, he ceased to speak even at night. At about that time, nevertheless, on a day when Mother Judith proved especially intolerable, when he saw her walking off between the rows of white beds, her head bowed, her shoulders shaken by strange tremors, he felt a tear filter from his eye and run off under the plaster mask, leaving a sweet wake.

That night for the first time Ernie's past invaded him like a river in flood, with torn tree trunks here and there, babies' cradles floating, animals belly-up, figures on the roofs, Ilse on a boat manned by grimacing creatures and the Levys' poor Noah's ark wandering among the flotsam, all of them raising their arms to God, who looked down inscrutably. The world was going to rack and ruin, though no one seemed to notice. Ernie's neighbors carried on their habitual conversations, always bearing on their pre-hospital lives or on the lives they would begin when they got out, as if they had been officially assured that the river outside would politely stop its rush to wait for them. No one noticed that the river was flowing beneath the beds, carrying off the whole hospital in its slow, cruel course. Over the bed across from him, Ernie had noticed two plaques, one above the other. One, in faïence, bore this wide, handsome inscription—"The Rothschild Foundation of the Meurthe." The other was a plain piece of yellow cardboard—"Reserved for Jews and Dogs." But the invalids never referred to the square of yellow cardboard hanging above their beds. They spoke of shops to be lost or saved, of legs, of arms, of livers, of lungs, of intestines to be lost or saved, of visas for Palestine and of women and children and food and sunshine and of a thousand things to be lost or saved, as if the river were not bearing all that away on one huge black wave. "Be careful," Ernie wanted to say to them, but he was silent, for death kept the words upon his tongue. And when the Levys came to visit, their mouths full of projects for emigration to Eretz Yisrael, they too with their eyes full of *serious* tears and their hands clenched in hope—"Be careful, they're deceiving you," Ernie wanted to say. "Things are not what they seem, they are this way or that," and so on. But he was more silent than ever, for the Levys would truly have been horrified to an extreme at discovering that muddy river beneath their feet in place of the terra firma they imagined—so naïvely, the poor dear mortals. . . . With his one eye, out of the wounded depths of his vision, Ernie stared at them now from a terrifying distance, which separated him from them more than the small death before his suicide—a distance filled little by little with an inexplicable resentment rooted in the pity he felt for them despite—*because of?*—their blindness.

It was the same for Ilse, whom he tried in vain to think badly of. Often when one bone or another ached, he passed judgment on Ilse in words borrowed from Moritz or from Mother Judith: "She is a this," he said with feverish industry, "she's a that, she deserves this and that, God will rip her to pieces like a fish," and the like. But immediately he saw before him a swift current carrying her off without her knowledge, and all the decrees of justice yielded to the horror of seeing the blond husk of his love floating in the common waters with a musical cry. Even when Ilse's applause awakened him at night, reminding him of the torture in his nerves and his bones, Ernie could do no more than give her a bitter, distant thought, softened by commiseration. For Ilse too had been carried off by the wide river.

One day Fräulein Blumenthal arrived to visit, leading her rosary of tiny Levys. The sight of Ernie seemed to terrify her. Her nose quivered like a fly. Finally she came forward and caressed her son's plaster cheeks, murmuring, "Everything will be all right. . . . You'll be home soon. . . . I'll make some noodle soup. . . ." Then her hand hung as in a dream and a tear splashed onto the mask, which she no longer saw. Fräulein Blumenthal's tears were particularly silent and transparent. They had the quality of disappearing at the slightest glance, so that Ernie always saw her with a serene face. But that day Ernie saw the drop of light fall, and his tongue functioned in spite of himself. "Everything will be all right," he said in a harsh, rasping voice that surprised him altogether.

But he was sorry for those words immediately. It seemed to him that he had just made an entrance in the old comedy.

When he returned to Stillenstadt after two years in bed, his old acquaintances did not recognize him: nothing was left of the little lamb but his curls.

Though emaciated and limping along on crutches, Ernie had come back from his bed taller than Moritz. A white line, like barbed wire, crossed the upper part of his forehead. A similar scar raised his right eyebrow, stretching the eyelid and making the eye seem now sad, now frozen in horror. The other eye was still as sweetly shaped as ever, but according to Fräulein Blumenthal, who was an expert here, "Those funny little stars—you know, like in summer" no longer glittered in it. From then on the irises were entirely dark. And as for that rasping, slow voice, disagreeable to the soul, Benjamin claimed that it reminded him amazingly of the young Galician's voice.

"The worst," Mother Judith said, "is this silence—not a word for three days. No, God should not have——"

"But just the same, think," Mordecai interrupted, "think what a miracle. If I had not been kept in by a fever, I would never have heard the sound of his fall, and if God had not inspired him with the idea of jumping from the window, he would have bled to death. And the same way, if the hospital in Stillenstadt had accepted him, even though he's Jewish, he wouldn't have been taken care of half as well as at Mainz. And finally, if——"

Judith took the bit between her teeth. "Enough, please, enough miracles. They hunt us down and they hunt us down again, children jump out of windows and break their bones and souls, and he shouts about miracles! When will God stop *miracling* us that way?"

"Tut-tut-tut," Mordecai said reprovingly.

Ernie, who was coming down the stairs, stopped.

"Tut-tut-tut," Mordecai repeated.

Now there exists so vast a multitude of tones, expressions, chants, singsongs, mimicries and accents with which the banality "tut-tut-tut" may be pronounced that the Talmudists have distinguished no fewer than three hundred varieties, subject to analysis or not. Mordecai fell upon just the "tut-tut-tut" to make Ernie's blood rise most quickly to his morose cheeks.

"My God, they're just as innocent as ever," he said to himself, flabbergasted, and afraid that he would break out laughing, he went quietly back up to his room, where he went on with the boxing lessons he had recently begun. Since discarding his crutches, he had devoted himself seriously to that project, conceived in the meditative immobility of the hospital. It was a question of becoming proficient enough to appoint himself defender of the Levys' ark. The latter, he had decided then, would compose his entire universe, from insects to stars. They were pure, gentle and silly, they knew only how to weep and extend their naked hands. He, Ernie, would protect them with his fists. After his return from the hospital, he inscribed in a notebook, basing his work on the fights he had seen, all the pugilistic problems that might arise. Then in the greatest secrecy, he gave himself his first boxing lesson in the second-floor room. There was, he had discerned immediately, a subtle way to deliver a blow, taking advantage of the momentum of the whole body, which, it seemed, nothing could stand up to. And dodging sharply to the side, he would avoid hostile blows. And so on and on. At night he revised his notes mentally. Several months afterward, judging that he was in good fettle, Ernie escorted his brother Jacob to school. The first battle took him by surprise. He had the enemy—a very young Pimpf—well in the path of his "jab," and all he had to do was bring his arm back slightly in order to give the blow all the force he could want. But at just that moment, he was not sure how, an enemy fist hit him full in the face. In his fall he thought that he must have forgotten something. Then he stopped thinking altogether and realized that he was on his feet again, using his fists with precision and even his feet, which he had never bothered to train. That first victory made him so happy that he took pity on his fleeing enemy. "You beat him, you beat him," Jacob kept shouting, ecstatic at his mysterious elder brother's technique.

"Yes, I beat him," Ernie said in a strange tone.

Two days later, during a rear-guard battle, he saw a corner of the sky, very high. Immediately he looked directly into the eyes of one of his assailants, and thinking that they were all boys like himself, swept along in the wide river under the round, immutable eye, he lamentably let his arms dangle beside his body. . . . That misfortune occurred again. At a distance he seethed splendidly with ardor, but in the fire of combat, and though great thoughts were far from him, he dropped his arms forthwith. When Jacob complained, he forced himself to hate —he apprenticed himself to hatred. One by one he enumerated all the past and present reasons for hating the Pimpfe, but it seemed to him that if those reasons were as numerous as the stars in the sky they would not rouse him to the feeling he needed. He went so far as to repeat to himself that the Pimpfe were beasts in the eyes of human beings, and he managed to believe it. But some small detail always came along to tear down his beautiful edifice—a childlike glance, a pout or simply a patch of sky intruding upon the fight. He fell back on an unusually subtle stratagem. When he was escorting Jacob, he squinted slightly, so as to see all things as if through a fog. But it seemed that it was impossible to hate a silhouette.

All that did not fail to worry Ernie greatly, particularly in regard to the future of the fragile ark commanded by the patriarch. Flashes of shame shot through him. He considered himself a traitor to the cause of the Levys. His tongue once more became heavy.

. 2 .

O N NOVEMBER 6, 1938, a Jewish adolescent, Herschel
Grynszpan, whose parents had just been deported to
Zbonszyn, bought a revolver, had its use demonstrated to him,
went to the German Embassy in Paris and shot to death, as an
expiatory victim, the First Secretary, Ernst vom Rath. The
news went through the Jewish hearts of Germany like a train
of powder. The faithful barricaded themselves hastily and cast
their most heart-rending prayers heavenward. Then they
waited for the storm. At Stillenstadt, toward five in the afternoon, they saw the first group of Nazi hunters.

That night the whole Levy family pressed together around
the small tripod stove in the kitchen, the last vestige of a
vanished comfort. On the table the old oil lamp brought from
Zemyock smoked without conviction, and while waiting for the
string beans, the only course, the babies gnawed greedily on
chestnuts that Mother Judith extracted respectfully from the
peat oven. Their faces were tired, their clothes frayed and in
threads, and chronic hunger kept the children quiet in spite of
the close quarters.

Ernie appeared in the doorway, his face blue, crowned with
snow. "Moritz, Papa, Grandfather, Mother Judith," he counted
off calmly, and casting a worried glance at the little ones, he
signaled the adults to follow him into the living room.

"And me?" Fräulein Blumenthal said.

Mechanically, Ernie raised his index finger to his brow and
drew it along the scar that ran like a white line back to his
temple. In his jacket cut out of a blanket, with the down that
shadowed the lower part of his face—as pale and ravaged now
as Mother Judith's—with the slow, positive, meditative movement of his wide, moist black eyes, he looked like a young
Jewish workman from Warsaw or Bialystok. Set squarely on
the back of his head, a beret served him as skullcap.

"No, Mama, not you," he said with a sad smile. "This is for the grownups."

Those grownups moved into the darkness of the living room, where Ernie, raising a corner of the curtain, showed them a reddish glow across the street, at the entrance to a hallway. A brief spark sprang out a bit farther along, replaced immediately by the red lozenge a cigarette makes at night.

"There are more of them," Ernie said. "You see, there? And there?"

"Are they after us?" Mother Judith asked.

"Who else?" Ernie said. "They're waiting for a signal. . . . But here, I found some iron bars."

"*For whom?*" Mordecai asked coldly. "Not iron nor fire will shield us from the hands of God. Let us eat."

They went back to the kitchen. Fräulein Blumenthal, who had been listening at the door, retreated blushing. The meal was particularly silent. A gusty wind had sprung up, ripping through the black air; it did not favor conversation. Mother Judith had one eye out for the meal, and the other, tender and brooding, for the frightened children. The old man was of marble, and from time to time he gave off a stony rumbling, as if from the belly of a statue. Benjamin Levy was calculating the pros and cons of heaven knew what, and Fräulein Blumenthal served the meal with her eyes averted, the large, dark eyes of a suffering female. And the little ones, aware of the menace, made themselves tiny, nonexistent.

Even the presence of God at the head of the table would not have induced Mother Judith to hold her tongue. "Here's the table, the bread, the knife—and none of us can eat."

"What can we do?" Fräulein Blumenthal sighed; her lips were compressed in anxiety. "Won't God have pity on the children?"

And as she threatened to pursue that plaintive reproach to the Divinity, the patriarch interrupted her sharply. "God does what God sees fit, but a penny in an empty bottle goes clink-clink"—with which the old man stared at her so severely that there could be no mistaking what he meant by the empty bottle. Contrite, she returned to the stove, her kingdom.

"Ai, ai," Mother Judith wailed suddenly, "Frau Wasserman said that there isn't a country in the world that wants us Jews! Even the little places where the savages live—in Africa, in Asia, how would I know where?—won't let us have visas. And Frau Rosenberg said to Frau Vishniac this morning that the English won't let more than two hundred Jews a month into the Holy Land. You hear that?—in the whole world, two hundred Jews a month. And how many German and Austrian Jews like us, and how many Levys? And that isn't all, but these merchants in human life only take the rich ones. At the border everyone has to show at least a thousand pounds. So how does it look for——"

"There's no border," Benjamin said. "It's only the ocean."

"Ocean or no ocean," the old woman flamed bitterly, "it costs a thousand pounds, my friend! And how would I know, an idiot like me, if they walk on land or on water in America, and in Africa, and in Asia? All I know, and all that matters to me, is that you need a thousand pounds to get there. Yes, for a poor Jew, land or sea, America or Palestine, the sun or the moon, it's all the same—one thousand pounds. God, God, God—the proverb is right after all. The poor man is followed everywhere by his poverty. Where can we go if we have to leave—down to the bottom of the sea with the little fishes?"

"And France?" Benjamin asked in a voice entirely devoid of irony.

"They love us the same way everybody does, scum of the earth that we are! In France it's another story altogether. Frau Wasserman says the French don't like the Germans one bit, not one bit!"

"But we're not really German," Fräulein Blumenthal said innocently. "Aren't we Jews?"

Benjamin could not help smiling at her naïveté. It always delighted his contemplative spirit, so respectful of all the Creator's fantasies. "Little woman, oh, my own little woman," he answered her gently while his parents restrained their laughter, "do you know, to the Germans we are only Jews and

to the French only Germans. Can you understand such a thing?
Everywhere we are what it is important not to be—Jews here,
Germans there. . . ."

"And poor in either place!" Mother Judith cried. Once she
had an idea, she did not give it up easily.

Fräulein Blumenthal was wailing, "My God, how stupid I
am, *how stupid!* Well, then, what can we do?" she added, crossing her long hands over the chronic roundness of her belly as if
to calm the child within her.

"Wait a little longer," the patriarch said.

"Cry out," Benjamin Levy said dryly. "As they did in
Proskurov."

"God help us," Mother Judith exclaimed, "that man would
make jokes on the guillotine!"

At those words Mordecai rose heavily, and leaning forward,
his hands together like those of a farmer's wife chasing chickens
before her, he sent all the children out of the room, with Ernie
in charge and with one candle. Then, closing the kitchen door,
he trained the heavy anguish of his gray eyes upon Judith.
"It's not altogether a joke," he explained in some embarrassment. "The Jews of Proskurov cried out for seven nights. Yes,
the rabbi of Cszeln told me that the houses in the ghetto were
one great cry from top to bottom. It was the Cossack Shelgin.
He came every night with his White Guards—may God forget
even his name!—so whole streets cried out one after another.
They could hear our Jewish women several miles from the
town. But the miracle was this: The bandits came and then
went . . . because of the cries. The story is well known, you
know," he finished anxiously.

Fräulein Blumenthal's hands flew to her throat. "And—and
the seventh night?" she choked out.

But neither the patriarch nor Benjamin seemed to have
heard that question, and doubtless they judged it unfitting to
describe what happened in Proskurov toward the end of the
year 1918, on the seventh night of Jewish clamor. . . .

There was a silence.

"Do you know, I'm beginning to be really afraid," Mother

Judith said, smiling at her daughter-in-law. "And I wonder, wouldn't it be better to be Germans in France than Jews in Germany? A choice between the frying pan and the fire, all right. But just the same . . ."

Elbows on the table, his head resting on the heavy pedestal of his hands, Mordecai seemed to be staring off into some ultimate nothing. He murmured wretchedly, "Night is descending, and the beasts are prowling outside. . . . And our children . . . our children . . ."

"Do you want me to go outside to take a look?" Moritz asked.

"No, no, that would be a luxury that . . ." Returning to the conversation then, plucking his thoughts from his head one by one with the physical pain of old men remembering, "Yes, we were talking about leaving for France," he murmured confusedly. "Right? Right? I don't think we ought to run yet. Tomorrow the Germans will calm down and the French will take up the sword of God. What did we gain by leaving Zemyock? As it is said, the wicked serve God's purposes, and all that happens is a punishment. And what then—would you escape *him?* (Blessed be his name throughout the centuries. Amen.) I know the Germans, and they are not altogether savages, they aren't Ukrainians. They'll take everything, but not our lives. So I say to you—patience, children, prayer and patience."

And interrupting himself suddenly, the old man threw a brief glance of anguish toward the door.

"Ha, ha," Judith burst out bitterly, "I know the Germans, ha, they're not savages, not Ukrainians . . ." And then, as if she too wanted to forget her fears, she went on in mounting anger, "Ha, you men! You talk and you discuss and the truth flows from your mouths like honey. I may not be *intelligent,* myself, but may I be turned inside out if you've said one sensible word tonight! And may I choke on my own bile here and now if——"

"Enough," Mordecai cut in. Pulling at his beard, he muttered indignantly, "On a night like this . . . to swear that way . . ."

Judith was afraid to look at the cold Jewish despair on his face. Leaning across the table just the same, she caressed the old man's forehead with a maternal finger and murmured tenderly, "Nothing will happen to them, believe me. What can happen to children? And I'm sorry for what I just said, my friend, my old friend. . . . It will never happen again, never again!" And carried away by her burst of good will, she added innocently, "May I turn into a toad if I ever swear again!"

Mordecai shrugged in resignation. "No, no," he said, "swear all you want, I beg of you." He rubbed a hand across his eyes, pale with fatigue, and suddenly dug his lumberjack's fists into the sockets as if to hide his face from the light. "Children," he murmured in a strange voice, "my dear children, there are days when I myself don't understand the will of God too well. For a thousand years all over Europe, how many of our women and children have been martyred—not with the peaceful awareness of the Just Men but with the terrified little souls of lambs? And what good," the old man went on in great grief, "is suffering that does not serve to glorify the Name? Why all the *useless* persecutions?" Exhaling a hoarse sigh, the old Jew caught himself up suddenly. "But after all, are we Jews not the sacrificial tribute, the tribute of suffering that man—uh—offers to God? Praised be his name . . . O Blessed . . ."

"Ah, my dear father!" Benjamin said then, brokenhearted, "if all that were God's will, who would not rejoice? But I think we are the prey of the wicked—simply a prey. And tell me, my venerable little father, does the chicken rejoice that it serves to glorify God? No, and you know it very well, the chicken is altogether sorry—and *reasonably* so—to have been born as a chicken, slaughtered as a chicken and eaten as a chicken. There is my opinion on the Jewish question."

"The Messiah . . ." Mordecai began without conviction.

"Ah, the Messiah!" Judith said sharply, her head nodding suddenly and her eyes dreamy. "Yes, yes, you're right, my

friend. Perhaps the Messiah is about to descend. Who knows—
today, tomorrow? We need help so much, and if he does not
come, who will help us? Do you know, my doves, I feel something in the air. . . ."

"Maybe he's behind the door," Fräulein Blumenthal said.
Mechanically, all the Levys turned toward the Messiah.

On November 10, 1938, at one-twenty in the morning,
Reinhard Heydrich, chief of the Gestapo, announced to each
of his sections by telegram that anti-Jewish demonstrations
were "to be expected" throughout the Third Reich. At two in
the morning, beneath a sheet of frigid sky, a strident cry rose in
the center of a tightly coiled Stillenstadt, a cry that persisted,
that unfurled in the streets to the gleam of dozens of torches,
like so many hateful eyes. It might have been a nighttime carnival. Above the Jews was the emptiness of a winter sky and
around them was only crime. The shouts seemed to echo from
house to house, a dialogue from hell. The Riggenstrasse sparkled as if in broad daylight. A wall of fire, composed of all the
Jewish libraries in the street, shot skyward in purgatorial flame.
Machines, bolts of cloth, even the cradle of the last-born Levy,
all the contents of Benjamin's shop were scattered upon the
sidewalk, delivered up to the rush for spoils. On the watch behind a shutter, Benjamin declared himself *particularly* grieved
to recognize a former customer. "Savage beasts," the patriarch
stated in learned tones.

When the first shocks of the battering ram shook the door
at the end of the hallway, Benjamin suggested nailing more
planks across it, and then when Mordecai simply shrugged,
the two men made for the attic, where the rest of the family
was already huddled. Mordecai turned a key in the lock. A
dusky glow filtered through the skylight onto the Levys, frozen
like statues by the intense fear that made Fräulein Blumenthal's teeth chatter in the darkness. The children gathered at
her skirts trembled, and Mother Judith, pressing a handkerchief gently over the mouth of the infant in her arms.

muted the baby's gurgling. The noise downstairs grew louder, swelled, burst in a shattering of glass. Mordecai went to the stack of sacred books and with blind fingers made sure once more that no Scripture had been abandoned to the looters. As the patriarch had ordered, Ernie had the scrolls of the Law in his arms, the same scrolls confided to the Levys' care after the synagogue had burned. Mordecai set the horns of his phylacteries on his forehead, girded his wrists with the holy laces, and covering his head with the great prayer shawl sat, only his lips in motion—a sleeping mountain in profile against the shadow of the attic. Little Jacob felt a scream rising to his tongue. . . . "Mama," he groaned suddenly, "I think I'm going to scream. Will you put your hand over *my* mouth, too?"

Ernie saw Fräulein Blumenthal's gesture vaguely, and then a shout blanketed everything. "They're up above!" cried a piercing voice on the stairway. Ernie set the scrolls of the Law on the floor and picked up one of the iron bars he had provided for the occasion. Seeing this, the patriarch stepped toward him and slapped him. "To save your life," he said, "would you lose all reason to live?" Blows resounded against the attic door. There followed a lively exchange of words, and the voice of the Riggenstrasse's old mattress maker came through the panel, bleating and begging. "Listen, Herr Benjamin, they're *all worked up,* at least you have to give them some prayer books for the fire in the street. At least you have to give them that, Herr Benjamin. . . ."

"Just the books?" Benjamin asked.

"The books first," said a mocking voice.

"No," the mattress maker's voice interrupted, "just the books and that's all. Over my dead body—" he began. Then his voice was lost in the growing altercation on the landing.

Mordecai stooped down, picked up the iron bar Ernie had dropped and with a slow but astonishingly supple step reached the door of grief. His head was erect, he seemed larger, his shoulders rolled lightly and when he turned toward the huddled, whimpering group in the shadow, Ernie noticed that his teeth, exposed in a grimace, gleamed silver while a sort of harsh laugh emerged uninterrupted, mingled with the half-insane statements he was making. "For a thousand years, ha, the Christians have been trying to kill us every day, ha-ha! And we have been trying to live every day, ha-ha-ha! And every day we manage it somehow, my lambs. Do you know why?" He was suddenly tall against the door, and he held the iron bar high above his head, and his phylacteries and laces and prayer shawl fell to the floor in his anger. "Because *we never give up our books,*" he cried with awesome strength. *"Never, never, never!*

"We prefer to give up our lives," he added while the iron bar, swung like an ax, split the door with a deafening crash. "We'll give you our lives, ha-ha," he finished in that same delirious tone, mingling violence and an incomprehensible note of despair.

Then he withdrew the iron bar and stood firmly before the split door, his legs wide, like a lumberjack drawing strength and firmness from his ax. Light flashed through the jagged hole in the door. The clamor echoed again, but this time on the stair-way and as if hesitant and dulled. Sweat gleamed on the patriarch's cheekbones and on the points of his thick mustache. Then Ernie noticed that it was not sweat but tears—the patriarch was sobbing sadly as he murmured, "But the shame of it, at my age, the shame of it . . ."

Ernie's clearest memory was of the minutes when, resigned to his own confusion and terror, he drove fear from his mind by a meticulous inventory of the setting and the characters. Thus, at the end of Benjamin Levy's nose the pearl of real sweat, as torturing as those cackles of death on the stairway; more frightening, as it gleamed, than the paving stone flung suddenly through the door; more baleful in another way than the silence that signaled the pogrom's end.

· 3 ·

ON NOVEMBER 11, 1938, over ten thousand Jews were greeted with the customary courtesies at Buchenwald alone while a loudspeaker proclaimed, "Any Jew desiring to hang himself is requested to be kind enough to put a piece of paper bearing his name into his mouth, so that we can tell who he was." On the 14th of November the entire Levy family, flying the pennon of the wanderer, crossed the bridge at Kehl, carrying all that remained of their worldly goods.

But six weeks later the Levys saw their pogrom as a frankly providential nudge. Mother Judith saw in it nothing less than the hand of God. The remote reason was that, paying Germany back in her own coin, everything under the skullcap of the heavens that called itself a democracy condemned her, in reprisal for her anti-Semitism, to keep her Jews. The punishment was brilliant. It was applied at the precise moment when Nazism, out of patience, suffocating with Yiddishness, opened Hamburg to Yiddish emigration. Draining toward that port by the tens of thousands, the German Jews were brought up painfully against democracy's order of the day—"No visa." A few handfuls set sail anyway. In the name of humanity they were not sunk, but were permitted to die at anchor in London, Marseilles, New York, Tel Aviv and Malacca and Singapore and Valparaiso and at any anchor they wished.

Democratic regulations not providing for funerals, pious German Jews buried each other, for better or worse, in the sea. Only the natives of the island of Borneo, always epicurean about new heads, granted the privilege of burial but retained the right—the only condition imposed—to skim off the handsomest "beards" of the lot. Called into telegraphic consultation, a famous New World Talmudist sliced (if the phrase is permissible) the Gordian knot in this manner: "Let them cut. God—blessed be his name—will put everything back in place."

An ark in the modern deluge, the St. Louis sailed around the world twice without evoking one flower for its women, one smile for its children, one tear for its old men. The democracies refrained from any vulgar show of emotion. After a pleasant cruise, the whole group returned by way of Hamburg to end their days in the motherland. Never in history had an embargo been so admirably observed. "And long live democracy," cried the democracies. And immediately, "Down with demobolshoplutojudeonegromongolo . . . cracy!" brutally answered the little corporal who, out of spite, "dealt with" a hundred thousand Jews immediately, beginning with those from the St. Louis. "Shocking, shocking," the editorialist of the *Times* ululated in answer, and with the honorable intent of initiating this improperly constituted regime to the rules of international cant, the Royal Navy sank in eight fathoms a small ship full of Jewish children, which had ventured within the territorial waters of the Britannic Mandate of Palestine—*but after the customary warnings.*

"Are the Nazis everywhere?" Fräulein Blumenthal asked.

At least the barbarians had not reached the balmy banks of the Seine, where the hours still passed so peacefully that the Levys were appalled. How could oases exist? So God was tracing lines of demarcation upon the earth, decreeing, "Here you will be hanged at any time of day, and there only at mealtimes. Farther on your heads will be cut off, and elsewhere it will be France . . ."?

"What a stupid vegetable I am," Benjamin said.

"How do you mean?" Mother Judith asked.

"If I had chosen France in Warsaw, in 1921, without knowing it we would have flown across a desert of tears and blood. We would never have known Stillenstadt and its delights. And yet they offered me France on a platter, like an egg from the Garden of Eden. And I said, 'No, I can't stand that kind of food, it doesn't agree with me.' A stupid vegetable . . ."

"We would have been spared all the misery we've been through," Fräulein Blumenthal said.

Benjamin stared wide-eyed at her. Mordecai said, smiling,

"If you hadn't chosen Germany, you would never have met the young Galician, who would never have established you in Stillenstadt, where you would never have come to know a certain Fräulein Blumenthal, who would not have given you the handsomest children in the world. Now we have all that, *plus* France. Blessed be the name of him who lives in eternity. Amen."

These considerations saw the light in a trim little summer house in the suburbs of Paris, where the Jewish Committee of Welcome sheltered, for better or for worse, a dozen or so refugee families. The town was called Montmorency, the house bore the name of the Hermitage, and the city clerk informed the exiles, with earnest intensity, that it had once sheltered a vague colleague "entitled" Jean-Jacques Rousseau. But the proximity of even more illustrious shades, such as the great Maggid of Zloczow or Rabbi Yitzhak of Drohobicz, would not have inhibited the survivors from savoring the exquisite, downy warmth that reigned in the garden at all hours of the day, under the leafy arch sheltering the old stone bench where the women knitted with their fingers and their mouths, heaving a long, solemn, grateful Jewish sigh at a well-turned stitch or a well-turned phrase. "Still," one of the women admitted, "if I learned that, for example, the Baal Shem Tov in person, or the gentle Rabbi Abraham the Angel, or some Just Man from Zemyock was sitting here where we have our behinds right now, I'd probably drop dead from shame." Mother Judith said nothing.

The whole group lived on subsidies extracted from the Consistory of Paris. Mother Judith particularly performed wonders. She requisitioned with such authority, mingling threats and prayers, the heart of God and the lightning of the Last Judgment, that there was no office from which she did not commandeer something edible. "And remember," she said on the doorsill as she left, "it is your place to thank me. For it is written, 'That which you give, God will return to you a hundredfold.' All I say is, until the next time. . . ."

But these maneuvers cost her more than she ever admitted,

and it was not without a tear or two that she learned of Benjamin's employment in a Jewish tailor's workshop. Moritz soon followed him into the same establishment as a presser and apprentice machine operator. And then Ernie, promoted to the rank of bicycle messenger. They lived in such abundance then that they no longer bothered to eat except when they were hungry. Even Moritz, the bottomless belly, who in the beginning never went out unless he was loaded down with snacks—he even stored them inside his shirt—arrived at the point where periodically he drew a croissant from his pocket and gave it only a nostalgic nibble, nothing more. Every morning, followed by the admiration of the whole house, the workers went to the Montmorency station and took that small, dusty, blustering train that the French call a *tacot,* distinguishing it from the one that took you from Enghien-les-Bains into the City of Light. The *tacot* had a great advantage—it was a double-decker with an upper level of seats, and pitching and rolling fearfully, it encouraged a Jewish imagination to venture without risk on a furious ocean. People stared a bit at our three heroes, but no one insulted them and no one seemed to be holding back a desire to spit in their faces. On the way back they went into any old bakery, now one and now another, to vary the pleasure, and without the slightest hitch bought some of those *petits pains au lait* so fragrant with French flour, so intoxicating to linger over on top of a rackety little train while the countryside unrolls at your feet like an honorific carpet. A heart-warming thing—sometimes an old commuter nodded amiably, and they returned his greeting, with the manners of a marquis, and Benjamin squeezed his sons' hands tightly (both of them were a head taller than he was) while he whispered in Yiddish, his tone implying that this was the ultimate revelation, "My little pigeons, this is the life."

Sometimes on Sunday Ernie went with the patriarch to reunions of the Paris Association of Old Zemyock. The Association comprised seventeen members at that time, but since there was not enough room for all of them in the narrow premises that took the place of a social hall, the reunion took place partly there, partly on the staircase, and partly on the sidewalk of the Rue des Ecouffes. Invited only as a guard and protector, Ernie never got past the staircase. But while the patriarch palavered majestically in the "office," and for the *n*th time refused the presidency of the Association, Ernie mingled with the commonalty on the sidewalk, seizing upon gossip, memories, gilded anecdotes of Zemyock, which, to hear the refugees, was a great metropolis, a true city of light beside which Paris evoked only belittling epithets. But occasionally the gossip bore on events in Germany, Austria, Czechoslovakia, and the "evil of the times" pierced Ernie's ribs like a needle.

"Do you know what?" someone said then. "Let's talk about something gay. What news of the war?"

Ernie laughed too while the needle slipped into him gently through the narrow path of his throat. "You mustn't think," he said to himself as he laughed, "you mustn't see, you mustn't hear *the cries*."

Knowing herself awaited, the war made a queenly entrance. But she was preceded by sinister heralds: A multitude of gas masks that the workmen on the *tacot* slung over their shoulders like a new kind of musette bag. When it appeared that the refugees at the Hermitage—all of whose passports were adorned with a swastika, though bearing the further decoration "Jew"— were not to be included in the distribution of these salutary snouts, a great chill came over the Levys. "There we go again," Benjamin said. "What a great God is ours," Mother Judith declared, "and how oddly he runs the world!" "And you," Mordecai said to her, "what a big mouth you have, and how often you open that mouth, and do you know what comes out of your mouth? Fire and flame, sulphur and pitch!" But when the summonses came streaming in, and the police visits, the searches, the veiled interrogations, he had to admit that in the eyes of this nation, geared for war, the gentle Levys of Stillenstadt had begun to look terribly like enemies. In August appeared the first notices inculcating fear: "Be careful, enemy ears are listening. . . ." No one now nodded to the three foreigners on the *tacot*. First it was gossip, murmurs. The word "internment" was on every lip, but no one dared pronounce it. One day the three travelers found the little train seething. Newspapers were changing hands. War had been declared.

In the great shed at the Gare du Nord, Ernie felt slightly sick. Moritz offered to escort him home, but at Ernie's repeated entreaties they left him in a bistro. His brother Moritz and his father Benjamin had barely left him—their figures merging through the glass with the gray-and-blue crowd of suburban workmen—they had barely disappeared, finally, from his sight when Ernie stood up, his eyes uneasy but his body suddenly hard and sharp. Half an hour later he passed through the gate of the barracks at Reuilly and took his place in the cosmopolitan line of volunteers.

"You're lucky," the sergeant major said. "You're just within the age limits."

"Luck like that," Ernie said, "is pretty rare."

"You're sure you want to be a stretcher-bearer? You know, they don't give you a rifle."

"I know that," Ernie said. "So much the worse."

"All right. What instrument do you play?"

His pen at attention, the soldier stared imperturbably at the pink enlistment blank. "If he wants to make jokes," Ernie said to himself, "let's make jokes."

"The drum," he said with forced gaiety.

"There's nothing to laugh about," the sergeant major said. "Next."

Outside, a little old lady pinned a starched patriotic patch on his chest. As he thanked her and made off in confusion, she held him back by a sleeve. "That'll be one franc twenty-five, for a Napoleon badge."

He was back in Montmorency before noon. The city clerk opened his eyes wide but yielded to the rather extraordinary requests of the glorious conscript. Wanting to avoid any chance meeting, Ernie covered the five miles to Enghien on foot. A few flags and some bunting striped the house fronts. The oom-pa of a patriotic carnival blared from windows open on the infinite tenderness of the sky, where small white clouds seemed to drip their milky peace upon the tiny houses at war. A little girl applauded as he passed. Ernie remembered the tricolor badge on his lapel. "Let's see," he said to himself, "what sensations having a country procures for you. . . ." A circle opened around him on the train to Paris. An imposing lady leaned toward her neighbor and, contemplating Ernie Levy's devastated features, remarked acidly, "You can't tell if he's going to war or has just come back. . . ." Someone shut her up. Ernie smiled.

He found himself again in the bistro across from the Gare du Nord and sat at the same table where the secret farewells had taken place.

With the end of one finger he rubbed the corner of the table where three hours earlier Moritz's stubby, reddish square hand had lain. The proprietress brought him paper, pen and an envelope and said, "So, *poilu,* you're writing to your sweetheart before you go?"

"It's a military necessity, isn't it?" Ernie said in his strange accent, where the fleeting vowels of Yiddish fought it out with slow German consonants.

He started a first letter but tore it up when he saw how his handwriting wavered. When he had conquered the trembling of his hand, the rapid, disorderly flight of his thoughts obliged him to try a third time. Then, taking great pains with each of the beautiful Hebrew characters, and repressing each ground swell of his soul, he wrote the following letter:

"Dear Parents, Grandparents, Brothers and Sisters, all wellbeloved. Once more I am making you suffer. When you receive this letter I shall be in a French barracks. Don't ask me how it happened. Ask me no questions, ask me nothing. Moritz and Papa know that this morning I felt dizzy. When I felt better I took a walk and the walk led me to a barracks and there the madness fell upon me. Afterward it was too late. Hard as I pleaded with the general to return my enlistment blank, he refused, the contract was signed. It is a madness that all the wisdom in the world could not resolve, so ask

yourselves no questions, cease to torture yourselves. Madness
merits only silence. You know well that I love you and that
leaving you is no pleasure for me. You must never say,
'Ernie didn't love us.' I think that I wanted to go to war because of the Germans and because of what they did to me. But
don't worry, Grandfather, above all don't worry. I shall not forget that there are men across from me, and besides I am a
stretcher-bearer—I carry no rifle, I carry only men. Don't forget to give Mlle. Golda Fischer the volume of Bialik's poetry.
Apologize to her for me about page 37, where I made a dog-ear
without thinking. And now something for you, venerable grandfather. I know how much I must have made you suffer since the
trouble with the grocer's wife. I know it in my fingertips. But
often it seems to me that the evil that I do is much greater than
the evil which is really within me. Listen. You know what?
Let's talk about something gay. What news of the war? Forgive
me for that joke, but I think it's good to laugh with at least one
eye. Your son, grandson and brother who loves you and kisses
you and takes you in his arms with all the strength of his soul,
and venerates all of you, and asks all of you once more to forgive him, Ernie.

"P.S. In this envelope you will find eight certificates from the
city clerk. For every one of you there is proof that your son,
grandson or brother has enlisted in the French Army. Take
good care of them, because with them you too are a little bit
French, and they won't be able to put you into a concentration
camp. At least for once a little good will come out of all the evil,
and seeing that the madness is already upon me, at least nothing will happen to you. Let the madness do some good anyway,
in return for all the suffering that I cause you today. But it's too
late, because I have signed my name. Your respectful and
loving and sorrowful, Ernie."

· 4 ·

FORTY-EIGHT HOURS after this relatively inglorious volunteer's enlistment in the French Army he ran up against his limitations again, in the ranks of the 429th Foreign Infantry Regiment. Sergeants born in Dresden or Berlin trained irritated glances upon him, and the lieutenant, a Burgundian as gnarled as a root from his native vineyards, warned them bluntly. He wanted no nonsense about the foreigners-draped-in-the-folds-of-the-tricolor. They had better watch their step, and moreover they were confined to quarters until further notice.

Like colonial troops, the 429th Foreign Infantry Regiment turned up regularly on the field of honor. Between battles Ernie banged stoically on a drum in the regimental orchestra—all the musicians, apparently, were not stretcher-bearers, but all the stretcher-bearers were required to be musicians. In that strange May of 1940, a letter reached Ernie on the Ardennes front announcing the internment of his parents, brothers and sisters, grandfather, even Mother Judith. It was from a neighbor of theirs in Paris. He made it superbly clear that the thing was sad and that it was painful.

All the more so, he went on, in that the legal regulation, though it had struck the Levys, was not aimed at them in the least. To tell the truth, no offense had been intended by the said "thing" and they had been locked up only to keep order and maintain respect for the law. Besides, Ernie must in all logic admit that if German Jews were Jews, they were no less German, and it was customary in France, and so on. A letter from his father followed, less serene. The camp at Gurs was described with great restraint, but Ernie in all logic deduced from that letter that what was customary in France conformed at times to the best German tradition. So he yielded to the truth of Benjamin Levy's concluding remark: *"To be a Jew is impossible."*

At the same time, the letter from Gurs aroused the analytic

verve of the captain, who read his foreigners' mail dutifully and enthusiastically. "It's in code!" he thundered desperately. "It might as well as be Hebrew for all I can make of it."

"It *is* Hebrew, Captain," Ernie said without malice, but with a dry touch of Yiddish accent.

Amazement, questions, it must be translated. By chance Nightingale Company also boasted its Jew; they looked for him, they found him, and in all essentials he confirmed Ernie's version.

"And yet, Major," the second Hebrew pointed out, "there's just one thing, a very little thing. . . ."

"In the eyes of France there are no little things. Speak, soldier!" the officer cried, stern and dignified.

"It's just this, General," the second Hebrew said, deeply disturbed. " 'Delicacy' is really an imperfect translation of *'hemdah';* a much better word would be . . ." The rest of his lecture was lost in a colorful outburst, predominantly purple.

The whole affair would have ended in the customary rites and ceremonies of the military art if, as he rewarded both Hebrews—one with two days and one with eight of guardhouse meditation—a singular thought had not crossed the officer's mind. It was this: if Corporal Ernie Levy's entire family had been *removed to an area of maximum security,* his continued existence as a uniformed soldier was a sort of furious, outrageous contradiction, unprecedented in the annals. Should he or should he not arrest Levy on the spot? In that cruel dilemma, with the question taking on national importance, he decided immediately to refer it to a higher echelon.

A courier is dispatched, crawls on his belly, is perplexed, is worried, is overcome by fear. But all the fear in the world is no help. There is no higher echelon. As a last resort, mortified, he grabs an orderly from headquarters who is about to flee by bicycle. Grimly clutching his orderly, the courier crawls back up to battalion—no major; wriggles down to company—no captain.

The rest can be read in the history of France. But not this— that Ernie Levy, placed in the custody of the battalion sergeant major (who had solemnly received him from the ranking officer candidate, upon whom he had been bestowed by the observation officer, who had inherited him directly from the captain)— that Ernie slid so smoothly down the hierarchical ladder that he finally landed in the arms of a private who disappeared suddenly and in a most shameful manner and without passing the orders along, not even to a Polish recruit.

After that his decision was easy. Knowing there was an excellent bicycle in a certain nearby depot, he judged that with his nourishment and means of transport arranged for, all he needed now was an honest traveling companion. But the second Hebrew, after a fond embrace, addressed him in approximately these words: "My dear sir, I shall never be able to tell you how deeply I am touched by your proposition, for I feel quite sure that it was not made simply to a coreligionist but somehow to the man *personally*. Let me therefore thank you for that mark of consideration. And yet . . ."

"And yet?" murmured Ernie, much more saddened by that flowery preamble from a mouth recently converted to French grammar than by the line of fire that was creeping up on them.

"And yet, considering that aside from you I remain the last follower of Moses in the battalion, it seems to me of the highest necessity not to leave the non-Jews with the impression that Israel is no longer with them."

"But there isn't even the shadow of a Frenchman in the battalion!" Ernie cried, finally and entirely out of patience.

"There's me," said the second Hebrew. "I've been in France since 1926 and I'm about to be naturalized."

Ernie smiled bitterly. "All right, we'll be naturalized together. And stuffed, if you think it would be impressive. By the way, do you know the prayer of the dying?"

"I know it. But . . ."

"So do I," Ernie Levy said gently.

"Don't be a defeatist," said the second Hebrew. "Man is weaker than a fly and stronger than iron. Tomorrow the soldiers of Verdun, Waterloo, Valmy, Rocroi, Marignan . . ."

*　*　*

The next day the Nazi pocket burst open, showering a rain of tanks on the Ardennes flank. Reduced to one company, and lacking officers altogether, the 429th Foreign Infantry Regiment elected three veterans of the International Brigade to its command. At the ceremony every man swigged down a large last gulp of *eau de vie,* and a flabbergasted Ernie saw the second Hebrew raise his thin fist above all the others, high above them toward heaven, while his features testified to a most lively satisfaction with himself and with everyone else. At that moment the Spanish officer cried, *"Compañeros!"* Ending a black mutter of conversation in which despair welled up like a bruise, "Comrades, among us there are Garibaldians, Austrian socialists, German communists, Spanish anarchists, Jews, refugees from all over Europe. We've been retreating for years, kicked from border to border. France was the last country, but today France too is betrayed, and the French are rushing toward the sea like sheep. We know that, we know the taste of treason—the ex-communist comrades here tasted it a while ago with the Molotov pact. *Compañeros,* I don't say this to revive old arguments. We're at the last gasp, and I feel hazy and silly, like an old lady's traveling companion. This speech is just to tell you that there's no retreat for us, there's no more emigration. France was the last blockhouse. If you've got thin skin, you can move out now. To the others, by way of a joke, I can offer this proverb from my own country, Catalonia: The man who has hair on his heart is never beaten until he is dead. And to those of you who fought for the Republic, I recall the words of Dolores Ibarruri, La Pasionaria . . ." The little man with a face wrinkled like a walnut shell bent double in a fit of laughter. He whinnied, "We're in great shape! From now on these words sum up our whole"—he laughed at the word— "strategy, and all our"—he laughed again—"revolutionary tactics!"

"What? What did she say?" several dissatisfied voices asked.

The little Spaniard recovered some of his seriousness. "My friends," he announced with some difficulty, "in Madrid La Pasionaria told us that it was better to live on our knees—no—

better to live on our feet—no—*better to die on our feet than live on our knees!"* he shouted suddenly and tensely.

A phrase that the fifty men echoed in one breath, while the tiny, tipsy, triumphant second Hebrew quite openly wept for joy.

A time of waiting followed. Stretched out in a ditch with his rifle beside him, his heart heavy with the thought of the camp at Gurs, Ernie felt the same old amazement that there was no rhyme or reason to the universe. . . . The patriarch hesitated for a second, his soul taut, then plucked a perfectly ripe quotation from the Talmud. Less austere, Ernie's father was happy with a legend gleaned here, with an anecdote picked up there—fruits fallen from the great tree of Jewish knowledge. One of those anecdotes sang in Ernie Levy's memory. It sang with the feverish, ironic voice of Ernie's father, with his bespectacled rabbit's face and his fingers, skilled at analysis as much as at needlework. . . .

"Hear me, brothers. A village rabbi in his sermon taught the perfection of all things: 'And why would the Most High— blessed be his name—why, I ask you humbly, why would he have made evil or imperfection? So, my lambs, the earth is so perfectly round so that the sun may freely and comfortably circle about it. So, you see, the sun is so perfectly round so that its rays, darting out in all directions, shine for everyone, *without exception,* and so that neither the bears at one end nor the Negroes at the other will be left out. And the moon? But what does the moon matter? Let it be enough for you to know that although the moon is not always round, it is always perfect.'

"Hear me, brothers . . . 'And the onions?' asked a child. 'The onions too,' answered the rabbi. 'And radishes with butter?' a second child asked. 'It is just the same for radishes with butter,' answered the rabbi. 'But above all,' he added, fiddling with his beard, 'remember that after him (blessed be his name), man is the most perfect thing in all creation. Man, my little goats—ah, man . . . !'

" 'And me, oh excellent rabbi?' cried out a tiny hunchback.

"The rabbi thought quickly: 'But little animal, sweet little soul,' he murmured with a delicate hint of reproach, *'for a hunchback you're as perfect as can be. . . . Right?' "*

The bittersweet delights of that philosophy suddenly repelled Ernie. That the world bore a fantastic, enormous hump of suffering was not a matter for joking. For his part, he knew that the Most High—blessed be his name throughout the centuries —had endowed him notably with a matrix made to measure, crystalline and cold and transparent as glass, imprisoning him body and soul, and reflecting with tearless perfection the white ward in the hospital, the gleaming lights of the pogrom, the delicately blue sky of suburban Paris, and this dawn, stinking delicately of blood and gnawed at by a swarm of Junkers. . . .

And this was added to his memories a few hours later—the dazzling end of the second Hebrew, recipient of a projectile in that region which the Zohar calls the Third Eye, or the Eye of the Center, or the Eye of the Interior Vision, for the obvious reason that situated as it is, precisely between the external eyes, with it is extinguished all human consciousness, "be it noble as the sun, be it pure as light, be it innocent as childhood," as had been demonstrated to the second Hebrew that morning. And this was added to his memories—the ritual burial of the second Hebrew in a grave dug miraculously by a bomb, his arms crossed upon his chest, phylacteries clinging like ivy to his forehead, and above them, enveloping him as if for the Prayer of Forgiveness, the gentle black-and-white shroud of the prayer shawl. And this was added to his memories—the no less admirable annihilation of the 429th Foreign Infantry Regiment. And this was added to his memories—the retreat, of an altogether Celtic innocence, half on the magic steeds of Providence, half on the bicycle noted above. The burial of a human trunk lying at the roadside near Chalon-sur-Saône. The last tribute offered to a child lying face down beneath a burst of gunfire from the sky. The cool fraternity of a yellow-gloved officer who said to him, "My dear fellow, the situation is desperate, but not serious."

And then was added the announcement of the French Army's surrender. The discovery of the sempiternal blue of the Riviera. The announcement that France had ceded half of herself to the conqueror. The apprenticeship in degeneration.

And finally the announcement in 1941 of the complete delivery—including the terms and conditions of transport—of the internees at Gurs to Nazi extermination camps.

Even imprisoned by his protective matrix, Ernie Levy felt that this last straw had broken the camel's back. Now, for the second time, the happy thought of hanging himself came to him. We hasten to add that he did nothing of the kind. "And why did he want to hang himself? And why didn't he hang himself?" Interesting questions indeed. But our space being limited, we merely point out that he never forgave himself for not going through with it.

· 5 ·

WEAK AND DIZZY, Ernie Levy invoked the domestic shades in these words: "Oh, my father, oh, my mother, oh, my brothers, oh, my sisters, oh, patriarch, oh, Mother Judith . . . How is it that losing you I cannot lose myself with you? If it is the will of the Eternal, our God, I damn his name and beg him to gather me up close enough to spit in his face. And if, as all my comrades in the 429th Foreign Infantry Regiment taught me, we must see the will of nature everywhere and in all things, I ask Nature humbly to make me an animal as quickly as possible. Oh, my loved ones, Ernie exiled from Levy is a plant without light.

"Which is why, with your permission, I shall do everything humanly possible from now on to turn myself into a dog. So, my beloved family, I ask you to consider this message as my last farewell."

We may mention discreetly, to his discredit, that a Mediterranean Indian summer, than which nothing is lovelier, added greatly to the sweetness of life.

"Let's see now, brother," Ernie Levy was soon asking himself. "How do you turn into a dog in this part of the world?" In the process he adopted a way of life whose logical refinement will be obvious to the reader. From Tarde's original experiments, we know that imitation is at least second nature, if not all of nature. Following that line of thought, and if it is established that one's way of looking at life, of plucking rose leaves or cutting up a chicken, is rigidly bound by biological frontiers, we may agree without cavil that, wishing to lose his human identity, Ernie could do no better than to work industriously at absorbing, with all his heart and soul, the local manner of being a dog.

To begin such an apprenticeship, the late Ernie Levy decided to answer to the surname of Bastard, which seemed rather appropriate to his new position. First name, Ernest. Man or dog, not to take him on his own terms would be to offend the creature uselessly.

But baptism entails sacramental rites, and as he had once been circumcised in his now rejected Levy skin, he redeemed that secret heresy by the progressive addition of a mustache most Catholic in its form, consistency and grooming. Rome thus acknowledged, he was also obliged to acknowledge that it was a bit ridiculous, that whimsical symbol, indeed frivolous without the strong support of a beard. Not the least effect of his mustache was to give him the look of a poodle. And his walk, until then a gloomy slouch, took on a friskiness that is surely not found once in a hundred years among Polish Jews, even converted.

Much transformed by all his new charms, the late Ernie Levy, toward the end of August, 1941, three months after his conversion to the canine species, entered a small bistro in the Vieux-Port of Marseilles, the city where he had established his

kennel. . . . His entrance triggered a few laughs. Despite the
torrid heat he was bundled up in his old, mangy, tattered,
patched Army overcoat, far more repellent than the coat of a
dog with ringworm. His collar was fastened with a safety pin.
A string supported his trousers at the waist. A forage cap covered his unkempt hair, and below that a kind of mustached
muzzle with drooping eyes seemed to be in search of some old
bone to gnaw on in a corner. Reeling with hunger, he stepped
to the bar and asked for a glass of water. The waiter, a ruddy,
fat, humorous man, first claimed—to the indescribable joy of
his other customers—not to have in stock one drop of that dangerous "medicine." Then he served the vagabond with a beer
glass full of the local red, and seeing him hesitate shoved his
nose into the wine, inciting him to drink. The poor unfortunate's
gurglings inspired the waiter. He raised Ernie's head and offered to "bottle-feed" him. Two red furrows ran from the corners of Ernie's mouth to his chin and neck. Carried away by the
joke, a customer slapped him on the back "to make it go down
better." The liquid sprayed all over his face.

"That'll be enough," a voice said from the end of the room.

The waiter stopped respectfully. Ernie swabbed his face with
a sleeve and discovered an elegant, swarthy, curly-haired gentleman standing with his back to a cheerful table where cele-
brants of both sexes were enjoying a noontime *pastis*.

"We didn't mean any harm, M. Mario," the waiter's hesitant
voice said at Ernie's ear.

"Good God," the man said in his singsong accent, "just to
look at you makes me feel bloodthirsty. You're fatter than any
pig." Then, coming toward Ernie in a slow, majestic stride that
seemed to consist entirely in the motion of his shoulders,
"What's the matter, soldier, famine on the land? You should
have pushed this son of a bitch's face in. You're a great speci-
men of manhood. It wasn't heroes like you that we needed to
win the war. You want to put away a *pastis* with us? We're all
veterans of the bicycle brigades except for the girls. At least you
don't have fleas?"

An hour later, his hair combed, his body clean, wearing a

two-toned shirt, Ernie was participating actively in a kind of family banquet on the second floor of a shabby restaurant. M. Mario had developed a strange affection for him since noticing the pink scar of suicide on the beggar's wrist. Later on Ernie was to discover an identical symbol on M. Mario's right wrist. M. Mario was left-handed. But for the moment he asked no questions, and gave himself over altogether to a mastication tenderly supervised by M. Mario, who leaned confidentially toward him. "Now let me tell you again—you eat, and you let it settle a little, and then you drink, then you take a little leak if you want. If not, pal, you're a goner. I've had it too, you know, in my time. . . ."

M. Mario's friends seemed to be celebrating recent high profits. At first restrained by the presence of a guest, they gradually generated an eloquent debate on business in general and on the traffic in cigarettes, milk products, leather and medicine in particular. The men loosened their belts, and the women laughed shrill laughs that ended sharply. Mélanie came and went up and down the stairway to the kitchen. She was a very dignified woman, although still quite young, and Ernie did not understand why, every time she passed, the men—under the blissful gaze of their wives—felt the need to make extremely bold passes at her, passes she did not seem to notice, keeping her head erect above the dishes. Yet he too fell to laughing at it, and intoxicated with joy, drunken-eyed, he decided to be a dog.

First it was vigorous "arf-arf"'s that he barked against his plateful of bones, then a spectacular tumble, after which he got up on all fours and, amid general hilarity, galloped grotesquely around the large table. One of the women threw him a bone, which he dug into, teeth flashing, in perfect mimicry. Screams of laughter. Ecstatic women writhing. Finally he springs at Mélanie on all fours, and tries to bite off a pretty chunk of flesh. Her back to the wall, the waitress protects herself and invokes his higher feelings. Waves of laughter. Finally Ernie gives in to her stirring pleas, sits up, delicately pinches Mélanie on the cheek and barks in her face. But suddenly feeling the extrava-

gant sweetness of a human face between his thumb and his index finger, he cries, "Mélanie!" flinging himself backward as if
the touch had burned his fingers. Laughter all around. Which
stops suddenly when they see that Ernie is galloping around the
table at a frantic, desperate rate and that tears from the depths
of his drunken soul are running down his cheeks while he barks
hoarsely, as if at death—barks, barks endlessly. . . .

The Veterans, as they called themselves ironically, gathered
often in a bungalow that looked out over the docks. They were
a dozen or so young men brought together by the military dis-
appointments of the Exodus, in a common awareness of absurd-
ity and of the secret shame of those who are defeated inglori-
ously. "We were sold down the river," some of them said, rat-
tling off the proof. "We were weak and naïve," retorted others,
more aware of moral frailty. "We were cowards," insisted a
third group, mostly escaped prisoners who drank more than the
first two groups to forget what treason, weakness and naïveté
could not absolve them of. These last seemed to be waiting,
alert to any signal for a new fulfillment. The black market
gilded it all with a comfortable, tolerable varnish. With these
people Ernie discovered that he had a cashier's talent, and the
sensitive antennae of the "universal snoop." But the primary
origin of the esteem they held him in generally was his capacity
for cold drink; the second, his capacity for raw meat. Although
this last talent offended the delicacy of some people, Ernie's
"raw meal" was a real circus act: bloody meats, sausages of all
kinds, lumps of fresh blood stuffed him to the ears. Strangers
admitted without explanation were frightened.

"The blood will be running out of your eyes," his patron said
to him one day, amused. "Don't you like anything else?"

"Only animal's blood, M. Mario," Ernie excused himself.

"All right, all right, what I was saying was for your own
good. . . ."

The Jews do not slaughter their own animals; a kind of holy
executioner does the job according to millennial ritual. Blood

being the basis of life, the animal is bled to the last drop. Then his blood, collected in a gutter, is buried. This symbolic funeral of a chicken, a duck or a calf marks the respect due to all the forms of creation. In appearance Ernie had been stringy, gloomy and puny as a result of the vegetarianism that a strict observance of dietary laws had condemned him to after his enlistment. Now he was beginning to look like a fat, good-natured, gluttonous, Rabelaisian personality. He had a huge, fat paunch, which in France is popularly called a *brioche,* as much for its characteristic shape as for the gentle good humor to which it disposes its owner. But was the word *brioche* really appropriate? Intellectual rectitude obliges us to set down a reservation on that point. For the *brioche,* that superfluous furnishing, grows pianissimo ("have a brioche"), in an always harmonious ensemble (pink, round, laughing, and so on.) . . . But if carefully observed, Ernie's face revealed its chronic sickly emaciation, and his eyes revealed nothing of the warm, emotional brilliance of a tranquil soul in perfect repose. Certain people (whose testimony we cannot trust absolutely) claim to have noticed that *the fatter the late Ernie Levy's paunch grew, the thinner grew his face.* And his companions accused him of chewing stiffly, even sadly. And then, they wondered, how was it that he could take in so much heady nourishment and yet not devote the slightest part of so much vital energy to love? In fact, despite his age, a certain vigor, and his extraordinary appetite, the late Ernie Levy seemed to be doggedly alienating himself from human affections.

In truth, the late Ernie Levy had deceived his audience from the first day. Passion was smoldering in his heart. Strangely drunk on the night of the fatal banquet, he lay sleepless afterward, with the feeling that between his thumb and finger there had momentarily been something supernaturally soft and smooth. Whether that sweet, tender something in Mélanie's face had clung to his fingers, or his fingers had been made tender by her cheek, he could not say. When he awoke the next morning he knew, though he was still a dog, that some new force was at work in his world. While he mused upon it, the lustrous sweetness of Mélanie's face at his fingertips reminded him of her presence. He rubbed his fingers together quickly, to make her disappear, but in vain.

That tenderness refused to leave him. Wherever he went from then on, whatever he did, even when he believed himself lost, body and soul, in one of his revels, he found himself sadly caressing Mélanie's face. When he saw her again a few days later he thought her transformed—all the facets of her careworn person glowed for him. She felt the difference, and showed him small attentions unnoticeable to the insensitive. But Ernie, troubled, thought it over. He suspected that even at the lowest levels of love there were phenomena that tricked the imagination and would tempt even a dog to thoughts dangerous to his future. And yet the longer he thought it over, the higher a frightening languor rose along his arm, weaving its threads one by one, enveloping the arm in a sheath that quivered at the slightest breath, at the most gentle motion. When Mélanie's face had reached his shoulder several months later, and invaded his breast, made his heart beat heavily, the late Ernie Levy realized in terror that he was in love with the girl!

Fearing the worst, he decided to offer his homage to a streetwalker as soon as possible. But when she left her post in the dark doorway he was moved by her animal lassitude, and when she stood before him in her garret, gossiping affably under the naked bulb that sharpened her features cruelly, the young madman's heart suffered excruciatingly.

"Pardon me, Mme. Whore," he said in his strange accent. "I've changed my mind. Be kind enough to take this money and let me go."

"Are you sick? Are you sad? Don't you like me? How sad your eyes are. You're a foreigner, you're not from around here."

"Sadness," Ernie said, "is not for me."

"Then do you hurt?"

Ernie sat down on the bed, considered, invented an autobiography. When he had finished telling her about his family in Marseilles he went on to his grandparents from Toulon, to the numerous relatives he had in the area of Nîmes, reeling it all

off like so many titles that would make him a man in the eyes
of the world. "And you?" he asked finally.

The girl hesitated, invented a child for herself, then another,
then augmented them by an aged mother, for these are among
the props that accent the pathetic. Then she began to joke, and
between wisecracks and caresses she turned out the light with a
kind of loving discretion. She babbled on even while she practiced the last outrages upon the poor madman.

When he came to himself in the street, feeling a certain new
and more complete sweetness, Ernie realized that he was
in love with the prostitute—or at least considerably more
taken with her than with Mélanie, who ran a poor second
now and for whom, in all honesty, he no longer felt more than a
small tingling in one finger. At an outdoor café his enthusiasm
cooled. As he sat down, his legs moist with tenderness, he noticed that one of the girls from Belle-de-Mai, the Negro section,
was seated near him. There were gilded whalebone combs in
her chignon, and her upswept hairdo seemed woven of black
silk above a face carved in rare woods of the Eastern isles. Immediately all his false tenderness, all the impious tingling disappeared, giving way to a yet stranger intoxication, this time
centered in his eyes, and he knew that the young Negress had
inspired eternal love in him. Then another, milky white, who
was gliding along the sidewalk like a ship, all sails full before
the wind, ravished his heart no less thoroughly. Then it was another, then still another. In the next few days he forgot all
about swigging cold drink and eating raw meat. Ernie wandered
like a troubled soul among the streets infested with faces,
dotted with eyes like so many stars twinkling in his night. Finally he decided to leave the city as soon as he could. For if a
dog, he said to himself in his delirium, gives in to love just
once, he soon thinks nothing of going without food. And from
fasting he backslides to temperance and breaking the siesta,
and from there to daydreaming and the impulse to write poetry.
And once on the downward trail, he never knows where it
might end. Doubtless more than one dog could date his fall
from some passing fancy that seemed unimportant at the time.

.6.

E RNIE spent the whole winter of 1942 roaming the Rhone
Valley, working upstream against the season's furious
mistral. At night its screaming winds mingled strangely with
the harsh, dark, shrieking wind that swept through his wounded
brain. His diet in Marseilles had filled him out. He had no trouble finding work in a countryside depleted of its men by the
German prison camps. He was in a black hole the whole time.
Systematically he cultivated his lowest instincts. Now and then
he brawled like an animal. His object, though unformulated,
was to bar any infiltration of light into the hole. One day he
surprised himself in a mirror. He was pleased to note that his
former face was somehow still hanging on the gallows of Marseilles. All the features that ordinarily compose a face—nose,
mouth, eyes, ears—were there in their proper shapes and usual
places, but they did not constitute a human face. They seemed
detached one from another, and the late Ernie Levy suspected
that it would have made no difference if he had worn his ears
where his eyes were, or his eyes in his dark nostrils, for example.

He wound up near Saint-Sylvestre on a small farm owned by
a prisoner's wife who, from the height of her weakness, ruled
with a rod of iron over the waifs and strays the invasion periodically sent her way. In a woman too weak to be captain of her
own fate, and too demanding to resign herself, delicacy is easily
transformed into treachery. Mme. Trochu had adopted a certain
independence since her husband's incarceration. She breathed
a bit more easily, even considering herself a free woman, and
between packages to Germany she slept with all comers among
her hired hands, while waiting for the man whom she would
now know how to domesticate, if he didn't kill her first. She was
a woman of Provence with eyes like black, sour raisins and a
harsh mouth, but paradoxically she was carved from fire and
ice. At first glance Ernie estimated that she could never make
him dream, so he considered her with no fear and took a fancy

to her. Restored to his bloody meats, he let a happy time go by. Then she commanded, and he obeyed.

As he did not love her in the least, the late Ernie Levy imposed a penance upon himself—to display a herculean passion, which she accepted without question. She was a modest soul, so exquisitely composed that in love she sought only the proofs of love, provided that they were sufficiently repeated: they called her the Glutton. We could have great fun showing how the late Ernie Levy established those proofs, and as his otherwise undemanding mare based all her reactions on that, nothing happened between them that did not relate to the disposition and management of those proofs. But we may pass along—such common things are not worth discussion.

"My love," the excellent lady asked, "a bit more kidney?

"A pepper?

"A little pheasant? It's three weeks old. It does that little god of yours so much good." And endearments—*"bijou, chou, caillou, pou, hibou."*

The late Ernie did not answer, opening his mouth only to champ at his food. But now and then, dreamily, helped along by nostalgia, he tried to figure out which meat, raw, roasted, or simply boiled, was most compatible with a bestiality that was aboriginal and therefore his own.

For the rest, domiciled, laundered, stuffed with food, honored by the whole village and respected in the connubial bed, he was what we on earth call (and have called since time immemorial) a happy mortal. Even better—his amorous benefactress, fearing to overwork him, took it upon herself—working it out by a private arithmetic—to spare him the pains of sowing, spading, planting, clearing fields, harvesting, digging potatoes, and the like; the bother of constant cold drink; and even the annoying necessity of getting out of bed.

"Look at the geese!" she cried on a note of triumph. "Follow their example!"

At which the late Ernie Levy dropped docilely to all fours, stumped out to the front yard, saluted his rooster colleague on his dunghill, cousin goose in its coop, threw an envious glance at the current capon, and finally, as always, pushed along to the pigpen, which evoked a cold fascination mingled with a hate so excruciating that at times, in a fury, he spat Judaically upon the impure beast.

That night he had a strange dream. As usual he was embracing a thoroughbred Airedale, and as usual he was amazed at the intensity of the joy he took in his beloved. If, he said to himself, the appearance of man had been denied him, at least his essence remained spiritual. Proof: the heights of joy occasioned by a bitch.

But at the very moment when, as the Zohar says, "All visible things die to be born again invisible," the bitch was transformed into a splendid cat whose eyes shone in the night; embodying the thousand twists and turns of desire, she enticed Ernie into the dance again. And why, too, by what malicious spell, did the cat, at the moment spoken of in the Zohar, become a rat, and then a beetle, a cockroach, a snail, and so on, finally melting against him in a living, seething mass, in a drunken, ameboid crawl toward oblivion in the sea of infinity?

Though she was inordinately proud of Ernie's proofs, the farmer's wife accorded him a new respect when he told her that he felt bad when he thought about the man whose bed and wife he was occupying. That's the height of *cynicism,* she told herself, impressed. For a long time she tried to make him admit it, acknowledge his cynicism, but when the sly fox refused, her respect became even greater.

In the same manner, he never admitted that he was not from Bordeaux (as a certain identity card in the name of Ernest Bastard stated falsely). So his admirable loyalty to his "Alsatian" accent made the woman think that he was an escaped prisoner. Giving her curiosity full rein, she deduced from a certain detail of the bedchamber that he was an Israelite, but as she preached the greatest tolerance in religious matters, she never mentioned her discovery—and anyway that peculiarity, taking one thing with another, added a certain spice. Since girlhood she had dreamed of meeting a circumcised man. The desire dated from her early catechism, the priest having imprudently mentioned the circumcision of the heart, at which the little Dumoulin girl had snickered, as she often did under the influence of her father, the teacher, who, unable to keep his pious wife from going to church, obliged his daughter, a little lady of no religion at all, to attend catechism and heckle the priest. The catechumens had assembled for an illegal conference on the theme of circumcision. Mlle. Dumoulin explained, on her father's orders, that the Israelites, the first monotheists, customarily sacrificed a small piece of their bodies to their God. And that the priests, the second monotheists, not wishing to be behindhand, and in any case rather timid, confined themselves to clipping a small curl of hair from the skull.

M. Dumoulin, a perfect layman, never called the Jews anything but Israelites. Way down deep he almost believed that the word Jew had been invented by the Jesuits to annoy the Freemasons. And from all that emerged one consequence quite distressing to the late Ernie Levy, who fell from his heights when, toward the end of an afternoon, as he was resting on the bed, his farmer's wife rushed in, her face afire, and addressed him in approximately these words: "You lied to me. You're a Jew."

"Oh, come on now. You mean you never had the faintest idea?"

"I know that you're an Israelite, because . . . yes. But I was just talking to the town clerk, and he told me that all Israelites were *automatically* Jews."

"That's possible. But what's the difference?"

"What's the difference?" she cried indignantly. "I can't have a Jew sleeping in my Pierre's bed and sitting in his armchair and wearing his clothes and his shirts! Ah, no, no, what you did was awful!"

"All right," said the late Ernie. He got up.

"Where are you going?"

"Away."

"But why? I can make up a nice bed for you in the barn."

"And the rest?" asked the young madman.

"Well, we'll have to be careful. You can't see poor old Pierre"—she always said "poor old Pierre," indicating as much her grief at knowing him a prisoner as the strange compassion that swept over her when she realized he was being deceived—"You can't see poor old Pierre finding out that we—that I—did it—with a Jew? No, no, we'll do it in the stable.

"And anyway," she added suddenly, "you've been taking it a little too easy lately. You'll have to do what I say now. And put a little less butter on your bread, too."

"And if I don't like it that way?"

"What's this I hear?" she said dryly.

"All right," said the madman.

With those slight alterations, life went on as before. The mistral had disappeared. A slow heat rose from the earth. The olive trees were no longer tormented, and sometimes in the evening all things seemed to rise toward the cheery happiness of the peaceful sky. On Sunday Ernie went into town, heard Mass vacantly, and then, between two dreamy *pastis,* went to watch the living play *pétanque* in the shadow of the church porch. One of the players threw a glance at him once that made him turn pale. It was the village blacksmith; he was a returned prisoner, and he bowled with his body rigid from the effects of a grenade. Ernie saw him again at his forge. By tacit agreement both kept silent about the mysterious thing that had brought them together. In a northerner's face the blacksmith had two warm, subtle, constantly flickering southern eyes. He was a big fellow with long limbs that ended in wide feet and thick hands, and he balanced himself carefully, like a tightrope walker, when he moved. When he spread his hands flat, they took up an impressive amount of space. Long fingers, pudgy at the base, tapered to flat ends with odd fingernails. Ernie thought they were like very sturdy pliers with the sensitivity of antennae. It was obvious that he had not been born with those hands, those two machine tools whose skin was thick, gray, stitched with burn scars and with nerves and muscles far more complicated, Ernie guessed, than any animal paw. Ernie watched them move precisely through the forest of controls of a multiple drill, or withdraw a glowing diamond from a wreath of sparks, and he felt that a considerable part of the blacksmith's intelligence had shifted to his fingertips, because he made his living with them. Which is why he followed their movements with more respect at each visit.

The blacksmith never asked him the questions that oblige a man to construct a more and more complicated scaffolding, at the mercy of the slightest breath of truth. Only the future seemed to interest the artisan, who occasionally let slip phrases heavy with hidden meanings, but without looking at Ernie. "My boy," he said, "there are things that make us feel they'll never end, like a good stiff mistral after a week of steady blowing. And then one morning the sun comes out. You understand?" Then he invited Ernie for a "drop" of *pastis,* and they went down the three steps at the far end of the shop. The fat, beribboned woman brought them a jug of cold water, and she, like the other, did not question Ernie about his past, as if she had joined her husband's conspiracy. When the children came back from school, they often kept their guest on for dinner, and even the children seemed to retreat from any innocent inquisitions, wanting only to have fun with the mad young man who occasionally emerged from his delirium and discovered, in one heart-rending flash, that impossible world under his very eyes—that unsuspected France, simple and good as bread. And though he was obscurely afraid that they would melt away the chains weighing on his soul, he could not keep himself from returning to that dangerous source of light.

"Listen," he said to his friend the blacksmith one day, "I feel somehow that you know me from somewhere. Even the first time . . ."

The blacksmith hesitated momentarily. "My boy, my boy," he murmured gently without raising his glance from the anvil, "I never saw you before, believe me. But I knew right away that you were Jewish."

"But I'm not!" Ernie cried in panic.

The man left his hammer on the anvil and crossed the room to place his heavy hands on the young Jew's shoulders.

"So it's that obvious," Ernie said in an odd voice, a slow, musical voice flowing from his throat with the moving ease of a remembered melody.

At which the blacksmith spoke. "I don't know what a Jew looks like," he said. "All I can see is the man. We had some in Stalag 17, but I never thought about it until afterward, after the Fritzes came and took them away. But when I got back from the prison camp I took a detour up toward Paris because of a buddy's wife—he was dead. She lived in Drancy. It was pretty early in the morning, and German motorcycle troops told us to line up on the sidewalk, and we saw buses zipping by in a hurry, full of Jewish kids with stars all over them. They were all at the windows, they looked out at us, and looked out at us, and looked out at us. And their hands were clawing slowly at the glass as if they wanted out. And I couldn't see any one face very clearly, but they all had eyes like I'd never seen before, and like I hope I'll never see again in this life. And when I saw you for the first time, my boy, it wasn't when we were playing *pétanque* but in church, at High Mass. And I couldn't see your face very well, but right away I *recognized your eyes*. You understand?"

"Ah," Ernie said, touched to the heart.

He got up and staggered out. Outside he heard the first cry, not right against his ear as before, but far off, still muffled by the tough shell of doghood that he was holding together with all his strength, though it was already crumbling. At the top of the path to the Trochu farm the cries, in spite of the flowering almond trees and all the other things that often distracted him, had become so loud that he stopped his ears several times. First he recognized the patriarch's cry, then Mother Judith's. Then he seemed to be coming out of a long dream and suddenly wondered if he was entirely sane. That question, as soon as he framed it, caused such atrocious pain that he brought both hands to his throat as if he would open it wider to the air. The farmer's wife thought he was sick. He stretched out in the barn and tried to escape the cries by covering himself entirely with straw. Now and then he poked his head out to breathe

the night air of Provence. When he fell asleep nothing within him had loosened. It was simply that the cries came from inside him now. He dreamed that he was a dog running along the boulevards of a great city while passers-by pointed to him, surprised but nonchalant: "Look there, a dog with Jewish eyes!" The hunt began without warning, and already people were running toward him from everywhere, brandishing nets that covered the whole sky. A cellar sheltered him, and he thought he was safe until the sound of his pursuers came through the door, demanding that he give them at least his eyes. "My eyes? But that's silly." And suddenly screaming at the top of his voice, "We won't! We'll never give up our eyes, never, never, never. *We'd sooner give up our lives,* arf, arf!"

Ernie Levy got dressed in the darkness and left the barn. The whole farm, the fence, the nearby olive grove were bathed in black water vibrating with milky currents. He opened the wooden gate, changed his mind and went to the house. The sound of a man's voice preceded Mme. Trochu's worried exclamation. "I've come to say goodbye," he said through the door.

A light gleamed. Mme. Trochu opened the door, furious. "What do you mean running off in the night like a thief?" She had thrown on a bathrobe that smothered her in red flowers, and over her shoulder Ernie discovered in his former place the naked body of a man he did not know. But though he recognized every object in the room, the luxurious oaken bed, the lampshade throwing that greenish light to the ceiling, the slippers into which he had placed his feverishly trembling feet many times, the nauseating odor of flesh against flesh in a room that was never really aired out, it seemed to him that this whole life had detached itself from him and was floating before his eyes like a dead fish. Mme. Trochu too seemed dispossessed of her customary personality. She was neither beautiful nor ugly, as he had tried vainly to define her before. She pitched and rolled gently in her poor female flesh, without destination, without moorings, drifting with the current.

"I wanted to say goodbye," he repeated. "I thought it was only right." He had spoken in a sweet, low voice that made her quiver. Bringing her hands suddenly to her exposed bosom, she cried, "My God, what have I done!" She wrung her hands furiously.

"Now, now, no need to cry," Ernie said. He took a step into the bedroom toward the farmer's wife, petrified by some unnamable grief. "You know very well that a woman like you will never want for men, right?"

"But he's a child! *He's a child!*" the woman exclaimed, staring at Ernie with wide eyes. Then she said nothing, and only her hands spoke, twisting together in fury against her breast while Ernie retreated timidly toward the door. At the last moment he turned for a farewell smile, but the woman's lips were twisting soundlessly.

On the wooded path down toward the village, he again had the feeling that he had forgotten something at the farm, but he did not know what.

"Dirty dog," he murmured suddenly.

And sitting down in the middle of the dark path, surrounded by shadows that seemed to be the shadows of his life itself, he hunched forward and strewed earth upon his hair, in the immemorial Jewish technique of humiliation.

That too left him dissatisfied.

Then, stretching out a hand in the darkness he slapped himself several times. But soon he felt that the slapper was himself, and the one who was slapped another himself, and it was like beating someone else—in spite of his cheek, which still stung. For which reason, he remained dissatisfied.

Then he scratched his left hand with his right and his right hand with his left, to cancel out the pleasure that the latter might have derived, so that neither hand could be considered the victor. But always there was born a third hand.

Then he tried to remember all the old-fashioned methods of self-abasement. And he invoked the name of God. And he saw nothing there before which he could reasonably abase himself. And he evoked the image of his own people, but doubtless they were too long dead for the image to be of much use.

Then he remained motionless and dry. And he stooped and picked up a stone, and in the pain he felt at cracking open his cheek, a tear finally escaped his eyes. Then two. Then three. And as he laid his cheek against the earth, sobbing, rediscovering deep within himself the source of tears that he thought had run dry when little Ilse applauded three times, and while Ernie Levy felt himself die, and come to life, and die again, his heart, sweetly, opened to the light, as it had done long ago.

VII

THE MARRIAGE
OF
ERNIE LEVY

*It happens that a people loses its sons:
That is a great loss, surely, and there is
no easy consolation. But here comes Dr.
Soifer, with his own loss. . . . For he is
one of those who are in the process of
losing their people. . . . What? What
is he losing? . . . No one ever heard of
such a loss!*

DAVID BERGELSON, A Candle for the
Dead. *Translated from the Yiddish.
Posthumous.*

. 1 .

THE OLD QUARTER of the Marais, once a resort of the nobility, is probably the most ramshackle in Paris. So the ghetto was part of it. On every shopwindow a six-pointed star alerted the Christian stroller. These stars were also displayed on the breasts of furtive pedestrians, who glided along the walls like shadows, but here they were pieces of yellow cloth the size of a starfish, sewn above the heart and bearing a hallmark of human manufacture: "Jew." Ernie noticed that the children's badges were the same size as the adults' and seemed to devour the frail chests, their six points dug in like claws. Ernie couldn't believe the sight of these tiny branded livestock; he thought he made out a dim halo of fear above them. But the disbelief faded fast.

The Association was on the Rue des Ecouffes, which seemed to him the most "picturesque" in the neighborhood, and the building in which it was quartered the most drooping and woebegone.

His heart pounding with curiosity, and with that moist anguish which rises from certain disused staircases, he knocked at the narrow door on the sixth floor. A little old man opened it. Over his shoulder Ernie made out three little old men standing in line, as if to review him. The master of the house raised a hand to his skullcap and tilted it forward a quarter of an inch, then dropped the hand to its ritual position.

"Pray come in," murmured the first little old man. His tiny, ceremonious voice reminded Ernie of the sour, temperately courteous voice of his father Benjamin. When his host had closed the door behind Ernie, he took a step forward, bowed almost imperceptibly, extended his right hand and said, "Good day, Monsieur!" Then the second, the third, the fourth old man greeted him. They all had the same pointed beard, the same small eyes buried deep beneath the majestic slope of the Israelite forehead. But the first attested his culture by pronouncing "Monsieur" in perfect harmony with its spelling and etymology, while the others were more easily satisfied, one with "Mossieu," another with "Moussi," and lastly and oddly, the third with "Missiou."

The master of the house introduced him soberly to those three personalities, who proved to be, in the order of pronunciation, vice-president, secretary-general, and treasurer of the Association. "As for ourself," he finished, raising a hand to his heart (this impersonal "ourself" seemed much more fitting than a "me" steeped in pride and complacency), "we are the president."

While his host completed this ceremony, punctuating each introduction with a respectful pause, Ernie took the liberty of examining the headquarters of the Paris Association of Old Zemyock: a cube seven feet on every side, a dormer window on the courtyard, a jug and a basin, a sewing machine with an unfinished garment upon it, fifty or sixty books on a shelf—Hebrew, French, German, Russian, perhaps Yiddish—a small table, a tiny wall cupboard, an alcohol stove in a corner, with a pot and a plate upon it, a bed, a chair. All of it meticulously disposed in the moonlike light of the room, and in the odor of antiquity.

"May I ask the object of the gentleman's visit?" inquired the president in a voice made thin by his worry at Ernie's silence. . . .

Abashed, Ernie could only answer "Yes, yes," and fell silent again, feeling in his confusion that he was an intruder.

"Feel free to speak. Have no fear," said the president with a sad, dry smile. "I have already guessed that you are here to arrest us, not so?" he finished with that same melancholy, shrewd smile in his small shining eyes.

"Oh," Ernie murmured.

"Have no fear, sir, we are quite ready," the president went

on, staring at him in sad fascination. "We were expecting you. . . ."

And with a gentle sweep of his foot, he pointed out four small bundles carefully lined up on the floor near the door.

"I beg of you," Ernie said in Yiddish. And unburdening himself beneath the calm gaze of the small shining eyes, he added, "I am the grandson of Mordecai Levy. My grandfather brought me here before the war. And . . . and . . ." he sobbed, "I beg of you. . . ."

The four old men immediately began talking all at once, and their voices, at first restrained by their emotion at Ernie's presence, soon rose to extraordinary heights, reaching the shrillness peculiar to old men and children, while a dance of lamentation took place in time to that discordant, plaintive concert, arms raised to heaven, hands twisting, small, skinny bodies swaying back and forth. From their eyes, turned toward a heaven momentarily quite close, fell those thin and transparent old man's tears, which linger glittering on the eyelids and then run off to disappear in wrinkles and beard.

When the first wave of emotion had passed, the old gentlemen turned to Ernie again. A ballet commenced, each of them attempting to show the greatest respect for the person of the Levys' descendant, to compose the most delicate tribute. The master of the house pulled a handkerchief from his pocket, dusted off the only chair carefully, as though it were a religious relic, covered it with a cushion of aged silk and begged Ernie at great length to do him the honor of sitting upon it. As Ernie squeezed back a tear the old man leaned toward him and stroked his cheek paternally, murmuring with a regretful smile, "Forgive us, we are so *permanently* afraid. May I hope . . . ?" The vice-president extracted a slightly flattened cigarette from a metal box and extended it to Ernie, his arm stretched to its full length, as an offering. The secretary-general opened a small bag of peppermints. And finally the treasurer trotted to Ernie, stared unbearably into his eyes, took his right hand in his own two gnarled ones and said, "Missiou, Missiou," and was then shaken by a brief sob.

Ernie noticed that they were all costumed for the slow, miserly death of old men. Missiou's shoes did not match—one was high, the other low. But it also seemed to him that on their caftans shiny with age the four yellow stars, sewed on with big, awkward stitches, were floating, even fluttering, with the fragile, innocent grace of butterflies. He had taken a seat on the cushion, and the four old men were sitting in a line on the edge of the bed.

"We had no idea," the president began, trying to put Ernie at his ease, "no idea at all that your father had a son thirty years old. It is true that before the war we were not yet president but simply assistant treasurer (which office no longer exists today). Alas! The day is not far when the Association will be extinguished, gently but physically, as a candle is extinguished—first myself, I hope, then another, then another, then the fourth. And tell me, what will be important then? Dead flesh cannot feel the sword."

Ernie wiped a hand across his eyes and murmured as if to himself, "But what are you saying? My father has no thirty-year-old son."

"Then how old are you?" the four cried together.

Ernie smiled to see them so lively and impetuous, so young, he thought irreverently. "Sometimes," he said, still smiling, "I feel a thousand years old. But from my father's point of view, may God take him into his gentle hands, I'm only twenty."

The president examined him with horrified attention, turned to the other three and launched a passionate debate in Polish, during which Ernie forced himself to remain politely detached.

Then renewing conversation with the visitor, "Then you escaped from *their* hell?"

"I've just come from the unoccupied zone," Ernie said flatly. "This morning. What hell were you speaking of?"

"Do you mean that you've come from *out there?*" the president asked, examining Ernie's face again as if a terrifying story were to be read upon it.

"My God," the secretary-general echoed, "he hasn't come from *out there!*"

"Then where has he come from?" asked Missiou in a barely audible voice.

The president was still leaning toward Ernie, sadness glowing from his discolored, gray-green, rainbowed eyes, like those ancient objects whose colors have melted into the patina of time. Because he was so close, Ernie saw the first sudden awareness in the old man's moist eyes, like a fish whose existence is first implied by a kind of watery trembling—a submerged idea rising slowly to the surface. "You wouldn't be Ernie?" the old man asked very gently.

Surprised, Ernie assented with a silent nod.

"Ah," the other said with conviction while tears of shame ran down Ernie's cheeks, "the old man spoke of you often. He always came to the meetings on Sunday morning, he was a real . . . Jew. Forgive me, I remember he spoke of his grandson—I mean, the son of his son—as if it was certain that the little one would be called to the destiny of a Just Man. 'Not a Just Man of the Levys,' he said, 'but a true Unknown Just, an Inconsolable—one of those whom God dares not even caress with his little finger.' But we are a long way from all that now, aren't we? Still, if I'm not being indiscreet, my child, my dear child, why have you come back to us, into the flames? Perhaps you don't know. They tell stories that raise every hair on your head. . . ."

"I know all that can be known about it," Ernie said. "Some of us read clandestine leaflets, some of us heard forbidden broadcasts. But the stories they tell are too much for the human spirit. They tell you this is what's been happening to us, but they don't believe it themselves."

"Do you believe it?" the president asked.

Ernie Levy seemed extremely upset.

"Then why did you come back?"

"That," the boy said, "I don't know."

"What you have done is very bad," the president said. "In Paris right now life is shorter than a baby's smock. And you're so young, you don't look Jewish, the whole future is running through your veins. It's really surprising how little Jewish you

seem. Listen to me, I'm telling you the truth," he said in
exaltation, "you look exactly like anybody else!"

Then, examining Ernie's disfigured face, he restrained a
shudder. "My child," he went on in a different voice, "it's
true, you know, you don't resemble anything or anyone. Were
you the little curly-haired boy who used to come with old Levy?
Don't say anything, don't wake up, don't wake up. . . . True,
it was in the old days, in the world that used to be, in my old,
dead memories, and if I didn't know that three years had
passed . . . Was it really you?"

He gestured absurdly in denial. "No, I beseech you, don't
answer, don't ever answer me. My aged soul prefers to remain in doubt about the hell they speak of and the hell they do
not speak of. Child Levy, do you know, it seems that I am
not a Just Man, for I cannot abide any sort of hell." And
dropping his gaze from the visitor suddenly, as if he could no
longer bear the sight, he clapped his skinny hands to his
wrinkled face and cried out in a kind of plaintive caterwaul-
ing, *"O God, when will you cease to stare down at us, when
will you grant us the time to swallow our saliva? O Lord,
Father of men, when will you forgive us our sins, and when
will you forget our iniquity? For we Jews will soon sleep in the
dust, and one day you will seek us. . . ."*

"Tut-tut-tut," Missiou interrupted reprovingly.

"*. . . and we will no longer exist,*" finished the president of
the Paris Association of Old Zemyock.

Furious, the three little old men advanced upon him, Missiou going so far as to tweak the president's elbow. "What is
this? Have you no shame? Do you take yourself for Job now?
And even worse, in front of a Levy . . ."

At that magic name the four old men fell silent on the edge
of the bed, two crossing their arms and two twisting their
beards in shame. The president lowered his eyes.

"We argue," he muttered without daring to look at the
visitor, "we jaw at each other like the old women we have
become. But that's because all four of us live in this little room,

two on the bed and two on the mattress we spread on the floor at night. . . ."

"Taking turns," Missiou added.

"And the esteemed Levy," the president explained, more and more embarrassed, "will perhaps understand that our obligatory close quarters force us into an excessive familiarity, which incidentally we are the first to regret. . . ."

"Particularly me," the secretary-general punctuated earnestly while Ernie Levy, squirming on his chair, thoroughly ashamed to see himself transformed into a supreme judge of these four harried existences, searched vainly for a polite phrase that would restore their dignity to them without denying his own insignificance.

"What am I," he said finally, "that my glance troubles four noble patriarchs like you? If you knew . . ."

At these words Missiou brightened, and chortling enthusiastically he cried, "These Levys! They're all the same! Ai, ai, ai, 'patriarchs'—did you hear him?"

"There is milk and honey upon their tongues!"

"If you ground up a Levy in a mortar," the president acquiesced without daring to look at Ernie, "amid the grains on the pestle would remain their gentleness. 'Patriarchs,' my God . . ." And with his nose still pointed at the floor he went on in a more peaceful voice, "My child, my dear child, it is not one but four miracles that we are here alive. If no miracle had come about, you would have found only the shadow of our precious Association, and in that case what would you have done?"

"I don't know that either," Ernie said smiling.

"Is it possible that . . . ?"

Missiou interrupted violently. "Don't interrogate," he yapped. "Don't ask questions of a Levy, let him go on. He knows his own way by heart! As they used to say at home— do you remember?—'It is useless to push a drunkard, he'll fall down all by himself.' Useless to push a Levy, he'll *fly on* all by himself! Hee, hee, hee!"

"Stay with us," the president said. He seemed to be speaking to the floor. "Truthfully, this room belongs to no one, it belonged to the Association. And as you see, we have made it our hiding place. They may come tomorrow, tonight, but today you are at home here. May we adopt you then? Perfect. Excellent. The perfection of excellence."

"But I——"

"Ah," Missiou said, "perhaps we're a bit too old for you, hey? It may not be too cheerful with four old sardines like us. I understand. But before, you know, there were young people in the Association too. My God, is that possible? I can remember a year when we had twenty-seven members enrolled in the Paris region!"

"And the dances . . ." the secretary-general said ecstatically.

Missiou did not let him finish. "Ah, ah," he yapped in excitement, "I remember the annual dances we used to have. Can it be? We held them in Belleville—simple family dances, not like the madness of big cities like Warsaw, Lodz, Bialystok, where nobody knew anybody else. And even so we had quite a few people, because people from Zemyock are known and loved in all of Jewish Poland. . . ."

"What a sardine you are," the president said dryly.

Missiou rolled his eyes wildly and then, with compunction, "Ah, ah," he said, "I beg your pardon, I meant to say *were* loved. Because from what I hear there is no one left to be loved in Jewish Poland, nor anyone to love. . . ."

The president raised his face finally, revealing the nostalgic moisture in his shining little eyes. "Do you accept our invitation?"

"It would be . . . my great happiness."

Trotting around the table, the president shuffled papers behind his guest's back. Later Ernie was to notice the cupboard cut into the wall, which contained the Association's archives. Returning to his place almost immediately, the president spread a black-bound register on the tiny table, and as he leafed through it gently, his lips went on plucking at his memories. . . .

"You understand, I was living with my son before the war. A beautiful apartment, with a tailor's workshop. And you know, they left me and tried to reach the unoccupied zone. I crossed several borders in my youth, but I had no more desire to run, so I stayed in the apartment. *May they rest in peace.* The concierge took the machines, and then the furniture, and then the dishes, and then the apartment. But she didn't turn me in. . . . We stayed on—the old books, the old papers and myself. Do you know? God was amusing himself. No, no, no, no, I think maybe it was 1938. Ah! Do you see? Mordecai Levy, 37 Rue de l'Ermitage, Montmorency, Seine-et-Oise. Shall I put your name next to his? Perfect. Excellent. The perfection of excellence."

"Only," Missiou interrupted worriedly, "you'll have to hurry and sew on your star."

"With pleasure," Ernie Levy said.

. 2 .

ERNIE was amazed that the men of the Marais never tired of God. In a tiny block of houses condemned to disappear shortly in the great flood of death, they went on waving their arms to heaven, clinging to it in all their fervor, in all their torment, in all their pious despair. Each day the Nazi raids netted relatives or friends, next-door neighbors, flesh-and-blood beings with whom only yesterday words had been exchanged, but the little synagogues in the Rue du Roi-de-Sicile, in the Rue des Rosiers or in the Rue Pavée were never empty. The four little old men escorted their guest to them regularly, inviting him to participate in their fiery affairs. Sometimes young people adorned with fleurs-de-lis were waiting for them when they came out, bludgeons in hand, elegant sarcasms on their lips. "It's like that every day now," the little old man groaned, trotting along close to the wall. "And yet we can't miss services. That's what they want, you know."

Between raids a swarming existence, as if in a human hatchery, went on in the branded alleyways and dead ends. Communal caldrons of soup appeared, no one knew how. In those springtime days of 1943 even the Jewish-starred small fry enjoyed the privilege of the pale sun that shone dimly through the medieval gray murk of the Marais. Ernie had found work with a furrier who had a green identity card. People were already passing word along that it was the white cards' turn next, but it turned out to be the red cards'. So the men on the riverbank confused their prey with an ambiguous bait—survival.

In the narrow garret on the sixth floor, Ernie's bundle had been added to the row of castaways' effects. It contained, like the other four, a prayer book, a prayer shawl, prayer ribbons, a spare skullcap and six lumps of sugar. When he got back from work one day he found the door sealed by a strip of linen with a German notice stamped on it. He hesitated, undid the seal and entered the room, which was essentially unchanged. Only the four little parcels of the last four survivors of the Paris Association of Old Zemyock were missing. They left a terrible vacuum around his own intact bundle.

Stretched out on the bed and shivering with a strange fever, Ernie waited his turn for forty-eight hours. His relatives and friends paraded before his eyes. Occasionally he thought he should go on downstairs and join one of the movements now forming in the ghetto and outside. There had been stories about the high deeds of certain young Jewish heroes. But all the Germans on earth could not pay for one innocent head, and then, he told himself, for him it would be a luxurious death. He had no intention of glorifying himself, of separating himself from the humble procession of the Jewish people.

When he realized that the Germans were not yet ready for him, Ernie walked down the six flights to go back to work.

That day, as he tottered along the sidewalk a little French-woman in mourning came up to him and shook his hand. The next week, in the Métro, another delight—an old workman in overalls offered him a seat. "They're human beings too," the man burst out, glaring furiously around him. "And, my God, nobody chooses his mother's belly!" Ernie declined that charming invitation, but he was still smiling when he started for the synagogue on the Rue Pavée for evening services. He found it almost deserted, and deduced that there had been a raid during the afternoon. There were only a few old men in permanent devotion haunting the dim stalls, and two or three women who wailed behind the segregating partition. Ernie wondered again what attracted him to the place. In spite of all his efforts he had not once been able to reach the person of God. There was an unbreachable wall between them, a wall of Jewish lamentations, rising all the way to heaven.

Outside, a crew of elegant youngsters were amusing themselves. One of them tried to tug at the beard of an old worshipper who, afraid of dropping his prayer book, defended himself fiercely. "Montjoie Saint-Denis!" the young man shouted spitefully, and an enthusiastic crowd came running to the rescue, crying, *"Pour Dieu et mon droit!"*

Drifting away from the scene of their exploits Ernie noticed a frail, bestarred girl in a doorway fighting desperately, the prisoner of two French "patriots" who were pawing her and laughing. He tolerated the sight for an instant. Then moving forward impulsively, he sent the two sprawling with a sudden attack, grabbed the girl's hand and dragged her after him in a mad flight through the mysteriously empty alleyways of the Marais.

At the Rue de Rivoli, as they slowed for the traffic, Ernie saw that the girl limped.

"I owe you great thanks," she said in Yiddish when they had stopped at the approaches to the ambiguous terrain of the Rue Geoffroy-l'Asnier. She was panting, and sweat was beaded on her forehead. Ernie thought she looked a little like a gypsy, with her disheveled red hair, a cotton garment floating around her like a tent, and the impertinence in her high, lusterless, Provençal cheekbones, the impertinence and candor that had been so attractive in the wild flowers along the roads from the Camargue to Saintes-Maries-de-la-Mer. The yellow star was like a gaudy trinket over her heart, a gypsy woman's showy jewel. "Not that they would have done much to me," she added with a smile. "I'm not pretty enough."

Ernie stared at her uncomprehendingly. Their hands separated in embarrassment. The girl began to speak rapidly, launching, as if blowing soap bubbles, vague acknowledgments of her *eternal* gratitude, and so on.

"You're not too tired?" he asked, interrupting her brusquely but gently.

"No, why? Oh," she said quite naturally, "because of my leg?"

The young man hesitated. "Yes," he said finally, "because of your leg."

"Don't worry about that. People think so, to look at it. But it's even stronger than the other. You got yourself broken once, my little one, but it won't happen again!" Bent over the offending leg she rebuked it gaily, even punishing it with a light slap.

Ernie said quickly, as if to divert her attention from it, "Do you live far from here, may I ask?"

She interrupted her game, raised her head, smiled. "No, no, it's just around the corner."

"Take my arm just the same, would you? Please?"

Abashed, suddenly blushing, the deformed girl slipped her arm wordlessly into the crook of Ernie's, and the two young people followed the Rue Geoffroy-l'Asnier as far as the banks of the Seine, where they promenaded under the bewildered eyes of the other strollers. Though she had granted him her arm, the odd young lady chose not to lean on him, so that their arms touched only when she stepped out with her shorter leg, barely hopping, resting her weight against Ernie for a brief instant. "It's only a tiny bit shorter than the other one, you know," he said naïvely, in an ordinary conversational tone. But as soon as the words escaped him the girl laughed gaily in answer, let go of Ernie's arm and took a few steps alone, in a deliberately rolling gait, as her glance maliciously took him to witness. "Only a tiny bit?" she said cheerfully. Then she was silent, and Ernie, taking her arm without permission, led her off again, but supporting her this time so that she rested much of her weight on him, quiet, bemused, following him unresistingly, her limp abolished. They broke into laughter at the same time, abruptly, and then were quiet, then laughed again, happy and embarrassed by the cascade of coincidences.

Ernie said dreamily, "Does it still feel shorter?"

"No, no," she answered in the same tone.

The sidewalk along the quay was strewn with feathery seed pods. They stirred at the slightest breeze, mingling with others that dropped from the plane trees in delicate spirals. Ten yards below them ran the waters of the river, imprisoned by the city. A chance taxi passed them, bearing away the vision of a young cyclist whose tongue was hanging out, and of his passenger, a fat lady regally enthroned in the sidecar, who seemed to be sniffing pleasurably at Paris in the spring. A few soldiers of the Wehrmacht were also strolling the quays, and Golda—that was her name—pointed out to Ernie that by supporting her with both hands as he was, he was dangerously masking part of his yellow star. Then she went on to create fantastic tales, among others that she was on her second husband now and had decided not to stop there, though new candidates were fewer all the time. Ernie let himself float along in the stream of gossip, concentrating exclusively on the pleasure he felt in breathing slowly, deliberately, with all the suddenly reborn vessels deep within his chest. "That's enough," she said every five minutes, "you can let me go now. Why are you taking all this trouble?" But those words too left Ernie unimpressed; they too were subordinated to the pleasure that Golda's presence lent all things, making houses dance in the warm air, turning the Seine into a modest village stream, melting the noises of Paris into a single triumphant harmony. At the most when Golda recited such inconsequences, Ernie straightened her up a bit with his right hand, holding tightly to her upper arm, and raised her from the earth slightly, as if to boost her words to a more aerial flight.

Cutting away from the quay, she led him toward one of the myriad blind alleys cut like drains into the rotten flank of buildings neighboring the Seine behind the Bastille. She teased him when he asked if he might see her again, as though this were a joke of the first order, and still teasing she agreed, asking about his work schedule, apparently juggling with the preposterous idea that her "savior," as she said sweetly, would tomorrow be at such and such a place at such and such a time, awaiting her good pleasure. But as she stood before the narrow iron door and offered her hand casually, she made a funny face and murmured, like a chatelaine, "Will you really come, Ernie?"

"Of course I will," Ernie said. "I can't very well send my shadow."

Attentive then, her voice trembling uneasily, "But why?"

"I beg your pardon?"

"I asked you," she went on gravely, "why will you come?"

"To see you," Ernie said softly, though with a suggestion of reproach.

At these words a second face appeared beneath Golda's features, etched in surprising clarity, a face of real beauty, implying a happiness so naïve that Ernie lowered his eyes in spite of himself. When he looked up, the girl was moving away in her birdlike hop, plunging into a corridor, turning back once and plunging away again in panic. From the far end a pleading voice reached him. "May I tell my father about it?"

"Yes," Ernie said.

Hearing nothing more from his friend, Ernie walked away without looking around. But at the end of the alleyway, convinced that she was staring at his back, he felt a nameless intoxication. And as he wept, standing on the sidewalk, he thought that it must be pity, a pity of very great sweetness, a pity being transmuted even now—he did not know how—into happiness. A pity so delicate, so subtle, that he was carried away by it.

· 3 ·

G OLDA was not born with a limp. When the passports of emigrating Polish Jews were revoked in 1938, and the new "Austrian" government sent them back to the Polish border, the Engelbaum family was swept up in the general expulsion. The story was well covered in the international press. On the first night, the Jews were deported to Czechoslovakia. The next day the Czechs sent them along to Hungary. From there they were shipped to Germany and then to Czechoslovakia again. They traveled in endless circles. Finally they retreated to fishing boats on the Danube. Most of them drowned themselves in the Black Sea; wherever they landed, they were expelled. In a violent eddy of the Danube, Golda was flung overboard. At the last moment her leg was crushed between the hull and a rock. They set the leg in wooden splints; she sang to drown her pain. After complicated wanderings, a few of the castaways found a footing on Italian soil, where they finally dispersed. One group entered France illegally, with Golda riding on a man's back. The wounded leg ceased growing—that was all.

But Golda never considered herself normal after that, and while there was no bitterness in her, the fine veil of that renunciation fell over her still smiling face, her still carefree, happy manner, her no less vivacious character. She was thenceforth shadowed by an imperceptible reserve that transformed her former waiflike prettiness into beauty. She suffered accesses of greed, eating fruit until she was sick or intoxicating herself on the melancholy strains of a harmonica, from which she drew unbidden love songs. She did all things without restraint, and bit into a wrinkled apple as though the whole world were between her teeth. Or she swigged down huge

quantities of water with no apparent thirst, in a dreamy frenzy
that terrified her mother. Each excess flung her up, satisfied,
on the banks of her desire, with no sadness and no regrets, as
though she had slaked her thirst at the most exhilarating springs
of life. "You're a featherhead," her mother told her. "You'll
never find a husband if you go on that way."

"So what else will happen? Who wants me with a leg like
that?" And Golda would laugh gustily while her mother, a
woman angular in shape and character, as if honed by life,
protested harshly and stubbornly, "May I choke on my own
juices if I understand this little animal! If you were as ugly as a
toad you could find a man to take care of you if you wanted
one! And what do you think I raised you for? So you could
rot where you stand? Look at me—and I managed to find
your father, didn't I?"

When M. Engelbaum was home he threw up his hands
fatalistically. "You found me, I found you, we were both
lucky . . ." And sarcastically, under his breath, "God save
you from that kind of luck. . . . Come here, my little one,
and tell me what kind of husband you want."

All these things passed over Golda's head without affecting
her, without even causing her to wonder, and it was only in
deference to parental eccentricity that she joined the game of
matrimonial hide-and-seek, asking her father, "But you're
my husband, aren't you?" as she glanced in friendly mockery
at her mother. And she added these words, which never failed
to infuriate her mother, "And you're my wife, my delicious
little wife. What more could I want?" In time, as if to show
indifference to her own femininity, she fell into the habit of
using that manner toward her parents, as if she wanted to
make them feel that, having married both of them, she was
doubly happy to be with them. Her imagination never dwelt
on the future, but always somehow on the satisfactions—
richer and fuller and more mysterious—of the present, which
bounded her world. Her "hungers," as she called them, her
"thirsts," her sudden "desires," bore only on objects near at
hand. When the cupboard was bare she treated herself to a

marvelous "fast" of dry crusts. Later, when her relations with Ernie were more tender, he asked her sometimes what thing she might desire. "Ask me for something impossible, something I can't give you. . . ." In the beginning she answered by embracing him. And then, as she came to know Ernie's odd personality, she asked him for things that existed, according to her, at the frontier between the possible and the impossible, like a toilet article, or more food than the ration, or a piece of fruit. Her lack of imagination was the despair of her Ernie; he read into it the gray humbleness of the poor. And sometimes he saw in it a kind of calculated wisdom, the spiritual usufruct of suffering. Which is how he interpreted Golda's resignation at unhappiness, her own and others'. He called her a "silly goon" freely, but one day after a long conversation on that subject, in which she had insisted on accepting, and he on denying, the will of God, he said pensively, "It's because I haven't even begun to know the first beginnings of what suffering is. But you, you know more than a rabbi." At a loss, she stared at him. Another time, in the Rue Pavée, when he asked her to name a "desire," she felt a sudden "wish": to walk through Paris together without their cloth stars. They did, the whole afternoon. That was her only impossible "desire."

The promenade took place on a Sunday in August. All their tattered outdoor clothing bore a star over the left breast. Golda proposed that they go out in shirtsleeves—without stars. The weather was fine, finer than it would ever be again in their lives. Ernie and Golda went down to the bank of the Seine, and in the shadows under the arch of a bridge doffed their compromising jackets, which Golda stuffed into a shopping basket, covering it with a newspaper. Holding hands, they strolled along the Seine as far as the Pont-Neuf, where in a delicious anguish they mounted the stone stairs to the surface of the Christian world.

In those days Ernie walked erectly, once again with the solemn stride of his childhood, and his long black curls—

carefully combed by Golda—fell over either side of his fore-head, screening the scars. His white shirt bright under the sun, his thin body straight and slim with the sinewy grace of a young cedar, he looked like any young man who loved life; like a casual leash, his fingers restrained the childish frisking of a red-haired animal with an equal claim on life. Golda seemed to dance. She glowed with a peasant beauty, her hair braided in a wreath and still glossy from the waters of the Seine, a trace of lipstick she caressed now and then with an amazed finger, and a blouse out of a dream—a brilliant white, dazzlingly starched, that two weeks before had promoted her to the rank of "young lady," and that she had insisted on iron-ing herself, delicately and lovingly, the iron heated by her own heart, according to M. Engelbaum.

In mingled agony and delight, not daring to look at each other, they strolled peacefully, knowing each other there, like two birds who fly in perfect formation by instinct. Forgetting his promise, Ernie occasionally swayed slightly toward Golda, who brought him to order with a slight squeeze of the hand. They reached the Place Saint-Michel and lingered in front of a movie. Golda broke the silence suddenly. "I've never been to a movie. Have you?"

"Neither have I," Ernie realized in surprise. "But as long as we don't have our stars," he whispered gently in Yiddish, "we can go on in for once. I can't even imagine what it's like. Look, I have four, five, seven francs left."

"It's much too expensive," Golda said. "And anyway I like it better outside, where life is."

She made a sweeping, possessive gesture. Ordering her to stay where she was, Ernie came back with two ice-cream cones. She chose the green one, and twisting her neck to avoid spotting her blouse, she bit into the ice cream and choked, strangled, spit up the delicious surprise. Then she followed Ernie's learned example, and as she ran her tongue around the cone he thought that she was savoring herself in the ice cream, as she seemed to in all things, in her slightest word or gesture, even in the greedy glances she trained on the nearby stalls of

a street, on the festive Boulevard Saint-Michel and on Ernie—
who felt that his whole body was living a dream and that there
was no longer the slightest trace of self-hate within him.

The ice cream devoured, they followed the Boulevard Saint-
Michel and arrived before the lion in the Place Denfert-
Rochereau, as majestic and dominant as the Lion of Judah,
guardian of the Ark of the Holy of Holies. Tempted then by
the neighborhood charm of an alleyway, they emerged at the
Avenue du Maine and saw an enchanting little plaza, a true
oasis surrounded by sunstruck buildings that, with all their
shutters closed, seemed to have fallen into a final sleep. They
took their time choosing a bench. Golda set down her basket,
and in the immemorial attitude of lovers in Paris they watched
—without seeing them—the children, housemaids and old
ladies who were also soaking in the happiness of the Square
Mouton-Duvernet.

"Imagine," Ernie said, "thousands of people have sat here
before us. It's funny to think about it. . . ."

"Listen," Golda said, "I existed before Adam was created.
I've always been one of two colors. Thousands of years have
gone by and I haven't changed at all. What am I?"

Ernie said, "My father had little anecdotes for every occasion. Yours has riddles."

"I'm Time," Golda said dreamily, "and my colors are Day
and Night."

The same thought drew them together while Time hurtled
by around them with cruel speed, branding their happiness
with a star.

"I wonder why they forbid us the public squares," Golda
whispered. "It's nature, after all. . . ."

A cloud of pink silk crossed the sky of Paris just above the
tall building outlined behind the foliage, on the other side of an
empty Avenue du Maine, and in his imagination Ernie followed
it all the way to Poland, where, under the same evanescent
August sky, the Jewish people lay dying.

"Oh, Ernie," Golda said, "you know them. Tell me why,
why do the Christians hate us the way they do? They seem so

nice when I can look at them without my star."

Ernie put his arm around her shoulders solemnly. "It's very mysterious," he murmured in Yiddish. "They don't know exactly why themselves. I've been in their churches and I've read their gospel. Do you know who the Christ was? A simple Jew like your father. A kind of Hasid."

Golda smiled gently. "You're kidding me."

"No, no, believe me, and I'll bet they'd have got along fine, the two of them, because he was really a good Jew, you know, sort of like the Baal Shem Tov—a merciful man, and gentle. The Christians say they love him, but I think they hate him without knowing it. So they take the cross by the other end and make a sword out of it and strike us with it! You understand, Golda," he cried suddenly, strangely excited, "*they take the cross and they turn it around, they turn it around, my God . . .*"

"Sh, quiet," Golda said. "They'll hear you." And stroking the scars on Ernie's forehead, as she often liked to do, she smiled. "And you promised you wouldn't 'think' all afternoon. . . ."

Ernie kissed the hand that had caressed his forehead and went on stubbornly, "Poor Jesus, if he came back to earth and saw that the pagans had made a sword out of him and used it against his sisters and brothers, he'd be sad, he'd grieve forever. And maybe he does see it. They say that some of the Just Men remain outside the gates of Paradise, that they don't want to forget humanity, that they too await the Messiah. Yes, maybe he sees it. Who knows? You understand, Goldeleh, he was a little old-fashioned Jew, a real Just Man, you know, no more nor less than . . . all our Just Men. And it's true, he and your father would have got along together. I can see them *so* well together, you know. 'Now,' your father would say, 'now my good rabbi, doesn't it break your heart to see all that?' And the other would tug at his beard and say, 'But you know very well, my good Samuel, that the Jewish heart must break a thousand times for the greater good of all peoples. *That* is why we were chosen, didn't you know?' And your father would say, 'Oi, oi, didn't I know? Didn't I know? Oh, excellent rabbi, that's all I *do* know, alas. . . .' "

They laughed. Golda took her harmonica from the bottom of the basket, flashed sunlight off it into Ernie's eyes, and still smiling brought it to her lips and played a forbidden melody. It was Hatikvah, the ancient chant of hope, and as she inspected the Square Mouton-Duvernet with uneasy eyes, she tasted the sweetness of forbidden fruit. Ernie leaned down and plucked a tuft of slightly mildewed grass and planted the blades in Golda's still moist hair. As they got up to leave he tried to strip her of that poor garland, but she stopped his hand. "Too bad about the people who see. And too bad about the Germans too. Today I say too bad about everybody. Everybody . . ." she repeated, unexpectedly solemn.

"Ernie, Ernie," the girl offered tenderly, "you know we're condemned."

She was sitting erectly, almost rigidly, on the small, gray-blanketed bed in the room on the sixth floor, and her clasped hands lay trembling on her knees in an attitude of supplication. The hem of her skirt was a modest half circle. Her red woolen jacket was an explosion against the somber shades of the room that had once been home to the four old men from Zemyock, and a random assortment of buttons fastened it as far as the gleaming, starched white collar of her blouse. A few blades of grass still hung in her hair, dry now after their walk, with golden glints tinting it, in the shadowy room, an autumnal red.

"Condemned, Ernie, condemned," she repeated, suddenly cold, while Ernie discovered the same tear in the corner of her eye that he had surprised during their silent return from the river; the same bitter clearness that had edged her eyes when, under the bridge, she had put on the red jacket marked with its star; the same willful, desperate spark that had livened her face a while before, when she had almost begged him to come to his room. And now, seated on the room's only chair, facing Golda as two months before he had faced the four little old men since gone from him forever, now, his hands heavy and flat against his trembling knees, Ernie Levy heard the mute cry exploding from Golda's lips—lips still stained with that scant maiden touch of lipstick.

"Of course," he murmured, forcing himself to smile, "we're friends to the end."

"No, no," she insisted. "You know what I mean. The end isn't far." She leaned forward and grasped his hands, then leaned back slowly, their arms a bridge between them.

"Right now," Ernie said, "it isn't far from anybody."

"Ernie, Ernie. But us, we're . . . sort of engaged, aren't we?"

"And right now," Ernie said, very pale, "are we the only engaged couple in the world?"

The tear Golda had been holding back since the Square Mouton-Duvernet slipped delicately down the shadowed curve of her cheek, and while she maintained her stiff, hieratic pose her lower lip sagged and she blurted, "No, no, there are others, so many others." Ernie had never seen Golda weep, and he found the tears of his beloved more bitter than death. And he thought, "Look now, my God, the oppressed weep and there is no one to console them! They are naked to the violence of their oppressors, and there is no one to console them!" And while Golda's tears flowed silently, he discovered that the dead which were already dead were happier than the living which were yet alive, and he squeezed Golda's hands so tightly that she raised her eyes and smiled through the tears and said, "Ernie, Ernie, I want to be your wife today."

He was breathless for a moment.

"Perfect," he said acidly. "Excellent. The perfection of excellence. And where will you find a rabbi at this time of day?"

Golda laughed, and threw him a glance of marked reproach. "You know very well," she said with heavy significance, "that there is no thought of a rabbi in my heart."

"Perfect. Excellent. Then what is in your heart?"

"Please," Golda said.

Ernie closed his eyes, opened them and seemed to recover his powers of speech with a jolt. "Tomorrow," he said abruptly, "you'll be sorry not to have been . . . before God."

"Tomorrow," Golda said calmly, "it may be too late." She detached one hand from the bridge of their arms, still connecting the chair and the gray-covered bed, and circling the free hand above their heads, she added, "And aren't we before God now? Would he abandon us at a moment like this? You know it as well as I do—when death knocks at the door, God is always there."

"If you like," Ernie said. "If you like. . . ."

Beneath its customary gentleness his voice carried a distant condescension that displeased Golda. "If God weren't here," she breathed in a tiny, indignant voice, "how would people stand it? You're crazy, Ernie, if you believe . . . If God weren't here right now, if he weren't helping us all the time, we'd melt into one tear, all the Jews, as my father says. *Ernie, do you understand me?* Or else," she added distractedly, "we'd all become dogs, like the Just Man of Saragossa, when God abandoned him for only one minute. Or we'd disappear into thin air. *Do you hear me, Ernie, do you hear me?*"

Worried, she set her free hand on the quivering bridge of their arms, and while he murmured, jolted out of his dream, "Of course, of course God is here," she surprised so cold a gleam in his eyes that she withdrew her hands, threw herself back on the bed, against the whitewashed wall, and sighed in desolation, "Then you don't want me for a wife?"

"You?" Ernie said.

He stood up suddenly, and as he whispered "You? You?" his eyes dulled and his cheeks seemed to soften, to swell. He shouted in a grating voice, "But my poor Goldeleh, don't you know who I am?"

"Yes, yes, I know who you are," Golda said, frightened. She felt as though she were in the presence of a shrewd madman— his conversation is a black night studded with sharp points.

One's own uneasiness is hard to define because he is gentle, sensitive, cultivated. Suddenly one finds that he lacks only rationality.

"No!" Ernie repeated harshly. "You don't know who I am! I . . ."

Then that abominable voice thickened and a third voice emerged, so thin that Golda had to lean forward to hear it. "Listen, Golda," it was whispering, "you have to know, believe me, there is no worse Jew on earth than I, truly, truly. . . . Because I . . . An animal wouldn't have . . . you understand? . . . And you, you're so . . . And I'm so . . . Now do you understand? Oh, Golda!"

"Don't say another word," she told him calmly.

And as he contemplated the girl, who seemed not at all alarmed, who smiled frankly at him, Ernie raised his hands. They seemed to float in the air for an instant before he fell, the whole weight of his shame crashing down at once, his head on Golda's knees, her hand combing through his hair, gently smoothing the black curls disheveled in the storm, the girl herself unembarrassed, feeling Ernie's breath against her thighs, savoring it, happy to know herself so fully loved.

"I know who you are, I know who you are," she repeated in delight.

Ernie discovered that his old mask of blood and earth was dissolving in Golda's words. Pulling back, he looked at her and saw something like a distant reflection of his own face deep in the girl's eyes. He did not know what his true face was composed of, the interior face he could sense confusedly within him, but Golda's eyes seemed to be smiling simply at the face of a man and, liberated, Ernie smiled.

"Maybe we should kiss at least once," Golda said.

"That's required," Ernie said. "Absolutely."

Facing each other, seated on the edge of the bed, they made an arch of their four hands, and each looked at the other's mouth. But the occasion was one of such gravity that finally Golda, confused, rose and retreated slowly toward the small square-paned window, against which her tawny head was framed on a background of sky.

"And now," she said, "what do I have to do?" As she spoke she saw an almost imperceptible smile flit across Ernie's lips like the stroke of a child's crayon. "Oh, yes," she sighed, stirred by that smile, "I've read that men undress their women. But what would you like—to undress me or to have me undress myself?"

"And you? Which would you prefer?"

Golda burst into cheerful laughter. "I'd rather undress myself." And then frowning, worried, "But maybe you want to watch me?"

"I want it if you want it," Ernie smiled.

Her laugh was more relaxed. "I'd rather you didn't."

When he too was naked, Ernie turned and saw that Golda was a tight face lying like a flower on the upper part of the bed. The gray blanket covered her to the chin. Suddenly regretful about his body, he was sorry for the long, livid scars on his legs and arms and trunk, the marks of old open fractures. Then he knelt near the bed, laid his cheek against the pillow, and rubbed his black hair against Golda's russet curls. "There is no tomorrow," he murmured softly. At those words the girl brought a milky arm from beneath the covers, and while she caressed Ernie's moist chest hesitantly, her eyes opened upon him and she courted him. "You're as handsome as King David, do you know that?"

· 4 ·

THE NIGHT WAS a transparent blue when the boy and girl came back to this world. It was past the hour of the Jewish curfew, and though Golda forbade it, Ernie could not resist following her, twenty yards behind, through the dark, empty alleys of the Marais. At the metallic tread of a patrol she dove into a doorway. Flat against a shadowed wall, Ernie congratulated himself that he had not let her face being arrested alone. But the patrol passed, and Golda's halting figure took up its journey through the night. When she reached her alley, she turned, to Ernie's amazement, waved one arm and disappeared.

Ernie made his way back to the Rue des Ecouffes without trouble and fell asleep the moment he closed his eyes. In the morning he found a few blades of grass on his pillow, left behind by his beloved. He rolled them carefully in a handkerchief, which he slipped between his shirt and his skin. Then he went off to work and began to construct plans for the future, plans that rose and fell into ruins, one after another, in his mind. His work consisted of stretching and tacking down untanned sheepskins, which M. Zwingler, happy owner of a green card, delivered to the German Army in the form of vests. His mouth full of tacks, the tiny furrier's hammer in his hand, Ernie fought off the rising temptations of "simple human happiness." "Logic," he had claimed the night before, "says that we'll all be arrested." "Logic," Golda had answered, "says that I love you and that I'll stay with my parents." Logic? In the long run they were risking death with that logic. And yet Golda was right. To flee was impossible, and all they could do was to love, on the fringes of their common fate—a few days, a few weeks. "Maybe even a few months, who knows?" Ernie cried enthusiastically, causing a stir among his fellow workers.

At noon the girl had not arrived, and yet she knew the price of a moment's anguish. Had her parents kept her home? Had she . . . ?

At twelve-thirty Ernie set out slowly for the alleyway. He took the last hundred yards at a dead run, but when he reached the corner he stopped. His back to the wall, he suppressed the beating of his heart. When he finally started through the courtyard, the concierge stretched her head out of a kind of porthole, opened her mouth, closed it. At the second floor Ernie clung to the banister, then he seemed to go up effortlessly, as if he were pulled along by a rope anchored to his own innards like an umbilical cord. He simply let himself be hoisted up by the horrible thing, and he found himself before the unassuming iron-latched door, on a corner of which he saw the seal of the Engelbaums' doom.

The concierge was waiting for him on the ground floor. Golda's harmonica lay in the flat of her hand. She was one of those Paris concierges—in a dressing gown, her hair in corkscrew curls—who never forgive you for confining them to a perpetual sentry box. The first time Ernie had bothered her, to ask where the Engelbaums lived, she had withdrawn her head from the porthole and answered furiously, "Still in the same place!" But today she stood modestly at the foot of the stairway, next to the knob of the banister, her exhausted, stringy hair limp on her forehead as if to hide her grayish flesh, and in the hollow of her hand Golda's little harmonica—broken, twisted as if by an iron hand—expressed all that the concierge might have said. But Ernie's silence was disconcerting. "I wanted to tell you before," she explained. "But this is the third time I've had Jews, and it's better to let people go upstairs first. I'm not very good at saying things, even if I'm not as bad as people think. Here."

Stunned, Ernie raised the harmonica to his lips. A shrill, unpleasant chord emerged.

"They stamped on it. She threw it to me and she said, 'The young man . . .' and I knew she meant you, because I know about life, I do. And one of the gentlemen picked it up to see what it was. Maybe he thought it was jewelry, or maybe just to see what it was. And he *stamped* on it. And then they all got into the truck. And . . . you know what that means!"

"It's nothing," Ernie offered. "It can be fixed." And as she stared at him in amazement he added, "Don't worry about it, Madame. All your Jews will be back. Besides, all the Jews everywhere will be back. All of them." Then, suppressing a shudder, "And if they don't come back, you'll still have the Negroes, or the Algerians . . . or the hunchbacks."

"What are you saying?"

"You're right," Ernie said. "Excuse me. I really don't know how to apologize. And thank you, thank you. It's— Really I don't know how to apologize!"

"Get out of here," she said, "before my charity runs out."

"So excuse me again," the Jew insisted awkwardly. "The words just popped out of my mouth. Honestly, just like that. Presto."

The name "Drancy" was merely an insignificant word on the pediment of an ordinary station in suburban Paris. With its unroofed platforms, with its patriarchical clock that ticked off time nonchalantly in the French manner, with its resigned crowd of commuters, with the man in a cap who collected tickets without even looking at them, leaning back against the concrete barrier that opened on the whole town basking in the mellow caress of an Ile-de-France sun—nothing seemed to indicate, even to knowing eyes, the existence of a camp the mere name of which terrified Jewish children far more than tales of the Devil. Once more Ernie felt as he had several times in his life—stupefied, overburdened by the extraordinary power of humanity to create suffering out of nothing, or almost nothing. The sky above the roofs of Drancy was no less sweet and pure and tapestried with promises than the sky that had witnessed the blossoming of a juvenile Hell on the banks of the Schlosse, no less serene than the clouds contemplating the annihilation of the 429th Foreign Infantry Regiment—the Exodus, the dog days of Ernie's despair. The day after a bombardment by American planes, the city of Saint-Nazaire, three-quarters demolished, according to the newspapers, awoke beneath a silken sky. Things took no part in the mischief of men. Somewhere Drancy harbored an abscess from which oozed an unbelievable quantity of suffering, but the town showed nothing of it nor did its sky. Ernie followed the ticket-taker's directions, walked for a long time, saw a mass of concrete rising to dominate the low roofs around it, turned off on a badly paved road and was suddenly standing before the

huge double block of buildings that seemed to have sprung
fully armed from the vast emptiness of back-yard gardens and
vacant lots among which it stood like a bronze fortress. A
cyclist coming up behind him passed at a leisurely pace,
riding halfway between the barbed-wired wall and the small,
snug homes opposite the concentration camp. As he passed,
the cyclist threw a brief gesture of greeting at the squad of
gendarmes posted in front of the gate (more precisely, in front
of a tiny door of white wood), cut off to his left, dismounted,
left his bicycle on the sidewalk and whistled a tune as he
entered the neighboring café, his cheeks sunburned and his
eyes shining with thirst, with life. The shadow of the barbed
wire lay lightly on the sidewalk.

Ernie halted before the two gendarmes on duty and said,
"I'd like to get into the camp, please. I'm Jewish." He wedged
the little bundle—his legacy from the old men of Zemyock—
firmly under one arm, and bowed politely.

"You hear?" the first gendarme said, pointing to Ernie's star.
"He's Jewish. It therefore follows inevitably that I'm a gendarme."

"Visits are not permitted," the other said sententiously.
"But you can leave packages. We could make a deal. . . ."
And he winked heavily at the first gendarme, who clapped
Ernie on the shoulder banteringly. "You can get in but you
can't get out!"

Ernie waited until their laughter had receded. "Exactly,"
he said then, his voice altogether deferent. "Exactly. I'd like to
go in and not come out." And inspired by the fat gendarme's
previous wink, he winked conspiratorially at the two of them
and then bowed his head slightly, smiling, as if inviting them
to make fun of him freely.

Their response was an appalled silence, and Ernie knew
immediately that these two characters had not received his
proposal kindly. By the irate explosion that followed their
silence, he understood, flabbergasted, that the gendarmes saw
themselves only as guards over the stock rounded up by the
Gestapo, and took great offense at being considered hunters.

"That's not our job! Go ask somebody else! We take receipt of the merchandise, and that's all we do!" And under the vehement phrases of refusal Ernie thought he heard a muted disapproval of the sacrilege he had committed in surrendering himself thus to the will of the German gods, instead of waiting humbly, like all the others of his tribe, for the day and hour appointed by competent authority. Finally the gendarme with the more officious face (on his sleeve Ernie saw the triangular patch of a four-striper in the cavalry) raised the butt of his carbine with a nervous gesture, and with the abrasive remark "These wise guys," he shoved Ernie into the middle of the street without further ceremony.

The bead curtains across the doorway to the café parted, and a few drinkers, one of them still holding his glass, gathered around the sentries to hear what had happened. And while their suburban accents rose in the warm air, mingling with the gendarmes' oaths, Ernie Levy—sweating in fear and strangled grief, in the oven of his black ersatz-wood-fiber suit, another legacy from the old men of Zemyock—Ernie Levy, standing in the middle of the road, wiped his cheeks slowly with the bundle, his eyes closed, his tongue hanging out as though he were drowning in the eternal immediacy of suffering.

One, two, three drinkers surrounded him, trying to drag this haggard, silent Jew toward the café. Close to his blurry eyes, stinging with sweat, Ernie saw the woebegone face of the young cyclist who had been whistling two minutes before, and who now could only repeat with the feverish insistence of a child, "Come along, come along, we'll talk, we'll talk," while Ernie, touched by the awkward compassion of these ordinary Frenchmen, clung to the doorjamb, smiled at the workingmen who were trying to drag him inside and assured them calmly, without the slightest offensiveness, as if he were stating a naked fact, "But you can't understand, you can't understand. . . ."

He was not sure how it happened. The hands released him, a purring throb echoed in his skull, and while he stood, amazed to find himself alone before the sunlit façade of the café— the bead curtain rustling against him—a low black sedan gleaming like a scarab came out of nowhere and glided to a halt at the camp gate, which opened with a shrill metallic scream. Then a short man in a Tyrolean hat stepped out of the car, examined the motionless Ernie with small, cold, official eyes; examined the young cyclist who was still on the sidewalk, his arms dangling in fear; examined the two gendarmes at stiff attention, whose rigidity masked the obsequious agitation behind their eyes fixed fearfully on the German inspector. Ernie raised a hand to his heart and tried to undo one of the points of the yellow star sewn to his jacket, but M. Zwingler, a man of caution, had crowded his tight stitches too densely. Exasperated, Ernie grasped the cloth in his right hand as though he were sinking claws into it, and ripped the whole star from the jacket in one strenuous jerk. With it came a shapeless patch of the thin, wrinkled ersatz cloth. Then with a slow, deliberate gesture that expressed a kind of wistfulness, he flung the rag to the street. The paving stones glittered in the raw sunlight, which touched all things with its enchantment—the street, the gendarmes, the great black insect buzzing before the open gate of the Drancy concentration camp. Ernie saw himself, with heart-rending clarity, as a ridiculously agitated ant at the foot of the redoubtable blocks of concrete. "*Was ist das?*" cried a harsh, angry voice curiously without timbre, the voice of the little man in the Tyrolean hat.

A young S.S. in a "death's-head" uniform jumped out of the car and dragged Ernie into the camp at a sign from the Tyrolean hat. There, the one raining blows on the other's back, they burst into the guard platoon's barracks followed by a small cortege that consisted of the Tyrolean hat complaining in German about the "unheard-of impudence," and the two gendarmes trailing along behind, wailing in voices low enough to imply humility but high enough to be heard, "With your permission, Herr Inspector! With your permission!"

The "correction" Ernie received in the guards' barracks seemed to him if not justly deserved at least in the normal order of things. But when it appeared that the Tyrolean hat did not yet consider that he had paid for his "impertinence" and was disposed, after a methodical interrogation of the two gendarmes (with the aid of an interpreter), to "beat it out of him," as he said, to force a confession of his "real reasons" for demanding entry to the camp, Ernie could not repress a thin smile. He nevertheless answered, with an earnest good will that might have seemed fearful, that he wanted to see someone, a person very close to him, from whom the camp unfortunately separated him. He excused himself; he had never dreamed that it would create such complications. It had seemed to him that the simplest way was to present himself at the camp gate. Whom did he want to see . . . ? But what good would it do to make trouble for that person—couldn't they take his word for it? What harm was there in a Jew wanting to get into the camp, he cried finally in mingled tones of vindictive bitterness and simple irony.

A few minutes later he was on the second floor of a building situated behind one of the two huge concentration blocks. They invited him into a luxurious room, illuminated—thanks to a steel shutter—only by a single arc lamp. The walls were of square white tiles, and the tiled floor was gently concave in the center, where Ernie stood. A light gurgle of drainage, as in a bathroom, echoed in the depths of a hole at the prisoner's feet.

"Let the creature strip," said the little man in the Tyrolean hat.

More than in the paraphernalia with which he surrounded himself, even more than in the torpid eyes of the S.S. aide (who had stripped down to shirtsleeves and was nervously slapping the blackjack against one of his boots), violence lay coiled nakedly in the thick, fair face of the seated inspector, a face rigid beneath the ludicrous hat, and in his eyes, seemingly cut from the limp cloth of German sentimentality but in which, behind the veil of his glasses, slender serpents ringed in green stirred momentarily. And above all, violence radiated from his small, childlike mouth, as if moistened by raspberry juice, which riddled Ernie constantly with glacial promises that would have seemed trite enough if the use of the word "creature," by which they designated the Jew, had not lent them a demonic significance. "Let the creature," said the little man in the Tyrolean hat, "let the creature explain the reasons for his request more clearly. Does the creature have friends in the camp? What messages was he to transmit, and to whom? To what organization does the creature belong? Hans, explain to the creature that all this is just an hors d'oeuvre, to be followed by the main course. Now does the creature understand?" And so on and on, as if in an inverted delirium, believing his victim and not himself possessed by a devil, the director intended to give greater force to the barrage of violence by that bizarre form of verbal exorcism, or as if, fearing the sudden manifestation of a human face in that lump of flesh offered up to his good pleasure, he was driving Ernie down all the steps that lead to nothingness, making him less than a Jew, less even than an animal, reducing him to a mere object.

"Let the creature strip," he said again quietly while the slender green rings writhed frantically and a savage anger muddied his sorrowfully moist eyes.

His aide leaned forward smiling. "Should I help him?"

Then he stepped back into the shadows, reading in his superior's unhappy features that he had just transgressed against some unwritten rule of the ceremony.

The techniques of torture are ridiculously limited. The most audacious, the most industrious imagination must limit itself to variations on a few fundamental themes bearing on the five senses—by the end of the afternoon Ernie Levy was chattering, chattering, chattering tirelessly.

Rolled up in a ball against the door, he was wriggling like a wounded caterpillar in its own juices. He had been stripped of all shame, his eyes were staring whitely and the only defense he offered was to cup his hands around his genitals. No Jewish name, no Jewish address, nothing but that infantile babbling, like a rushing spring, irresistible.

"What do you think of it?" the little man in the Tyrolean hat asked suddenly in a soft voice.

The aide snapped to attention. "I don't think anything of it, Herr Stoekel," he said, panicky.

Wallowing delightedly in the *fauteuil* that had been his throne for the afternoon, the little man smiled. "Oh, yes, yes, I'm convinced that you have an opinion. I permit you to state it. I even order you to."

"Really?" said the aide.

And when the little man shot an imperative glance at him, the aide shuffled his feet, embarrassed and coy, and at length said timidly, "With your permission, Herr Stoekel . . . when I was in Poland, every time we had an outdoor *Aktion*, at the last minute there was always—when the whole sector had already been 'handled,' you know?—there was always an animal or two who came out of his hole and just walked up to the ditch or the truck, and they wanted the 'special treatment' too. And this reminds me of it. . . . That's all."

The little man leaned back in the armchair and chuckled in pleasure. "And just when did you think of that?"

"With your permission, Herr Stoekel . . . it was when the animal"—he pointed to the now unconscious body—"said, 'Where are you? Where are you?' It was then, Herr Stoekel."

"And I," the little man said, "I thought so from the beginning."

"Really?" his aide cried, dumfounded. He shook his head while he recovered from the shock. And then guessing by his superior's chuckles that he was expected to show admiration for a *Witz* so well contrived, the aide raised a hand to his mouth politely and said, "With your permission, Herr Stoekel, I feel a tremendous laugh coming on."

· 5 ·

WHEN HE CAME TO, he thought that he had been carried back several years, to the hospital at Mainz, not so much because of the whispering Jewish voices busy around his bed as because his body felt as it had then, because he recognized the old desire not to cry out, though his mouth was exhaling God knew what larval gurgling that might have been a cry. Then he made out the deep gray of the concrete ceiling, the yellow stars gleaming on the nurses' white blouses. A fantastic, enormous hypodermic needle danced above his body, naked under the bloody sheets. He felt it enter his thigh, and with it a trickle of cool silence invaded the already vanquished citadel of his body. He closed his eyes on that liquid sensation and fell asleep. And while they inspected all the wounds of his flesh, while they washed and disinfected and anointed his skin, while they checked his stitches and his bones, he dreamed that he was being married, as trumpets of joy sounded upon the air.

. . . That morning before dawn, before the morning star, he bathed himself so thoroughly that no human being (or divine) was ever as pure in the flesh as Ernie Levy is at this very moment, a unique moment, when the dream is an official promise of happiness. Guided by a spirit, the crystal cake of soap glides over his skin, and he makes no movement except to raise himself quite gracefully when the soap manifests an intent to lave his back. (With a gesture of his red beard the doorman at the baths points the way to the synagogue.) "Do not believe," Ernie says, "that my gratitude ends as I leave the baths. I am not one of these young bridegrooms who confine the universe within a wedding ring, and I beg you to permit me never to forget your beard. What will it profit you to sell

cakes of soap if no one in the world cherishes you in memory?"
"Then cherish my beard," the doorman answers simply.
"And yet," he adds, "permit me to thank you for having expressed your gratitude. I shall never forget the cake of soap I
sold you. *Mazel Tov.*"

As the doorman of the baths offers that benediction, *"Mazel
Tov,"* two Stars of David illuminate his eyelids and Ernie knows
that the doorman is a Just Man. "So," he thinks, "my ancestors are rejoicing with me, and I deduce from that that I am
the just heir of the Just Men and that I must be happy for all
of them with my beloved." "Rejoice in your fragile glass of
elegant crystal," the doorman goes on, smiling in approval,
"even if it is only for a single day."

"Please don't believe," Ernie says immediately, "that I have
any desire to rejoice in my beloved. My beloved is not a fragile
glass of elegant crystal for drinking wine of the best vintages.
Nor is she . . ."

But the doorman clucks ironically while his two stars stare at
Ernie as if to say, "You, my boy, you would teach me how the
seed of the Eternal is planted?" And then, a fat yellow-gray
bird, he flies off toward the moldings of the ceiling, wings
trailing through the shadows of the synagogue.

The rabbi's pointed red beard is also like a beak and the
black flaps of his *tallis* reveal his swallow's belly. Ernie prays,
to drive from his body, from his heart, from his soul, any
Christian temptation, any Christian influence, and so that he
may receive his beloved as a beggar receives the light of the
Lord. To the rabbi's left, here is Mother Judith, smiling, her
wig unfurled in long tresses, enveloping her naked body like a
dress with a train. In her right eye is a tear of blood, in her left
eye a pearl of milk. And in a corner of the synagogue, surrounded by a dozen friends, is the bride, so beautiful that
everything around her disappears, so beautiful that she herself
blurs, thins, vanishes, leaving an admirable hollow in the air
so burdened with faces.

"Let us have music," the rabbi says. "Let us celebrate."
He extends a glass of wine to the beloved, who drinks off a

modest half, her lower lip thrust forward like a little spoon. Ernie wets his lips in turn, then flings the glass of fragile crystal to the floor at his feet and turns to the beloved, whose soft and tender flesh is visible now, though the contours of her face remain unknown. "So that no woman," he says boldly, "will ever drink from the cup upon which you have set your lips, and so that no man will ever set his lips on the cup from which I have drunk. And may this broken cup be resurrected in spirit in our hearts, and may the spirit of the cup remain inviolate in our life and in our death. For it is made, my beloved, of a matter that the human eye cannot grasp and that the human foot cannot crush. Amen."

They all applaud so vigorously that Ernie persuades himself that he invented the words. "It's a beautiful wedding," Frau Feigelson says. "May the evil eye stay away," Mother Judith answers. "Since heaven has been heaven and earth has been earth, Ilse and Ernie were made for each other."

"I thought," Frau Feigelson says, "that her name was Golda?"

"Didn't I say Golda?" Mother Judith answers gently.

And as the procession arrives at the Riggenstrasse, exposed to the four winds, though the day is gaily sunny, tinted with blue and with the green of the chestnut trees, Mother Judith wraps the garment of her wig more tightly about herself. The tresses of her train are studded with apple blossoms and with those winged seed pods that flutter down from the plane trees upon the whole procession. Behind Mother Judith, the beloved advances on Benjamin Levy's arm. He struts and puffs as though he were the groom, not his son, Ernie the Blessed. And then comes the beloved's mother, a celestial creature whose hands, on Ernie's elbow, are as light as cobwebs. Her face cannot be seen. It is entirely covered by pink, dainty, happy tears. They sense that she is flattered in a son-in-law like Ernie Levy.

And marvel of marvels, the fiddler appears, with a white belly and a light black prayer shawl. He dances and twists, and pirouettes and turns as if he truly took himself for a swallow. A sharp stroke of the bow begins the nuptial song. "Who is she that comes up from the desert, holding the arm of her beloved? *Oi vai, oi vai, oi vai* . . ."

And here is our swallow now, stopping in the middle of the road, waiting for the procession, hopping beside it with tiny steps, as if for a cold Catholic procession, while heads appear at the windows and fists spring out.

> *Set a seal upon your heart, ha-ha!*
> *Like a seal upon your arm, ho-ho!*
> *For love is like death. . . .*

All of them now would prefer that the fiddler manifest his nuptial joy more discreetly, but they are unable to stop singing because the fists are rising. Ernie judges that it would be fitting if one of those fists approached politely. "My dear Jewish ladies, my dear Jewish gentlemen," the Fist would say, "the world is not gay enough to warrant so many violins. Each stroke of the bow pierces our hearts. Have you no pity?"

But as the fists always rise at a distance, stubborn, silent, the procession continues imperturbably, each couple ambling along gracefully and apathetically while their legs rise and fall lazily, as if in a purposeless stroll. Even that fiddler-swallow has slowed his flight to mark clearly his disapproval of the fists. On a long stroke of the bow, in a long, mournful voice, he enters the Levys' living room:

> *The great seas cannot reach love*
> *And the rivers cannot drown it—*
> Oi vai . . . Oi vai vai—
> *But who is she that comes up from the desert*
> *Holding the arm of her beloved?*

Where did Herr Rajzman find that sumptuous top hat? And dear Frau Tuszynski the fox bonnet that hides her withered dewlaps so badly? And that poor beggar of a Solomon Vishniac the gold-headed cane that he holds between his legs with both hands as if he were afraid it would fly away? Happily the little whore from Marseilles answered his invitation in a quite simple dress, and the second Hebrew in his muddy uniform. But alas, this fellow cannot help foundering in excuses at each drop of blood that falls to his plate from his forehead. Why does he make excuses? You could die hearing such a gentle, pure fellow excuse himself that way. Nevertheless, he is not too preoccupied with his manners to sing. Rising on his chair he begins, in the shrill voice of a little housemouse, learnedly psalming an odd love song that no one has heard of until now. Between verses, excusing himself a thousand times for the interruption, he wipes away the trickle of blood running into his mouth. And when the last verse ends in the death of the lovers, he has a charming smile that wins forgiveness for that sad ending. "Pardon me," he says before sitting down, "pardon me, my friends. It's only an old local song, a penny ditty—you know, the kind where you say, 'If they finish badly, at least they're well finished.' "

The second Hebrew sits down to thunderous applause. Then Herr Benjamin Levy, red as a cherry, undertakes to explain something to the groom. But constantly interrupted by the malicious laughter of the women, he can say only this: "My son, I recommend to you . . . For the divine instinct . . . enlightened by a shadow of worldly knowledge," upon which he collapses into his chair and is also generously applauded. Ernie thanks him with a brief nod and then concentrates his attention on the fiddler, who has sprung onto the table and is scraping vigorously at his instrument, hopping about among the dishes, smirking. After a vibrant ghetto melody the fiddler climbs up the neck of a bottle and breaks into an old-fashioned dance on tiptoe. Caught up in the celebration, Ernie has not glanced once at his beloved, but at his left he senses the misty pressure of her elbow. "May I die on the spot," Mother Judith says, "if the lovers have said one single word!"

"And yet I have not ceased to speak to my beloved," Ernie says.

"Nor I to hear him," says the young bride.

"May my insides rot!" Mother Judith begins indignantly,

but Ernie interrupts her with a smile, his eyes still staring straight ahead. "Where are the words?" he asks in a tone of amused confidence.

"Yes, where are they?" murmurs the beloved in echo.

"At least look at her once," Mother Judith says plaintively.

"I have not ceased to," Ernie says.

"He has not ceased," the voice says.

"Then all happiness," Mother Judith says, embracing him.

And the whole company lines up instantly behind the plump woman, waiting for her to finish so that they may do as much. "All happiness, all happiness," they all say one after another, weeping. And then in the hallway that leads to the couple's room, the beloved murmurs, "My feet are bearing me to the place that I love."

The bridal chamber is so small that it is cramped by a sewing machine, a bundle, and a miserable cot with a gray blanket. As Ernie and Golda enter, the room, as if by the pressure of their calm breathing, distends, swells, grows to the dimensions of the couple's happiness. Now it is the immense hall of a palace in the center of which reigns a canopied bed under a sky glittering with stars, a few of which drop softly to the sheets. Golda glides toward the bed with the requisite humility and good breeding, and truly Frau Levy is right to say that she has been brought up to share the bed of a prophet (although Mordecai claims that the prophets, even for a girl of such saintly beauty, would have only the cold eye of the spirit). And now Ernie takes his beloved by the hand, and between their fingers dappled butterflies are born, fluttering off to the heavens above the bed. And now Golda's hand is lost in Ernie's, and from the warmth of their hands a dove is born, which contemplates them with a wide, peaceful eye. Then a hen, a white rooster, ruby-crested, a fish squirming with life spring up between the lovers. But when Ernie draws Golda's body to himself, the body is suddenly cold. He opens his eyes to find that he is embracing a scant handful of faded grass.

What has happened? Can such things occur on the banks of the Seine? And the wedding, what has become of it? Dropping the handful of grass, Ernie dashes into the corridor, groaning sadly, "Where are you? Where are you . . . ?" But the corridor is as empty as the bridal chamber, and empty the dining room, the wedding guests perhaps years gone, for cobwebs cover the walls and veil the corners of the ceiling and scrolls of mildew rise from the once joyous banquet table. Ernie dashes into the Riggenstrasse stark naked, pleading with passers-by to tell him which way the procession went. But why do the passers-by answer with comments about the weather? And with indifferent shrugs, with glances that pass through Ernie as though he were made of glass, phantom glances, purely and simply the absence of glances? Lowering his eyes he suddenly discovers the bloody, lacerated surface of his body as textbooks of anatomy would show it, muscles and nerves exposed.

Demoralized by that discovery (or perhaps deriving fresh strength from it), Ernie makes his way, without falling too often, to the modest waiting room of the Drancy station, which is shimmering pleasurably, washed by the syrupy effluvia of the sun, undulating and ceremonious. But no attendant will offer him the slightest information. It is a point of honor with them to close their wickets in his face, and one of them is even preparing to have the monster without skin expelled, on the pretext that the sight of him is offensive to the travelers, when Ernie feels a hand upon the striated muscle of his shoulder. "We had to wait for the creature," the German soldier says. "Let him hurry up. The *little train* is about to leave."

The little train stands patiently in a station within the station, a sort of secret station. Ernie has barely reached the platform when the little train quivers passionately, spitting and thundering on both levels. Ernie leaps onto the last step, pushes open a door—the whole wedding party is in the compartment.

"We were waiting for you," they shout enthusiastically. "We thought you weren't coming. . . ."

"Should I be the only Jew left?" Ernie sighs. "Every drop of my blood cries out for you. Know that where you are, there am I. If they beat you, am I not in pain? If they gouge out your eyes, am I not blind? And if you take the little train, am I not aboard?"

"You are, you are," the wedding company cries, all but Fräulein Blumenthal, huddled in a corner with the newborn at her breast and her bundle timidly lodged between her knees. She wails in a small, despairing voice, "Oh, my angel of God, I had so hoped that you wouldn't come. . . ."

"But why?" Ernie asks. "Isn't my place with you?"

"Put on this garment," says the patriarch, "and instead of listening to empty bottles, sit down with Golda, who saved a place for you like the good Jewish wife she is, though she is not the daughter of a prophet."

"I did the same," Ernie says to Golda. "I saved you a place."

The girl squeezes his hand without answering, and leaning from the window shows him the extraordinary length of the little train. Other trains then appear in the distance, in echelons as far as the eye can see, all converging toward a central point far ahead of the locomotives—in Poland, according to Mordecai.

"I don't know where we're going," Mother Judith says. "I'm not a fortune-teller like some people, but we're going there together and that's good."

"It's in Poland," Mordecai repeats. "God is calling us all to him, great and small, Just Men or not."

"Yes, there will be an emptiness in the shape of a star," says the second Hebrew sententiously.

"But God will make them pay for it," Moritz growls. "He'll crush them all, just like us."

At that point Ernie feels constrained to reveal the great thought that has come to him long before. "Moritz, Moritz, if God exists he will forgive everyone, for he threw us into the stream blind and he will pluck us out of it blind, as on the day of our birth."

"Then what will he do with us if he forgives the others? Will he put us in a special de-luxe paradise?"

"No, no," Ernie declares calmly. "He will say to us, 'See now, my beloved people, I have made you the lamb of the nations, so that your hearts may be forever pure.' "

"Oh, my friend," the second Hebrew cuts in, "just the same, why this journey? Why?"

No, no, no, none of Ernie's words can calm the second Hebrew's heart, or halt the terrified rolling of the infants' eyes. The little ones are silent between Mother Judith and the patriarch, each clinging solemnly to his exile's bundle. Shivering suddenly, Ernie moves closer to Golda, who slips her hand beneath his jacket lovingly, seeking the hollow of his chest. But in spite of the happiness in his soul, the touch of that hand upon his nerves, upon his skinned flesh, is so insidiously cruel that Ernie chokes back a cry as he smiles at Golda, garlanded with grass. The fiddler strikes a note then that reduces the whole wedding party to tears. His voice swells in a fullness they have never heard before:

> *Oh! Can we rise as far as heaven*
> *To ask God why things are as they are?*

The train disappears along the track, but the violin music rises like smoke in the sky. Flung back into his solitude, naked and bleeding on the roadbed, his legs spread wide between the rails, the wind plucking at every naked fiber of his body, Ernie thinks that separation from a loved one is the most painful foretaste of death. Then the smoke of the violin also disappears, and Ernie cries out in his dream. Cries out. Cries out. Cries out.

VIII

NEVER AGAIN

. . . The sun, rising over a town in Poland, in Lithuania, will never again greet an old Jew murmuring psalms at the window or another on his way to the synagogue. . . .

Isaac Kacenelson, Song of the Assassinated Jewish People. *Translated from the Yiddish. Posthumous.*

. 1 .

A FEW FREIGHT TRAINS, a few engineers, a few chemists vanquished that ancient scapegoat, the Jews of Poland. Taking strange roads (rivers to the sea where all was engulfed —river, lifeboat, man) the ancient procession of stake and fagot ended in the crematorium.

In the process of exterminating the Jewish people, the camp at Drancy was only one of many drains inserted into Europe's passive flanks, one of the assembly points for the herd being led to the slaughter, quietly and without fuss, toward the discreet plains of Silesia, the new pastures of heaven. The Germans reached such perfection in *Vernichtungswissenschaft* —the science of massacre, the art of extermination—that for a majority of the condemned the ultimate revelation came only in the gas chambers. From profane measures to sacred, from registration to the Star of David, from assignment to transient camps, a prelude to the final mopping up, the mechanism functioned admirably, extorting obedience from the human animal, before whom a shred of hope was dangled to the very end.

So it was that at Drancy a belief was current in a distant kingdom called Pichipoi, where the Jews, guided by the staves of their blond shepherds, would be permitted to graze industriously on the grass of a fresh start.

And even those who had heard about the "final solution" did not trust their senses, their memory, their alerted minds. An interior voice reassured them, arguing plausibly that these things did not exist, that they could not exist, that they would never exist as long as the Nazis retained the faces of human beings. But when that voice was silent they foundered in the

351

refuge of madness, or flung themselves from a seventh-story window onto a certain cement slab that became sadly famous in the camp. And yet they were silent to the end, leaping with lips sealed on their terrible secret. And if they had spoken it aloud, none would have believed them, for the soul is the slave of life.

In the infirmary Ernie was offered a review of all the mental and physical distress that can afflict the human creature, from sick old men plucked out of homes for aged Jews in Paris to madmen plucked from their asylums, to women in childbirth and to scabby, purulent children whose seraphic faces, like those of the women, were deformed by venomous bedbug bites. Day and night the long room's crude cement walls echoed to complaints eased by the yellow-starred nurses, all of them reputable physicians who once occupied important professorial chairs and who contemplated the double- or triple-decker beds with impotent, terrified, blind expressions. Hell, Ernie discovered in the infirmary, the real Hell, is simply the vision of a hell, nothing more than that, and to struggle in Hell, he came to understand as he watched the fights break out around the garbage cans that served them as cooking pots, is to play the Devil's game.

The "nurses" had nicknamed him Gribouille, which means simpleton. One of them in particular, a Catholic of vaguely Jewish ancestry, hovered constantly at Ernie's bedside as though he were fascinated by the insane act that had led the young Jew to the infirmary. "But it's madness," he said, raising his gold-rimmed glasses as if to get a better look at the prostrate patient. "It wasn't enough just to be Jewish, but you had to come straight to the camp?"

"And everything that's happening right now," Ernie answered one day, "don't you think that's madness too? Look, you've got a medal of the Virgin hanging around your neck and you have a yellow star on your jacket—is that reasonable, being born one-eighth Jewish?"

"I know, I know," the nurse said. "In the old days, if you people wanted to escape the fate of a persecuted man, you could do it by baptism, but now it isn't your souls they're after, it's your blood. They think you people don't have souls."

"And do you still believe in . . . uh . . . ?"

The madman on the upper bed of the double-decker bayed loudly from deep within himself. Without changing his heavily dignified expression the Judaeo-Christian doctor excused himself to Ernie, set one foot on the bed, hoisted himself up and said a few words to the madman, who had only wanted to make his existence known and who, satisfied, was then silent for an hour. The nurse came down to Ernie's bed again, and while he answered his patient's question the latter, ill at ease, a bit distracted by the veneer of pedantry masking the ex-professor's rank of prisoner, noticed behind the gold-rimmed glasses a vague trembling in the protruding, myopic eyes—so perfectly blue, so perfectly French—a vague terror revealing, as if through a gap in a tapestry, the compact, suffering mass of the man's being.

"Do I still believe, my poor Gribouille? It depends on the circumstances. When I was a gentleman, as you put it, one of my friends used to tease me by asking if God, in his omnipotence, could create a stone so heavy that he couldn't lift it. Which is my position—I believe in God, and I believe in the stone."

Ernie thought it over and decided to smile. "I don't understand at all, M. Jouffroy. You're not mad at me?"

It was said in such a way that the nurse did not consider it undignified to chuckle briefly, covering his mouth courteously with one hand. "Gribouille," he said finally, "Gribouille, you're right. We French are often *intelligent for no good reason*— that's the expression you use, isn't it? To tell the truth, I don't know any more whether I'm Catholic or not. When I found out a year ago that I was one-eighth Jewish, at first I was very ashamed. It was stronger than I was—I had the feeling that I'd crucified Our Lord, that . . . you understand, don't you? I was still on *the other side*. And then I came here and I began to be ashamed of the part of me that isn't Jewish. Terribly

ashamed. I kept thinking of those two thousand years of catechism that prepared . . . the ground . . . that allowed . . .
You understand, don't you?" His face was even more open.
"Two thousand years of Christology," he said dreamily, as if to
himself. "And yet—I know it's absurd but I still believe, and I
love the person of the Christ more than ever. Well, except that
he's not the blond Christ of the cathedrals any more, the glorious Saviour put to death by the Jews. He's—" Gesturing at the
infirmary, he leaned forward above Ernie's suppurating elbow
and said, his face altogether open, "He's *something else,*" in a
suddenly Jewish tone, the miserable tone of a prisoner.

And then, surprising Ernie and the neighboring patients and
perhaps himself, he raised his hands to his temples to hold his
glasses firm, and broke into sobs.

The October sky was like a sheet of dirty snow waiting to
drift down over the vast emptiness of the courtyard. Gusts of
wind like human voices raised black dust from the slag gravel
that carpeted the camp. There were only a few children in front
of the dormitory for the "normal" prisoners, running around on
the cement slab with their mufflers flapping; the slab was the
internees' authorized promenade. Near the gate, S.S. men
gleamed in all their leather and all their steel; they had replaced the French gendarmes, who were found to be seriously
lacking in enthusiasm. Dr. Louis Jouffroy, one-eighth Jew, supported an emaciated, pallid Ernie, grotesque in his black suit,
whose condition no longer justified the privilege of a stay in the
infirmary. They shuffled along beside the Technical Building,
past the little red-brick kiosks, and set out on the promenade of
the "normal."

Ernie's head was shaved, but a quarter-inch fuzz covered all
traces of torture. His right ear, though, imperfectly sutured,
hung loosely, as if exhausted, and his smile disclosed several
black gaps, giving him an old man's mouth. As they approached
one of the doors, a boy of about fifteen emerged excitedly, his
hair upset by the wind, his face a frosty blue, and, waving a pair

of huge gloves tied to his forearm, shouted triumphantly, "I'm not cold any more with my gloves! I'm not cold!" He ran the length of the promenade screaming, "I'm not cold, I'm not cold!" and disappeared into another doorway.

The one-eighth Jew commended Ernie to the care of the floor supervisor, Stairway A, second floor. But when the inmates heard the name Gribouille they surrounded his bed, laughing, and brought him bread, soup, vitaminized crackers, and a generous sprinkling of advice—how to avoid hunger, thirst, sickness, death, and so on. The room differed from the infirmary only in that it was calm and silent by contrast. Some played cards, read, prayed aloud. One little group huddled around a stove that radiated nothing but smoke. When they left him alone for a while Ernie, shivering, slipped from under his single blanket and went upstairs, where he haunted the women's dormitories, inquiring whether anyone had seen, some three months before, a "pretty redhead named Golda." Only once did he dare to mention that she "hopped" a bit, but in such a pretty way, so amusingly. . . . They answered him evasively. In three months so many convoys had left so much emptiness, so quickly filled by new arrivals, that they didn't know, no one could keep track, no one remembered anyone. And behind his back, they whispered. At the door to Stairway B he hesitated. He was drunk with all those feminine dormitories in indescribable disorder, where a thousand little signs betrayed the desire to hang on to this fur coat, that makeup kit, this ludicrous or charming knickknack—the flotsam of the sex. Yet his heart beat rapidly when he entered a new room, even before he recognized Golda's hair against a distant bed in the shadows of the row nearest the windows.

Seated on the edge of the bed, lifeless, her head in her hands, she did not hear him approach. He touched the hem of her red jacket to make sure it was real, and only then did she unveil a face at once swollen by fleas and bedbugs, and gaunt, bony, yellowed by misery. Frost had purpled her beautiful hands, which she brought to her mouth, stopping a shriek. Ernie sat down beside her and wept. When he could see her he realized that her eyes were dry, examining him with the sad indifference common to all the internees.

"You too," she articulated coldly.

"And your parents?" Ernie said.

"Gone a long time ago. Pichipoi." She ignored Ernie's hopeless wringing of his swollen, reddened, frozen hands.

"Have you been here long?" she asked politely, and without waiting for an answer she went on in the same neutral tone, "I hardly recognize you, poor boy. You look as though you'd been run over. All you have left is your eyes. And do you still think I'm pretty?"

"Golda, Golda," Ernie said.

Curious groups gathered at a distance; a woman with disheveled hair peered down from the upper deck. The girl nodded slowly. "There's no more Golda," she said. "It's every man for himself here. But I'm glad to see you anyway. You mustn't think . . ."

"Are you hungry?" Ernie asked.

She stared helplessly, a dawn of understanding in her eyes.

"Wait," Ernie said, rising.

And tapping her nose in good humor, he managed to reach the exit door without betraying his weakness. But outside, in the icy wind of the assembly plaza, the aftereffects of his dysentery bent him double, hands clawing at his belly. Yet there was a strange peace within him, for it seemed to him that nothing, not men, not the circumstances that make and unmake men willy-nilly, could ever again exile him from that great Jewish ark where, since his admission to the infirmary, he had come to rest side by side with the invisible shadows of his own people; where, since a few moments before, he could touch Golda, whether or not she had become ugly, soured, indifferent to the past. With joyful gestures he raised his blanket and found the chunk of bread, the vitaminized crackers, intact. With a grimace that was almost a smile, his tone quite natural, he asked around if anyone would be good enough to make him a gift of a piece of chocolate or some other goody that would "gladden a heart." His immediate neighbors turned, outraged.

"You were right," a cardplayer said in Yiddish, "this one's a comedian. You could split your sides."

"But it's not for me," Ernie protested, tears in his eyes. "I swear it, it's to give away!"

Hilarity overcame them. In the wink of an eye Gribouille's latest performance was being reviewed at the far end of the room. But a man with gray temples, stretched out on a bed nearby, slipped a hand into the secret opening in his straw mattress and extracted a spectacle case containing two lumps of sugar and a few moldy pieces of candy. Emptying it into his hand, he paused to reflect and slowly put one piece of candy back in the case. Shuffling up to Ernie, who stood haggard and trembling at the foot of his bed, his shoulders bowed under the gibes, he smiled and handed the boy his small fortune. "Brother," he murmured with a note of almost imperceptible regret, "brother, little brother, you're the one who's right. It's very important to give"—he hesitated, his smile widened—"when you have nothing."

Ernie guessed immediately that the women's attitude had changed while he was gone. A group of them awaited him on the landing, and they all stared in melancholy, familiar, emphatic attention. One of them, a tiny, hooded dumpling, withdrew her hands from the blanket that shrouded her like a burnoose, clapped vigorously and shouted stupidly, "Bravo!" Then the others giggled conspiratorially, but there was nothing disagreeable about all this strange behavior, and when he went into the dormitory Ernie had another surprise—a troop of magpies chattering around an embellished Golda, to whose mouth a young internee was solemnly applying lipstick. At his approach the whole group fluttered away, and even the tenants of the neighboring beds strolled to the far end of the dormitory, abandoning Golda, painted and coiffed like a madwoman, in the middle of the aisle that separated the cubicles of white wood. When she saw the lump of black bread and the goodies he was clutching to his chest, her eyes, mottled by some impro-

vised purple cosmetic, gleamed so feverishly that she became
beautiful again. Pulling Ernie to her with one finger, she bade
him sit, and while he spat on his handkerchief and silently removed her makeup with cautious delicacy, she kept repeating, only half embarrassed, "They wanted to make me pretty.
. . . They did it. . . ." And then she had to laugh, a velvety,
gentle laugh, and rubbing Ernie's hand against her cheek, she
said, "I didn't know that Gribouille was you. . . . Did you
come to the camp because of me?"

"Oh, no, believe me," Ernie said in a tiny voice.

Amid the powder and the hideous whiteness of her face the
girl's eyes were as loving, as clear, as mysteriously bubbling
with life as they had been under the arch of foliage that had
shaded them in the Square Mouton-Duvernet. "Then there are
other skies," she sighed, "another earth, other thoughts than the
ones that come to you in Drancy?"

Toward the middle of October the Feldgrau buses deposited
fifteen hundred orphans in the snowy assembly plaza, orphans
between four and twelve, arriving from the collection camp at
Pithiviers. They were jammed like insects into the special dormitories, so many stalls, of the Technical Building, and as they
went on screaming pathetically for their parents, it was decided
to tell them that they would meet them again soon in Pichipoi,
which was evidently the next, if not the last, site of their incarnation on this earth. Many of the smaller ones did not know
their own names, so their companions were questioned, and
they supplied bits of information. Names and surnames thus
established were inscribed on small wooden medallions strung
around the children's necks. A few hours later it was not un-
common to see a little boy bearing a medallion inscribed Estelle
or Sarah. The innocents played with the medallions, and
swapped them for fun.

Five hundred adults were added to this group for the ship-
ment scheduled at dawn the next day but one. When he learned
that Golda was on the list, Ernie paid a discreet visit to the sec-

retariat, where he found a dozen postulants like himself, only
female. Some wanted to join their husbands in a common fate,
others felt pity for the children. The superintendent of docu-
ments held forth in a minuscule room at the end of a corridor on
the ground floor, a kind of office for notices and dossiers, illuminated by a single red bulb that gleamed like a bloodshot eye
above a funny little puppet with a pince-nez, the sleeve-garters
of a city clerk, a skull of glittering, soft pink skin, and tiny
porcelain-blue eyes that examined you with the disembodied
benevolence of a nineteenth-century photograph. The yellow
star on his meticulously pleated shirt seemed a stroke of pure
malice.

"You're out of your mind," he muttered in a thoroughly
French voice when Ernie stated his strange request.

"Yes, that's right," Ernie agreed, breaking into an idiotic
laugh. "I'm completely crazy—you guessed it."

The charm of the bureaucrat's face thinned in suspicion.
"Unless," he said, pointing his pen at Ernie, "you believe in
that kingdom of the Jews? But suppose it was . . . *something
else?*"

Overplaying his part slightly, Ernie applauded three times,
and terrifying the superintendent altogether by an attempt at an
entrechat (his toothless smile and emaciated body, ghostly in
the black suit, made the gesture seem perfectly demented), he
shrilled a piercing laugh: "M. Blum, wherever there are Jews,
there is my kingdom!" The homunculus shrugged, and when it
appeared that the applicant for that kingdom obstinately refused to make his own choice, the superintendent hunched over
his lists, sucked at his pen, and suddenly noticing a namesake of
the young madman, struck out the word "Hermann" and wrote
in above it, in a good round hand, "Ernie."

The search took place early in the afternoon.

As usual, the inspectors of the French Police for Jewish Problems officiated in the barracks adjoining the S.S. building. A
table was set up near the door, and there, all afternoon, volunteers undid and redid, one way or another, the children's bundles. The little girls' brooches, earrings and bracelets went the

way of the adults' jewels. A ten-year-old girl left the barracks with a bloody ear—a searcher had ripped off an earring that, in her terror, she had not removed quickly enough. Ernie also noticed a six-year-old boy, tousled, dirty, wearing a cute little jacket ripped at the shoulders, a good shoe on his left foot and none at all on his right, barehanded, the proud possessor of nothing under the sun.

After the search the two thousand souls were herded into the Technical Building, thenceforth isolated from the rest of the camp. The stalls in these special dormitories were not even furnished with straw. The tumult soon became indescribable; terrified by the search, the children were beside themselves. While the adults formed teams, Ernie, with the help of a woman doctoi and a few nurses and teachers, arranged the distribution of children around groups of adults. Then, until night fell, the few owners of pens or pencils that had escaped the search filled out the farewell forms. Thoughtful housewives and little old illiterate women crowded around Ernie, who could do no more than repeat the same formula, of an atrocious banality: "We leave tomorrow for an unknown destination. . . ."

"My handwriting is a little shaky," he said, smiling, "but that's because I have such a tiny pencil."

He and Golda slept with two children between them. In the darkness he stretched out a hand and found Golda's, waiting for it. Now and then a breath of panic followed a shriek, and forests of little arms rose in the suddenly clamorous darkness. He had to get up and spread the balm of an adult voice. But women too, turning their backs on life, were losing their reason, dying of fear in the shadows, and the only remedy, the only way to quiet the storms swelling in their throats was to place a child in their arms. Occasionally a neighboring roomful of people exploded in the night, and jerked out of their torpor, restored to the cold, to the hunger, to the incomprehensible destiny hovering above them, the children answered with equally dreadful wails—a strange dialogue that several old internees had described in Ernie's presence, but whose colossal horror he had never suspected. At dawn the children were sleeping so deeply that the S.S. death's-heads had to drag them out of the room when they awoke and realized what was happening in the adult world. But in the courtyard all was silent, as if by magic. Quietly clutching an adult's hand or arm, they answered the roll call as distinctly as possible. Those who did not know their names took their cue from the adults, who deciphered the medallions in the yellowish clarity of the floodlights set up on the observation towers. Then the stars were snipped off and thrown to the center of the courtyard, which was soon like a field carpeted with buttercups. Finally the machine guns were trained on the flock, the gates opened and the first delivery buses drove into the yard.

At the last moment the Germans ganged up on an internee wearing a derby and sporting a display handkerchief in his breast pocket. He was thrown into the snow, stamped on, struck with rifle butts, but he was most outraged by the way an S.S. man, to start things off, bashed his derby down over his skull, flattening the last vestiges of his dignity. A few children gave in to shrill laughter. Ernie realized clearly that he was entering the last circle of the Levys' hell. And when, an hour later at the Drancy station, the sliding doors closed over the dark night of the Jews packed into freight cars, Ernie could not help shouting, he too shrieking his terror with the whole flock in a single breath: "Help! Help! Help!" As if he too wanted, one last time, to stir up a void against which the human voice could echo—however feebly.

. 2 .

HIS HEAD on Golda's knees, he emerged from his glacial torpor, and thought that the soul must be woven of nothingness if it was to bear, without breaking, the trials God reserves for men of flesh and blood. "You were crying in your sleep," Golda's remote voice said. "Your tears never stopped. Can't you dream?" she finished in a plaintively reproachful tone. Ernie, arching up on his elbows, again discovered—without believing it—the fantastic darkness of the freight car, which seemed to be rolling by itself in a clacking of wheels and axles, delivered up companionless to the locomotive, an antediluvian beast breathing fire, dragging to its lair the hundred or so bodies stretched out on the jolting floor. They were like frozen corpses, though there were only a few dozen who had found true consolation—cadavers heaped up pell-mell, their limbs intertwined and skulls knocking, in a corner of the car first established for sick children, which had imperceptibly become a morgue. "Wait, let me wipe your eyes first. They're all red." Laying his head in her lap, the girl blew on her stiff, cold handkerchief and wiped her lover's inflamed eyes. Suddenly aware of a presence, he awoke completely and discovered the sparse circle of children surrounding the couple. There were about fifteen of them, of all ages, crammed together in various attitudes, their bodies interlaced by the same reflex that brought men and women together in compact masses under a common covering. In blue faces ravaged by dysentery, their eyes were black in the shadows, staring at Ernie with animal patience. Some opened their mouths or let their lower lips hang, and threads of vapor, gray as smoke, escaped their silent lips.

"They're waiting for you to say something," Golda told him, and moved by the fierce, rather childish rancor that had raged in her for twenty-four hours while most of the beings imprisoned in their compartment of doom had ceased to be human, she added spitefully, "I can't have you to myself any more." As she said it, other children's figures emerged from the gloom, moving closer on their knees or crawling on their elbows across the straw blackened by cinders and soiled by human filth. "What time is it?" Ernie asked. "It's the third morning," Golda articulated with an effort. "And it still hasn't rained?" "No, but the dew made icicles." From a crack in a panel, she ripped off with numb fingers one of the stalactites that the night had formed in a groove and held it to Ernie's lips. Before the envious eyes of the children, Ernie, still dulled by sleep, sucked at it slowly, sadly, deliciously, his palate seared by the cold, his thirst slaked in unspeakable joy. "So I'm nothing to you?" Golda said. Ernie understood that she wanted consolation before he turned to the children. Jacking himself to a sitting position, he embraced the masses of cloth that enveloped her, parted the wool—borrowed from the dead—that hooded her face and kissed her marbled blue cheek, and clung to her, cheek against cheek. "You're everything to me," he began in the slow, chanting voice that was his only balm for the flayed nerves of the unfortunate in his charge. "You're more to me than bread and water and salt, more than fire, more than life. . . ." He went on without paying much attention to the meaning of his words, trying only to recapture the solemn, soothing rhythm of Biblical verses while Golda, exhausted by her sleepless night, set her forehead against Ernie's shoulder and sank into the oblivion of tears. "All this," Ernie said—the children were hanging on his words—"is because you believe in this train and everything that's happening, and they don't really exist. . . . Right, children? All this is because you believe your eyes and your ears and your hands. . . ." As he spoke, the children in the first rows let their jaws drop, and while some of them wagged their heads left and right, as if to sink more quickly into the dream flowing from Ernie's mouth, others came closer greedily, craning their necks, lips already moist.

"You're not talking for my sake," Golda sobbed, "you're talking for the children."

Frightened, the nearest children retreated with a horrifying, slow passivity, backing away on their elbows or knees without a word while they stared intently at Ernie's mouth, and Ernie was once more amazed at the extraordinary toughness of his soul. "O God," he thought, "you have given me the soul of a cat; it must be murdered nine times before it dies." Golda was still lying against his shoulder. He stroked her cheek, stretched his lips in a scant, blackish, sweet smile, winked cunningly at the first row and murmured in Yiddish, "Don't run away, little ones, don't mind her. Come closer, and I'll tell you what our kingdom is like. . . ." A little boy in the first row opened an eye—swollen by a blow during the explosion of panic the night before—and whispered tonelessly, as though his tongue were unable to form sounds against his dry palate, "It's not for us, mister, it's for the other one, the one who's sick. He's asking for you." "Why didn't you wake me up?" Ernie asked. "I thought because it was only the first time . . ." Golda said, ashamed. Ernie released her without answering and, suddenly aware of the torn muscles in all his limbs, crawled through the crowd of children, who pressed away to make room for him, or whom he straddled so as not to deprive them of the advantages of immobility. The child was lying a body's length from the morgue, and an old woman doctor was sitting next to him, her back to the wall, her face rigid and masklike beneath the white cap adorned with a red cross that she insisted—strange compulsion—on wearing, though since the night before, her functions had been reduced to rubbing the icy bodies of victims of dysentery and watching them die. She was staring into the distance in the murk of the sealed freight car, and did not even blink at Ernie's approach. "He's dead," she said simply. The old woman's face was a desiccated bone blue with the cold, and her nostrils were pinched like the dead child's. Sensing the children's stares behind him, Ernie said clearly and emphatically, so that there would be no mistaking him, *"He's asleep. . . ."* Then he picked up the child's corpse and, infinitely gentle, set it on top of the growing heap of Jewish men, Jewish women, Jewish children joggled in their last sleep by the train's jolting.

"He was my brother," a little girl said hesitantly, anxiously, as though she had not decided what attitude would be most fitting before Ernie.

He sat down next to her and set her on his knees. "He'll wake up in a little while with all the others, when we reach the Kingdom of Israel. There children will find their parents, and everybody will rejoice. For the country we are approaching is our kingdom, know it well. There the sun never sets, and you can eat anything that comes to mind. There an eternal joy will crown your heads. Happiness and joy will come to you, and pain and lamentation will flee. . . ."

"There," a child interrupted happily, repeating the words rhythmically as though he had already said or thought or heard

them several times, *"there we will be warm day and night."*

"Yes," Ernie nodded, "that is how it will be."

"There," said a second voice in the gloom, *"there are no Germans or railway cars or anything that hurts."*

"No, not you," a nervous little girl interrupted, "let the rabbi talk. It's better when he does it."

Still cradling the dead boy's sister on his knees, Ernie went on. Around him the heads of his young audience wagged feebly, and he noticed that farther off a few men and women had begun to eavesdrop. Their eyes gleamed vaguely with the same delirium that was exciting the little ones. The girl on his knees broke into dry weeping, as all of them wept who had wept too much the first two days. Her eyes staring at Ernie, her fists balled against her chest, she fell asleep.

"And me too, mister," a dying voice whispered, "would you make me sleep? I haven't slept since the beginning." The voice belonged to a boy of about twelve with a face so emaciated that his protruding eyes seemed to hang in place only by a miracle.

"And why?" Ernie asked.

"I'm afraid."

"But you're too big for me to rock to sleep," Ernie said, smiling in spite of himself. "I wouldn't know how to do it."

"Just the same," he begged, dying of dysentery, "even if I'm big I want to sleep."

Ernie slipped the little girl under a blanket of clothes, and after strenuous efforts on both sides he managed to hoist the boy onto his thighs, but he himself was so weak that all he could do in the way of rocking was alternately to raise the sick boy's head and then his knees, glistening with excrement. With the help of a few women who had somehow managed to stand up, Golda began rubbing the limbs of the children closest to death. *"When we reach the Kingdom of Israel . . ."* Ernie murmured, hunched over the boy, whose eyes were filming over, yellowish, dreamy, peaceful. Suddenly the doctor's arid, ravaged face was close to his own. "What are you doing?" she whispered in his ear while the children retreated in fear. Ernie looked down and discovered that the living corpse he was rocking had become a dead corpse. The doctor clutched at his shoulder; her fingernails dug into what remained of Ernie's flesh.

"How can you tell them it's only a dream?" she breathed, hate in her voice.

Rocking the child mechanically, Ernie gave way to dry sobs. "Madame," he said finally, "there is no room for truth here." Then he stopped rocking the child, turned and saw that the old woman's face had altered.

"Then what is there room for?" she began. And taking a closer look at Ernie, registering every slight detail of his face, she murmured softly, "Then you don't believe what you're saying at all? Not at all?"

She was weeping with bitter sorrow and laughed a short, terrified, demented laugh.

· 3 ·

THE HOURS that Ernie Levy lived through in the sealed freight car were lived through by a host of his contemporaries. When the fourth night fell on the chaos of tangled bodies —a Polish night squatting on their smashed souls like some fantastic beast against which some of the adults were still struggling, blowing on their hands or rubbing frostbitten limbs—no complaint, no protest, no lament issued from the children's half-open mouths. Even gentleness was powerless to make them speak. They stared expressionlessly. Now and then those who were cramped against an adult's body scratched at random with their insensate talons like little animals, not to remind the world of their existence but, rather, in spasms born in the still tepid depths of their entrails, in a kind of attenuated pulsation that prolonged circulation artificially—a vague rush of life perpetuating itself in bodies abandoned by their extinct souls but still without the consolations of God. Inert, his back to the wall, Ernie did not dare to search for a breath of life in Golda's face, resting against his shoulder, to see if she had not been silently drained of what made her—because of, in spite of, the horrors

of the flesh—the object of his love. But for some time he had
been incapable of the slightest movement, and only the upper
part of his body floated over the mass of small bodies clinging
to him, bodies that had slowly enveloped him. One clamber-
ing over the other, attracted by the memory of his words, they
had then frozen in position as they were now, a wave of cold
flesh stabilized at the level of his heart, binding him in a net-
work of hands flat upon his skin or clawing deep into his flesh.
Occasionally, thinking that one of them might be able to hear
him, Ernie created gentle, happy words in the ice palace of his
mind, but in spite of all his efforts the words never issued from
his sealed lips.

The locomotive whistled, shuddered, ground reluctantly to a
halt. A ghostly tremor ran through the car. But when the first
barking of dogs was heard, an electrifying, fluid terror struck
the outstretched bodies one by one, and a leaden Ernie stirred
too, supporting Golda, who had been jolted out of her stupor.
The surviving children screamed with all their poisonous breath,
surrounding Ernie with a gaseous ring of decomposing entrails.
Outside, pincers were already snipping through the seals affixed at the Drancy station, and the doors slid back, admitting
the first S.S. death's-heads in a blinding flow of light. Carrying
whips and bludgeons, restraining black mastiffs on taut leashes,
they plunged with gleaming boots into the stormy tide of deportees, channeling it out onto the platforms with shouts and blows
that roused even the dying, setting them suddenly into motion
like a flock of sheep jostling and crushing. At dawn the platforms seemed unreal beneath the floodlights, and the jerry-built
station opened out on a strange plaza bounded by a chain of
S.S. men and dogs, and by a barracks dimly visible in the agonizing fog. Ernie never knew how, with Golda and a child
clinging to his arms, he succeeded in running the length of the
platform amid the mad panic of the survivors, many of whom
were absurdly dragging bundles or suitcases. In front of them a
woman tripped over her valise, which had burst open; her skirts
flew up to her waist. Immediately a German stepped forward
with one of those savage animals baying on his leash, and obvi-

ously addressing himself to the animal, he shouted before the terrified eyes of the motionless group, *"Man, destroy that dog!"* At the poor woman's outcry, Ernie started running again, aware of nothing but the crackle of his flaming brain and the pressure of Golda's and the child's hands. He wondered suddenly if that tiny, sharp shriek belonged to a girl or a boy. . . .

Beneath the blackish heights of the dawn, the plaza, trampled by hundreds of Jewish feet, also seemed unreal. But Ernie's wary eye soon noted alarming details. Here and there on the hastily swept pavement—just before the train's arrival, it was obvious—there still lay abandoned possessions, bundles of clothing, open suitcases, shaving brushes, enameled pots. . . . Where had they come from? And why, beyond the platform, did the tracks end suddenly? Why the yellowish grass and the ten-foot barbed wire? Why were the new guards snickering incomprehensibly at the new arrivals? These, catching their breath, were trying to settle into their new life, the men wiping their foreheads with kerchiefs, the girls smoothing their hair and holding their skirts when a breeze sprang up, the old men and women laboriously trying to sit down on their suitcases— silent, all of them, in a terrible silence that had fallen over the entire flock. Aside from the snickering and the knowing laughter, the guards seemed to have exhausted their anger, and while they calmly gave orders, blows and kicks, Ernie realized that they were no longer driven by hate but were going through the motions with the remote sympathy one feels for a dog, even when beating him. If the beaten animal is a dog, it may be supposed with a fair degree of probability that the beater is a man. But as he examined the barracks building, again a vague gleam shone through the fog, high in the gray sky, capped by a cloud of black smoke. At the same moment he became aware of the nauseating odor that hovered in the plaza, which differed from the stagnant effluvium of dysentery in that it had the pungency of organic matter in combustion. "You're weeping blood," Golda said suddenly in amazement. "Don't be silly,"

Ernie said, "nobody weeps blood." And wiping off the tears of blood that furrowed his cheeks, he turned away from the girl to hide from her the death of the Jewish people, which was written clearly, he knew, in the flesh of his face.

The crowd was thinning out in front of them. One by one the deportees passed before an S.S. officer bracketed by two machine gunners. With the end of his swagger stick, the officer directed the prisoners distractedly to left or right, gauging them with a quick, practiced glance. Those on the left, men between twenty and forty-five whose outward aspect was relatively sturdy, were lined up behind the chain of S.S. men along a row of roofless trucks that the lifting fog had just revealed to Ernie's haggard investigations. On one of those open trucks he even noticed a group of men apparently wearing pajamas, each of whom was holding a musical instrument. They composed a kind of peripatetic orchestra waiting farcically on the truck, wind instruments to their lips, drumsticks and cymbals raised, ready to blare forth. The prisoners on the right, all children, women, old men and invalids, huddled together raggedly near the barracks, shrinking before a wide grating set directly into the wall of that strange building. "They're going to separate us," Golda said coldly. And as if echoing her fears, the few children who had mysteriously found Ernie's trail through the crowd pressed closer around him, some of them simply offering the mute reproach of their heavy eyes, swollen like abscesses, and others clinging to his sleeve or the tail of his pitiful black jacket. Quite sure now of their imminent destiny, Ernie caressed their little heads, and contemplating Golda's anxious face and widening his eyes fogged by the blood congealing under the lids, he drank deeply one last time of the girl's beloved features, of her soul so well made for the simple marvels that earth dispenses to men, from which the curt movement of the S.S. doctor's swagger stick would shortly separate him forever. "No, no," he said, smiling at Golda while a fresh flow of blood streamed from his eyes, "we'll stay together, I swear it." And to the children, many of whom were now risking feeble groans, "Children, children," he reassured

them, "now that we've come to the kingdom, do you think
I'd stay out? We shall enter the kingdom together," he went on
in the solemn, inspired voice, the one thing that could touch
their souls so full of darkness and terror. "In a little while we
shall enter it hand in hand, and there a banquet of tasty foods
awaits us, a banquet of old wines, of tasty foods full of marrow,
and of old wines, clear and good. . . . There, my little
lambs . . ."

They listened without understanding, gentle smiles shadow-
ing their tortured lips.

·4·

I AM SO WEARY that my pen can no longer write. "Man, strip
off thy garments, cover thy head with ashes, run into the
streets and dance in thy madness. . . ."

Just one incident interrupted the ceremony of selection.
Alerted by the smell, a woman suddenly cried, "They kill people here," which gave rise to a brief panic in the course of which
the flock fell back slowly toward the platforms masked by the
strange floodlit façade, like a stage set for a railway station. The
guards went into action immediately, but when the flock was
calm again, officers went through the ranks explaining politely
—some of them even in unctuous, ministerial voices—that
the able-bodied men had been called up to build houses and
roads, and the remainder would rest up from the trip while
they awaited assignment to domestic or other work. Ernie
realized joyfully that Golda herself seemed to grasp at that fiction and that her features relaxed, suffused with hope. Suddenly
the band on the truck struck up an old German melody.
Stunned, Ernie recognized one of those heavily melancholy
lieder that Ilse had been so fond of. The brasses glittered in the
gray air, and a secret harmony came from the band in pajamas and their languidly glossy music. For an instant, a brief instant, Ernie was certain in his heart of hearts that no one could

decently play music for the dead, not even that melody, which
seemed to be of another world. Then the last brassy note died
and, the flock duly soothed, the selection went on.

"But I'm sick, I can't walk," he murmured in German when
at his turn the swagger stick had flicked toward the small group
of healthy men who had been granted a reprieve.

Dr. Mengele, the physician in charge at the Auschwitz extermination camp, conceded a brief glance to the "Jewish
dung" that had just pronounced those words. "All right," he
said, "we'll fix you up."

The swagger stick described a half circle. The two young S.S.
men smiled slyly. Staggering with relief, Ernie reached the sad
human sea lapping at the edges of the barracks building. With
Golda hugging him and the children's little hands tugging at
him, he engulfed himself in it, and they waited. Finally they
were all gathered together. Then an *Unterscharenführer* invited
them, loudly and clearly, to leave their baggage where it was
and to proceed to the baths, taking with them only their papers,
their valuables and the minimum they needed for washing.
Dozens of questions rose to their lips: Should they take underwear? Could they open their bundles? Would their baggage be
returned? Would anything be stolen? But the condemned did
not know what strange force obliged them to hold their tongues
and proceed quickly—without a word, without even a look behind—toward the entrance, a breach in the wall of ten-foot
barbed wire beside the barracks with its grating. At the far end
of the plaza the orchestra suddenly struck up another tune and
the first purring of the motors was heard, rising into a sky still
heavy with morning fog, then disappearing in the distance.
Squads of armed S.S. men divided the condemned into groups
of a hundred. The corridor of barbed wire seemed endless.
Every ten steps, a sign: "To the Baths and Inhalations." Then
the flock passed along a tank-trap bristling with chevaux-de-
frise, then a sharp, narrow, rolled-steel wire, tangled like a
briar, and finally down a long open-air corridor between yards
and yards of barbed wire. Ernie was carrying a little boy who
had passed out. Many managed to walk only by supporting
one another. In the ever more crushing silence of the throng, in

its ever more pestilential stench, smooth and graceful words
sprang to his lips, beating time to the children's steps in reverie
and to Golda's with love. It seemed to him that an eternal silence was closing down upon the Jewish breed marching to
slaughter—that no heir, no memory would supervene to pro-
long the silent parade of victims, no faithful dog would shudder,
no bell would toll. Only the stars would remain, gliding through
a cold sky. "O God," the Just Man Ernie Levy said to himself
as bloody tears of pity streamed from his eyes again, "O Lord,
we went forth like this thousands of years ago. We walked
across arid deserts and the blood-red Red Sea in a flood of salt,
bitter tears. We are very old. We are still walking. Oh, let us
arrive, finally!"

The building resembled a hugh bathhouse. To left and right
large concrete pots cupped the stems of faded flowers. At the
foot of the small wooden stairway an S.S. man, mustached and
benevolent, told the condemned, "Nothing painful will happen!
You just have to breathe very deeply. It strengthens the lungs.
It's a way to prevent contagious diseases. It disinfects." Most
of them went in silently, pressed forward by those behind. Inside, numbered coathooks garnished the walls of a sort of gigantic cloakroom where the flock undressed one way or another,
encouraged by their S.S. cicerones, who advised them to remember the numbers carefully. Cakes of stony soap were distributed. Golda begged Ernie not to look at her, and he went
through the sliding door of the second room with his eyes closed,
led by the young woman and by the children, whose soft hands
clung to his naked thighs. There, under the showerheads em-
bedded in the ceiling, in the blue light of screened bulbs glowing
in recesses of the concrete walls, Jewish men and women, children and patriarchs were huddled together. His eyes still closed,
he felt the press of the last parcels of flesh that the S.S. men
were clubbing into the gas chamber now, and his eyes still
closed, he knew that the lights had been extinguished on the living, on the hundreds of Jewish women suddenly shrieking in
terror, on the old men whose prayers rose immediately and

grew stronger, on the martyred children, who were rediscovering in their last agonies the fresh innocence of yesteryear's agonies in a chorus of identical exclamations: *"Mama! But I was a good boy! It's dark! It's dark!"* And when the first waves of Cyclon B gas billowed among the sweating bodies, drifting down toward the squirming carpet of children's heads, Ernie freed himself from the girl's mute embrace and leaned out into the darkness toward the children invisible even at his knees, and he shouted with all the gentleness and all the strength of his soul, "Breathe deeply, my lambs, and quickly!"

When the layers of gas had covered everything, there was silence in the dark sky of the room for perhaps a minute, broken only by shrill, racking coughs and the gasps of those too far gone in their agonies to offer a devotion. And first a stream, then a cascade, an irrepressible, majestic torrent, the poem that through the smoke of fires and above the funeral pyres of history the Jews (who for two thousand years did not bear arms and who never had either missionary empires or colored slaves) had traced in letters of blood on the earth's hard crust—that old love poem unfurled in the gas chamber, enveloped it, vanquished its somber, abysmal snickering: "SHEMA YISRAEL ADONOI ELOHENU ADONOI EH'OTH . . . Hear, O Israel, the Lord is our God, the Lord is One. O Lord, by your grace you nourish the living, and by your great pity you resurrect the dead, and you uphold the weak, cure the sick, break the chains of slaves. And faithfully you keep your promises to those who sleep in the dust. Who is like unto you, O merciful Father, and who could be like unto you . . . ?"

The voices died one by one in the course of the unfinished poem. The dying children had already dug their nails into Ernie's thighs, and Golda's embrace was already weaker, her kisses were blurred when, clinging fiercely to her beloved's neck, she exhaled a harsh sigh: "Then I'll never see you again? Never again?"

Ernie managed to spit up the needle of fire jabbing at his throat, and as the woman's body slumped against him, its eyes wide in the opaque night, he shouted against the unconscious Golda's ear, "In a little while, *I swear it!*" And then he knew

that he could do nothing more for anyone in the world, and in
the flash that preceded his own annihilation he remembered,
happily, the legend of Rabbi Chanina ben Teradion, as Mordecai had joyfully recited it: "When the gentle rabbi, wrapped
in the scrolls of the Torah, was flung upon the pyre by the Ro-
mans for having taught the Law, and when they lit the fagots,
the branches still green to make his torture last, his pupils said,
'Master, what do you see?' And Rabbi Chanina answered, 'I
see the parchment burning, but the letters are taking
wing.' " . . . *"Ah, yes, surely, the letters are taking wing,"*
Ernie repeated as the flame blazing in his chest rose suddenly
to his head. With dying arms he embraced Golda's body in an
already unconscious gesture of loving protection, and they were
found that way half an hour later by the team of *Sonderkom-
mando* responsible for burning the Jews in the crematory ovens.
And so it was for millions, who turned from *Luftmenschen* into
Luft. I shall not translate. So this story will not finish with some
tomb to be visited in memoriam. For the smoke that rises from
crematoriums obeys physical laws like any other: the particles
come together and disperse according to the wind that propels
them. The only pilgrimage, estimable reader, would be to look
with sadness at a stormy sky now and then.

And praised. *Auschwitz.* Be. *Maidanek.* The Lord. *Tre-
blinka.* And praised. *Buchenwald.* Be. *Mauthausen.* The Lord.
Belzec. And praised. *Sobibor.* Be. *Chelmno.* The Lord. *Ponary.*
And praised. *Theresienstadt.* Be. *Warsaw.* The Lord. *Vilna.*
And praised. *Skarzysko.* Be. *Bergen-Belsen.* The Lord. *Janow.*
And praised. *Dora.* Be. *Neuengamme.* The Lord. *Pustkow.*
And praised . . .

Yes, at times one's heart could break in sorrow. But often
too, preferably in the evening, I can't help thinking that Ernie
Levy, dead six million times, is still alive somewhere, I don't
know where. . . . Yesterday, as I stood in the street trembling
in despair, rooted to the spot, a drop of pity fell from above
upon my face. But there was no breeze in the air, no cloud in
the sky. . . . There was only a presence.

André Schwarz-Bart

was born in Metz in 1928 to a family of Polish Jews who had arrived in France in 1924. By 1941 he was alone in the world, his parents having been taken in a Nazi roundup and deported to an extermination camp. Schwarz-Bart joined the Resistance, was arrested in Limoges, escaped, and rejoined the Maquis. After the war, he worked as a mechanic, salesman, foundry laborer, miner and in a library, where he developed an irresistible hunger for books. He entered the Sorbonne, turning again and again to his favorite works of literature—*Don Quixote, War and Peace,* the books of Thomas Mann, Stendhal, Georges Bernanos, Dostoevski, and, above all, the Old Testament. He wrote five different versions of *The Last of the Just* before he was satisfied to have it published. His second novel, *A Woman Named Solitude,* appeared in 1972.